Sheila & Jerry

My best

Decoration for Valor

Joe Cassilly

Strategic Book Publishing
New York, New York

Strategic Book Publishing
An imprint of AEG Publishing Group
845 Third Avenue, 6th Floor — #6016
New York, NY 10022
www.StrategicBookPublishing.com

ISBN: 978-1-60693-701-3
SKU: 1-60693-701-4

Printed in the United States of America

In Memory of Virginia Kirsch,

American Red Cross Doughnut Dollie

I met her in Cu Chi Viet Nam August 1970

Spec/4 Ronald A. Spudis, who was a friend and a hero

And Spec/4 Mayo McClinton, Jr., who was a better friend than I knew.

God keep them all.

"War spares not the brave, but the cowardly."

—Anacreon around 500 B.C.

Dedicated to my Diana,

whose love inspired the end of the book.

Contents

Chapter 1—On Good Legs 1

Chapter 2—Old Men's War, Young Man's Fight 7

Chapter 3—The Second Goodbye 11

Chapter 4—Christmas Presence 15

Chapter 5—The First Goodbye 19

Chapter 6—Her New Start 25

Chapter 7—The Bed Bath 29

Chapter 8—The Purple Heart 35

Chapter 9—Despairing of Forever 39

Chapter 10—The Hell in My Mind 45

Chapter 11—Veteran's Hospital 49

Chapter 12—Three Nurses 53

Chapter 13—Pigeon-holed 59

Chapter 14—Morning 61

Chapter 15—Wheels!!! 65

Chapter 16—Ben 73

Chapter 17—HRONK!! 77

Chapter 18—REMFs 81

Chapter 19—Life in the Real World 89

Chapter 20—Motives 97

Chapter 21—Slow Dance in a Wheelchair 105

Chapter 22—Happy Birthday, Baby 113

Chapter 23—Flushing Out the Doc 121

Chapter 24—Left Behind 125
Chapter 25—A Mother and Child 133
Chapter 26—To Look Normal 139
Chapter 27—A Bachelors' Party 145
Chapter 28—The Ultimate Humiliation 151
Chapter 29—The Phone Call, the Bathroom, and the Orphanage 155
Chapter 30—The Feeling of the Grey House 163
Chapter 31—The Body Image 173
Chapter 32—Adventures in Wheelchair Land 177
Chapter 33—Little Old Aunt 185
Chapter 34—What I Deserved 193
Chapter 35—Growing Older 201
Chapter 36—A Thanksgiving Party 207
Chapter 37—Against Medical Advice 215
Chapter 38—Lt. Donovan 221
Chapter 39—Flo's Determination 229
Chapter 40—Graduation 237
Chapter 41—Looking for a Love 243
Chapter 42—A Last Goodbye 251
Chapter 43—A Father and a Son 257
Chapter 44—Back on the River 265
Chapter 45—Widows, Orphans, and Cripples 269
Chapter 46—October 1987 273
Chapter 47—The Reunion 277
Chapter 48—No More Goodbyes 287
Epilogue 293

1

On Good Legs

Most of the patients on Ward 11 of the Walter Reed Army hospital suffered spinal cord injuries. A row of beds ran down each of the long walls. At 11:30 on Christmas Eve 1970, the ward was dark except for the colored lights on an artificial tree and a glow from the nurses' station.

I had elevated the head of my bed so I could watch the lights slowly hypnotically blink. Sleep would not come. I held my hand up in front of my face and concentrated on making a fist. My arm and shoulder muscles tightened, the fingers flexed slightly and trembled. The thumb hung away from my palm. The message from the brain never reached the hand.

"Please, God, if you're there," I said aloud. "I mean, I know you're there!" *Oh my God,* I thought, *I doubted God. There goes my chance for a miracle.*

"It would be a great Christmas present if I could just make a tight fist." I concentrated and stared at my fist as if my eyes could send the nerve messages that could not get past the bruise on my spinal cord. "Come on God, do this for me and I'll never think about sex and I'll become a priest," I bargained. I thought for a second and then said out loud, "Okay, I'll be a priest."

"C'mon, hands, damn it," I swore, as if the obstinate arm had ears and a brain and would perform like a trained pony. Nothing. I let the hand fall to my chest. There was no skin sensation or muscle control from the armpits down. What had been pretty good muscles in the legs had atrophied.

I stared into the slowly blinking tree lights. My mind left my body's prison. I traveled back eight months from the cold, snowy darkness of Washington. I was standing on young, strong legs in the hot California sunshine along the Coast highway near Santa Barbara. The road burned through the soles of my boots. My feet itched and stuck to my socks. I would have taken off my boots and gone barefoot but I had enough to carry with my duffel bag.

The road was flanked with hitchhikers, thirty or more. They were laden with knapsacks, bags, bedrolls, and the rest of their possessions. I was wearing jeans and a T-shirt, but I felt out of place. My regulation haircut was in stark contrast to theirs. Some of the women had longer hair under their arms. My spit-shined boots and huge, awkward, olive drab duffel also marked me as military. Not that olive drab was out of place; the crowd looked like models of clothing for a military surplus store. The duffel made me so clumsy that I had missed several rides because of it. Cars chose to stop nearest the hiker with the least luggage. A seventy-pound bag seemed to scare drivers.

Suddenly there was the screaming of brakes as a car swerved to avoid a collision with an old Volkswagen bus that had roared from a garage across the highway. The bus came toward me and slid to a stop on the gravel shoulder, almost striking me. The women driver leaned to the open passenger window and yelled, "Throw it in the back!"

I threw it through the open sunroof. She screamed, "NO!" and watched with a pained expression as it landed in an open space among stacks of boxes.

I opened the front door. She started forward. I ran beside and leapt into the seat. She jammed the bus into second gear and sped off before the swarm of hikers could envelope her car. I slammed the door, flopped back in the seat, closed my eyes, and drew a deep breath. She shifted into fourth gear. I opened my eyes and looked over. She had soft brown skin, black hair, and a thin pretty face with great brown eyes that so commanded attention that it was as if the rest of her face was designed only to frame them. Then, I became aware that I was being stared at. I turned and looked in the back but there were only stacks of boxes and an old suitcase.

My gaze fell into the space between the two seats. On the floor sat a child duplicate of the driver with the same big brown eyes. She regarded me with suspicion. The result of a runny nose had reached her lower lip. I arched out of my seat and dug a crumpled Kleenex out of my pants pocket. I wiped her face. This service convinced her that I could be trusted. She climbed onto my lap, stuck a grimy thumb in her mouth, and laid her head on my chest.

"Why did you stop for me?"

"I was across the road at my uncle's shop picking those up." She tossed her head toward the boxes. "I felt sorry watching you stagger around with that elephant." She meant the duffel bag.

"Yeah, but why pick up just me?"

"There isn't room for anyone else. Those boxes are full of glass lampshades. By the way, I'm glad you didn't smash the whole works, throwing that bag like that. You can pay for gas, can't you?"

We looked at each other. "Yeah, sure." I shrugged.

The bus had climbed several hills from the coast. Heat distortions danced above the hot road to an audience of tall brown grasses on either side. I watched out the window. There is something about a VW engine straining up a long grade that is hypnotic. My head snapped forward and opened my eyes. The lack of talk made me uneasy.

"What is the little one's name?"

She looked fondly at the baby, who had fallen asleep. "Elana."

"How old is she?"

"Two and two months. What's your name?"

"Jake, Jake Scott."

"Are you going to Fort Ord?"

"No. Oakland Army Base. I'm getting shipped overseas."

"Vietnam?"

"Uh-huh. What's your name?"

"Bibi."

We drove on in silence. My eyes crept closed. I woke, trying to figure out where the hell I was. My shirt had lines of sweat and my back stuck to the seat. There wasn't a drop of blood left in my butt; at least, I could no longer feel it. My pants felt wet. The sun hung over the Pacific Ocean and glared through the driver's window. Bibi had taken off her shirt. Her naked breast showed through her fishnet tank top. She followed my stare to her bosom. She smiled, reached over her shoulder, and brought her long black hair forward so that it covered her.

"Where are we?"

"On a side road near Santa Cruz."

"Can we pull over? I gotta stretch. My pants are soaked with sweat."

"Oh no," she whispered and laughed. She turned onto a narrower road.

"What's so funny?" I wasn't in the mood for inside humor.

"I'm afraid it may not be all sweat," she said nodding toward Elena.

"You mean she isn't housebroken?" My eyebrows arched.

"Well, sometimes when we are both bouncing in the car, we forget." For the first time, we smiled at the same thing. The small road wound and dove toward the ocean and where the asphalt ended, the bus dropped down into two ruts, which woke Elena. She promptly popped her thumb back into her mouth.

"Where the hell are you taking me?"

"To my grandfather's."

By the edge of the ocean, I could see a long, low building built up on timber piling with a corrugated tin roof and wood plank walls. Elena looked up and took the thumb from her mouth long enough to say "Poppa's" and wave in the direction of the shed.

"We can spend the night here and I'll drop you off tomorrow."

As we pulled up, Elena squirmed out of the front seat and ran, calling, "Poppa, poppa."

I expected to see an old, bent Chicano. Instead, a tall, athletic man with silver hair emerged. The man swept Elena from her feet, tossed her into the air, and hugged her in a well-rehearsed motion.

"Bibi, I knew you would be stopping by today," said Poppa.

"Poppa, this is Jake—Jake, Poppa."

The old man did not acknowledge me, but put an arm around the woman and started inside. As they reached the doorway, Bibi turned and called, "You'd better bring in some dry pants." They disappeared inside.

I dragged my duffel out of the back and started thrusting my hand into it. You know there's something to be said for suitcases. You can lay them down, flip them open, and see just what you want. I didn't want to unpack the whole bag just to find one pair of pants. I slid my hand down the side, stopping every few inches to feel the clothing. Raincoat belt. Patches on a shirt. Socks. Underwear. Shaving kit. I pulled that out. Then I began working my hand in again. When I was about to my shoulder, I felt belt loops. The stitching was jeans, not fatigue pants, and I felt the frayed edges of cutoffs. I slowly dragged them out, trying not to dislodge everything in the process.

My watch read 6:30. The sun seemed only an inch above the ocean, ready to ease in and set the sea boiling. I went inside. The front of the building had display space for all items that were Mexican: flags, streamers, piñatas, costumes. No one was there so I walked through a door to the rear. The back was used for living space. There was one large room, half kitchen and dining table, half living room with a bed. Bibi and her grandfather were sitting at the table drinking iced tea, speaking in low tones. I stood there for a minute, hoping that someone would offer me a drink. The old man pointed to a door at the far end of the building. "There is a shower out there, go clean up." It was an order, not an invitation, to leave them alone. I kept going and found myself back outside, blinking at the sunset.

I was about to storm back inside, tell them both to go to hell, and start walking to San Francisco, but then I saw the shower. It consisted of a frame of two by fours with pieces of corrugated tin on three sides, strategically located for privacy. The water came from a garden hose with a spray nozzle. I looked both ways and saw only deserted beach so I got naked and started the water. It was a little colder than I wanted. I put a mirror from my shaving kit up on a nail and was concentrating on shaving around a mole on my neck when Bibi walked out. I shaved the mole off.

"Can't you knock, damn it?" I sputtered, holding a washcloth over my crotch.

"I came out to get your clothes to wash them with Elana's."

"Yeah, well that doesn't mean you can't knock." I tried to win the argument while feeling decidedly foolish standing there stark naked.

"Don't be a jerk."

"Wanting a little privacy isn't a sin."

"Look, you haven't anything I haven't seen. You'd better wad some toilet paper and stick it on your neck before you bleed to death." She grabbed my pants and slammed into the house.

"What a blabbering idiot I am," I swore at myself. In my fantasies, I had been naked with a beautiful woman. She had been overwhelmed with desire. Instead, I was humiliated by the fact that she could not have cared less. I had acted like a jerk.

2

Old Men's War, Young Man's Fight

Dinner was eaten in icy silence, except when the old man would bark some angry sentences in Spanish. Elena would babble, happily unaware of the tension between the adults. Dinner was hotdogs wrapped in tortillas, beans in spicy sauce, and rice. I felt relieved when it was over. The old man stood at the sink washing dishes. Bibi and I sat at the table with a couple of beers. I was staring into the glass trying to determine if bubbles follow the same path to the top. A Spanish language radio station was doing the news.

She leaned over and whispered, "Don't mind Grandfather—he's had a bad day. My mother called him today. She had my father arrested for beating her up. She is Grandfather's only daughter. He is still angry at her for running away with Father. He's angry at Father for all the years of abuse. Mother sent me to live here when I was about ten." Bibi stopped talking and slowly, deeply inhaled, as if she was drawing on an imaginary cigarette, then added, "to get me away from my father." I wondered if this was so she would not see the abuse or be abused.

The old man finished at the sink, walked to the refrigerator, and took out two beers. He poured one for himself and the other into my glass. "Where are you going?" The old man's gesture and calm voice took me off guard.

"Vietnam," I answered. "I mean, Oakland Army Base to be shipped overseas in a couple of days."

"And you're going to report like a sheep to a slaughterhouse?" mocked the woman.

"What do you mean?"

"I mean, why don't think for yourself and get away from them," she said, nodding at the duffel, a symbol of the Army.

"You mean desert. Are you crazy?"

"Not as crazy as you are if you go off and get yourself killed in some fight we have no business in."

"No business there! Look, if you were walking down the street and some guy attacked you and you were screaming for help and I was standing by, don't you think I ought to help? I mean, maybe there is no duty for me to help, but isn't there at least a duty to call the cops?"

She frowned, "What ARE you talking about?"

"Put that example on a global scale. Here you have a country—South Vietnam—where millions of people ran to after the communists took over the north. Now the communists are trying to take over the south by killing their leaders, teachers, and anyone else who disagrees with them. And if the communists take over the south, where will those millions of people have to run to?"

Bibi fixed me with a glare. "The Pentagon can't bull their way around the world trying to make every country into a good military base for the U.S. You can't tell me that their corrupt puppets are morally any better than the communists; they would just as easily murder to maintain their power. We aren't the world's policemen."

"Mommy, mommy." Elana had been frightened by the anger in her mother's voice. Bibi picked her up and carried her into a bedroom. I swallowed the rest of my beer and walked outside. I sat looking out over the dark Pacific Ocean wondering about a little war on the other side.

I didn't need to hear Bibi's criticisms on top of the doubts I really felt. I was trying to convince myself. I had read a lot about Vietnamese history and the U.S. reasons for being there. My father would go on about the need to stop the Russians from moving into other regions of the world. The closer I came to shipping out the stronger the fears and misgivings bothering me. Yet, I had this curiosity to know what was really happening or maybe just to know war. I sat there for a long time. The sounds of the ocean and the wind were healing some part of me that was not body or mind. I heard the door open. The old man stepped out, lit a pipe, and stood staring out at the ocean by the edge of the porch.

I cleared my throat. "Where's Bibi's husband?"

"She was never married."

"Then Elana's father."

"He is in prison. The same kind of man as Bibi's father. I thank God she never married him."

"What did he do?"

"He shot a storekeeper to death during a robbery."

"What happens when he gets out of jail?"

"If he comes for my Bibi I will kill him." The old man was not just talking, his tone was serious and he had thought over his response. The old man held out his hand. I could see a piece of metal, a ribbon. It was the Silver Star. "I was in a war once, like your war." The old voice had changed; it was tired and discouraged. I looked into his face, trying to see his eyes.

"Korea?"

The old man nodded. "I thought like you. But we fought half a war for half a victory and young men die because old men can't remember history's lessons."

We sat there, two spirits being healed by nature's rhythms. Then, the old man stood, put his hand on my shoulder, squeezed it, and walked back into the house. The breezes pushed me down onto the bench and hummed me to sleep.

3

The Second Goodbye

I woke up on the bench. Someone had put a blanket over me. I must have been exhausted; I'd slept outside the whole night. I was about to get up when I heard stirring inside the house. I pulled my arm from under the blanket and tried to focus my eyes on the luminous hands of my watch. It was 5:15. The sun was only a possibility in the eastern sky. The door opened and Bibi walked out wearing a bathrobe that belonged to her grandfather. I closed my eyes and pretended to be asleep. I remembered how we ended yesterday and I didn't want it to start up this early. She sat a big mug of coffee beside me and reached out and softly stroked my hair.

She hung the robe on a nail by the shower, walked down the steps, and ran into the ocean. I shivered as I watched her dive in and swim through the swells. She came out and went into the shower and struggled out of the wet swimsuit. *Drat,* I thought, *this was the time for x-ray vision.* She lathered shampoo into her hair. Quietly, I rose from the bench. I took a sip of the coffee and walked down the porch and stood watching her. She was beautiful. There were goose bumps on her soft brown skin, her nipples hard. She rinsed the soap from her hair and opened her eyes. She was startled to see my grinning face.

I stepped forward and offered her the robe that was draped across my arm. She jerked it away from me. "If my grandfather had seen you just then, he would have killed you."

"Why, you haven't got anything I haven't seen before." She faked a smile. I walked into the house and quietly closed the door.

By noon, the VW was parked outside the Oakland Army Base. I stepped out, slid open the back door, and pulled out my duffel. Then, I reached back in the front and picked up Elana. I held her very close and kissed her on the cheek before sitting her back in the bus. Bibi had walked around and slid the back door closed. She turned and I held out my hand with a twenty-dollar bill. "What's that for?" she asked.

"Gas money." She shook her head. "Go on take it," I said. "I understand this is an all expense paid trip, so there probably won't be any place to spend it." I grinned, but she didn't. She took the bill and turned and walked around the bus. I felt slighted. I thought we knew one another at least enough to say goodbye. I bent down to pick up the bag when she reappeared.

"How old are you?" Her voice was gruff with maybe a touch of hoarseness.

"Nineteen," I said, "How old are you?"

My question surprised her and she stood blinking as if trying to remember. "Twenty-three." Our faces were only inches apart. Tears began to go down her cheeks. "Damn you, I wish I had never stopped to pick you up yesterday. I'll spend the rest of my life wondering if you got yourself killed or what!"

"Do you want me to write?"

"No!" She pointed to the gate. "I just want you to walk through that gate and get the hell out of here." I shrugged and bent to pick up the bag. She pulled at the shoulder of my shirt and I stood upright. She looked into my eyes. I pulled her towards me, intending to kiss her. She pushed softly against my chest, stepped back, took a breath, and walked around the bus. Then, she was in and it roared away. As I stood watching, a small hand came out the window and waved.

I picked up the duffel and swung it up onto my shoulder and walked toward the gate. The MP there asked, "Your wife and kid?"

"No, just a girl I met yesterday."

"You wouldn't like to give me her name and phone number would you?" he called after me.

"I don't know her name."

The noise of the door to the nurses' station closing brought me back to Christmas Eve. Lieutenant Staunton was coming around for one last check before she went off at midnight. I liked her. She was shy and soft-spoken. Her dark brown hair was cut short. She was too skinny for her starched white uniform. She folded it at the sides back under her belt.

I watched her work her way down the line of beds. When she got to my bed, she turned and watched the blinking lights on the tree. "Hey," I whispered loudly. She jumped, startled from her thoughts. "I'm sorry; I didn't mean to scare you. If you stand there like that, Santa will know we are not asleep and he won't come."

She walked back beside me. "Santa isn't going to bring you anything anyway from what I've heard," she said smiling.

"Yeah, and what have you heard?"

She tapped the mistletoe, which was tied to the frame above my bed. "I hear that you and your deadly plant have gotten a kiss from every nurse on this ward."

"Everyone but you and Captain Rogers," I corrected, "and I don't think Captain Rogers has lips." She covered a laugh with her hand, not wanting to wake any patients. There was an awkward silence, but I could not think of what to say. She reached out and touched my forehead. "You are still running a fever." I knew. It was a bladder infection. I put my hand over hers and held it against my head. "I was fine until you got close."

She pulled her hand away. "I am a married woman," she said gently.

"Oh come on, Scrooge, it's Christmas—mistletoe—custom." I reached over with both hands and took her hand between them. There were no calluses on my hands and I was self-conscious about how smooth they must feel. She looked around to see if anyone was watching. She sat on the edge of the bed and kissed me. I slid my hand up her back and into her hair and pressed her face toward me and felt her mouth open for my tongue. We were breathing quickly. She put her hands on my cheeks and pushed me away. She straightened her cap and hair and fanned her face with her hand. She sat still on the bed and held my hand.

"That's all I wanted for Christmas," I said and I fluttered my eyelashes.

She ignored me and pointed to something near the head of the bed. "Can I look at this?"

I could not tell what she was pointing to but I said, "Sure go ahead."

She reached behind me and took a black beret that was hanging at the head of the bed. She felt the heavy wool and fingered the small metal crest pinned to the front. She put it on her head and it slipped down over her eyes. "Jeez, you have a big head."

I reached up and adjusted it. “It’s mandatory for all Rangers to have big heads, you develop it during training.”

“What do Rangers do?” she asked.

“Most of the time we did recon, six- to eight-man teams sneaking through the jungle looking for trouble.”

“Suzie,” a woman’s voice called from the nurses’ station.

“Oh my god, the next shift is here,” she whispered. She hurriedly hung the beret up.

“Your first name’s Susan, huh?”

“Yes, I gotta go. Merry Christmas.” She double-timed back to the nurses’ station.

I lay back. I wondered what kind of relationship a guy whose body was three quarters non-functional could have with a woman. I was finding out all over again who I was. I’d have to sleep on it.

4

Christmas Presence

The time at Walter Reed was twelve hours later than in Vietnam. I watched "A Christmas Carol" until 2:00 a.m. Then, I went to sleep, but that was an afternoon nap by my body clock. I was awake at six. The Christmas tree was dark and the ward was all shades of gray in the early dawn.

Men were still sleeping in the other fifteen beds. Someone at the end was snoring and choking. I could not see the rest. Most of us just knew the others by their voice or by the visitors they had.

I held my arms up in front of me and rocked from side to side to roll off my back. I reached for a water pitcher on the stand beside my bed. My hand would not grasp the handle, so I had learned to slide my palm between the pitcher and the handle to lift it. I sucked on the thick plastic straw and tasted the icy cold water. I swished it in my mouth and swallowed; then, I dipped my hand into the pitcher and wiped it over my face and neck to cool my fever.

It made me think of the water in Vietnam, and the lack of it. Maybe it would figure in the outcome of the war. The presence or absence of water at crucial times had certainly caused death and had been a factor in my own injury.

Maybe I could write a book about water and the war. You always—and never—had water at the worst time. There were big trucks and two wheeled tank trailers with "POTABLE" and "NON-POTABLE" stenciled on the sides that were constantly filled and emptied. My unit had a shower with 55-gallon drums on the roof, which were painted black to absorb the tropic sun. If you weren't in the field then, the best time to shower was around 5 p.m. when the sun had all day to warm the water. Unless, of course, it was raining and then it was always a cold shower.

One time, I had come in from the field desperate for a shower. The heavy rucksack and equipment had rubbed my skin rash to a bloody mess. When I pulled off my shirt, it tore open the raw flesh. I went to the shower at about 11:00 a.m. for some relief. The water was so refreshing. I had my eyes tightly shut with soap on my hair and face. I heard the screen door on the hut open and shut. Someone had come in but they didn't say anything. I continued lathering and scrubbing. Finally, I pulled the chain to get water to rinse with. It was then that I found that my audience was four mama-sans squatting on the floor washing clothes.

The rains in Vietnam. There was never a mist or a shower or a gentle rain. There were only downpours. They might be ten minutes or ten days long, but it always rained as if God had a surplus and only one place to hurry and get rid of it. In the jungle, the sound in a single second of a billion raindrops striking every tree, bush, leaf, your hat, rifle, pack, and friend was a roar. Like standing beside a passing train. It was a dangerous time to be on patrol. You couldn't hear yourself go through the brush and you could not hear the bad guys coming up on you. If the shooting started, you had to yell into the radio to be heard and there was no air support or reinforcements.

Once, on the move, I stepped on a root, which snapped under the weight of me, my pack, gun, and ammo. I quickly sunk up to my thighs and it suctioned around me. I had to take off all my equipment and then it took two guys pulling on me to get me out of the muck. There were creeks on maps that, during the rainy season, were rampaging rivers that carried trees along. There were rusting vehicles and corroding ammunition that did not work. And when the sun came out, the temperature would soar from the eighties to a hundred and something. The moisture in the air was so thick that it felt as if tiny spider webs were brushing over your skin as you walked through it.

There was water taken from streams and treated with iodine tablets to make it safe to drink. But if I drank it too fast, it made me throw up. And there was running out of water and licking the sweat off your arms and the backs of your hands just to moisten your lips. I put the straw back between my lips and took another deep drink. "*Water and Warfare*" I would call my book.

At 7:00 a.m., the lights came on. I could not believe I had been daydreaming for a whole hour; maybe I had gone back to sleep.

The daily routine began. A nurse pushed a cart down one row of beds. She gave each patient a thermometer, took their blood pressure, and then gave them a small paper cup of pills. Down the other row of beds, an orderly pushed a big bucket on wheels. He wore a rubber apron and gloves. He stopped at each bed where a patient was connected by a catheter through a tube to a small plastic bottle, which had filled with urine overnight. He emptied it into the bucket.

Christmas started quieter than other days; most of the staff was off. Lunch was delicious. I could not believe that the U.S. Army had actually served lobster and a glass of wine. I think it was lobster; there was no shell, but it was white and orange and you dipped it in butter and it looked too big to be a shrimp. Lunch was served by an older man who explained that he was a volunteer who had come with a church group from New Jersey. They had come to keep the patients company and fill in for the staff on Christmas. I listened while the man told stories of Christmas in World War II. I kept looking past the man toward the entrance, wondering if they would come. "I mean, Christ, it is Christmas! You'd think that they'd come on Christmas," I muttered.

The man stopped his story. "Did you want something?"

"Na, just talking to myself."

The man picked up the tray of dishes. "I better clean these up," he said. "I'll stop back later."

I nodded. I hoped I hadn't hurt his feelings interrupting his story, but his story just made me feel lonelier. Almost all the patients had visitors. Wives with children carrying presents to show Daddy what Santa brought. Girlfriends. Mothers. Fathers. Sometimes, the children spoke loudly, but mostly it was hushed tones about "Howya doin'? What the doctor say? Whenya gettin out?" I fished in the drawer beside my bed and reread some letters from my mom and friends that I had received while I was in Vietnam. The folks from the church group came through with a guitar and sang carols. I looked at the door a dozen more times. Still, no one came for me. I felt lonely. I felt tired. It was after two in the afternoon, the middle of the night to me. I rolled onto my stomach and went to sleep.

5

The First Goodbye

Someone had touched me. I strained my head back to look out of the window. It was just getting dark. In December, that would make it about 5 p.m. The last two months had taught me to hate hospitals. They were always waking you up and telling you to get some rest. A hand shook my shoulder again. I rolled over and started to say "What!" but Lt. Staunton slid a thermometer under my tongue, picked up my wrist, and looked at her watch.

"You have a visitor," she said softly.

I raised my head and looked around the nurse. There on a folding chair sat my mother. She wore a red dress with a white sweater. There was a holly sprig tied with a striped ribbon pinned to the collar. In her lap she held a folded topcoat. Her blond hair was streaked with gray and worn pulled back. Her eyes were red and puffy—maybe she had been crying or was just tired.

"Bing hur lung?" I asked with the thermometer still in my mouth. She shook her head "no," but I felt that she had probably been there for sometime watching me sleep. The nurse took the thermometer and noted the reading on the chart.

"Lt. Staunton, this is my mom—Mom, Lt. Staunton." The two women shook hands and the nurse answered a few questions. I looked toward the door for the presence of another visitor. The nurse excused herself and moved to her next patient. My mom pulled her chair close to the head of the bed.

"He didn't come, did he?"

She dabbed her eyes. "No."

My father and I had always had a, a...I don't know what word to use, "confused," "uncomfortable," "adversarial" relationship. I keep trying to do something or be someone that would win his approval.

After two months in the Army, they gave me some tests. The results were good. I was told that I was eligible for helicopter pilot training or Officer Candidate School. I was so excited at the chance to fly helicopters. When I had joined the Army, I never thought of myself as a pilot. This was wonderful. I wrote home and told my parents of the news of the test results and that I had decided on flight school. I thought I had finally done something that would make my father proud.

I was surprised the next weekend when my father showed up at my barrack. It was the first time anybody had visited me since I had been in the Army. My father had come all that way to ridicule my decision to become a pilot. In his opinion, I had to think about what I would do when I got out of the Army. A prospective employer would not be impressed by the fact that I had become a pilot, which was nothing more, in his opinion, than a glorified truck driver. I had to be able to put on my resume that I had been a U. S. Army officer, a leader of men. I started to tell him what I wanted but he was in a rush. He had a plane to catch, but he would get back to pin those gold bars on. My father left.

I was so damn mad. My father would not take the time to listen to me. He left assuming that I would follow his "advice." If he had stayed a few more minutes, I could have told him I had already ruled out being a leader of men. I was eighteen years old. I didn't want to be responsible for bringing another bunch of eighteen year olds out of combat alive. I walked out to the PT course, pulled out a rum-soaked cigar, and argued with myself. I could not find it in myself to do what I wanted to do in the face of my old man's objection. But I'd be damned if I were going to do what he wanted me to. So I found another school to go to. The Rangers. I never found out what my father thought about that school.

After I became a Ranger, I got a two-week leave before shipping out to Nam. I was home for three days. My father never spoke to me. I kissed my mother goodbye and left to spend the rest of my two weeks hitch hiking to California.

When I had first arrived at Walter Reed, my parents came to visit. My mother stepped beside my bed and saw the tongs fastened into my skull. The tongs went into holes that had been drilled into either side of my skull. A rope was tied to the tongs and went over a pulley to weights to pull my broken neck into line. My mother broke down crying and sat beside me, holding my hand between hers. My father stood at the foot of the bed. He looked at the tongs, the hose going from the urine bag up under the sheet, but he did not see me, his son. He walked to the end of the ward where I could see him talking to the doctor. He walked back to the bed.

"The doctor says you will probably never walk again," he paused and then added for effect, "for the rest of your life." I had the sense that he was telling me that this was my punishment for not following his advice. We looked back at one another. There was a long silence.

"I know," I said, "they told me that in the hospital in Japan. I just laid there for a while trying to understand and when I did, I just cried."

"What, a Ranger cry," my father said mockingly. I was so angry with myself for thinking I could talk to him. "Did you say that to make me feel bad or make yourself feel good?"

My father stepped forward, grasped his wife's arm, and began pulling her toward the door. I had not seen him since then, but I would, if it would make my mom happy.

I looked back at my mother. She was gazing at the Christmas tree. She looked back at me. I felt as if she had been reading my mind for the past several moments. We talked about Christmas presents, the relatives, the tree they got this year, and the Christmases we remembered from past years. My mom took the tray from the nurse and fixed the hamburger and fruit salad for me. I told her that the Army must have spent all its money on lunch. After dinner, she began gathering her things to leave; it was a three-hour drive home.

I cleared my throat. "They tell me that after the first of the year, they will be sending me to the V. A. hospital in Richmond. That's another two hours of driving."

"I'll be there," she said as she pulled on her coat.

"I know. Thanks."

She walked up the aisle and stopped by the nurses' station. I could see her speaking with Lt. Staunton. My mom was holding her hands in front of her as if she was preparing to catch a ball. The nurse would nod. Suddenly, it appeared that my mom was crying. The nurse stepped forward and hugged her, patting her back. After a few seconds, my mom squared her shoulders, wiped her eyes, and left. The nurse looked at me and went back to her desk.

Just before 11:00 p.m., the nurse made her rounds. I wanted to stop her and ask her about my mom, but she seemed in a hurry. She ignored my attempt at small talk. She probably wanted to get home and enjoy what was left of her holiday. I watched the late news. There was a story about how the troops in Vietnam had celebrated Christmas.

It was after midnight when Susie Staunton slid a chair beside my bed.

"Your mom asked me not to say anything to you, but I think you should know. She is very depressed. This thing between you and your father is tearing her apart. She doesn't know how to get through to either of you. She doesn't think he will let you come home."

"So who said I wanted to go to his house," I said with irritation in my voice.

"That's beside the point. Your feelings for each other are destroying everything she values in life, being a wife and mother." She paused and stared out of the window. Without looking back, she asked, "What is it you want to do later?"

"Well, didn't you know I'm gonna try out for the Baltimore Colts," I said caustically. She would not look back at me. I softened my voice and lowered my eyebrows. "I guess I'm going to college since it appears my brain is the only part of me that works like before."

"You need to tell your mom this. Let her know that you have ambitions and plans and are thinking of life outside of the hospital."

I nodded in agreement. "Thank you," I whispered. She reached over and patted my hand. Then there was a silence.

"I thought that you would have been home with your husband today," I said.

"My husband had a paper that has to be at his publisher's and exams to grade, so he stayed at the university. It's in Illinois."

"I can't believe it. If I were your husband, you'd never be alone at Christmas." She smiled but her face was sad and thoughtful.

"So you gonna take any time off?" I asked trying to change the mood.

"Tomorrow, I am going with some friends to Vermont to go skiing. You want to come?"

"Sure, you think anybody would notice you smuggling me outta here?"

She stood, her face moved down toward mine. She studied my features. Her eyes looked into my eyes and then at my mouth and she gave me a very soft kiss. Her tongue licked my lips.

"Goodnight, Jake."

"Goodnight, Suzie."

As she walked away, I traced the feeling of her lips on mine with the tip of my finger. "I'm going to miss you," I called out in a loud whisper. I knew that she heard me.

6

Her New Start

She had not gone to Vermont. Instead, she was watching small mountains of snow flash past the jet windows as it landed in Chicago. She had burned with resentment over her husband's excuse to avoid being with her over Christmas. Then Jake's remark about how Jake would not have left her alone compelled her to come home. She had not let her husband know she was coming. She did not want him to have several hours to prepare for the coming confrontation. She took a cab from the airport.

Blowing, swirling snow was hitting her eyelashes as she walked up the front walk; the windows were dark and forlorn. She pulled her car keys out of her pocket and found the key to their Chicago townhouse. She twisted it in the lock but it didn't turn. She pulled the key out and looked; it was a different brand from the lock. The bastard had changed the locks. She felt under the metal railing and pulled loose a small magnetic box. She removed the key from it and quietly opened the door.

She gently put down her bag and stood in the dark foyer listening. There was a woman's coat on the hook and a small bag on the table. There was music playing upstairs. She moved up the stairs, putting her feet next to the wall where she thought the steps would be less likely to make a squeak. She moved down the hall toward some muffled sounds. She opened the bedroom door a crack and peered in. She heard grunting and saw her husband's naked back, shoulders, and head moving to and fro above the bed. She softly closed the door.

Her throat tightened and tears pushed out of her eyes; they were not from sorrow but from rage. She quietly made her way downstairs and went to a desk. In the top drawer, she felt around until her fingers closed on the cold steel of a pistol. She would kill him and then the bitch he was humping. She drew the slide back to put a shell in the chamber, but there was no bullet. She thumbed the release and the empty clip dropped into her palm. She caught herself as she was about to throw the useless thing through the window.

She reached back into the drawer and slid the contents forward, looking for a box of bullets. There weren't any, but there were bank savings pass books, the deed to the townhouse, and some bonds, a checkbook and cash and his wedding ring. She stuffed the pistol and all the papers into the pockets of her coat. She heard the water running through the pipes. Someone was in the shower.

She called a cab but they told her it would be thirty minutes or more before they could get though the snow. She told them to pick her up at the Dublin Pub on the corner. She left her house and made her way across the street and down to the small neighborhood bar on the corner. She took a table by the window where she could watch for the cab but she could also see the front door of the townhouse. She ordered an Irish coffee and a bowl of chowder.

She was warming her hands around the large mug and sipping the whipped cream from the top when the door to the townhouse opened. It was difficult to see what the bitch looked like in the dark, obscured by snowflakes. The woman crossed the street and was going to pass right in front of her window seat. Suzie peered out, wanting to see what her husband had thrown her over for. The dark figure walked into a streetlight's glare. It was a girl, young, pretty, maybe eighteen or nineteen. Just as quickly, she walked into the darkness.

"You all right, Miss?" asked the bartender, looking at her ashen face with her mouth hanging open. Her hands were shaking and she was spilling her drink. Not only was she being cheated on, but that God damned piece of shit was screwing his students.

"Oh God," she muttered, "I hope he had not been doing that while we were living together." Of course, that was how she met him, as his student. She wondered if the girl knew he was married. Then she thought, *That is how old Jake is*. It was an hour before the cab got there.

The cab slipped, slid, got stuck a few times, but finally arrived at another house. She saw the glowing Christmas tree through the front window. Green and red lights lit two trees on either side of the front walk. Her knock on the door was answered by her mother who began laughing and crying, pulling Suzie inside, calling for her husband and Suzie's sister, taking her bag from her, and pulling her coat off. Before Suzie could remember how she got there, she was seated at the dining room table with smiling faces on every side, a plate of meat loaf and mashed potatoes and Christmas gifts that her sister had brought out from under the tree.

They had talked and laughed, looked at photos and Christmas gifts. Her mother handed Suzie the Christmas stocking she had made for her daughter even though Suzie had told her mom she would not be home for Christmas. Her dad went to bed. Her mother, sister, and she were on their second bottle of wine when her mother asked, "So, Susan?"

It was the Irish; that question could get you all the knowledge in the universe. When her mother called her "Susan," it meant she'd take no nonsense or lies and probably knew the answer already. Suzie told her everything.

The next morning, they started at the bank where they closed out every account and cashed every bond. She pawned his wedding ring. Then, her mother took her to a lawyer. By the time she caught the plane back to Washington, the process for the divorce had begun.

7

The Bed Bath

A few weeks earlier, before Christmas, just after Thanksgiving, they were getting ready to operate and remove a piece of bone that was pressing on my spinal cord. I was flat on my back. A cable system attached to the tongs pulled my neck into line. I could not sit up or roll over. They would put a mattress on me with a hole for my face, lock it into place, pull pins holding the mattress I was lying on and roll me over every four hours and four hours later roll me back over. That day, I woke up freezing. I had pulled my blankets up over my head. I was shivering violently. A man's voice spoke to me, "Aren't you a little cold?"

"I yi yamm freezing."

Hands gripped the blanket and tried to pull it off of my head. "Nnnno, I'm too cold don't take it off."

"Well the reason you're so cold," the voice explained, "is that your head is the only part of you that is covered. The rest of your naked body is lying here turning blue for all the world to see."

The hands re-arranged the sheets and blankets over me. I saw that the hands and voice belonged to Doctor Butcher. Why a guy with that last name would become a surgeon I always wondered. The doctor touched my head. He then walked to the cart that the nurse was pushing around and took a thermometer. He slid it under my tongue. "If you get sick, we will have to delay the surgery," he said. A few minutes later he came back with an armload of blankets. He put three of them over me. Then, he looked at the thermometer. "Ninety-four!" He put two more blankets over me.

I grinned at the doctor. "Does this mean my fever has broken?"

"It means that you're dead."

The nurse had reached my bed and the doctor ordered a couple of hot water bottles to be tucked in with me. A short time later, one of the student nurses who came to the ward three days a week carried in hot water bottles. Her name was Cynthia Ward. I had called her Cindy once and received a haughty glare and silence. She never stopped just to chat with the patients, never said "Hello" or "Good morning." She did what she was assigned to and got the hell out of there. I wondered if she thought spinal cord injuries were contagious. Maybe she thought smiling caused wrinkles.

"I guess you won the raffle to get me as a patient," I said, trying to break the silence. Her upturned nose parried my attempted humor. She kept working as if she had not heard a word. Her manner made me uncomfortable.

"This our last class here before the end of the semester," said a voice from the next bed over. It was another student nurse named Cathy.

"Thank you," I said. "It's so nice to hear the sound of a human voice." Cynthia roughly shoved the water bottles under the blankets. She looked at me to see if I felt anything. "Am I your assigned patient today?" No response. Each student nurse was assigned one patient to care for and write notes on.

"If I die today, do you have to repeat the course?" There was a laugh but it came from Cathy; Cynthia strutted away.

At about 10 a.m., Cynthia came down the aisle pushing a cart with two basins, two towels, and two washcloths. Harvey, a loudmouthed patient that I had never seen because of the position of our beds, called, "Look out Jake! She's coming for your body."

Cynthia pushed the cart next to my bed. She then went and pulled the long curtains, which slid on tracks in the ceiling around the bed. She dipped a washcloth into a basin, wrung it out, and handed it to me. "For your face" were the first words that she had spoken to me. I scrubbed my face and handed it back. She put on a pair of rubber gloves. She then wet the washcloth, rubbed soap on it, and took my hand and pulled my arm outstretched. She then began roughly scrubbing, working between each finger and up to the shoulder. I grinned to myself and wondered if she would like the story of the last time before I was injured that a woman gave me a bath.

In the base camp at Cu Chi, there were two steam baths. I had always heard stories about the one nicknamed "Steam and Cream" down the road from our company area. I had never gone there. One night, though, I was sitting with the Dutchman drinking straight scotch, because there was nothing else to drink. The Dutchman was shipping home in a week. He could not take his stash of liquor with him. He had divided it into equal portions for each night he had left in country. This particular evening, it was a fifth of scotch he had to finish to stay on schedule.

His name was van Jooser something or other, which everyone gave up on and called him the Dutchman. He was a great horse of a man and would have probably killed the scotch all by himself but he had poured me about six ounces in a water glass and asked me to sit with him. The Dutchman was reminiscing about all the good times he had with the Rangers in Vietnam. He said he would sign up for another tour, but this was the end of his second tour. He hadn't seen his old lady in almost two years. She had already told him if he didn't come home after this tour, she would leave with the kids and he would never see them again.

All of the sudden, in the middle of his memories, he jumped to his feet, grabbed my arm, and pulled me to my feet.

Cynthia had finished rinsing one arm and had taken hold of the other.

He breathed his booze-soaked breath into my face and said, "I want to go to the Steam and Cream one more time."

I had finished most of my scotch. I felt tipsy and tired. I let myself be pulled out the door. The pouring rain and driving wind quickly sobered me up in the few minutes it took to walk there. I stood dripping wet in a little entry room. The Dutchman must have been a favored customer because the old pap-san at the table beamed with recognition. The Dutchman, feeling the effects of the scotch, marched over and picked the Vietnamese, who was a foot and a half shorter, right off the floor in a bear hug.

"Papa-san," he boomed, "I bring baby-san," pointing to me. "We want numbah one girls." He pulled out his wad of military script and counted out some bills. I figured the storm must have been keeping anyone with brains away since it looked like we were the only ones there. Around another small table sat four Vietnamese girls playing cards, chattering, and watching the Dutchman out of the corners of their eyes.

He roused me with a slap on the back. "Hey, kid, we're lucky. Papa-san was just gonna close the place down 'cause business has been slow, but he says 'cause I'm such a good tipper, we can each have two girls." He started toward the table, but before he could reach it, one of the girls, the prettiest by my thinking, jumped up, ran over, and grabbed my arm. She began hollering at the old man, the tone of her voice fearful.

The old man translated, "She say you crazy, you drunk, you hit her and hurt her." *That was the Dutchman all right*, I thought. When he had been drinking, he could get real mean.

"Why you little bitch," said the big hulk, starting toward her. She jumped behind me and pushed me into his wrath.

"Dutchman, Durtchman," I hollered into the face of this homicidal maniac, trying to get his attention away from the girl. "You brought me down here to show me a good time, the good old days. Look, why don't you take the other three girls and I'll take this one. That's fair, right?" I was saying anything that came to mind and hoping that it would knife into that booze-soaked brain before he knocked me through the wall and stomped the shit out of the girl.

Suddenly, the Dutchman's face brightened, "Yeah, I never had three girls." He turned and pulled out his wad and handed each of the three girls some bills, glaring at the girl behind me to emphasize that she would not be getting any of his money. I breathed a long sigh of relief.

Cynthia pushed down the blankets and started scrubbing my chest. I should have been thankful she wasn't using steel wool.

The Vietnamese girl took my hand and led me into the back. I stood there beside some lockers not sure what to do next. She reached up and began unbuttoning my shirt. The Dutchman and his three girls came back and, while they were trying to undress him, he would pat their asses and squeeze their tits. They kept dodging him and working. The next thing I was aware of, my girl had unlaced my boots and was trying to get me to lift my feet out of them. She put the boots in a locker with my shirt. She unbuckled my belt and I pushed her hands away.

I reached over, grabbed a towel, and draped it over my shoulder. I turned toward the locker and took my pants off. I had stopped wearing underwear right after I got in country. I wrapped the towel around me and turned around. She led me into a steam-filled room. My chest heaved to breathe in the heavy, hot, wet air. The heat intensified the effects of the scotch. I was drunk. The room had little tin panels in it, which served as dividers. She took me to one area and I sat on a stool.

The Dutchman walked by to the other side of the room and sat down behind another panel out of sight. The girl went and brought a large sponge and soap. As she moved around the room, I stared at her white T-shirt and very tight fitting white shorts. Two of the Dutchman's girls walked by carrying buckets and my girl grabbed two buckets and followed them. I heard a door bang open and the howling wind. When they walked back through carrying full buckets of water, they were soaked from the rain. She sat the buckets beside me.

Cynthia had rinsed my chest and stomach. Although my head was immobilized and I could not look, I knew what she was doing from the pressure on my body or from being able to see in a small mirror that hung at an angle above my bed. Cynthia then pulled all the blankets off the bed, leaving only the sheet on me. She then moved to the foot of the bed and folded the sheets up, exposing my legs. She began to scrub my feet, working in between the toes and up the leg.

The steam had done its job; the sweat was pouring out of me. The Vietnamese girl moved beside me and reached down and pulled off my towel and tossed it over the panel. She dipped the sponge into the bucket several times and, each time, squeezed it over my head. Her wet shirt clung to her body and her breasts jiggled each time she held out the sponge. She soaped up the sponge and briskly scrubbed down my back. Then, she came up over my shoulders and started lathering my chest and working in small circles down my body.

I could hear the Dutchman moaning and crying out short yelps. I began trembling, my heart was pounding, and I was breathing through my mouth. I watched the girl's expressionless face as she slowly washed me. I slid my hand up and down the inside of her thigh. With my other hand, I grabbed her wrist and pushed her hand.

When it was over, I found myself gripping the stool. I felt numb and dizzy. I stood and dumped both buckets of water over myself. I took the towel and walked to my locker. I was pulling my pants on when I realized that she was watching me. I started blushing. I suddenly felt guilty.

"Hey, Jake," the Dutchman hollered. "Did she jerk you off yet?" I was embarrassed. Damn, I didn't want to be hassled, I couldn't talk to him. I shoved a wad of script into her hand. I grabbed my boots and shirt and ran back to the company area.

When the Dutchman came into our hootch, I pretended to be asleep. I lay there wondering how many soldiers she had washed before me. What did she think of GIs? What would she be doing when we all went home?

Cynthia was pulling the sheet down over my legs. With no feeling below my armpits, I had no sensation of anything south of my chest. After almost two months of bed baths, I had tried to discard modesty as a ridiculous virtue in my circumstances. But I always felt a deep embarrassment when they uncovered me and began to wash me. I hoped maybe they were embarrassed too and might say something that acknowledged my feelings. They treated me like a thing.

Cynthia moved up beside me and folded the sheet down. I watched her reflection in my small mirror as she took my penis into her gloved hand and cleaned the discharge off the catheter that ran into my bladder. I had no feeling there. She wiped down my penis, scrotum, and between my legs. I began to have an erection. I did not understand my body. Sometimes, I stayed soft when they washed me and other times I responded like this. But I wished it were not happening now. I could not endure the embarrassment any longer.

"Look, that's good enough. You don't have to wash me anymore," I said in a hoarse whisper. Her expression never changed. She wasn't going to hear me. She began rinsing the soap. The blood pulsing through my penis made it throb and arch each time she touched me. I closed my eyes and thought, "*If I can't see it, it isn't happening*." I felt my jaw clench with anger, anger that I was so dependent on others and yet I had no control of how they treated me.

I felt her rearranging the blankets over me. I would not look at her. Just before she pulled open the curtains, she came around the bed and leaned forward to look into my eyes. "You're just a job. I'm not at all affected by how you look," she said with what looked like a smirk. At that instant, I wondered if everyone I met in life would just regard me as a job.

"I knew a girl like you in Vietnam," I said from my still-clenched teeth. I wasn't sure she heard me over the noise of the curtains sliding in their tracks.

The surgery went okay. They removed the tongs from my head and I was able to slowly begin sitting up. After I was able to sit, I took over my own washing.

8
The Purple Heart

In the days after Christmas, all over the world, normal people were driving home from the relatives, throwing away tons of wrapping paper, returning gifts. The days up to the New Year were the loneliest of my life. My despair was so deep. I cursed the doctors in Vietnam for not letting me die. No one came to visit. Although nurses and volunteers would stop and chat, I wanted a friend. I needed to know that I could have friends in spite of my body.

I wanted to get out of bed, but the doctors said it would be another month before I could get up in a wheelchair. On New Year's Eve, a major and a first sergeant came to the ward and held an award ceremony. It was attended by the staff, some patients, and their visitors. I had been told about an hour before that they were coming. I held my electric razor between the palms of my hands and shaved. My hair hadn't grown back enough to need combing. Finally, with the help of Cathy, who was my assigned student nurse for the day, I put on a clean T-shirt. It was the first time since I had been hurt that I had put on any clothing. Then, we arranged a surprise.

The major read the proclamation. I heard something about "injuries received in combat" and "presented to Specialist Fourth Jake Scott." My mind was on what I was about to do. He stopped reading and took a small blue box from the first sergeant. He opened it and produced the purple ribbon from which hung the Purple Heart edged in gold. I had the sheet pulled up under my chin. When the major stepped forward to hand me the medal, I pulled the sheet down to show my T-shirt. The major and everyone but the first sergeant broke into big smiles.

On my T-shirt, Cathy had drawn an Army uniform with a magic marker. On my left chest, she had written "U.S. ARMY" over a drawn pocket and a rough approximation of the combat infantry badge. Down the center were a row of "buttons" and over the right "pocket" was written "SCOTT." On the left sleeve was a scroll with "AIRBORNE RANGER, F CO., 75TH INF." and under that was the taro leaf with a lightning bolt of the 25th Infantry Division. The major pinned the medal to the shirt and we shook hands. Everyone congratulated me. I laughed and joked with them. This medicine could not have come at a better time. The laughter gave me new energy and strength. It felt good.

Cathy stopped by at the end of the day to ask if I needed anything before she left.

"Are there any Red Cross volunteers on the ward?" I asked.

"I don't know. What do you need?"

"I think I need to write a letter home to let my mother know I'll be okay."

"I'll see if I can find someone to help you." She walked down the aisle.

About an hour and a half had passed and no one had come. I was struggling to hold a pen with my crippled hands and write on the pad lying on the bed. It was slow going and frustrating. I kept trying new grips, between both palms, woven between my fingers on one hand. I kept thinking, *You can't be beaten unless you let your mind tell you to give up*.

Suddenly, hands reached to take the pad and pen from me. "Could I help?"

It was Cathy, but she had changed from her student nurse's uniform to a bright white sweater over a blue turtleneck with blue jeans and knee boots. She sat down beside me and crossed her legs. She placed the pad on her knee and waited with the pen poised above it. She tilted her head so that her hair fell forward and looked at me. I then realized that I was staring with my mouth open. "What are you doing here?"

"I couldn't find anyone to help you with your letter. So I went to my apartment, changed, and picked up some things."

"You think anybody can read that scrawl?" I asked. "Should I get you to do it over?"

"Dear Mom and Dad," she read, "I know I haven't written since the hospital in Vietnam. If I don't say this now, I may never find the courage to again. I was thinking today that I have lost so much this year that's ending. I don't want to lose my family too. I know we're stubborn but I need to ask for your..." I had stopped at that point. She looked at me.

"You ready to dictate?"

"I don't know now. What I want to say is hard enough to write to my parents, but I may have a little trouble telling a stranger."

"I'm Cathy Creel. I am 21. I'm from Frederick, Maryland. I'm studying nursing and, this morning, I helped you take a bath. I think we're a little passed the stranger stage." She had a very pretty smile.

"Okay, the next word is—support."

"Support! That's stockings for old women. If you want to be honest with them, tell them you love them and need their love."

"Who's writing this letter anyway?"

"We are."

"In my whole life, I have never told my father I love him. He pisses the hell out of me." I looked away from her and out of the window. "I can't help but think that what he says and what he does is because it's his way of trying to give me love. Why is it so hard to say 'I love you' to someone you have lived your whole life with," I said, looking back at her, "and so easy to say to some girl you met three hours ago."

"Maybe, if she doesn't say she loves you back, it won't hurt." Her eyes looked down at the letter. "I don't have any answers. You want to finish this letter?"

"Yes. Tell them I learned that they are sending me to Richmond in early January. That I am going to start college this fall and that I will probably study teaching and history." I stopped and watched her as she wrote. Her sandy blonde hair curled over her shoulders; when she worked, it had always been done up under her hat. Her sweater fit nicely to her body and her jeans were tight. She finished writing.

"How tall are you?" I asked.

"I'm five feet ten inches tall. How tall are you?"

"Six feet one or about ten inches lying down. Depends on your perspective. Start a new paragraph. Please. "Please, send addresses for all the aunts, uncles, and cousins and let them know I'd like to hear from them. Mom and Dad, I know Richmond is a long drive, but I'd like you both to visit. Please, I need you to."

I watched her writing. Why had she come back? I could smell fragrance. A tear ran down her cheek. She glanced at me and saw that I had seen the tear and wiped it with the back of her hand.

"You okay?"

"Yes, I was just thinking about what you were saying."

"That bad, huh?"

"No, it's nice."

"It sounds awkward, but I don't know what else to say. Sign it 'Love Jake.'"

"No, you sign it." She handed back the pad and pen. I fumbled with the pen but I got it done. Cathy pulled the curtain forward on the track a little bit. "Watch out for the nurse."

I kept an eye out while she reached into her shoulder bag. She pulled out a small bottle of champagne and two paper cups. She twisted out the cork, poured it into the cups, and handed me one.

"What's the occasion?"

"I thought we would toast in the New Year. May you have a really great one." She held out her cup.

"Well, it has got to be better than the old one; it couldn't possibly be worse." I tapped her cup and we drank it down.

"I'm sorry it's not chilled."

"I'm sorry it's not beer."

"Next time, it will be beer." She picked up the envelope. "You want me to address this?"

I nodded. "Mr. and Mrs. David Scott, P. O. Box 927, Castle Crossing, Pennsylvania."

She sealed the envelope, put the stamp on, and placed it in her bag.

"You picked a great evening to come. Thank you very much."

"I was with you all morning and you never spoke to me. I was very worried. But when I saw you scheming this afternoon and laughing at your joke, I knew you were all right. I'll be your visitor if you need one."

"I need one."

"I'll see you." She stood and walked out. Her long legs moved gracefully and her hips were…well, I decided I was in love with tall women. The next two days passed quickly. I hadn't seen Suzie since she said she was going skiing. Cathy stopped by each day, but I kept feeling she was only bothering because I would be gone shortly. Try as I might to drive it away, the depression began crawling back into my life, like rust slowly eating at my will. I did not have a chance to say goodbye to anyone when the orderlies came in very early on the third of January and packaged me up to ship to Richmond.

9

Despairing of Forever

I arrived at the VA hospital around 8:00 p.m. There was a heavy fog and drizzling rain as the orderlies lifted the stretcher from the back of the ambulance. You get a very different view of the world moving through it on your back; looking up the men's nostrils, the peeling paint on the porch roof, the top of the door frame and the glaring lights and fire sprinkler nozzles on the ceiling of the hall. We stopped by the door to an office and the orderly went in. Then, I heard the voices.

The man, "We brought you a war hero out here."

A woman's voice, "Put him in the first room on the right."

They wheeled me out of the pale green hallway into a pale green room and slid me onto a narrow hospital bed. I was left alone. Fluorescent lights gave the room an uncomfortable starkness. I pulled a cloth laundry bag open that contained all of my belongings. I fumbled around inside it until I found a small transistor radio. I slowly edged the round tuning knob through the static until I got a clear station. It was a basketball game. I laid the radio on the pillow near my ear.

After awhile, a nurse came in. She was in her mid-fifties, brown skin, thin frame, a long face, and gentleness in her eyes. She brought in a pitcher of water. She helped me lift my head so that I could take a drink.

"Did they get you supper, boy?"

"Yes, ma'am."

"Tomorrow, we'll move you out on the ward with the other boys so you won't be lonesome."

"Thank you, ma'am."

She left the room and was almost immediately replaced in the doorway by a big, heavyset man in a large electric wheelchair. "New guy, huh? My name's John Byrd, Big John they call me." His conversation was quick, as if he did not care about a reply.

"How long have you been here?" I asked. I expected the reply to involve months, at the most a year—or two.

"Sixteen years," he boomed matter of factly.

"Sixteen years!" My voice was suddenly hoarse as if I had just heard a prison sentence from a hangin' judge.

Big John said goodnight. I think he was miffed at my startled reaction. "Sixteen years," I repeated softly. I wondered if all my plans for college and life were just dreams out of my reach. I prayed.

"Oh please, dear God, please help me, just cure my hands. You can keep the legs if that is part of some big plan You have, but give me my hands." The long day of travel had exhausted me. I fell asleep as the Philadelphia 76ers were beaten by somebody. I slept soundly—at first.

The dream started. It was the dream I was terrified of. As soon as it started, I knew how it would end. Somewhere deep in my subconscious, a part of me did not want to relive the feelings, the sights, the smells, the tastes, the sounds. It began screaming at me to wake up, telling me I did not have to let this happen again. But it had started.

I was sitting on the edge of the open door of a Huey helicopter. My legs were dangling out over the jungle two thousand feet below. The ground was pocked with artillery craters, which had dried to light tan starbursts on the dark green jungle floor. I cradled my M-60 machine gun in my arms. A heavy pack pressed into my back. The team of seven Rangers and a Vietnamese scout were on our way to be dropped into the jungle to ambush a Viet Cong supply trail. This was my eleventh mission. I worried about number thirteen. I had been in country for five months.

I looked around at the other faces. Two were eighteen years old, two were nineteen, one was twenty, one was twenty-one, one was twenty-four, and the Vietnamese scout was sixteen. It was a war like all wars, fought by young men who were such great warriors only because we did not understand that we could be killed.

The chopper banked left and I looked straight down at the ground below. Now, we lost altitude sharply, dropping, dropping, until we were flying below treetop level. I sat, thrilled at seeing trees pass within feet of the chopper at fifty knots an hour. The adrenaline was surging and I tightened my grip on the big gun. Any second, we would spot the landing zone. It was coming, coming, coming. My heart was pounding. I was breathing through my nose and mouth. I wanted a drink of water. There wasn't time.

I felt the chopper nose pull up, the tail swung around, and we were dropping sideways into the jungle clearing. The ground was rushing up. My eyes peered into the nearby tree line. Searching. Were they in there? Waiting? Aiming their guns?

"YES, YES," screamed the voice in my head. "Wake up! Wake up! Don't dream on. I don't want to know! I don't want to see!"

I was breathing hard. Lying in a bed. "In Richmond," I said to myself. I was afraid to go back to sleep, afraid the dream would start again. "Jesus Christ, why are you doing this to me," my voice was silent but desperately, angrily pleading. The sky gradually lightened. I would not dream in the daytime. They brought me a breakfast tray. Everything but the orange juice was cold. A cold sausage paddy with congealed grease. Cold grits. Cold dry toast. Cold coffee. If I had to eat to get well, then I was definitely in trouble. And grits. Nobody eats grits. Nobody with taste. I drank the beverages. An aide came to clear the tray.

"Not hungry, huh?"

"I'm starving," I emphasized. "Got any food?"

The aide wrote something on the chart at the end of my bed. I could not see it, but I suspected he told the rest of the staff that I was a restaurant critic. He then hustled off with the tray.

By nine that morning, they had moved me to a bed on the ward. I figured the building had been built in the 1940s. The spinal cord injury center was a parallel series of six, single story, long rectangular, wooden buildings joined by a hall, which crossed through the middle of each of them. To each side of the hall were offices and small rooms like the one I spent the night in and bathrooms and showers. Next were the wards, two in a building and at the ends of those were dayrooms. A ward had twenty beds lined up against the walls. As I lay there looking at the other patients, I noticed a crowd of seven men and women dressed in white uniforms enter the ward. They shuffled together from bed to bed. They would greet each patient, look at his chart, and talk to each other about the man without bothering to talk to the man. They worked their way down one row of beds and back up the row to my bed. A nurse in the crowd said good morning.

That was her job. No one introduced themselves. Anonymity was company policy. Another nurse was carrying my file from Walter Reed. She flipped it open and the three doctors gathered around her, staring at the reams of paper.

"C-7, T-1," said the first, the leader.

"Mmmm," said the other two nodding in agreement.

"Came in last night," said the nurse.

Another lifted the chart from the foot of the bed. "He's running a fever."

"Mmmm," said the three doctors, nodding. One of them leaned forward and looked at the urine in the bag hanging on the bed. "Cloudy," he said and scribbled in the chart.

They closed the file and were preparing to move on when I spoke. "How long will I be here?"

They all stopped in mid-step. The leader took the file from the file bearer. He opened it but the two inches of paper were too awkward to hold in the flimsy folder so he was unable to turn the pages. The first assistant page-turner quickly lent a hand. "David Jacob Scott," the leader read aloud from the file.

"Jake," I corrected sharply. "It's just Jake Scott."

The leader arched his eyebrows and peered over the top of his glasses at me. "I see they had plans to get you up in a wheelchair at Walter Reed."

"Oh, I was already up in it," I lied. "They were letting me get used to it a few minutes at a time."

"Too soon?" said the first assistant page-turner.

"Too soon," said the leader. The pen-bearer presented the ceremonial black U.S. government pen. The leader scrawled on one of the pages. Then, they started to walk away again.

"How long will I be here?" I asked again.

Slightly annoyed, the leader said, "At least until December."

"But I have to start school in September or even summer courses."

They smiled and knowingly shook their heads and walked to the next patient. "This is Mr. Burnie, L-4, been here nine months," one of them said about a big dark-haired man who was getting ready to transfer into his wheelchair. The group moved onto the next patient, a tall lanky guy with pale white skin, lots of freckles, and long strawberry-blonde hair.

I lay there watching Burnie lift his feet onto the footrests of the wheelchair and then fit the arm on. "You going to be getting out of here soon?" I asked.

"Soon as the doctors clear it," he said positively. "I broke my back in a car accident. The doctors say it will be a few more months." His big hands firmly gripped the wheels and he pushed down the aisle and went off to his routine.

"He'll never leave," said the guy with the freckles looking after Burnie. "He's waiting for these goofball doctors to make him well. They have him thinking that if he stays here long enough, they'll have him walking out of here." He pushed his chair up beside my bed, put out his hand, and flashed a broad grin. "Joe White." I thought how the name "White" was so fitting with his very pale skin. I returned his greeting. He noticed the weak, soft handshake. "Partial quad, huh?"

"Yeah," I acknowledged.

"How'd you get hurt?" asked Joe.

"Vietnam, How about you?"

"Motorcycle accident. Some girl pulled out in front of me. You're the only guy on the ward from Nam."

"Really. Where'd all these other guys come from?"

"Car and motorcycle accidents mostly. Two diving accidents. A few falls and one gunshot. Look, I gotta run to therapy. I'll check on you at lunch." The wheelchair spun around smartly. He rocked it up on the rear wheels and, with a few strong shoves, glided from view. I envied the grip he had in his hands.

I had been awake since 4 a.m. My eyes closed.

10

The Hell in My Mind

I had been asleep for a couple of hours when the dream came. The Huey helicopter, with its big side doors removed and stripped of the backbenches, clawed its way into a headwind. Raindrops hit my pants with such force that they went through and stung my legs. My hands were numbed by the wind and rain. The two Rangers on my left sat watching the green below change from open clearings to jungle. Beyond them was the chopper's door gunner leaning on his mounted machine gun. I looked back over my shoulder. On the opposite side of the aircraft sat three other Rangers in the doorway. In the middle of the floor sat our team leader and our Vietnamese scout. The team leader had a map spread on the floor and, from time to time, would lean over to peer out the door, trying to recognize landmarks. I could understand his worry. More than once, the choppers had dropped us off in the wrong area. The fear was that there was no way to get artillery or air support if you were hit going in and they did not know where you were.

We had one landmark to the east, a huge mountain that rose out of the flat landscape, Nui Ba Dinh. Even at night, the lights of a fire support base on the top were beacons to steer by.

As I felt the chopper losing altitude, my grip tightened on my machine gun. I checked the ammo belt that fed the gun from an ammo box on my hip. Jim, who sat beside me, wiped the beads of water from the silencer of his .45 caliber submachine gun. He looked at me. We both managed a grin, but his eyes showed the tension.

The chopper banked sharply and only the centrifugal force kept us from free falling to our deaths. Just as quickly, the bank swung in the opposite direction. The chopper was plunging toward the jungle. I leaned my head out of the door and saw that we were heading down a canyon of trees. Suddenly, there were green blurs flashing past us. The nose of the chopper pulled up steeply and then it flared sideways and dropped into the clearing.

The voice at the back of my consciousness began screaming at me, pleading, "Not the dream, not the dream." It was a sobbing voice, a voice full of fear, not of what would happen—the voice knew that was history—but fear of the sights, smells, and sounds, the memories of which were trapped in my mind and about to be released.

I peered toward the edge of the jungle. Something had moved. Maybe it was a plant being whipped by the downdraft. No! There was someone there. The chopper bumped the ground. I wanted to turn and holler at the team leader, but he had already gone out of the other side. Jim, in a crouch, was running away from the chopper. I jumped off instinctively as the chopper started to lift up. As I came up to Jim, I felt something wet and hard hit me in the face. Jim was falling into a prone position. Over the roar of the chopper, I could not hear Jim's silenced gun but I could see it bucking in his hands as Jim fired into the tree line. I also saw the gaping, bloody hole in his cheek. I reached up and wiped my face. I had been splattered by Jim's flesh, blood, and teeth. The rattling of the door gunner's machine gun made me grab the trigger of my own gun. The calming feeling of the big gun's power took away my fear. I settled to the job at hand. I directed the tracers from the barrel into the spot where I had seen movement. Pieces of rotted wood flew up. The man tried to crawl away from the fire, but I stitched him from the hip to shoulder. The air around me was buzzing with bullets, but most of them were being fired at the chopper.

We had landed in a semi-circle of bad guys. Those in front had shot the windshield out, killing the pilots. The nose dropped and it slammed into the ground from about twenty feet up. The door gunner was thrown back into the wreckage. He managed to pull his gun from its mount and continued firing. The door gunner on the other side had been thrown out and was hit by the main rotor blade which had sheared off. The Rangers who had gone out of the right side had a little luck and reached a huge downed tree for cover.

The team leader was screaming into the radio to two gunships that were about two miles out backing us up. The Cobras had already started toward the landing area when the Huey did not come back up.

Once the Huey was down, the bad guys turned their fire toward the Rangers. I was quickly going through ammo in the box on my hip. I had to drop the box on my other hip so that I could get it in position to feed it into the gun. While still firing, I grabbed the quick release on my pack and let the pack slide down my right arm. Jim was having a hard time breathing as his face and throat began swelling shut. He was going into shock. The clouds above had suddenly released torrents of rain that washed streams of blood down Jim's neck. I knew I had to kill the bad guys quickly so I could care for my friend before he lost consciousness and bled to death.

A Viet Cong soldier near the front of the helicopter stepped into the open and aimed his rifle at me. I swung the machine gun toward him, but I snagged the ammo belt and the gun jammed. At that instant, the lead Cobra leaped over the treetops, dropped its nose, and the roar came from its mini-gun. As I watched, the man dissolved into a bloody mist hanging on the raindrops. The Cobra swung out of the way to let its sidekick come up and take a shot. Just then, one of the bad guys fired a rocket-propelled grenade at the Huey. The missile exploded on the fuel tank, which blew up in a fireball covering the door gunner in burning fuel. He jumped from the burning chopper. In my dreams, the burning man seemed to float slowly through the air. His dying scream filled my ears; the reeking odor of burning aviation fuel filled my nostrils.

Suddenly, hands grabbed my shoulders. The voice in my brain pleaded with me to wake up. These were the sights, sounds, and smells that terrorized me. My own crying voice reached my ears. Joe White's face was looking into mine. His mouth growled, "Shit man what kind of fucking dream are you having?" I looked at the faces of others around my bed looking at me. I reached into my water pitcher and wiped water over my face. My fever seemed to have gotten worse.

11
Veteran's Hospital

The cold, dreary days of January settled into a monotonous routine that offered little hope. I was wheeled on a gurney to therapy after breakfast. There, a red-haired therapist named Florence with a high-pitched voice and a Virginia accent worked on my hands and arms. She flexed the muscles and balled my hands into fists, stretching the tendons. Flo chatted with the other therapists as she worked. They talked about soap operas that they were never home to watch, Florence's soon-to-be ex-husband that she hadn't seen in years, and all the sluts they knew in Richmond. It was a distraction to me, but I felt ignored in the room of patients and staff. They talked over top of me but not with me. At the end of the hour, I was wheeled into a line of other gurneys and elderly patients in wheelchairs by the door to wait for an aide to push me to my next stop.

The next stop was occupational therapy for an hour. There were guys making leather billfolds, while others made patterned cloth on a loom or painted landscapes or still lifes. The therapists fitted wide leather straps across my palms and fastened them with Velcro at the back of my hands. Into slits in the palms they slid a spoon or a fork and I practiced picking up marbles or some food substitute. After an hour of this, I had reached the limits of boredom or frustration. Then, it was back in the line and back to the ward for lunch.

Whatever else there was on the plate, I could always count on grits being there and, at least one meal a day, there was a slice of purple pickled apple on a wilted lettuce leaf. I wanted to have somebody investigated for taking kickbacks from the grits supplier. I sent so many lunches back untouched that the dietitian came to me after a couple of weeks.

The tray was sitting beside me still wrapped in cellophane. The pudgy woman regarded me through watery eyes set above her rosy cheeks and said, "The food we send to the ward is scientifically selected to provide the nutrition you need to get healthy."

"Yeah, well let's see you eat it," I said.

She glanced sideways with disgust at the cold blob of grits. "How do you expect to get well if you don't eat."

"I don't expect to get well eating that crap."

"We'll just wait until your hungry enough, mister." She waddled from the ward as though she had a rash. Of course, I would never get hungry because all of the other guys who went to the mess hall brought me sandwiches, fruit, and anything else they could smuggle out, including hot coffee, which is a real trick if you think about pushing a wheelchair with a cup of hot coffee.

The afternoon was my best time. I was wheeled into a small gym of specially adapted exercise equipment. Flat on my back, I was rolled under a barbell that was suspended by ropes from the ceiling. A well-muscled black man named Sam fit the right amount of weight on and I started lifting. My arms had grown weak so I only lifted fifty pounds in sets of ten. I rested and then did it over and over until my hands and arms started to shake and would not do what I asked of them. I felt good here. I was finally doing something that I could feel making me stronger so I could get out of here. Sam would keep an eye on me. I think he appreciated that I did not want to leave after an hour but wanted to stay all afternoon. One day, my arms gave out and I dropped the weights.

"Hey, white boy, you're gonna hurt yourself," called Sam with relief when he realized I hadn't. I shook my head. If I could control these muscles, then they were going to do what I told them to.

After the barbells, Sam strapped light weights onto my wrists and I did curls or other stretching exercises. After dinner on the ward, I would talk to other patients who might come by my bed or watch my small television until lights out. Then, I would lie on the bed, fighting sleep even though exhausted. I had started to pray every night. I could not let the dream start. Sometimes, I made it through the night, but other nights, I was awakened by an aide or nurse because I was crying or talking in my sleep.

I was there for six weeks. I had not had any visitors. I finally got a letter from my mother. It was lying on my bed when I came back for lunch. My crippled fingers fumbled frantically to open it.

> "Dear Jake,
>
> Thank you so much for your beautiful letter. It meant a lot to me. I want you to know I love and miss you. I am sorry I haven't written or visited you, but we have had a tragedy. Just after the first of the year, your father had a stroke, which has left him paralyzed down his left side and partially blind and unable to speak. I know that you will understand that he requires round-the-clock care."

I could not read on through my tears. My lips trembled. I buried my face in my pillow to hide my sobs. *That son-of-a-bitch*, I thought, *he wanted to keep Mom away from me and see me in this dungeon. Now he has his way. I hate him. I hate him*. When the aide came to roll me to the gym, I shook my head and waved him away. I was giving up. *What the hell's the point*, I thought. *I'll live here like the rest of these bastards who have no one on the outside. God, why in the hell are you doing this to me. What did I ever do that was so bad that you should punish me like this? I believe in you, God. I believe you have the power to make me better. Please, in the name of Jesus Christ, I beg you—please help me out of here. Send me some hope*.

§ § § § § §

It had been a long drive. Suzie had thought of turning back several times when her car had become enveloped in swirling snow. She was not sure why she wanted to see Jake, but she was hurting and needed a friend, but not someone too close. She thought of him because she had helped him over some bad days and it seemed natural to collect on the debt. Her passenger was napping in the front seat. *Poor kid*, she thought as she remembered her own all-niters cramming.

Suzie was surprised at how easily she found the hospital. Finding Jake was a different story. The hospital had miles of corridors. When they finally got to the spinal cord injury wards, they were sent to the gym. The therapist told them Jake had not come in today. They walked back to his ward. Every man on the ward, patients and staff, watched the two women walk to Jake's bed.

§ § § § § §

The dream had started. The chopper ride, the landing, the shooting, the drenching downpour beating relentlessly on us, the smells of gunpowder, of burning aviation fuel, of burning flesh, the sights of pain and blood and death. I turned away from the image of the burning door gunner. I thought of Jim. Jim could not breathe now. He was lying on his side. His face was gray. Blood was bubbling from his nose and mouth. He was fighting to suck air, but bits of bone and teeth had exploded into the back of his throat and were obstructing his windpipe. I was kneeling, trying to unjam the gun. I knew I had to help Jim. My mind was overwhelmed. The burning chopper exploded again. I never saw the chunk of metal that was blasted off of the chopper that hurtled toward me and slammed into my back just between the base of the neck and top of the shoulder blade.

I did not know how long I was unconscious; face down on the jungle floor. The rain was still beating down. I tried to raise myself, but neither my arms nor legs would respond to the messages my brain sent. The area around my face had started to fill with water. It was making it difficult to take a breath. I had to turn my head sideways or else I would drown in a puddle. I went to turn my head, but a horrible pain almost made me blackout again. I moved my bottom jaw sideways, opened my mouth, dug my chin into the earth, and then pushed with my chin and moved my jaw across. By repeating this process several times, I managed to push my head enough to the side that I could escape the water. But then I wished I had not, for when I opened my eyes, I saw Jim. The eyes staring into my own were lifeless. The hideous hole, where his cheek should have been, had the gray pallor of death. If I had moved faster to save my friend, then I would not have been hurt and I could have saved Jim. I began sobbing. "Jimmy, Jimmy," my hoarse voice called.

"Jake, Jake."

I heard the voice. I was confused. It was not the little voice at the back of my mind that called. It was a familiar voice. My mind began to pull back from the soggy, cold clothes and rain. Jimmy's eyes were replaced in my vision with big, soft brown eyes in a pretty face with short brown hair. "Suzie, oh God, it's Suzie." I grabbed her head and kissed her lips and cheeks carelessly. Then, I looked around on the chance that maybe I was still at Walter Reed and this whole experience at the VA hospital was some other bad dream I kept having. Suzie was surprised, but she remained close to me and slid her arms around me in a hug, a tight embrace. "Thanks, God," I whispered.

12

Three Nurses

I started shivering. Suzie brought her hand up and touched my short stubble of hair. "Bad dream, huh?" I nodded. As she held me, I looked up and saw Cathy standing by the foot of the bed. I stretched out my hand. She came forward and took it and I pulled her so that she sat on the edge of the bed.

Suzie looked at me. "I'll help you with your bad dreams if you'll help me with mine." I did not understand the remark but it was the wrong time for questions.

When I could speak, I spoke hoarsely, still trying to clear some of the emotion from my throat. "What in the world are you two doing here?"

Cathy flashed a big smile. "Suzie asked me if I wanted to go south between semesters. I thought she meant Fort Lauderdale; next thing I know, she's turning in here."

The men around my bed started drifting away. Joe White asked if I wanted him to bring something back from chow, but I said I was fine. I asked how things were at Walter Reed. First, Suzie and then Cathy took turns telling me about the staff and patients. I looked at them attentively, the short brown hair, the long blond hair, the soft brown eyes, the pretty blue eyes. I wasn't really listening to them because I was trying to figure out why these two women had driven all this way. When I had despaired of anyone caring, why had they appeared that day? Maybe God does know our limits.

Then, there was the sound of a throat being cleared. Standing at the foot of the bed was a short, stocky nurse. While she was on duty, she made herself useful by being in charge of everything and everybody. She enjoyed making it clear to the patients that she would tell them what to do. The previous Saturday, a patient, who had been there for months, had returned from his first evening out of the hospital with a few too many drinks. She had gotten on his case and he had mouthed off. She wrote him up and, by Monday, he was told to leave the hospital. The patients always referred to her as "the Bitch," and even some of the staff did, as well.

"You women may not sit on that bed," she commanded.

I was embarrassed, but it quickly became an angry response. "Where the hell do you get off with this crap? Guests sit on the bed all the time. There aren't any chairs on the ward."

"If they do not get off of the bed, I will call security and have them escorted from the hospital grounds," she snorted. Suzie and Cathy stood up. She began to walk to the nurses' station.

I was fed up. "You officious little bitch." She did not acknowledge it, but I knew that she had heard me.

"Want to show us around the hospital?" asked Suzie to distract me.

"They haven't let me up in a wheelchair yet," I said. "Besides, the only places that I have been since I got here are this ward and therapy."

"Then we'll show you around the hospital." She winked and walked down the ward to a gurney and pushed it back to my bed. Cathy unhooked the urine drainage bag from the bed, moved the gurney close to the bed, and hooked the bag to the gurney. As the women helped me slide onto the gurney, the sheet did not slide with me. For a second, I was naked before them. I struggled to pull the sheet over me, but my crippled hands would not grab it. Suzie pulled it over me. My mind told me not to get embarrassed or feel humiliated; after all, they were both nurses and had seen me naked at Walter Reed. I was no longer their patient, however, and I wanted to be their friend.

"Damn it to hell," I muttered too loudly.

Suzie saw the color in my face and the clenched jaw. She put her arm around my shoulder and gave me a squeeze. She put her lips close to my ear and whispered, "I'm sorry we embarrassed you."

My God, I thought, *after all these months, somebody actually noticed what I've been feeling*. As the women started to pull the gurney away from the bed, I pointed to a small canvas bag on the bed stand. "Hand me that little bag, please. It's got everything I own and I don't want to leave it." Then, Cathy took one side and Suzie the other and they wheeled me from the ward, down the hall past the door I had come in that first night. The hall went for maybe two hundred feet before making a left turn and widening into an area about twenty-five feet wide and fifty feet long, where lines of patients were waiting to go into the mess hall. As we went by, I could hear a few comments and whistles for the women. I looked up at their faces to see if they had heard.

"These boys been locked up too long," said Cathy.

"Horny bastards," said Suzie with a growl.

"They just appreciate pretty women," I said in their defense.

"You're probably the horniest of them all," said Suzie. I immediately wondered what I had done to give myself away. We went by the gift shop and a snack bar. Then, we turned into a lounge area with big windows. It was dark outside. For the first time, I saw the snow swirling in the lights of the parking lot.

"Aren't you guys worried about driving back in this snow?"

"There is a motel back by the interstate. We're gonna stay over there and drive back tomorrow," said Suzie. I could not keep the smile from spreading all across my face. I could have visitors on Saturday. Maybe my luck had changed. The thought salved the pain I was still feeling from my mother's letter.

"Are you hungry?" asked Cathy. "'Cause I'm starving."

"We passed a pizza place about two blocks from here. I'll run down and get one," volunteered Suzie.

"Okay, but I'm buying," I said.

"Where you gonna get money?" Cathy wondered.

I pulled open the bag. First, I pulled out my beret. Suzie grabbed it and put it on so that it slipped down over her eyes. Cathy laughed. Next, I pulled out a pack of photographs wrapped in a rubber band and, finally, a camouflage patterned nylon wallet. My clumsy fingers fumbled with the snap. Suzie reached for it to help me but I pulled it back from her.

"It may take me a minute, but I can get it." When the wallet was unfolded, the girls were stunned to see a stack of fresh green bills, several hundred, mostly twenties. "Five months worth of Army pay and not a damn place to spend it.

"To hell with pizza," said Suzie, "I'm gonna find carry-out lobster."

I slid out $60 and handed it to Suzie. Her eyebrows became question marks. "I'm not really getting lobster."

"No, but I also want to pay for that motel room." I pushed it into her hand. "I'd rent it for a month if I could get you two to stay." I rubbed her hand softly between mine. There was a silence between the three of us for a while.

"How about everything on it," said Suzie, pulling on her coat. Cathy reached for her coat, but Suzie said, "No, no, you better stay here with him. I think that this is a tow away zone. If we leave him, they'll put the hook on this thing and drag him down to the impound yard."

Cathy and I watched out the window as Suzie ran through the snow to her car. Cathy sat on top of a table and pulled her knees up under her chin. We watched as the wind lifted the fallen snow up into the lights so that it looked like a crashing wave against the darkness.

Cathy scooted around on the table so that she could look at me. "You know that you don't have to give us all that money. I mean, what are you going to do for money when you get out of the Army?" I was touched by her concern. I imagined she thought my future involved selling pencils from a tin cup.

"I am out of the Army. It was a singularly anti-climatic event. Some VA clerk came in back in early February and handed me a piece of paper that said I was retired with a medical disability. So I'm nineteen years old and retired already."

"What are you going to do for money?"

"Ohh, being crippled is a real racket. First of all, I get almost a thousand dollars a month disability pay." I put my hand beside my mouth and in a stage whisper said, "That's the going rate for two legs and a couple of crippled hands. They're going to pay for job retraining so that I can make beaded wallets, and get this: they're going to buy me a car!" She knitted her eyebrows to see if I was serious. "Yeah, really. The benefits clerk said they will pay for a brand new car with hand controls and everything." My voice took a sarcastic tone. "I'm telling ya, if I had known it was gonna be this good, I would have become crippled years ago."

My sarcasm made her uncomfortable; maybe she thought I was mocking her concern. She turned her head and stared back out the window. I was distracted by the stitching on her jeans. I noticed how it came up the insides of her thighs and joined with the stitching that came down from the zipper. The convergence of the thread provided a focal point for my eyes.

Cathy broke through the trance. "Can I look at these?" She had picked up the pack of photos.

"Yeah, sure."

She pulled off the rubber band and took off a piece of protective cardboard. She realized that I could not see the photos so she dragged the gurney closer to the table. The first photo was of me and another guy playing guitar and a girl in a Red Cross uniform singing.

"Who are they?"

"Well, her name was Connie. She was a Red Cross girl and he is a chaplain's assistant. If I was in base camp, we would go play together at Mass. Connie was the singer."

The photo made me remember my times with a guitar, practicing to fill the hours in Vietnam. I would sit on top of a sandbagged ammo bunker, in the darkness, the humid air moving softly through hairs on the back of my arms, playing until the calluses on my fingertips had grooves in them. One night, I felt someone watching me. I spun around, ready to bash the guitar over some bad guy's head.

The first sergeant had come up quietly and was sitting on the bunker. He leaned forward and spit a long stream of tobacco juice. "I been sitting here listening," he drawled in a Georgia twang, "and you ain't half bad." Then he slid off and walked into the darkness. That was the only time he had talked to me before he came to see me in the hospital in Long Binh.

I had held a guitar in Walter Reed once, but the calluses were gone and my fingers would not curl around the neck. Tears had run down my cheeks. A lump in my throat made it hard to swallow. I pushed the guitar back into the hands of the volunteer who had let me hold it.

"Where was this?" Her question brought me back. Cathy was holding a photo of some Vietnamese children and a Ranger kneeling in their midst, all smiling at the camera.

"That was in Cu Chi, the village outside our base." I laid there watching her eyes studying the photos. She became aware of this and looked back at me.

"Having you girls come see me is the best thing that's happened to me since I got to this concentration camp." I took a breath. "But why did you come?"

"Well, it was Suzie's idea. The day they shipped you out, we were both off. The next day, we arrived on the ward at the same time. I went down to your bed and Suzie was standing there. She seemed upset and she asked me where you were. I told her I didn't know. We checked at the nurses' station and found that you had been sent here."

She paused to brush her hair back off her face. My blue eyes were fixed on her, waiting for more. "At lunch, I sat with her and we talked about you. I told her about you receiving the Purple Heart and she told me about Christmas Eve." There was a sly twinkle in her eye when she said that. "Anyway, I could tell that something was bothering her and I asked if she wanted to talk to me, since you weren't there. So she told me that, instead of staying in Vermont skiing, she decided to go see her husband in Illinois; apparently, something you said about being with her at Christmas." She arched an eyebrow.

"She had a key to their townhouse and let herself in. She found the rat in the bedroom doing an extra credit project with one of his students. He didn't know Suzie had seen them. Suzie said she felt faint and went down and sat in the living room for a while to think. Then, she went to his desk and took out their joint bank accounts, some cash, and his wedding ring and walked out. The next day, you'll love this, she hocked his wedding ring and used the cash to make a down payment on a divorce lawyer." Cathy was gleeful when she related this last bit of information. I decided you had to be a woman to really appreciate it.

"For the past few weeks, we would talk and we got to be friends." I shook my head. "Then this morning, after my exam, she all the sudden says let's go to Richmond and here we are. Although, until she told you about the motel, I didn't know we were spending the night."

"You don't mind, do you?" I asked, afraid there might be a change of plans.

"No, I want to see you too." She slid her hand across my cheek and rubbed the back of my neck. I shivered.

13
Pigeon-holed

"Hey, hey, hey, no sex in the lounge, please, or I'll have to call that charming little nurse." It was Suzie back with the food. She slid it onto the table. Out of a paper bag she pulled a six-pack of beer.

"Whaddya think this is?" I asked, pushing the bag in front of the beer to conceal them from passersby. "An Army hospital," I said. "That little bitch sees this stuff here, she'll tie a knot in my catheter." The two women looked at me with wide eyes and arched eyebrows and then burst out laughing.

Suzie dabbed her eyes and gasped, "I gotta go to the bathroom before I pee my pants," and ran out of the room.

Cathy leaned over to me. "Look, don't let her know I told you about the divorce. It might be something she wants to tell you or not."

The three of us ate, drank, and told stories about home, school, and the Army until almost nine o'clock. I explained to them about being retired and about disability pay. The women were surprised that the VA didn't give the patients beer. The Army provided two beers a day for their patients. We started laughing, talking about the time I was flat on my back with tongs in my head. Suzie was holding a can of beer with a straw in it for me. I blew bubbles into the can and it foamed all over me.

On the way back to the ward, the women went into the gift shop and bought toothbrushes and extra large T-shirts to use for night-gowns. Then, they helped me back into my bed to a chorus of kidding from the other guys. They kissed me goodnight and turned to leave. There stood Miss Adams, the nurse who had first greeted me upon my arrival at the hospital. She said goodnight in response to the women's greetings. Then, she moved up beside me, slipped a thermometer under my tongue, and turned to watch the women walk down the ward.

"Now, Scott boy, are you going to tell me one of those girls is your sister?"

"No, ma'am."

"Cousin?"

"No, ma'am."

"Damn, boy, I'd a never thought it to look at you. You're a ladies' man?"

"No, ma'am, Just lucky."

"So what did you do to the short nurse?" The sudden change of topic, as well as the change in the tone of her voice, took me off-guard. The only response I could come up with was a wide-eyed, innocent "who me?" stare. She continued, "When I came on tonight, she was working overtime typing something into your file."

"I called her a bitch."

"Are you ready to be thrown out into the cold, cruel world?"

"No, ma'am."

She took a typed sheet of paper from her pocket and crinkled it up and tossed it into the trash. "Try and stay out of trouble."

"Yes, ma'am." I lay back on my bed and decided it had been a very profitable day. I was ahead in this world by three friends.

§ § § § § §

In the motel bathroom, Suzie stood naked in front of the bathroom mirror. She knew she was too thin. She turned sideways and looked at her profile. Why had that son-of-a-bitch soon-to-be ex-husband preferred sex with another woman to her? She closed her eyes and wrapped her arms across her breasts. She remembered the places where Jake's hands had pressed against her back.

14

Morning

I slept well that night and did not dream. I was up early watching for the girls. At about eight, Suzie walked in. She caused a little commotion. It was before visiting hours and some of the guys were still getting dressed. She pulled the curtain around the bed to give the other guys privacy. She sat on the bed and pulled two large coffees and doughnuts out of a bag.

"Where's Cathy?"

"We were up all night talking so I left her sleeping."

While she fixed her coffee, she told me about the divorce—how she had suspected and was glad it was over. She told me about her plans to leave the Army in June. I liked listening to her. She had come all this way to say these things and I was flattered.

"By the way, how's your mom? Does she get down on the weekends?"

The question ruined the beginning of the day. My visitors had quite erased the memory of the letter of the day before. I opened the drawer of my bed stand, took out the wadded ball of paper, and handed it to Suzie. She pressed it flat against the mattress and read it. Tears formed in my eyes and crept down my cheeks. I lay back in my bed and put my forearm across my eyes. I felt her fingers pulling my arm down. She had finished reading and she looked at me.

I felt the tears leave cold trails across my cheeks. "You're the first visitors I've had since I've been here. You don't know how lonely the last several weeks have been."

"Oh, but I do," she responded softly. Then she kissed me, a soft, friendly kiss that neither of us hurried to end. Finally, she moved back. "Are you still planning to go to school?"

"Yeah. That is the one thing your visit has reminded me of. No matter how bad this place sucks, I'm getting out. I don't know how I'm gonna manage or where I'm gonna live, but this is all going to be behind me soon."

"That's the way I feel about my marriage."

We retreated into ourselves and thought for a minute about the similarities of our loss and loneliness. "Look, I'm going to drive back to the motel and pick up Cathy and we'll grab something and come back for lunch. Then we have to start back to Washington. I'm afraid to drive when it gets dark. The roads may freeze."

She started to get up, but there was something I needed to say to her alone. I took her hand between my palms. "I know it's a long drive down here. We hardly know each other and you don't owe me anything." I was doing it again, rushing my words. I took a breath, trying to slow down. "Please, ***please,*** promise me you'll come back again, sometime. You don't have to say when. I just have to have hope."

"Jake." Her tone was that of an impatient teacher with a dim-witted pupil. "Aside from my mom, my sister, my lawyer, and Cathy, you're the only other person I've told about what led to my divorce. I haven't even found the nerve to tell my father. Of course, he had the good sense to be suspicious of my ex from the beginning." She was trying to look through my eyes to see if anything was being registered in my brain. "I drove all the way down here and stayed overnight just to see you. I don't know why you're different from all the other patients I've had. Maybe it's because of the determination I see in you, or maybe it's because you made me feel special when I needed it."

"Suzie, when my own mother can't come see me anymore and I haven't had so much as a note from anyone else," I paused, "I'm scared to death you won't be coming back. I'm pretty damn insecure."

"Jake do you know why I came to see you?" I had no idea and I wondered if Cathy had told her that I asked that. "To me, you are the answer to a question I asked night after night in the hospital in Vietnam as I packed broken, torn, and disfigured bodies of young men for shipment stateside. I wondered," she continued, her voice grew hoarse with emotion, "what the hell is going to happen to these people?

What kind of life are they going to have? If I don't hang around you, I'll spend the rest of my life wondering what the answers are."

I stopped listening after she said the word Vietnam. I shook my head and said incredulously, "You were in Vietnam?"

"What did you think I meant yesterday when I said you could help me with my bad dreams?"

"I don't know—the divorce."

"I meant that I have woken like you from the memories of little boys with stumps instead of hands and feet, from the sound of the silence when their breathing stopped, from the smells of death." She was going into a trance as she said this, as if one of her own dreams were starting. I shook her arm. She looked out the window and bit her lip. She had probably seen me tossing in my sleep at Walter Reed. Our friendship contained a lot of common ground that I was not aware of yet. She grinned at me to signify that she had had enough of this getting serious so early in the day. "Well, Doctor Freud, next time I come back, we'll do some dream analysis. I will be back. Promise."

Before they left that day, both women had promised to come back and see me, but they would take turns. Suzie gave me her phone number in case I needed a pep talk between visits.

Monday, I received a letter from my Ranger team. Actually, it was a Christmas card that had been chasing me from Walter Reed. It was mailed in late November. It was signed by a lot of the guys in the company, so there was not much room to write anything else. I took a pad of paper and wrote to tell them I was okay and that when they got stateside, they should look me up. When my hands grew tired, I pulled out the photos. I was even able to look at the one of me and Jim out in the jungle with the butts of our rifles resting on our hips. My free arm was resting on Jim's shoulder and my fingers formed a V.

"When I get out of here, buddy, I'll look you up. It's a promise." My throat grew tight and I felt the tears on my cheeks. I reached out with my tongue and tasted them.

I went back to writing.

15

Wheels!!!

On Monday, an aide woke me at 6:30. It was bath morning. The aide rolled a gurney covered with a rubber sheet beside the bed. He unhooked the catheter from the drainage bag and clamped the catheter. Then, he slid me onto the gurney and covered me with a sheet and rolled me into the shower room. There is something really weird, odd, and peculiar about rolling along lying down. I think that our balance has evolved to want to be able to see what is beneath us.

The patients on the ward were divided into groups and each group had its day to go to the showers. It did not apply to guys in wheelchairs, who could take showers whenever. To keep everything, and I mean everything, on schedule, a suppository was shoved in my rear when I arrived in the room next to the showers. Ralph, a jolly man with pockmarks across his black face and a big belly, went through an endless supply of examining gloves. He rolled me on my side and, even though I had no feeling there, I could feel him shoving. This was an assembly line operation. Ralph would stick a blue disposable pad under your butt and move onto the next man while the suppository had its effect. There were always the same old jokes about the situation. Ralph was the "King of Crap" who had a real shitty job working between the cracks. And they always wanted him to make sure he had not lost any gloves. He came back in a while and cleaned me up. I was rolled to the next man, Lavassuer.

Lavassuer wore rubber boots, a rubber apron, and rubber gloves. He held a rubber hose with a spray attachment. I used to imagine myself as a '57 Chevy convertible with a chrome grill and mag wheels being pulled through a car wash. He wet each man down from head to foot, then he grabbed a soapy sponge from a bucket and lathered you everywhere. There were times when I thought that I would just slide off the rubber sheet onto the concrete floor. He gave me a cloth for my face and then he rinsed me. I was covered with a towel and rolled out to dry myself the best I could. Then, it was back to the bed.

I arrived at my bed just as the troupe of doctors and nurses came by. The short bitch nurse handed the doctor my file and then stood with a smug look, waiting for the doctor to finish reading her report of Friday evening and anticipating the lecture I would get about being thrown out for not respecting her authority. The doctors hemmed and hawed, murmured, and never even glanced at me. They returned the file to her and prepared to move to the next patient. With a puzzled expression, she flipped through the file to look for the page she typed, her jaw tightened, and she glared. I knew my troubles with her were beginning, but I had business with the doctors.

"Doc," I addressed the chief page-turner, "I think it's time for me to get up in a wheelchair."

"It's too soon," he barked curtly.

"No, it's not. Look how long I've been here!"

The doctor was perturbed that a patient would dare to question him. He grabbed the file and licked his thumb before flipping over each page. He and the first assistant pen-carrier read something and exchanged glances. I could see his brain transmitting the word "NO" to his lips so I volunteered, "I have been sitting up in my bed; so I would probably do real well in a wheelchair."

The file was closed. "Have this patient put up in a wheelchair today," the chief page turner ordered the short nurse. I was so glad.

These doctors aren't so bad if you can just show them a reason, I thought. On the other hand, the doctor was walking away thinking, *I've had it with this jerk. Let him fall flat on his face and I won't have to listen to his crap any more. He'll do things by my schedule.*

The aides showed up that morning to help me dress. They strapped a bag on my leg and attached the catheter to it. They put tight elastic stockings on me to force the blood from my feet and help my weak veins return it to my heart. Finally, I got the first pair of pants I had had for months. Funny, the things that become symbols of success.

They did not come take me to therapy that morning. I waited in bed until almost lunch. Sam came in with a wheelchair. The chair had a tall back that had been adjusted so that it was at a forty-five degree angle.

He lifted a stainless steel contraption from the seat. It was a brace to support my head. A pad went on my chest and a second pad went between my shoulder blades. The pads were connected by straps that went over my shoulders. Two metal rods came up from each pad. The rods on the front pad pushed a curved pad into my chin and the rods on the back pad pushed a pad into the base of my skull. Those were also attached to each other by leather straps that went around my head. After Sam had this in place, he took me under the arms and an aide grabbed me under the knees and they sat me in the chair.

I grinned. I saw colored lights. It went dark. When I came to, I realized that Sam had rocked the chair back on its big wheels so that my feet were higher than my head. Sam's face was smiling down at mine. "This ain't gonna be easy, boy. You tell me when you feel faint." I nodded weakly.

Sam worked patiently with me for almost an hour until I could sit up. My breathing was labored. My weak stomach muscles were exhausted from pushing and sucking air through my lungs.

"I gotta go back to the gym," said Sam. "You want to go back to bed?"

I shook my head no. "Let me go with you."

When we got there, Sam put my feet up on an exercise mat. "If you feel faint, put your head between your knees." Sam patted my shoulder and went to work with other patients.

The triumph I felt was incredible. I had made a major step toward getting back in the world, even if I did frequently put my head between my legs during the next hour. By then, I was exhausted. Sam rolled me back to the ward and guided the chair beside the bed. He placed a smooth board from the edge of the bed to the edge of the chair. I was supposed to slide across to the bed. I was so tired that I just fell to the side and Sam grabbed my legs and rolled me onto the bed. Maybe it was the sound of the rain I heard as I drifted to sleep, but the dream began immediately.

I was lying in the jungle. The rain was beating in my face. My boonie hat had blown off. I opened my eyes and saw Jim's face. I closed my eyes. There was the sound of an occasional gunshot. I couldn't make out whether it was the Rangers or the Viet Cong shooting. Who won the fight? Would the Viet Cong find me alive and shoot me? Did anyone know that Jim and I were there or would the jungle just grow over our bodies?

I was thirsty. I remembered being thirsty in the helicopter. I opened my mouth so that the rain would fall in. I stuck my tongue into the puddle but it tasted of blood. I heard the sound of choppers. They came over the clearing and hovered. Ropes came out of each side and Rangers climbed onto the skids. They rappelled down into the clearing. They spread out into the woods. One of them came upon Jim and me. "Hey, Doc there's two guys over here." The Ranger moved to stand guard between the jungle and the medic who ran up. He knelt over Jim. "Jesus Christ," he gasped. He pulled Jim's poncho from his pack and spread it over his head.

He reached over and felt my neck for a pulse. There was a stab of pain and my eyes opened. "He's alive." He called to the radioman, "Get a dust-off in here."

The radioman yelled into the mouthpiece, "Five-o, five-o, this is Cowboy. We need a rabbit. Over."

"Roger, cowboy," came the reply through the handset, "one is inbound." The medic started looking for injuries on me. He cut off the harness that carried my ammo boxes. Then, he saw the edge of a dark red mark with the faint purple of bruise starting by my collar. Gently, he pulled back on the shirt. "Shit." He put his face right in front of mine. "Can you move your legs?"

"No," I said quietly, "or my arms." I could see my team leader and Snake, another team member, holding a poncho over me and the medic to keep off the rain. I could hear the radioman talking to the rescue chopper, assuring the pilot that the landing zone was secure. Two choppers came in. Into the first one they dragged six lifeless men, Jim and five VC, wrapped in ponchos, and it lifted off. The medic ran to the second chopper and came back with the stretcher.

"Okay, you guys lift his body and I'll handle the head and we'll just roll him back on the stretcher," the medic directed. They tried to be careful, but a surge of pain shot through my brain and I blacked out. When I came to, I was in a chopper bouncing through the dark. They landed. I was wheeled into a brightly lit room. A nurse and a medic cut off my clothing. A portable x-ray machine was rolled in and they shot me from every angle. My head was shaved. A doctor leaned over and looked into my face and explained that I had a broken neck and they were going to drill two small holes into my skull. He held up a device that looked like small ice tongs and said that these would be put into the holes in my skull and that weights would be hung on a rope tied to the tongs to pull my vertebrae into alignment. Those tongs would be in my skull for six weeks. I was too tired to care what happened and his voice was like a dog growling into an empty can. When they moved my head to align my neck, a wave of pain broke over me and I passed out.

"Hey, wake up." Someone in the VA hospital was shaking me. It was nine o'clock at night. I had slept through the dinner. It was an aide waking me up to undress me. I went right back to sleep. There was no more dream.

The next morning, I was up early watching for the first aide to come on the ward. They got me dressed and strapped the neck brace on. I noticed that the chin pad was beginning to rub a sore, but I was too anxious to get back into the chair to worry. The aide showed me how to use the trapeze that hung above my bed to get into the chair. The trapeze was an iron pipe suspended by two chains from the ceiling. A loop of web cargo strap hung from the pipe for me to put my forearm in and swing over to the chair and lower myself.

For an instant, I started to feel light-headed, but I quickly put my head between my knees and took some deep breaths. Then, I pushed against the chair frame and sat up.

"Are you okay," asked Joe White, who was an early riser.

"Yeah, could you do me a favor and see if you can adjust the back of the chair so it's more straight up."

"Roll out here so I can get behind you."

My smooth palms slipped on the rims so I put my hands on the rubber tires and pushed into the aisle. Joe loosened the clamps and pushed the back of the chair forward. "Howzat?"

"Yeah, that's good, thanks."

I slowly pushed back and forth on the ward. I stopped often to catch my breath. I was surprised at how many muscles tired from working to pump air. I looked at the people and places I hadn't seen on the top of the gurney. I stayed up until about ten. Then, an aide helped me back into bed for a nap.

After lunch, I decided to push and see Sam. I rolled to the hall that divided the ward. From this point, the hall sloped downhill on either side of me. To my right, it went fifty feet to the hall that ran to the mess hall. To my left, it went down to the other wards and the therapy rooms. I turned left and the chair quickly began picking up speed. I tried to slow it by dragging my palms against the pushrims, but the friction started burning my hands. It was now a runaway wheelchair. I grabbed the brake handles and jammed them forward, unfortunately not at the same moment. The right brake bit into the tire first causing the chair to make a sharp turn and slam into the wall. A nurse, who had suddenly walked from a door and just missed being run over, put her arms across the front of my shoulders and helped me slide back into the chair. “Still on your learner’s permit, huh?”

My initial fright went to embarrassment and started to become anger, but her tone was friendly and she was trying to make me smile. She backed me away from the wall. “Been driving long?”

I heaved a long sigh. “No, that was my first time coming down hill.”

“Are you going to PT?” I nodded. “Ask them for some wheelchair gloves. They’ll help you get a better grip on the wheels. How about if I steady you the rest of the way?” I nodded again. She held onto the chair until we turned into Sam’s shop. She left me there so I could push in by myself.

Sam looked up from strapping weights onto a patient’s hands and smiled. He grinned broadly. “Hey did you come down by yourself?”

“Not quite,” and I related my almost disaster. Sam walked over to a drawer and took out a pair of black gloves with thumbs but no fingers that closed on the back with Velcro. I put them on. They gave me a grip on the pushrims and that helped push and stop the chair. I pushed around the gym, practicing turns. When I stopped to rest, I sat watching two guys standing in metal frames. “Hey, Sam.”

“Yeah,” he said as he helped a patient roll under the barbells.

“When do you think I can do that?” He had to turn around to see what “that” was.

“Kid,” he said with disbelief, “you just started sitting yesterday. Don’t start bugging me.”

“No, Sam, I was just wondering what the schedule was.”

“When I think you’re ready, and you’re not ready.”

I pushed back up the hill but I had to stop every ten feet and lock the brakes and put my head between my knees and suck my breath in. Friday, I managed to push to the mess hall. It took me almost ten minutes. I did not use the gloves so I could start building up some calluses. For grip, I would spit on my hands and wipe it on my pants. I still had to stop constantly for breath; I could not believe how out of shape I was. All of my exercising had not strengthened my diaphragm and my hands would get ice cold because of the poor circulation. You do see the world from an interesting angle with your head hanging below the seat of the wheelchair. Even with the stockings on, my legs were not in shape to return the blood and my feet would grow very swollen.

Trains of three and four wheelchairs would go sailing by. The guy in front pushed with both arms. The guys in the following chairs held onto the handles of the chair in front with one hand and pushed their own chairs with their free hand. One of the trains stopped to ask me if I needed a tow. I tried to hold onto the last chair but my crippled hands could not grasp and they pulled away.

The daily routine went on with the doctors and me trying to avoid one another. Everyday, I learned new ways to do the simple tasks and they grew easier.

16

Ben

The wheelchair had given me the ability to find distractions. Every time the despair started crawling from the dark areas of my mind, I was on the move. One day, I went from my end of the ward across the hall, past the nurses' station and the showers, and into the other end of the ward. The patients here were, for the most part, horizontal. Some had pressure sores so severe that they had to lie on their stomachs on gurneys and push themselves along with canes. Others were severe quadriplegics.

As I pushed slowly along down the aisle, a big voice boomed, "Hey Jake, come on over, boy!" I screwed up my face and cringed. I recognized the voice. It was fat Harvey from Walter Reed. I wished I had explored someplace else. I was sure Harvey was not my kind of people.

I came over to Harvey's bed and smiled weakly. "Jake, this is Ben," said Harvey, pointing to a frail black man in the next bed. "Give him a hand will ya?"

I rolled up beside Ben's bed and watched for a few seconds as Ben tried to scratch his nose with his upper lip. "My nose itches terrible. Can you scratch it?" I took a Kleenex off the bed stand and reached over and rubbed Ben's nose. "Harder," said Ben. I rubbed more vigorously. After a few seconds, Ben nodded and I stopped. I sat there studying Ben's mustache. It was a pencil thin line of white hair that went from corner to corner of his mouth following the contour of his upper lip. His closely clipped hair was also white. I wondered, if Ben could not scratch his own nose, then who took care of his mustache.

Harvey was yakking on about Walter Reed, but I wasn't paying attention. "Gimme a drink a water, please," asked Ben. I clumsily slid my palm into the handle of the pitcher and moved it toward Ben until the straw brushed Ben's lips. Ben caught the straw with his lips and drank deeply. As I held the pitcher, I noticed a small gold statue of a man with a baseball bat. The inscription on the base: "The Best Coach Ever, Roanoke Boy's Baseball League."

"Howd ja get hurt," asked Ben. I could see he had a problem breathing.

"Vietnam," was all I said. To change the subject I asked, "What about you?" The question took Ben off guard. I realized he was trying to get me to talk about myself. His story was a package; once begun, it had to be told from beginning to end the way it had been told a hundred times before.

"I loved to play baseball. I played Double A ball a couple of years ago. How old do you think I am?" He paused for an answer. I knew from the way he asked the question that my answer would be wrong. "In your sixties, I guess."

"Forty-eight. Forty-eight, I am a young man. I was coaching little league." His pupils crowded into the corners of eyes straining to see the statuette. "I loved to run. I loved to hit. Damn, I could hit. I was coaching for ten years, ever since they wouldn't sign me to semi-pro no more." He laid his head back in the pillow, staring at the ceiling. Sometimes, his voice would grow hoarse with emotion. I noticed dampness filling the sockets of his eyes.

"I loved them boys, too. They was all poor boys—white ones, black ones—but all dirt poor. But they love that game of baseball 'cause they thought, like me, maybe if they play that game they could get outta being poor. Two and a half years ago, I was driving home and I picked up this nigger hitchhiking. He pulled a gun and wanted money so I gave him all I got." He began sobbing and the tears ran freely. He turned and looked into my eyes. "He shot me anyway. What he want to do that for?"

Suddenly, Ben began choking. He could not say anything and could not roll over to clear his throat. I hollered, "Nurse!" My wheelchair was jerked backwards out of the way, almost out from under me. Miss Adams grabbed Ben by the shoulder, rolled him over, and slapped him between the shoulder blades. I heard him take a deep breath. She sat on the bed and stroked his hair and then took a Kleenex to wipe his face.

I turned and pushed back to my bed and sat reading. About an hour later, Miss Adams stopped by. "Scott, boy, if ever there was a magnet for trouble, you're it." She grinned; I liked her soft Virginia drawl.

"I been sitting here," I said, "thinking that two arms and crippled hands are better than no arms and no hands."

She nodded and told me, "Ben is worried that he scared you away. He wants you to come back." I pushed back to Ben's bed and sat beside it until he turned to look at me.

"I ain't gonna visit if you start dying on me," I said, trying to be funny, and I forced a smile. He tilted his head back into the pillow. I rolled up by the head of the bed. We started talking for more than an hour, again about baseball. I had played second base in the Army. I learned that Ben liked checkers. I said I'd come back. I got one of the patients to get me a checker set from the activity room and every two or three days I went down to play with Ben. He told me the move to make for him and I moved. I did not win often and I never again asked someone how they ended up in a wheelchair.

17

HRONK!!

The trips to the chow line helped break the monotony. I was still struggling, stopping very often to catch my breath and put my head between my knees. If I could not even push this far, how could I get out of the hospital? The neck brace had rubbed through the skin on my jaw and there were spots of blood on the padding. I had loosened the straps over my shoulders so that the pads barely touched my head. Eating had become my new learning experience. Each food was a new rehabilitative challenge. Like the time they served barbequed ribs, one of my favorites.

I saw Dave sitting off by himself. A firefighter in the Air Force, Dave had been in Vietnam at Nha Trang when a wounded Army plane had come in. It crashed and Dave's truck responded. The plane caught fire and the pilot could not get out. Dave took off his glove to unbuckle the man's seat harness and his hand had been badly burned.

I rolled up with my tray in my lap and lifted it onto the table. We talked while I tackled the ribs. I had brought the leather cuffs that strapped to my hands to shove a fork and knife in. I placed the fork against the rib and pushed with the palm of my hand until the fork slid in. I then took the knife and started to saw the meat but, instead of the blade sliding on the meat, the knife twisted in the cuff and lay sideways. After several attempts, I took off the cuff and wove the knife handle between my fingers and tried to cut the meat from the bone. The neck brace prevented me from tilting my head forward to look down at the plate. I looked down with my eyes but they kept focusing on the end of my nose and I would go cross-eyed. The knife continued to slip and my hand was covered with sauce. The fork had slid into the other cuff until it too was covered. I removed that cuff and grabbed the fork between my teeth and the cuff between my palms to pull them apart.

Next, I took the handle of the fork between my palms and tried to cut the meat with the edge of the fork. The rib slid around the plate and suddenly pushed the beans and the cole slaw off the plate. Dave offered to cut the meat for me, but I wasn't beaten yet. I grabbed the rib between my palms and brought it to my mouth. I bit as savagely as I could into the meat. I ripped with my head in one direction and my hands in the other. A piece of meat tore off and the greasy, sauce-covered rib squirted from between my palms, flying straight at Dave. He could not move fast enough and it caught him right between the eyes.

A startled Dave gasped and stared at an embarrassed me. Dave broke into choking laughter and the milk he had been about to swallow came out his nose. "If you are gonna grovel with your food and wrassle it around the floor," he gagged through his laughter, "I'm getting a shield." I ignored the rib on the floor and started with another rib with more success. Dave feigned ducking from imaginary flying food and said, "I'll bet you're a real adventure when they serve corn on the cob."

In traveling to and from the mess hall, I learned of one potentially fatal hazard. The hospital staff loaded stainless steel carts with the meals to be sent to the wards. These carts were hooked in strings behind an electric tractor to be towed to various ends of the hospital. Each cart was unhooked at a different ward and the tractor left to deliver the rest. The danger was that the train delivering to the spinal cord injury section turned a blind corner into the hallway that the men in wheelchairs used. Rather than stop at the corner to see if anyone was coming, the driver of this train had solved his problem by attaching a bicycle bell to his tractor. This he rang vigorously before entering the hall. It was up to the people in wheelchairs to get out of his way. Complaints to the hospital staff about the danger of this brought no response. So the patients decided to solve things in their own fashion.

The staff should have guessed that something was afoot by the size of the crowd outside the mess hall so early. The driver climbed aboard his tractor and pulled away. As he approached the corner, he began ringing the bell. But today, the sound of his bell was answered by the sound of an air horn. "HRONK, HRONK!"

He attempted to stop the tractor, fully believing that he was about to be struck by an eighteen-wheeler, but the carts slammed into the tractor, shoving it into a concrete wall and throwing the driver up onto the steering wheel. The carts banged into one another and the side doors flew open. The trays came sliding one after another off of the racks inside, shooting down another intersecting hallway. Two nurses walking up the incline had to jump several runaway trays. From around the corner came a train of wheelchairs, each occupant going, "chugga-chugga, chugga-chugga." As they came alongside the electric tractor, the leader pulled out a can of compressed air and let out a "HRONK."

The effect on the patients was pandemonium. Guys on crutches fell down. Guys with breathing problems almost passed out laughing. I could not see for the tears of laughter and I had to put my head between my knees to catch my breath. It was an event that became a legend, funnier and grander with each re-telling.

One evening, I sat outside under the roof that covered the sidewalk and watched the cold March rain. Dave went by pushing two empty wheelchairs. "Where the hell you going with those?" I called after him.

"Come on, you gotta see this."

I struggled to keep up with him. "Slow down."

"I can't. I gotta get to those idiots before security finds them."

"Who?"

"Marv and Duke wanted to go buy some beer. They found one of the electric tractors and took it."

Just ahead in the dim light, I saw the bright yellow tractor on the side of the road. As it happened, they were going fine until they got to a speed bump. Fearing that the low frame of the tractor would get stuck on the speed bump, they had driven off the road to go around, but the tractor had sunk into the rain-soaked earth. The two men had been sitting in the drizzle for forty-five minutes trying to figure a way back to their wheelchairs when Dave came along and rescued them.

The VA hired a psychologist, a female in a wheelchair, to work on the spinal cord wards. She wanted to take me and some of the other guys out for a ride one evening. The only vehicle the hospital had that would hold us and the wheelchairs was a station wagon in which the police force had put a cage across the back of the front seat and against the windows to haul their K-9 dog in. One Saturday afternoon, three of us struggled into the back seat with the help of some aides. She drove us out toward the park. It felt weird riding in cage. At a stoplight, a car with a family in it pulled up beside us. We could not resist and opened the window. We grabbed the cage and started growling, howling, and shaking the metal bars. One of the kids started crying and we went into hysterical laughter. Her task of making us sane was overwhelming.

The stories of this insanity were the best medicine and so the patients were constantly devising and scheming. As I looked back years later, I wished that I had done some serious work with that psychologist, but I did not know how much I needed the help.

18

REMFs

I called Suzie once a week, but it was a month before she got back to Richmond. In that time, I had progressed from the four-post collar to a hard plastic cervical collar. I only had hospital pajamas to wear until a few days before Suzie got there when I went to the hospital store and bought a gray sweat suit.

That Saturday morning, I was sitting by the door to the parking lot at eight o'clock, I was very anxious. My hair had grown back to about an inch on top, too long to stand up and not long enough to lie down; I had done my best with water to plaster it down. I hadn't said anything to Suzie about going out. I hadn't bothered to get a pass from the nurse. But I had brought my sliding board with me. As I sat there, I remembered waiting for a ride at the main gate at Cu Chi.

There was a covered space inside the gate where guys who were hoping to catch a ride could ask outgoing vehicles for a lift. I was dressed in a clean set of my dress camouflage fatigues with colored patches on the sleeves. My black beret, which was only worn when a Ranger was not in the field, and especially when he was hoping to meet women, was set at an angle with the crest over the left eye. I carried an M-16 rifle with a clip of ammo in each pocket and a bandolier of clips under my jacket.

I was going to Long Binh to see Harry, a guy from the unit who was due to be sent stateside. *Of all the dumb luck*, I thought. We had all been playing football in the company area when Harry went out for a long pass and fell into a drainage ditch that ran across the end zone. Harry ended up with a compound fracture and had to have a pin put in his leg. The next day, I went out on a mission and when I came in, I asked about Harry. They told me he was to be shipped home any day. I hadn't bothered to get a pass or say anything about going to Long Binh. I just walked down the road to catch a ride.

It was getting toward 5:00 p.m. and, any second, the guards would close the gate and no more vehicles would leave. Even in the summer with the longer days, it was just too dangerous to travel in the evening. Just then, a jeep pulled up, but it wasn't like any I had seen before. The back had been extended to hold stretchers. There were a man and woman in the front and a man and two women on the benches in the back. "Where are you going?" one of them called.

"Long Binh," I replied.

"That's where we're headed," they said, and they waved me in. I climbed in the back. As we rode, the man in the back explained that they were doctors and nurses from Long Binh and they had spent the day visiting the hospital in Cu Chi. I told them that I was going to visit my friend who I guessed was in their hospital. They weren't from that hospital, but they had to drive by it on the way in and would drop me off. No one bothered to introduce themselves.

I sat back and laid the rifle across my lap. The doctors and the head nurse, a major who appeared to be in her early thirties, started talking about what they had seen that day. The two younger nurses were not included in the conversation. They sat watching the passing countryside. I sat watching the nurse across from me.

She had an unusual shape to her mouth. It was as if she were pouting. I could see the inside of her lip. I was staring at her lip, wondering if it got windburned. I realized that she was aware that I was staring and she was glaring at me. I shifted my gaze around the jeep. Suddenly, it struck me and I interrupted the conversation in the jeep and blurted out, "Hey, you guys aren't carrying any guns."

The driver responded in a superior tone. "We're medical personnel. We don't carry guns." I was more surprised by the tone of his voice than what he said.

"What, you think the gooks won't shoot at you because you got that big red cross on the front of this thing?"

The driver proclaimed, "I don't care for that word 'gooks.' It's demeaning."

I mumbled to no one, "You want demeaning, you ought to try shooting at them—that demeans the hell out of them."

The nurse beside me leaned over and spoke into my ear. "The reason we stopped to pick you up was because you are carrying a gun." I sat in silence, looking out the back of the jeep at the flat expanse of rice paddies on either side of the road. We drove past the 11th Armored Cavalry base camp. We were halfway there. The conversation in the front droned on, and then the topic changed to stopping to get a soda. I looked out of the windshield and saw a small grove of trees by the side of the road. Standing near it was a boy of about ten or eleven years old holding two bottles of Coke in one hand and waving them to stop with the other. The driver was already slowing down and pulling to the shoulder of the road. I glanced fore and aft and saw no other vehicles on the straight stretch of road.

"Hey," I called out. "This isn't a good idea. Why don't you wait till we get to Long Binh to get some sodas?"

But Doctor Demeaning was not listening. He was digging military script out of his pocket. As the other doctor climbed out of the back, he queried, "I wonder where they get cold sodas way out here."

I grumbled, "Off supply trucks they ambush." But no one was paying any attention to me. The two doctors and Nurse Pout were walking up to the soda vendor. Major Nurse and Nurse Reassurance stayed in the jeep. Once they reached the soda vendor, about forty feet away, I could hear them arguing about the price; the little pirate wanted two dollars a bottle. The doctor was insisting on no more than twenty-five cents.

I felt uneasy. These situations made me feel like a target. I liked being out in the field where the odds of being a target were less because usually the bad guys did not know that the Rangers were there. Then I heard it. You have to have been shot at a few times to recognize the sound of a bullet whining past you. It was followed by a "pop" sound off to the left. I could not place it exactly but I guessed that the shooter was in a tree line that was three to five hundred yards across the rice paddy.

I slid off the bench onto the floor of the jeep, brought the rifle to my shoulder, and fired short automatic bursts toward the trees. I hoped that by returning fire, the sniper would get rattled and lose his aim. "Shit!" I cursed as I saw my bullets send up little puffs of dust from a dike halfway across the paddy. I dropped the empty clip out and pulled a new one from my pocket and jammed it into the receiver. As I did, I glanced around to see what everyone else was doing. The soda vendor had vanished into his clump of trees. Doctor Demeaning was about to holler at me for scaring the boy when several more bullets came whining in. This time, the sniper had corrected his aim from being too high to being a little too low. The bullets kicked up dirt along the road between the jeep and the doctors. "Sniper!" I screamed. I unloaded the whole clip out across the field. By this time, there was a steady sound of "pops" coming from the tree line. The nurse who had been sitting by me was still sitting on the bench with her mouth hanging open. I reached up, grabbed the neck of her shirt, and jerked her to the floor. The doctors and the other nurse had run into the clump of trees.

The only one whose brain was still thinking was Major Nurse. She climbed into the driver's seat, started the engine, and pulled up beside the trees. Meanwhile, I was firing clips of ammo as fast as I could load them into the rifle.

"Get in," Major Nurse hollered at the other three who were crouched behind a tree. They ran out and crawled over the side. One of them rolled onto me and knocked me forward. I put out my hand to catch myself and caught my hand on a piece of metal on the floor, which neatly sliced my palm.

"Get off me you dumb son of a bitch," I shouted. I grabbed the rifle, thumbed the selector switch to semi-automatic, and kept firing as the Major went through the gears going faster and faster.

I put the weapon on safe. I rested my forehead on my knee and let the adrenaline rush subside. Someone took a hold of my right wrist and pulled it. I looked up. It was Nurse Reassurance. She had a first-aid kit and wanted to bandage my hand. The pistol grip of the rifle was coated with blood, which was dripping onto the floor. I realized I was cut. She rested my hand on her lap and poured hydrogen peroxide across the cut. She dabbed at it with a gauze pad. I looked around at everyone else. Major Nurse was in the front by herself, jaw clenched, knuckles gripped white on the steering wheel and foot stomping on the accelerator. The doctors and Nurse Pout were sitting on the right bench. I caught Doctor Demeaning's glance for a second but then he turned and rested his elbows on the back of the right front seat and stared out the windshield.

I grinned at the nurse on the floor beside me. "I call that the pause that refreshes," I quipped, trying to lighten things up. She was trying to open a bottle of iodine when I saw her hands start shaking. I took the bottle and unscrewed the cap and handed it back. She tried to get some onto a cotton swab but ended up spilling the whole bottle all over my hand and her uniform. The iodine hit the cut like boiling water. "Shit, fuck, damn!" I jerked the hand back and started blowing on it. The nurse lost her composure and started sobbing. I wrapped my arm around her shoulder and pulled her against me. "First time getting shot at?" I asked.

She nodded, "I've only been here two weeks."

"Congratulations, you'll probably get a medal," I said, still trying for a smile. She lifted my arm over her head and put my hand back into her lap and began taping a clean gauze pad to the cut. Then, we got up and sat on the bench. She pulled my hand back to her lap and kept adjusting the bandage. I could feel that her hands were like ice and were still trembling.

As we neared Long Binh, the other doctor said to me, "They won't let you bring that rifle onto the base."

"What are you talking about?"

"The commanding general has a standing order that you can't carry weapons onto the base."

I was incredulous. "What is it with these rear echelon mf'ers? You live in some kind of wonderland down here? Do you think there isn't a goddamn war going on?"

"I'm just saying that you will have to leave the rifle with the MPs at the gate."

"I ain't leaving my rifle with nobody."

I figured that if I left it with the MPs, they would sell it or lose it. I took my shirt off and took the bandolier off. I handed the bandolier to the nurse beside me. "Put these clips back into this, will you?" I paused. "Please." Then I took the rifle apart. I unfastened my pants and began to hide the barrel down my pants leg. I glanced at the nurse who had stopped putting the clips into the bandolier. She had noticed that I was not wearing underwear and was watching the barrel sliding into my fly. She looked up and we made eye contact and she started blushing. She looked down and started putting the clips away. I got the barrel hidden, but the bulky bandage on my hand made buttoning my fly difficult. I tried with my left hand, but that was a bad angle.

She scooted forward on the bench, turned sideways, and buttoned my fly. I looked over and saw the doctor and nurse watch her help me. When she finished, she turned and faced the front of the jeep and stared out. I put the bandolier on and put the stock under my arm under the shirt. I had more difficulty holding the stock in place and buttoning the shirt. Rather than ask for help, I just held the front of the shirt together. I wondered if the soda seller had been a decoy or just smart enough to get the hell out of the way when the shooting started.

We pulled up to the gate. An MP stepped out of a guardhouse and saluted the major. “Do you have a weapon in the truck?”

“No,” said the major firmly.

“Well, ma’am, where did all those come from?” he asked, gesturing toward about one hundred and fifty shell casings strewn over the rear floor.

“We’ve been out at the firing range today,” said the major, “and we had to clean up our brass.” The MP walked to the back of the jeep and looked under the benches. Then, he suspiciously eyed me; my camouflage fatigues and black beret did not belong to a medical unit.

“I’m just a patient,” I said holding up the bloodstained bandaged hand.

The MP knew he was being lied to, but there was no tactful way of questioning the major’s honesty, so he waved us through the gate. The major drove to their hospital area first where she dropped off the others. They all silently moved passed me, not even looking at me. Doctor Demeaning went to the front and started whining about having signed out for the jeep, but the major cut him off with an arched eyebrow.

She drove me to the other hospital. I got out and laid the stock of the rifle in the back of the jeep. I reached in my pants and pulled out the barrel. I tried to assemble it, but my hand would not work. The major walked back, took the pieces, and snapped them together. “Where are you going for dinner?” she asked.

“I hadn’t thought that far ahead.”

“I’m supposed to go to a cookout at the First Aviation headquarters. You want to go with me?”

“Sure.”

“Can you find your way back to where I dropped them off?” I nodded and reached for the rifle. “No, I better keep this,” she said, sliding it into the back of the jeep. “Let me take these,” she added as she slid my shirt off and then pulled the bandolier over my head. She helped me get my shirt back on and began buttoning it. I was very aware of how close she was standing and the softness of her fingers as they brushed against my chest and stomach.

I walked to the hospital and spent about fifteen minutes trying to find the right ward. When I got there, they told me that Harry had been shipped to Tahn Son Nhut airbase that afternoon to be sent home. As I walked back, I watched the sun slip below the horizon. I found the jeep where she had parked it and sat in the front seat to wait for her. She came down the hill from the nurses’ quarters wearing a white blouse and a khaki skirt. Her auburn hair was still wet from the shower.

"I didn't expect you back so soon," she said with a questioning look.

"They already shipped my friend. I didn't have any place else to go." She started the jeep and, in a few moments, we were at the Aviation battalion. There were about thirty men and half that number of women. I was amazed at the selection of food: steaks, lobsters, three kinds of pie, a bar with everything. *These bastards don't know there's a war on*, I thought as I fished a beer from a tub of ice. While we waited for the baked potatoes to be done, I picked up a guitar, found a thumb pick and tried picking a melody. She recognized the song and started singing "Leaving on a Jet Plane" and I followed her. With the bandage on my hand, I could only strum the song. Her voice was very good; she soared through the high notes and when she finished, I realized that everything had grown still and everyone was watching us.

"That was great," I said to her. She pretended not to have heard and picked up a plate to get in the serving line. She arranged for me to sleep in a spare cot at the Aviation battalion. The next morning, I got up and took a hot shower, a really *hot* shower, the first in three months. "These bastards don't know there's a damn war going on," I said out loud to nobody.

I hiked over to the hospital. The Major had said that she would take my rifle to work with her. When I found her, she told me that she had lined up a ride for me back to my base on a medivac chopper that was bringing a patient in from Cu Chi. She walked with me to the chopper pad. As we stood watching the chopper come in, she touched my arm. "Thanks for yesterday," she said.

"Hey, I'm not sure that I did any more than shoot up a bunch of ammo. You were the one who was cool-headed enough to get us the hell out of there."

"I'm still glad that you were there." She stood on her toes to kiss my cheek. I figured what the hell. I wrapped my arms around her and kissed her full on the lips. Her lips parted. My tongue tasted hers. She was cooperative. *I haven't had a kiss like this in too long a time*, I thought.

When I stepped back, she asked, "How old are you?"

"Nineteen."

"I'm thirty-two."

"Does that bother you?"

"Why did you do that? Kiss me."

"'Cause I could be killed next week and I didn't think there was nothing you could do to me for kissing an officer that was worse than that." I said it loud enough to be heard above the chopper. I turned and walked to the chopper and climbed aboard. I looked over to wave goodbye, but she was already gone.

19

Life in the Real World

When Suzie arrived, it was a learning experience. It was the first car ride, if you did not count the ambulances that I had encountered since that ride with Major Nurse. I had rehearsed it in my mind during the preceding week. I would sit by the back door watching other paraplegics get into their cars. Even so, there was still some experimenting to be done. Did I leave my feet on the footrests and slide my butt into the car or put my feet in first and scoot my butt after them? I decided on one foot in the car and the other on the wheelchair. I never thought to ask her what kind of car she drove; a VW bug swung into the parking lot. I had a bad feeling.

"Can we take a ride?"

"Your car, sir." She held open the passenger door. I rolled up and positioned my feet. Then, I rested the sliding board from the wheelchair to the car. I did not really slide across the board. I just fell sideways and then dragged myself in with my arms.

Then came the problem of getting the wheelchair into the backseat of a VW bug. I told her how to take the footrests off and she put them on the floor. No matter how she turned or angled the chair, she could not get it into the backseat. I felt useless; all I could do was offer words of encouragement. Finally, she popped the hood and shoved the chair under it. She could not get the hood closed so she tied it shut with a piece of cord. The car looked like a frog that had eaten too large of a bug and could not swallow.

She slumped into her seat. "Okay, where to?" she gasped, still out of breath.

"I was hoping that we could go clothes shopping. I need something to wear when I get out of this place," I answered.

"Shopping!" Suzie's voice was enthusiastic, "Honey, honey, honey, have you come to the right woman! Do you still have that wad you had before?"

"Well, actually, I started getting a check from the VA for about $800 a month, so I opened a bank account and got a credit card."

"A credit card!" The way she repeated it made me think that I had revealed a magic incantation. "That's even better than cash. We'll have that sucker worn smooth by the time we get finished." The little car made a throaty roar as it headed into downtown Richmond.

"Do you know where we're going?" I asked.

"To the best department store in Richmond."

"Have you been there before?"

"No, but when it comes to shopping, I have a special sense of direction." True to her words, within minutes, she was pulling up in front of a building with big display windows showing fashionable clothes, hats, and jewelry. In the next block, she zipped into a parking space left by a big Cadillac pulling away from the curb. Suzie struggled with the chair again and got it back together. Then, she put it on the sidewalk and brought it up to my open door.

With the wheelchair sitting on the sidewalk, the top of the cushion was a good foot higher than the seat of the car. The sliding board was not going to be of any help. I was going to have to lift myself up. I heaved a sigh. "Here comes the tricky part," I said. I had a hard time trying to figure out where to put my hands for leverage. I tried a couple of different handholds, but even with my arms fully extended, I could not get my butt to the wheelchair seat. Suzie had an idea.

"Lift once more," she said. I took a deep breath and lifted. When I did, she grabbed the waistband of my sweat pants and pulled my rear end up into the chair. In pulling me up, Suzie had pulled the pants halfway to my armpits.

"Thanks," I said in a high, squeaky voice. "You wanna pull those pants back down a little?" She was laughing and every time I lifted up so she could tug them down, she started laughing again.

She started to push the chair toward the store. I tried to turn to talk to her but I could not with the hard plastic collar. So I put on the brakes. "I need to learn to do this and, besides, I need the exercise." I pushed as far as the intersection but there was no way to get the chair to the street level.

"Can I try something?" asked Suzie, hesitating to take hold of the chair.

"Whatta you going to do? Get a running start and jump the whole street?"

"No, I'm going to back it down."

"Okay, give it a try." She spun the chair around and backed the big rear wheels off of the curb onto the street. Then, she spun me around while keeping the chair up on the rear wheels.

"AAWK," I squawked, not feeling very comfortable with this maneuver. She raced us across the street and put the front wheels up on the opposite curb and lifted the back wheels up. She had too much momentum, though, and almost pitched me out of the chair.

"Hey, you're pretty strong for a skinny woman," I said.

She feigned a frown and a pout and said, "I ain't skinny, I'm wiry," and she flexed her biceps. I shook my head and smiled. I pushed up to the door. It was a revolving door. Suzie went and explained to a security man that I was in a wheelchair and wanted to come in.

"No problem," said the guard. He walked to a regular door beside the revolving door, unlocked it, and pushed it open. It was too narrow to get the chair through. "Wait a second, this revolving door folds up." The security man struggled and fumbled with a release lever, but it had been so long since anyone had used it that he could not operate it.

"Look," he said, "go around the corner. There is a door with a ramp there. I'll go through the store and let you in."

There was a door around the corner, all right. It was a loading dock. The ramp was so steep that when I tried to push up it, the front wheels came off the ground and the chair started to go over backwards. "You sure this place is worth all the trouble?" I blinked at her with the sun behind her head.

"Aw, sure, I mean, we're here. Once we get in, it will be fine. Hang on." She grabbed the handles, backed the chair up a few feet, got a running start, and zipped up the ramp. As we waited, there was a pungent aroma of dirty dumpsters and industrial cleaners. The walls were adorned with various splotches of spray paint, numerous words that you would not say around your mother, and a large profile drawing of the male anatomy. A few grimy windows peered down from the top of the wall. Suzie wrinkled her nose in the foul air and quipped, "This must be the foyer for their most exclusive clients."

"Now I know how a black man told to go to the back of the bus felt," I said starting to get angry. Suddenly, we heard the doors being unlocked inside. The guard pushed them open.

"Sorry it took me so long, I had to clear a path." We wound our way between stacks of cardboard boxes, through big double doors, and into "Intimate Apparel." "When you folks are ready to leave," said the guard, "I'll be by the front door and I'll let you out."

On a mannequin's torso was a black lace bra and panties. "That's what you need," I said, "to wear under that boring old nurse uniform to give you some pizzazz."

"What difference would it make to you what I wore under my uniform." It was part statement and part question.

"Well, not much when you wear white, but I seem to remember a nice royal blue set." Her eyes grew big and color rushed to her face.

"You could not have seen them." She was almost convinced that the dark undergarments had been perfectly visible through the white uniform for everyone at work to see.

"Actually, I looked up your sleeve one time."

"How did you see the panties, then?"

"I didn't. I just figured they were a matched set." She punched me in the arm. "Ow, damn it, are you trying to make me a cripple? If I can't use this arm, I'll have to push in circles." I said this loudly, attracting the attention of nearby shoppers. I looked at a young woman and an older woman who were shopping together. "Please, help me. She beats on me and abuses me all the time."

Suzie pressed her hand over my mouth. "Be quiet you maniac." She spoke to the women, "Don't pay any attention to him, he's delirious." I started laughing and licked the palm of her hand. Then, she started laughing. "I gotta go to the little girls' room," she gasped between giggles.

"I know or you'll wet your pants." She went to the ladies' room. I decided to use the opportunity to empty my leg bag. I found the men's room. I tried the door to each stall but I could not get the chair through any of them. So I rolled up to one of the sinks and laid my leg across it. I fumbled with the clamp for a while before getting it to release. A guy came in and gave me a curious stare before going into one of the stalls. It was embarrassing, but I thought, *what the hell.* I would never see the guy again and it was the store's fault for not having accessible bathrooms. I finished draining it into the sink and left.

We asked for men's clothing and were told it was on the second floor. There were escalators in the center of the floor, but we were directed to the elevators in the far corner. The pushing was starting to tire me. When we got to the men's section, we were approached by a salesclerk that I just knew I was not going to like. There was his shoulder length brown hair that curled up smartly where it hit his shoulders. While I tried to ignore the nauseating power of his cologne, I looked at his clothes. Somewhere in this department stood a naked mannequin while this guy pranced around in its clothes. Everything matched too well. He walked to within an inch of me and looked directly at Suzie's face. "Good morning, Miss, may I help you?"

He was looking beyond me. I was trying to get over the shock that I did not exist. He was making a point of ignoring me. I coughed. "I'd like to look at pants." Still, the clerk looked past me. I suddenly realized how weird I looked in my plastic collar, short buzzed hair, and black fingerless gloves with my crippled fingers showing. The clerk launched into a spiel about a sale that the store was running, but he was looking at and talking to Suzie. It was becoming painfully obvious that he was not going to acknowledge me.

"I want to see some khaki pants," I said louder.

The clerk asked Suzie, "What size does he wear?"

"I don't know what size *he* wears," she spat through clenched teeth. "Ask him."

As the clerk turned and walked down the aisle, he said over his shoulder, "Those pants are down here." The path through the racks was too narrow for me to get through and I felt sure he knew that. My face burned with the humiliation and the muscles in my neck grew taut. I wanted to scream after him but my brain would not come up with a response. I turned the chair and pushed as hard as I could for the elevator.

§ § § § § §

Suzie started to run after Jake, but she turned around and ran all the way back down the aisle to the clerk. She grabbed his lapel and screamed, "YOU, asshole." Suzie ran to the elevator, but when she got there, Jake was gone. She went to the escalators. As she stood there riding down, she could see Jake pushing through the "Intimate Apparel" section. At the bottom, she ran for the revolving door, planning to meet him on the sidewalk.

§ § § § § §

I pushed passed the stacks of boxes to the exit to the loading dock. I did not see the sign that said "Opening Door Will Sound Alarm." As

I hit the crash bar, a loud bell went off. I pushed across the dock to the steep ramp. It was a mistake. I picked up too much speed and the incline threw my weight forward onto the front wheels. When the chair hit the alley, one of the front wheels struck a small pothole. The chair jerked violently sideways and flipped. I put out my hand to try to protect myself, but the glove tore away and my hand slid across the surface of the alley. I hit the concrete and rolled out of the chair. The breath had been knocked out of me.

I rolled onto my back, trying to suck in air. I rocked from side to side to sit up. Then, I scooted backwards to lean against the wall. I had torn a big patch of skin from my hand and I laid the flap of skin back over the cut and pressed my palm against my chest to hold it in place. "Goddamn this shit," I screamed. "Why, God, why are you screwing around with me?" My face was covered with tears and mucus. To emphasize my frustration, I hit the wheelchair as hard as I could. "You stupid piece of junk."

Suzie came walking around the corner. When she saw me, she broke into a run. "Are you okay?" she asked, kneeling beside me.

"This was a dumb idea to come here. I should have just stayed in the hospital," I muttered. She took Kleenex from her pocket and wiped my face. Then, she noticed the blood on my shirt and pulled my hand so she could look at it.

"Oh, Jake," she said with compassion. At that moment, the security guard, summoned by the alarm, looked out of the door.

"You folks need some help?"

"Please," said Suzie. The guard walked down the ramp. He set the chair up and put the cushion back into it.

"Can you get back in it?" I shook my head no. The guard told Suzie to grab under one of my arms and under my knee and he took the other side. They lifted me into the chair.

"Thanks," I said.

"My uncle is in a wheelchair," said the guard. I nodded. "If you want a store that's easy to get into and a darn sight cheaper than this place, go left at the street and it's in the next block."

"Thank you," said Suzie.

"Look, son," said the guard, "don't lose heart. You got a real pretty wife here and you both will get through tough times."

I started pushing the chair. It cheered me to have the guard think that Suzie and I were married, and more so because she did not correct him. I had hit hard on my ribs and shoulder and my hand was throbbing. Every push brought pain, but I was not going to ask for help. We got to the curb. I just sat there staring at the eight-inch drop. Another wave of helplessness broke over me and tears started down my face anew. Suzie took the chair off the curb and across the street. We found the store, which was called "Rebel Country."

"Stop a minute," I asked of Suzie, who had been pushing since the corner. I wiped my face with my shirtsleeve. Suzie then realized that I had been crying again. She stepped beside me and gave me a hug, but in doing so, she pulled my face into her breast. I wrapped my arms tightly around her waist. Then, I started laughing. She was startled by my sudden change of mood. She stepped back and gave me a quizzical expression.

"What?"

"I was thinking that I would smother in the expanse of your bosom."

"You are absolutely insane," she said, blushing as she realized where my face had been.

"I know, but it's all I've got going for me."

We bought a jacket, jeans, shirts and a pair of cowboy boots. Then, we went to lunch. I marked this in my memory as the first meal that I had eaten outside of a hospital in over five months. I ordered pizza and beer; I was relieved that they did not card me. When we got back to her car, I just fell from the chair into the front seat.

As she pulled from the curb, she asked, "Where to now?"

"Are you going to stay over until tomorrow?" I asked.

"I don't know."

"I would like to get a motel room."

"Jake, I'm still married and I'm working through a lot of emotional stuff with the divorce. I don't want to confuse our relationship."

"It isn't that. I just don't feel like going back to the hospital, but I need a place to lie down."

We got a room. I was very sore and exhausted. I struggled from the chair to the bed. Suzie lifted my legs onto the bed. My eyes closed.

20

Motives

I started dreaming, only, this time, the sequence of events was different. This time, I got to Jim. I knelt beside him. The shooting had stopped. I wrapped my arms around my friend and gently rolled him over. I looked into the gaping, bloody hole. I dug a first aid kit from a pouch on my belt. I stuffed gauze pads into the hole. "Medic!" I screamed. It echoed from the trees in the forest.

The little voice inside my head kept telling me that this was wrong, that this was not what had happened, but I ignored it. I wanted to see how it would end. The "doc" ran up to me. He quickly examined the wound and felt for a pulse.

"He's dead," said the medic, "nothing you coulda done." I laid Jim back, sat in the mud and pouring rain and started crying. The phrase, "nothing you coulda done" kept rumbling through my ears. It woke me up. I laid there with my eyes shut. *What about Jim's mom and dad? Where is he buried? Had they heard how he died or would they want to?* The thoughts crowding my head made me dizzy and I had to open my eyes.

The room was lit only by the sunlight seeping in around the heavy drapes. Beside me, Suzie lie sleeping. I quietly got off the bed. I left the collar lying on the table by the bed. I went to the curtain and peeked outside. The sun was low over the building next door. I guessed it was about 5:00 p.m.. I went into the bathroom. I washed the dried blood off my hand. I pulled off my shirt. A large bruise darkened my shoulder and rib cage. I sat there staring into the mirror.

I did not know how long I had been sitting there grinding thoughts through my head and sifting my emotions before Suzie came walking in. She pulled my chair back from the sink and sat in my lap. "Am I too heavy?"

"No."

"Nasty bruise." She took a washcloth and ran cold water on it. She tenderly wiped the bruise and then my forehead and cheeks. The softness of her hand on my shoulder and the coolness of the water stirred me from my thoughts, but still I kept staring at the man in the mirror. She looked into the mirror and asked, "Why are you sitting in here?"

"Thinking."

"About what?"

"Thinking that I could not get out of that car, or cross the streets, or get in that store. Thinking that today that clerk treated me like shit, like I don't exist because I am in this wheelchair."

"Come on. You're just having a bad day."

My jaw drew tight and my voice became bitter. "When your legs don't work, your fingers won't do what you want them to, and you have to piss through a tube, *everyday* is a bad day. It doesn't make any difference how hard I work to get out of there. I'm better off in that damn hospital, because I can't get around in the outside world."

"You don't mean to say that."

I jerked my eyes from the mirror and looked into hers. "Why? Why can't I say that? Afraid I'll mess up your psychological self-help program. If 'Jake is doing all right'—when I'm smiling and doing fine—then all those other cripples that haunt your dreams are out there somewhere smiling and doing fine too. Isn't that it?"

Her hand left my shoulder as if I had caught fire. She brought her hands to her face and sobbed deep wracking sobs that shook her body. She struggled to get up but I wrapped my arms around her shoulders and pulled her firmly against my chest. After awhile, she took her hands from her face and put her arms around me and laid her head on my bruised shoulder. I knew she was still crying, though; I felt each tear drop onto my skin.

"Look, I am incredibly frustrated, but I didn't mean to hurt you."

There was a long silence. "The dream was driving me crazy," she said in a hoarse voice. "I asked to work nights because I was afraid to go to sleep, afraid it would wake me up. I'd be alone and I'd lie in the dark and see the dream even though I was awake."

I shivered.

"I thought that I was going mad. I mean, nurses work in emergency rooms and operating rooms and see things as bad, if not worse, all of the time. We're not supposed to be bothered by that stuff, but it got to me. I didn't think other medical people would understand. They would say I wasn't cut out for this work." I looked into the mirror; her eyes were closed and I felt her draw a long slow breath. "One night at work, I heard you crying. I asked what was wrong but you didn't answer. I saw you were having a bad dream. I realized I wasn't the only one it had made crazy."

It made me smile to be called "crazy" and I thought for the first time I had more than a physical disability.

"I didn't know if I could help you or if I even wanted to. Then, there was Christmas Eve and those killer blue eyes shining in the dark. I was so lonely that holiday, I wanted so badly to mean something to someone, to feel a hug." Her arms tightened. "Or a kiss. When we talked after your mother's visit, there was something positive. I knew that if you made it, if I helped you, my dream would be over. Since I've been coming to see you, I haven't had that dream. But if you get depressed, then I can't come see you anymore."

"Why?" I tried to keep my apprehension from sounding.

"It's all I can do to deal with my own head. I don't have enough strength to pull you up out of your depression and I can't risk letting you drag me down." She ran her hands up my neck and massaged the back of my head. I watched us in the mirror, me sitting there in a wheelchair with this very pretty woman sitting in my lap.

"I am sorry for what I said."

"Why? You're right. I feel better now that it's all been said. I never told anyone about the dream. What I want to know is how you knew."

"It was what you said about me helping you with your bad dream. That kept bugging me and then I figured that was the reason that you would drive all the way down here to see me."

"What you figured was that I must be crazy to hang around with some cripple," she said as she leaned toward me and placed her lips next to my ear. "Sweetie, we gotta work on that low opinion you have of yourself. Do you think you can't be attractive without your legs?"

"I can't figure some woman driving to the store to buy damaged goods."

"I knew you didn't know anything about shopping for bargains. I had a man with two strong legs and a lying, hateful heart. You've got it all over him. Flat on your back, you did more to make me feel good about myself and make me realize that I'm special than he ever did."

"But I am confused. Am I your patient, your friend, or your therapist?"

"Couldn't you be all three?" The room was quiet for a few minutes. She turned to look at us in the mirror. "You feel better?"

"Look, I am glad you come down here, but you're not being fair. You can't expect me to just slap on a smile 'cause you come walking in the door."

"That's not what I expect. I know this is tough for you. Today was awful, but you have just begun your rehab, you will learn. Just please." She took my chin in her hands and turned my face toward hers. "Please don't give up on yourself. Promise me."

"I'll try." She shook her head no, indicating that that was not enough. "Okay, I promise." She gave me a hard hug. "You know, I haven't had a hug like that since I said good-bye to a nurse on a helipad in Vietnam." I tilted my head and kissed her—a long kiss. I licked her lips and her mouth opened. When we stopped for air, I asked, "I hope this is the right way to say," I began, pausing to make sure I wanted to say what came next. "…I love you."

"I love you too, but don't go too fast." She stood up. "I'm getting too heavy for you."

"What? A wiry woman like you, heavy?"

She glanced in the mirror and saw the smile brighten my face, but she knew it was an ornery smile. "What?"

"Royal blue, right?"

She pulled out the front of her sweater and looked down. "You pervert, how do you know?"

"Come on." I started backing the chair out of the room. "You gotta help me with an experiment." As I pushed out of the bathroom, I explained that I was tired of being told by the hospital staff that I could not do this or not do that. "They don't let you move ahead or try anything if it's not on their schedule. If you ask to do anything new, they always ask, 'How many months have you been here?' just to see which pigeonhole you belong in."

I put the collar back on. I swung the footrests of the chair off to the side and slid my rear end off the seat until my knees hit the floor. Then, my butt dropped and hit my heels and my knees cracked loudly.

"Ow, ow, ow," said Suzie, "doesn't that hurt?"

"How can it hurt? I don't have any feeling down there."

"But that doesn't mean that you can't hurt yourself." I pulled myself forward until I was lying on my stomach. "Okay, now slide my legs apart." When she had done that, I did a push-up and tried to get up on my knees, but my legs slid backwards. I laid down, rolled over, sat up, and threw my legs so that my feet were against the wall. Then, I rolled back over. "Okay, let's try it again."

This time, I got up on my hands and knees. I steadied myself. I strained against the collar so that I looked down between my arms and along my body to see my legs bearing my weight after so many months. I looked over at the motel room chair and asked Suzie to slide it over in front of me. "Put it so that the seat is under my chin and then hold on tight and don't let it move." When the chair was positioned, I quickly lifted one arm and put my forearm on the seat. I steadied my self, then the other arm. I lifted. I was kneeling up. "Slide the chair closer." Unfortunately, my hips went backward and I ended up sitting on my heels again. Suzie moved the chair and I went through the exercise again, but this time I went off to the side. I fought the impulse to express a profanity. Third time was a charm.

"My therapists say I'll have to wait another few weeks before I can try this at the hospital. Wait till I tell them Monday morning. Once I can do this, they will let me stand up in a frame."

Suzie sat cross-legged on the floor beside me. "How long are you going to kneel there?"

"As long as I can."

"There's something I want to talk to you about."

"Okay."

"How do you feel about Vietnam?" she asked.

"You mean, was it worth spending the rest of my life in a wheelchair?"

She nodded.

"I don't know the answer to that. I liked my Ranger unit and I liked the work we did. I learned a lot about myself, stuff I would never have learned under other circumstances."

"Like what?"

"Like watching out for my brothers and trusting them to watch out for me. Like esprit d' corp. Like bravery."

"Yeah, what's bravery?"

I grinned. "Bravery, my dear, is not having sufficient time to realize that you should be scared shitless. Why do you want to know all this?"

"I want you to talk to Cathy. Tell her not to go to Vietnam."

I cautiously turned my head so that I would not lose my balance. I did this weird thing I can do with my eyebrows where one brow goes up and the other comes down. "How the hell is Cathy going to Vietnam?"

"Dummy, didn't you know? After she finishes nursing school, she owes her Uncle Sam a few years in the Army and she wants to volunteer to go to Vietnam."

"I volunteered to go to Vietnam," I said softly.

"Oh, great," she paused, shaking her head. "Look, she's a sweet kid. I just don't want her to see the things that I've seen and have the dreams that I have had. At least tell her," she added as her voice grew angry, "that it isn't all fucking red, white, and blue." I watched her draw her knees to her chest and sit rocking. She looked at me. "Well?"

"Okay, I'll talk to her." I watched her continue to rock. "Who was hurt worse in Nam, me or you?" She put her forehead on her knees and didn't answer.

I changed the subject. "Do you wonder what happened to your marriage?"

She looked up and heaved a sigh. "Maybe we never gave it a chance. I left him right after we were married for Fort Sam Huston for training, then two weeks leave, then Vietnam and then back to Walter Reed. We probably didn't live together for more than a month at a time. Hell, I'm in the war and he's home protesting it; not much in common."

I knelt beside her another five minutes and then I noticed my hands were growing cold and my circulation wasn't getting blood to them. "Can you help me up?"

"How are we going to do this?"

"Well, I thought that I could get into this chair because it isn't as high as the wheelchair, and then I can lift over into the wheelchair."

"Okay, so what do I do?"

"You could grab the back of my pants and lift my butt when I lift with my arms and pull my rear end around into the chair." We tried that but the sweat pants slid up and around me without lifting. I caught my breath. "Okay, I got another idea." I could feel myself blushing. "Clasp your hands between my legs and lift from there."

I counted to three and lifted with all my strength and we almost had me into the chair when Suzie said, "Did you go through all this just for the cheap thrill of having me grab you between the legs?" We started laughing.

"Don't make me laugh, you goofy broad, or I'll fall on the floor." I managed to fall forward into the chair. Suzie let go and ran into the bathroom. I could hear her peeing. I dragged my legs around so that I was sitting in the chair. When she came out of the bathroom, I said, "You are the only person I know whose sense of humor causes bladder spasms."

21

Slow Dance in a Wheelchair

We were driving back to the hospital after dinner. We had talked for hours in the restaurant about our families, hometowns, and growing up. Suzie asked again if I had heard from my mother. "No, not since the letter that I had showed you." It was 10:30 when we parked. While Suzie was getting the chair out of the car, I turned the key so that the radio was playing. Suzie wheeled the chair next to the door. She went to put the sliding board from the car to the chair.

"Let me try it without it." I found some handholds and tried to throw myself at the chair. I landed half in and out. Suzie went to drag me in. "No, no I got it." I twisted, I wiggled, I struggled, and I made it, though the sweatpants started sliding down again. I fitted the arm into the chair and used it to pick up so Suzie could tug the pants back in place. I set down and took a deep breath of the cool evening air. "Damn, I hope this gets easier." We started to back away from the car. "Wait, listen." It was the radio. "This is a great slow-dance song." I closed my eyes. "I'm gonna miss dancing."

Suzie sat on my lap and put her arms over my shoulders. "Maybe not so much." I wrapped my arms around her waist and we leaned toward one another until our foreheads touched. We moved slowly from side to side in time with the music. When the song ended, we kissed.

We were still kissing when a voice said, "Boy, I think you best come inside." Suzie jerked with fright and would have screamed except that she bit my tongue, which was in her mouth. I was startled, but the sudden pain on the tip of my tongue made me forget about the surprise. I looked over. It was Miss Adams, walking in for the night shift. She had not stopped, but glanced back before she went inside and then stood just inside the door, looking out of the window.

"You bit my tongue," I said, trying to rub the pain into the roof of my mouth.

"I know," she said impatiently. "I'm sorry, but can't you ever get away from these crazy nurses."

"Oh, she's all right." I pulled her toward me and held her very tightly. "Thank you for everything today."

"I think that we're even." She glanced toward the watching nurse and then kissed me softly. "Good night. See you in the morning."

"Good night." As I pushed towards the door, I heard the VW roar out of the drive.

Miss Adams held the door open for me. "Scott, boy, you are a mess."

"Yes, ma'am, and how are you?"

"And I suppose that that wasn't your cousin either?"

"No, ma'am."

The next morning, Suzie and I went to Mass in the hospital chapel. She asked me if I was Catholic or just liked guilt. I said I was Catholic and asked her if she was or was just keeping me company. The priest gave an interesting sermon about how when Jesus came from heaven and took a human body, He became disabled. The priest explained that a disability meant not being able to do what you were once able to do. Therefore, Christ becoming man meant that He suffered the frustrations of not being able to use His divine abilities. I listened; maybe God did understand what I was going through.

We had coffee from the vending machines. Suzie said she had to start driving back because she had to work that night. I pushed out to her car with her. I pulled her onto my lap; it was beginning to feel like a very normal position for us. "When can you come back?" I needed to know.

"In a couple of weeks. Next weekend, I want Cathy to come down so that you can have that talk with her, okay?"

"Yeah," I said.

I spent the rest of the morning polishing my new cowboy boots, reading the paper, and writing a letter to my mother. Then, I thought it was time to get beaten at checkers by Ben. I rolled to the other side of the ward. Ben was sitting up in his wheelchair. I dragged a table up next to him where he could see the board. I set the board up and then Ben would tell me what to move. We were into the game when he suddenly looked at me and he must have just realized that I wasn't wearing hospital clothes. "Where'd you get them new duds?"

"A friend of mine took me out of here shopping yesterday. It was a disaster. I flipped the chair and fell out. Tore my hand up, got treated like crap. I tell you, after yesterday, I had real doubts about whether I got what it takes to survive outside of this hospital."

"Are you crazy?" said Ben, sounding annoyed. "You must be crazy! If I had your arms, I'd lift outta that bed and push me outta this dump and down to the Richmond stadium. I'd get a big beer and a chicken-fried steak with hot sauce all o'er it. I would watch a ball game."

"You want to watch a game? The Orioles are playing a spring training game." I interrupted Harvey's son and asked him to push Ben to the dayroom. We sat watching the television in silence. The game got to the top of the ninth and it was a foregone conclusion who was going to win. I had a question I needed to ask Ben.

"How do you keep from getting, like…" The word I was going to use did not convey my meaning but I could not come up with another. "…Down?"

"What makes you think I don't get down?"

"Well, I don't know. Every time I come in, you always have a smile—except when you have your teeth out—and you know more funny stories and jokes than anybody I ever met."

He finished watching the game and then he turned and looked out the window for a while. I thought he was ignoring my question, but he turned back to me. "Everybody at sometime has to fight their way out of despair. Maybe it is being crippled or losing someone you love. We all do what is easiest for us. You can either smile or be bitter, you do what comes easiest, you don't plan it. To me, it would take too much energy to be bitter or blue." Then, it was my turn to sit and think. What would be easiest for me?

Ben interrupted my thoughts. "Do you believe in God, Jake?"

"Yeah, but I sure as hell wish I knew what He has in mind for me."

"It helps to know, whether you get any help from anyone else or not, you are not going through this alone."

I remembered the priest's words. I thought that if anyone had a right to be bitter it was Ben, yet he just kept plugging along. Maybe he was getting help from God. I asked one of the visitors to push Ben back to his bed. I stopped at the foot of his bed for a second. "You know, Ben, that little trophy is right. You are a great coach."

As I rolled back to my bed, I made plans to get the paperwork started to get my car. When I got that car, I'd get Ben to the stadium for a ball game. Monday morning brought a fresh determination to challenge the hospital. When they brought the gurney to take me to the showers, I asked for a wheelchair. It was sort of a clunker chair they used just for showers. I think the bearings were rusted; it felt like pushing a brick. Once I was wet, soapy, and slippery, my butt kept sliding forward in the seat. I had to hook my arms over the chair handles and slide myself backward. My life was becoming one long checklist of things to master in order to get out of this place.

I was still having trouble getting dressed by myself. The elastic support hose that they gave me to prevent my feet from swelling were so tight that even the aides had trouble getting them on. I also had trouble fastening the straps to the leg bag around my leg and hooking the catheter to it. I was able to get my shirt and pants on, but it took both hands, a lot of grumbling, and many attempts to button the buttons and pull up the zipper.

That morning, as every morning, they brought me a little paper cup of pills. The nurse handed them to me. I looked in. Eight pills.

"Can you tell me what these are?" I asked.

"They're the same thing you've been getting since you got here."

"I know that, but nobody told me what they are for."

She picked up a small pill. "This is valium."

"Valium, how?"

"Five milligrams."

"Why do I need valium?"

"It's to control muscle spasms."

"But I've hardly had any spasms since I got here and the ones I have had help tone my muscles."

"They give it to everybody as a precaution."

"Well, they could take everyone's appendix out as a precaution."

"The doctors write the prescriptions, I just deliver it." She was starting to lose patience.

"Doesn't this stuff cause depression and isn't it addictive?"

"Look, if you don't want to take it, don't. I'll just mark 'medication refused.'"

"Then I refuse that pill." The rest of the pills turned out to be vitamins, something to make my urine acid, a stool softener, and a laxative. *The breakfast of sprinters*, I thought. "Look, I really don't like pills. How about I take the vitamins and then I'll eat some prunes and cranberry juice for breakfast?"

"Suit yourself."

After breakfast, ("No grits, thanks") I pushed down to physical therapy, trying to think of a way to convince Flo to let me show the new trick I learned over the weekend. I was in luck; there was a bunch of student therapists. Flo was running from one to the other, watching them. All I had to do was get her to watch something besides me until I was ready. Ben was by the door. I went to him. "Ben, when Flo starts working on you, can you get her talking?"

"Get her talking! I'd like to see how to get her to shut up."

Ben was rolled in and a student started raising his arms back over his head to stretch the shoulder and back muscles. "Ow, ow, ow, ow," said Ben. I never asked him if stretching his muscles actually hurt or if Ben was anticipating the possibility. I went and slid out of my chair onto one of the platforms that had exercise mats on them. The height of the platforms was the same as the seat of the wheelchair.

A student with bright red hair and lots of freckles came over with Flo. Flo instructed the student, "Just start with stretching the legs and I'll be back in a few minutes."

I lay on my back and the student took my leg and put my heel on her shoulder and straightened my knee. She brought my leg up over my body and then out to the side and then in and repeated this ten times. Then, she did my other leg. Flo stopped back and watched as she took my fingers and rolled them into a fist and flexed my wrist forward.

When Flo walked back to Ben, he looked at me and I nodded. Ben asked her, "Flo, what kind of hot dates did you have over the weekend?" Flo was hysterically funny. She told the most outrageous stories about the men she had been out with. He might have been a rednecked truck driver, and she would tell how they got it on while she was sitting on the steering wheel of his Peterbilt as they were going 70 miles per hour. Or maybe she had been with Richard Nixon with her explanation of why they call it the Blue Room at the White House. Of course, the more the crowd laughs, the more she goes on. The really strange thing was that she was so convincing that there was always a suspicion that she might be telling the truth.

Once she was distracted, I told the student that I wanted to stretch my back. I rolled over onto my stomach and pushed up on my arms. While I was stretching there, I looked at the freckles all over the student's and arms and legs. I thought to myself that I could never remember seeing a centerfold of a naked woman with freckles all over her body. I wonder if there was some sort of prejudice to photographing them. I checked on Flo. The whole therapy session was in an uproar, except for some students who were blushing and looking at each other with questioning glances. Flo was telling how she had been locked in a freezer all weekend with her butcher and his knockwurst. I pushed back up onto my knees. The student put her hand on my hip to steady me, but she did not know it was not part of my normal routine. Flo started to pull her skirt up in the back to show where she got freezer burn, but changed her mind when she told them it was too painful to wear panties.

"Can you please put the stool up on the mat?" I asked the student. In another minute, I was kneeling up.

When Flo got around to checking on the students, she looked at me and frowned immediately. Then, she snapped at the student, "What is he doing up there?"

"Oh, come on Flo, you know it was my doing," I said gruffly to get her focus away from the student.

"You know you're not ready to do that yet." She was gritting her teeth with anger.

"Flo, gimme a break. Look at me! I am doing it! Not only that, I did it this weekend. I stayed up for a whole hour on Saturday and Sunday." (So I lied a little.) "If I think I can do something new, why not let me try it? Everybody doesn't have to go through this place at the same crawl."

She looked around and directed the student to go start with another patient. "Suppose you had fallen and hurt yourself?" She sounded concerned.

"Then all the doctors would have said that I'm an idiot for rushing things."

"Yeah, but I'm the one who will lose her job." She sat on the mat beside me. She put her hand over mine. "Look, I have a seven-year-old mongoloid son at home whose old man hasn't been back since he first saw him. I can't afford to lose this job."

"I'm sorry. I don't want to get anybody in trouble. I just want to get well and get the hell out of this place so I can start college in a couple of months. The doctors want me to wait for nothing." I felt bad that I could have gotten her in trouble. "I won't try new stuff if you're not around. On the other hand, maybe you'd like me to try new stuff when you're on a coffee break." She smiled and shook her head. "You gotta let me move on. I'm getting bored with the same old stuff."

She turned away and looked down thoughtfully. "Are you okay up there?" she asked.

"Yeah, thanks." She motioned for the red-haired student to come back. Flo walked to another student.

I looked at the freckled face beside me. "If you play your cards right, you can look forward to this excitement every day." That student never worked with me after that, but Flo was friendlier from then on and took more of an interest in how I was doing.

That afternoon, I convinced Sam to let me stand up in the frame. I put my knees against the pad and Sam grabbed the waistband of my pants and pulled my butt up. I pushed my chest up and stood for about five seconds before I passed out. It was the same routine as I went through when I first got up in the wheelchair, but it took loads more time and more energy. By the end of that first hour, I could only stand for about thirty seconds before I had to sit down. That evening, I was too tired to go to the mess hall. I fell asleep with my clothes on. An aide woke me up at about 10:00 p.m. and got me undressed. I had no trouble going right back to sleep.

22

Happy Birthday, Baby

The monotony of the hospital's routine crawled through the last two weeks of March, but, for me, there were a few changes. I was able to stand in the frame for almost a half hour. I could push to the mess hall with fewer stops to catch my breath. And I was developing a weak grip in my right hand. If I slid a soda can so that it was wedged against something, I could push my thumb to one side and the knuckle of my index finger to the other side and, by flexing my wrist back, could force a grip and pick it up. I was also becoming more coordinated at using two hands to do what I had done with one. When the hands failed, there were always my teeth to grab, lift, or pull. I graduated from a hard plastic collar to a soft foam rubber one. Finally, the hospital gave me a smaller chair without the reclining back. It was much shorter and lighter.

Thursday, April 1, 1971 was more than just April Fools Day. It was my twentieth birthday. I was aware of its approach, but I had taken pains to keep it a secret. I had been watching for a card from my parents. This really was my first birthday—of my life in a wheelchair. That thought did not make for a happy birthday. The VA had a sense of timing, though. A therapist came in to measure me for my own wheelchair, one of two I could get from the VA. What a macabre birthday present; it would not come in for a few weeks. I ordered dark blue and the narrowest chair I could get, better to get through narrow doors like men's room stalls.

The student therapists did not come on Thursday. Flo sat and flexed my hands. “Where does your son go while you’re at work?” I asked.

“He goes to a special school or stays with my mother.” She went on telling me about his classes, the things they did together. I was impressed about how important it was for her to be there for this little person. She told me about Saturdays. They would go to a stable and ride horses and go out on trails together. I felt melancholy when I thought that was her hot date on the weekend.

I stopped by my bed at lunch. I hoped to find a letter, but mail had not come around yet. I changed from hospital clothes into jeans and boots and a jacket. I went to the phone and called a cab. Recalling how much trouble Suzie had with the chair, I suggested that they send a station wagon. I had my own birthday celebration planned.

I packed my wallet and some papers into a canvas bag that hung from the handles of my chair. Outside, the sky was full of puffy white clouds moving quickly in a steady wind. The cab arrived in thirty minutes. The driver was a short, round woman. She had a red face with bright blue eyes and a big smile—but no teeth. It looked like some plastic surgeon had taken a tuck in her cheeks and pulled the corners of her mouth back toward her ears. I was not sure if she was happy or deformed. It turned out she was cheerful, very cheerful, one of those people who, when you are near them, you start feeling better and I realized I was smiling. I did not know why—maybe her energy and attitude were contagious.

She opened the back door as I pulled up to the cab. I tried several approaches, but I could not get around the rear wheel well. “Can I ride up front with you?”

“Don’t make no never mind to me, darling. I’ll tie you on the roof rack if you want me to.” She grinned wider. I could not help smiling more.

“No, the front seat’s fine.” After I got in, she handed me my cushion and bag. Then, she folded the chair and deftly swung the ungainly mass in through the open tailgate. She slid into the front seat, wedging her round shape behind the steering wheel. I looked down at the brake and accelerator pedals. She had wired a thick block of wood to each one so her short legs could reach them. She expertly slalomed through the cars and curves of the parking lot on the way to the exit.

“Okay were you wanna go?”

“Do you know the Pontiac dealer down by the interstate?”

“Have you there in a second.” The friendly driver introduced herself as Delia. She’d been driving a cab for twenty years. There wasn’t any history or part of Richmond that she did not know. Her daughters owned a beauty shop (they did her hair) and they furnished her with all the gossip in town. Her son was in the Navy in Norfolk. She reached over and flipped down the visor in front of me. It was covered with snapshots of her four grandchildren.

It was 2:30 when we got to the car dealership. I had seen it when I had been out with Suzie. Mostly, I had noticed a dark blue LeMans on the front lot. "That's $8.50."

I handed her a ten-dollar bill. "Keep the change."

"Are you sure?"

"Yeah, it's only money. Besides, I'm hoping I could ask you to stop back at 4:40 and pick me up?"

"I'll be here." She pulled the chair out and held it for me. I had improved since my effort with Suzie, but the exercise of getting into the chair was part lifting and part falling sideways and then squirming side to side to drag my butt onto the cushion. As I worked to catch my breath, I felt her pat my shoulder, and then she slid behind the wheel and was gone. I pulled on my gloves and pushed across the pavement. The LeMans reflected the sun and the other cars. I peered through the windows at the white upholstery. I read the sticker on the window. The car was loaded; no option had been left off. The price was $4,595.

I saw the reflection of someone coming up behind me, a tall man with salt and pepper hair. "I'm Herbert Walters," he introduced himself and held out his hand. I was aware how weak my own handshake must feel. "Do you have any questions?"

"I like it." I thought that was probably a mistake to tell a car salesman that you liked the car, but it was my first time.

"She's a nice car, only been here a week or so. Would you like to drive it?"

"Well, I couldn't drive with out hand controls, but if you wouldn't mind, I would like to get in and see how easy it is to get the chair in and out."

"No problem. When I saw you head straight for this car, I went ahead and brought the keys out." The salesman opened the door and stepped back. "I don't want to get in the way, but I'll help anyway I can."

I looked at the gap between the LeMans and the car next to it. "You're gonna have to back it up so that I can get the door to open all the way so I can get close enough to get in." That being done, I rolled to the open door.

"Need any other help?" he offered.

"Thanks, but I have got to see how much of this I can do by myself." I had watched Joe White and some of the other guys load their chairs into cars by themselves. I had practiced the routine in my mind. I pulled the right arm off and laid it on the backseat. Then, I got into the car. It was much easier getting into the driver's side because I had the steering wheel to pull on. I placed the cushion on the passenger seat. Then, I folded the footrests and collapsed the chair. I put my hand under the footrest frame and lifted the front wheels. I pivoted the chair on its rear wheels and put the front wheels on the door edge behind the front seat. Then, I slid across the front seat, slid the seat forward, and leaned the back of the seat forward against the steering wheel. I reached behind the front seat, hooked my hand under the toe strap on the front edge on the footrest, and pulled so that the rear wheels rolled up onto the door edge. This sounds simple because I haven't described in detail the many times then and thereafter that I pinched my fingers, crushed my hands between the car and the chair, had the chair flip sideways, lost my hold and had it fall out and roll away, and all the other causes for silent swearing and, at times, violent cursing.

"Can you guide it in?" I asked the salesman. "I don't want to scratch the upholstery or the paint."

"You do very well," he complimented as he steered it into the back. I was feeling pretty proud just then, one more little mountain conquered. I settled back into the driver's seat and felt the steering wheel against the palms of my hands. I shuddered.

The salesman had come around and gotten into the other side. "It has a 350 V-8, three speed automatic, air, power steering and brakes, AM-FM stereo and cassette player."

I nodded appreciatively. "I am a veteran and the VA gave me the paperwork to get a car—but I'm not sure of all of the procedures."

"Oh, but I am," assured Mr. Walters. "When I saw you getting out of that cab, I thought you might be from the hospital up here. In all the years that I've been here, I've sold more than a few cars to veterans. Do you have your own hand controls or do you need to get them?"

"I need to get them but I don't know who sells them."

"Well, I can have some installed by a shop across town that does a nice job. Their controls are black and blend in with the car." I dug my paperwork and Pennsylvania license out of the bag and handed them to the salesman. "Do you want to discuss the price?" asked Mr. Walters.

"Why, it's the VA's money," I said.

"Do you want to come into the dealership and I'll fill out the forms?"

I looked at the front steps. "How?"

"Oh, we can bring you through the garage and into my office."

I shook my head. "Actually, I'd just as soon sit here in my new car and listen to the radio, if you would bring the paperwork out here to sign." The salesman smiled and tossed me the keys. I found a good radio station and marveled at the smell of a new car. If buying a new car puts pride in the heart of any red-blooded American male, then at this point in my life, I was soaring in great arcs high above the earth.

I was reading the owner's manual when the right door opened. I looked over and saw a very lovely female backside in a beige knit dress sitting down on the bucket seat. Then, a pair of long legs swung into the car. "Mr. Walters thought you might like some coffee." She had a cup and some packets of sweetener and creamer.

"Just black, thanks."

"I thought you might like to try out the tape player so I brought some of my tapes." She handed me a couple of cassettes. "If you don't need anything else, I'll go finish typing your forms."

"Thanks very much." I watched her get out of the car. "Oh, God, thank you for women, especially when they look like her." I watched her in the rear view mirror. I shuddered. After I finished the coffee, I noticed that my leg bag needed to be emptied. The driver's door faced away from the dealership, so I looked around and, not seeing anyone, I opened the door, pulled the hose from inside my boot, and drained it onto the ground. I thought I had done this very unobtrusively until I looked up and saw a stream of liquid running from under the car and heading across the parking lot. "Damn," I thought. I started the car and turned on the air-conditioning. Maybe anyone who saw it would think it was from the system.

About an hour had passed when Mr. Walters came walking from the office carrying a clipboard. "Sorry it took so long, but I got through to the guy that installs the hand controls. Their man is off next week so they can't get to it until after Easter." He placed the clipboard on the seat and indicated all of the places I had to sign. Every place had carbons under it and I had to grip the pen with both hands to get enough pressure.

"After Easter is not a problem," I said, "if you don't mind keeping it here and delivering it to the hospital when the controls are on."

"By the way, happy birthday," he said. I looked puzzled. "It's on your license," he explained. Mr. Walters sat and talked. He wanted to know how I got hurt and about Vietnam. I answered his questions but I was uncomfortable talking about it. Delia came driving in right on time. I got the chair out, said good-bye to Mr. Walters, and handed him the cassettes. I waved to the beige dress through the window. When Delia and I had gone through the operation of getting me and the chair into the cab, I pointed to the LeMans. "I bought myself a birthday present. Whaddya think?"

"That kind of car can get you into trouble."

"And the sooner the better." We started driving back. "Delia, do you get a break for dinner?" I forgot I was not going to get a "yes" or "no" answer.

"Well, I was gonna drop you off and go home and fix a can of soup. See, my husband works for Phillip Morris and on Thursdays his V.F.W. has bingo at the V.A. hospital, so I just work a few extra hours." I thought that was a "yes."

"It's my birthday and I was hoping to celebrate with something better than hospital food, but I don't feel like eating alone. How about having dinner with me? My treat."

"Oh, I don't know."

"Come on, there's a steak place right up here."

Delia helped me cut the steak so I did not make a mess. It was 7:00 p.m. when Delia got me back to the hospital. I knew everything worth knowing about Richmond. She had talked my ear off but it was better than sitting in a hospital feeling lonely.

I handed her another ten-dollar bill. "No, no. I can't take this. That dinner was the best tip I ever got. My husband will never believe that a fare invited me to dinner and I had lobster." Delia was not timid at the table. I thought, *if she keeps eating like that, she's going to have to drive from the backseat.*

There were three envelopes on my bed. From the shape, I knew that they were birthday cards. The return address on the first one told me it was from my parents.

"Happy Birthday, son. Your father and I are sorry we haven't been to see you. (Yeah, I'll bet he's all broken up.) I feel sorry about missing your birthday for the first time in twenty years. (She forgot that she didn't make last year's birthday at Fort Benning.) I plan to come down for Easter. I hope you can use this to buy yourself a birthday present. Love, Mom and Dad." There was a twenty-dollar bill in the card.

There's the cab fare back, I thought.

The next return address was Suzie's. The card was a picture of Cathy and Suzie. Cathy was dressed in a man's suit with wide lapels. She was wearing a fedora with the brim pulled to the side and holding a Thompson sub-machine gun. Suzie was dressed as a flapper with her foot on a chair and her leg showing through a slit in the skirt, a glittering garter on her thigh. Inside, the card read, "Youse bedda have a Happy Boitday." Suzie had written, "I'll bet you didn't know we knew it was your birthday, but it was on your chart. Cathy and I went to a place in downtown D.C. where they dress you up in costumes, take your picture, and make it into a card. I'll be down in a few weeks. Love, Suzie." Cathy had written, "I can't come this weekend because my family is having an eightieth birthday party for my grandmother. I promise to be there on Good Friday. Love, Cathy."

The last card was a surprise. The return address was "Sheila Scott, 1011 Mariposa St., Tucson, Arizona, 85710" Sheila was my Uncle Jake's daughter. I hadn't seen her since I was ten and she was about eight. Her dad did not get on with my dad any better than I did. Her family had moved out West, but her mom and mine were best friends and they never lost contact. I remembered Sheila as being a stork with long hair that her mother kept in braids. I opened the card and a photo fell out. She still had long hair and long legs but she was no longer a stork. She wore a T-shirt with "Wildcats" on the front.

> "Dear Jake,
>
> I know it has been a long time but your mom wrote and said you would like to hear from the cousins. I am a freshman at the University of Arizona in Tucson. I am studying elementary education. Your mom said you are planning to start college this fall. You should think about Arizona. It's great here. We could share an apartment. I hate the dorms. I could show you around. Also, it would be nice to have some family near. I still get homesick. Please, write to me if you get a chance. Good luck, Sheila."

Arizona. Hmmm. At least I would not have to worry about getting to class through the snow.

23

Flushing Out the Doc

Friday, I was exuberant. Happy. Feeling better than I had felt in a long time. The new car and the birthday cards had been pick-me-ups for the spirit, bright thoughts to distract me from my gloom. I had to find someone to tell about the car. At lunch, I trucked the brochures to the cafeteria and found Joe White. "Not bad for a GM product," Joe said, then paused and leafed through the pages. "Course you'll never catch my Charger." Joe had a bright orange Charger in the parking lot. He spent hours in the evenings and weekends waxing it, cleaning the chrome, dressing the tires, and cleaning the inside and the glass. He had shown me how he pulled his chair into the car and even offered to let me put my own chair in. When I reflected on the possibility of being harangued for the rest of my stay at the hospital for any nick to his car, I declined.

I showed Joe the photos of Suzie and Cathy and Sheila. I explained that Sheila had suggested I come to college with her help. "Too bad," said Joe.

"Whaddya mean too bad?"

"Too bad anything that looks this hot is your cousin—unless you're up for a little incest."

"Get the hell outta here—you're sicker than I am." I decided I might get a more enthusiastic reception from Ben. When I got there, I thought that Ben did not look so good. "You all right?"

"I don't know, maybe I'm just tired."

"Look at this; it'll make you feel better. Is she pretty or what? I bought it yesterday for my birthday."

"Not bad." He paused and struggled to take several deep breaths. "I guess this means you're planning on getting out of here and leaving me behind." I was stung by the remark and I did not know how to answer him. It had not occurred to me that, during Ben's stay, he had made a number of friends, only to see them leave him here in this hole.

"I gotta get down and see Sam. He is going to work with me on something." I rolled away. I went back towards my bed and put the letters and stuff in my locker. On the way out, I came upon Joe White outside the ward doctor's office, knocking on the door

"Jake, I need your help."

"What's up?"

"That son-of-a-bitch doctor is in there, but he won't answer the door and I need him to sign this so I can get some supplies from the pharmacy to go home for a week," he said in a low voice.

"What do you want me to do?"

"Go down and ask Ben to ask to see the nurse—he knows the routine. Then, when she goes to Ben, you go into the nurses station and dial 5575, that's his office number."

"What do I say when he answers?"

"Don't worry, he won't answer."

I pushed down to Ben. "Joe White sent me to ask you to call the nurse."

Ben grinned. "They gonna have you call the doctor's office?"

"Yeah, have they done this before?"

"Every time they want to flush him out."

I went back to the nurses' station. The short nurse was on duty. "Ben asked me to ask you to come see him. I don't think he looks too good." She gave me a suspicious look and then got up from behind her desk and went down the ward. I reached across the desk and lifted the receiver. I had trouble using my finger in the dial so I used my thumb. I heard the ring. I looked down the hall to where Joe and two other guys in wheelchairs were sitting. By the third ring, the door to the doctor's office opened and the doctor walked out to be immediately boxed in by wheelchairs. I hung up just as the short nurse was coming back up the ward.

When she reached me, she said, "What were you doing on that phone?"

"It rang and I figured I'd help out, 'cause you were busy, but I guess they thought they had a wrong number 'cause they hung up."

"Well it is a good thing I went to check on Ben. He's running a fever of 103." She walked down and got the doctor just as he finished signing Joe's papers and brought him back to see Ben. I headed down to Sam. I stood up for about fifteen minutes and lifted weights for a few minutes, but I had something else I wanted to do that afternoon.

Later, I pushed to the counselor's office. He gave me a book of wheelchair accessible colleges and I looked up the University of Arizona. "Can I come over and use your electric typewriter some afternoon?" I asked him. "I would like to write to some of these colleges."

"Sure," he replied, "the afternoons are good. A lot of the times, I am out of the office anyway, so just let yourself in. Here's some paper and envelopes. You can leave the letters on the desk and I'll mail them for you."

I had to arrange for insurance for the car so I rolled to the public phones and flipped the yellow pages open to the insurance section. I called a couple of the big companies whose ads said they covered everyone. Once I told them I was in a wheelchair, though, they told me that company policy would not let them sell me insurance. "Wait a minute," I tried to explain to the third agent I called. "I've never had an accident. I was licensed to drive tractor-trailers in the Army, but you're telling me that, because I'm in a wheelchair, you can discriminate without a reason."

"Look, mister," he said defensively, "I've got nothing to do with the decision. Some guy at the head office says I can't sell you insurance. I'm sorry if you don't think it's fair, but there isn't a thing I can do about it."

Joe White gave me the number of his insurance agent.

24

Left Behind

During the next week, the hospital grew quiet. Joe White and a number of other guys went home for Easter. The students were on spring break. I was very worried about Ben. They had discovered he had pneumonia.

The weather finally turned sunny after a rainy Palm Sunday weekend. I started going for a push outside after Sam was finished with me or after dinner. It was so good for the spirit, the green buds on the trees, the birds and squirrels. When Good Friday arrived, the hospital was deserted. Most of the employees were off. That morning, the nurse told me that I no longer had to wear a collar. *Another mile pebble*, I thought. There was no therapy that day so I hung around the mess hall after breakfast, having another coffee and working the crossword puzzle, in ink, because I had trouble with a pencil. Before lunch, I pushed back to the ward. I wrote a letter to Sheila, asking for a university catalog and admissions material and for her to please write again.

I heard one of the guys tell another patient to look at something so I looked up. Cathy was walking toward me. I could not believe that I had forgotten that she was coming that day. I felt as though my smile would split my face in two. She was wearing a floral print dress and white heels. It had been six weeks since I had seen her and she was even prettier. All the guys on the ward had stopped what they were doing and were watching her.

"Hello, gorgeous."

"For that, I'll go out and come in again."

"I wouldn't if I were you. You walk up and down that aisle again and some of these guys will go blind from the strain of staring." She blushed. I liked that. It was pretty framed by her long blond hair.

She sat on the edge of the bed. "What would you like to do? We don't want to hang around here all day," she said.

"Come on," I motioned. "I want to introduce you to someone, take you to see my latest trick, and show you my birthday present." We went down the aisle, crossed the hall and into the other side of the ward. I took her down to Ben's bed. Ben looked worse. There was an I.V. drip into his arm and oxygen going through a tube to his nose. I rolled up beside him and called softly, "Ben, you awake?"

Ben's eyes opened and he spoke weakly. "Hey, buddy."

"Ben, I got someone here I want you to meet."

Ben looked passed me and smiled. "Is that your Easter bunny?"

"This is Cathy," I answered.

"Hi Cathy," he tried to speak a little louder, but his voice was hoarse and he had to take a deep breath. "You scared me," he said to her. "I thought Jesus sent an angel to take me home."

"Hi Ben," her voice said with tenderness. She stepped up on the other side of the bed. She lifted his hand and shook it. "Can I get you anything?"

"I need a drink." I picked up his water pitcher and held it towards his face. Cathy slid her hand under his head and lifted it and guided the straw between his lips with the other hand. When he had taken several deep swallows, she laid him back. Ben smiled faintly. "So, boy, this the girl you told me you're gonna marry?"

"Ben, I never told you that," I said feeling flustered. "I *never* told him that," I said to Cathy.

"How many girls named Cathy you engaged to, boy?" I think being ornery was medicine for Ben's soul; the twinkle was back in his eyes and Cathy was enjoying Ben's sense of humor. "You take good care of this boy now, Miss Cathy. He's a virgin and he won't know how to treat a real woman like you.'

"Ben, you old bastard, you see if I ever bring any women down here again." Ben took a deep breath and closed his eyes. The effort of teasing had left him exhausted. Cathy looked at his I.V. and pulled his sleeve up to see where the needle went into his arm.

"Jake, buddy, I'm awful tired," he whispered.

"No problem. Get some sleep. I'll check on you later." As we walked passed the nurses' station, Cathy spoke to the nurse behind the desk. Ben's drip had run out and he had blood backing into his I.V. tube. The nurse headed for Ben's bed.

"Come on, I want to show you my trick." She followed me down the hall to the empty therapy room. I went over to the stand-up frame. I fit my feet into the bottom of the frame and put my knees against the padded board. I got my arms over a strap at waist height. I pulled myself forward and up so that my legs straightened and my butt came up. I was still bent forward at the waist. "Take the other strap around behind me and hook it to the other side of the frame," I said. When that was done, I tried to straighten up, but my stomach muscles would not relax. "Do me a favor, please," I grunted. "Put your hands on my shoulders and push me up." She walked around to the front and ducked into the frame with me. She got a hand on each shoulder and we pushed together. "Wheew," I sighed.

She looked into my eyes. "I didn't realize how tall you are," she said. She reached up and smoothed down my hair. "You have a part in your hair. I can't get over how far you've come." She suddenly stepped forward and hugged me tightly. I almost lost my balance and went over backward, but I recovered. We were looking at each other. I wondered if she would let me.

I had to hold onto the frame with one hand to keep my balance, but I chanced letting go with the other and put it around Cathy. I was hugging her, but I was also using her for balance. Under the circumstances, it was not graceful, but I kissed her. Then, before I bent forward again, I let go of her and pushed against the frame. She brushed her hand softly across my cheek. "Hey Ranger, do you think you can just start kissing every woman who comes to visit you?"

I looked puzzled. "Don't think Suzie and I don't compare notes," she said.

I blushed. "What did she tell you?"

"She told me about going shopping with you."

"And that's all?"

"She told me not to let you get me into a motel room." The tone of her voice changed. "And she said you wanted to talk to me."

"Damn," I thought. I hadn't any idea what I was going to say, so I said the first thing I could think of. "Just hug me. Please?" She stepped close to me and laid her head on my chest. I inhaled her fragrance, feeling it fill my head. I slid my hands up her back, pulled her close, and brushed my cheek against her hair. Then, for an instant, I saw death; I smelled its smell and heard its sounds. I knew what I wanted to say.

"I didn't know that you had to go into the Army when you graduated from nursing school."

"Yes, I'm hoping you could come to my graduation if you're up to it."

"Yeah, I'd like to do that. Where are you going to be stationed?"

She pulled back from me, tilted her head, and looked up at me. "Are we about to talk about Vietnam?" Then, she stood on tiptoe and looked me straight in the eye. "Did Suzie put you up to this?" When I hung my head and looked guilty, she didn't wait for more of an answer. "Jake, I love Suzie. I have three brothers, but I never had a sister until her. But she's got to realize that we are all different. I don't know if what bothered her will upset me, but I think I could be a good nurse."

"I know you're going to be a good nurse. I could see that at Walter Reed and with Ben just now." I paused to collect my thoughts. "All I know was that I saw men dissolved by death. I laid there and looked into the dead eyes of a friend. I was a good soldier, Ranger, trained to kill and be tough about it, but I'll never be the same. As long as I live, there will be memories, dreams, and anguish. You're so sweet and innocent. Neither Suzie nor I want to see you scarred like us." Suddenly, I thought of Bibi trying unsuccessfully to talk me out of going and I knew I wasn't doing any better with Cathy.

"Jake, who do you remember after you got hurt and got to the hospital in Nam?"

I thought for a second. "The nurses," I answered.

"And suppose they hadn't been there?"

"I would have been miserable."

She reached up and wiped some moisture from the corner of my eye and said, "I'll be okay, just promise to write me when I get there."

"Promise."

"I know it upsets Suzie to think about me going to Vietnam, but a lot of that has to do with trying to sort out her own feelings. She's pretty mixed up about Vietnam, nursing, marriage, divorce and…" She paused and put her finger in my chest. "…And you. I don't know what to do for her."

"What do you mean she doesn't know how to feel about me?"

Cathy smiled. "I guess she hasn't given you the 'I hate those lying, heart-breaking bastards' speech. She's very bitter about your gender, but I think she's falling in love with you." She pouted and had a mock tone of reproach. "Jake, she's five years older than you."

"Is that a reason not to love her?"

"I just think that there is a lot more in your relationship with her than being friends or lovers."

"Like what?"

"Like being a patient and a therapist. There's something in psychiatry called 'transference.' They say nurses should not fall in love with patients."

"But I'm not her patient."

"I'm not sure both of you aren't patients."

"How do you feel about me?"

"I love you as a friend, but I don't need you. I see the same things in you that Suzie sees. I love your guts and determination, your specialness." She stopped and looked out of the window.

"Go ahead," I urged her.

"Suzie uses you as a drug to kill her pain. She can't see it. Maybe when she has had enough medicine, she'll get better, or she could become addicted, but that won't be love."

I began to feel light-headed. "I have to sit down."

"I didn't mean to hurt you."

"Actually, you haven't told me anything I haven't already suspected, believe it or not. I just think we're making each other feel better and there's no harm in that. This place might make my body better, but I need her and you for my self-image and spirit. You're a reason to keep trying."

"That's what I am, huh, a carrot?" She stepped back so I could lower myself into the chair. The mood changed and she asked, "Do you want to take a drive?"

"Yeah, I have something to show you." We went outside. She was driving a pick-up truck. "Where'd you get that?"

"It's my dad's. He let me bring it to school so I could start moving some of my things home this weekend. I only have another month until exams are over."

I reached into my bag and pulled out a loop of strap attached to a metal hook, the latest cripple tool that I had been given. "This is to help me transfer into cars. Here." I handed it to Cathy. "You put the hook into the rain gutter of the truck." After she had it hooked on, I rolled beside the truck, put my right arm through the loop, and flexed my hand down. Then, I pulled up with that arm as I pushed down on the truck seat. I got my butt up to the truck seat when suddenly my legs stiffened and started spasming. It was taking all my strength to hold me where I was. "Help," I gasped. Cathy put her arms under my knees and lifted my legs and shoved my butt onto the seat. I sat blowing breaths. "On the return trip, just throw me up in the bed of the truck."

She threw the chair in the back and I directed her to the Pontiac dealer. The car had been moved to a side lot. "What do you think of the dark blue one?"

"It's nice."

"I bought it for a birthday present."

"You're kidding," she said with a look of doubt.

"Nope."

"Why didn't you buy the red convertible?"

"There is no pleasing some women. Now you probably regret telling me you didn't need me."

"You goof." She got out and went over and looked through the windows. "It's very nice. Do you think you'll be able to drive it to my graduation?"

"When is it?"

"May twenty-seventh."

"If I can escape, I'll be there. Do me a favor, don't tell Suzie about it. I want to surprise her." We drove around Richmond and stopped for a late lunch. Cathy parked beside the curb, which put the wheelchair on the same height as the truck seat. It made getting out easy. Just before I ordered a cheeseburger, my Catholic conscience reminded me not to eat meat on Good Friday. "I'll have a tuna salad on toast and an iced tea." I said to the waitress. Cathy followed with "I'll have the same."

I looked across the table. "I didn't know you were Catholic."

"I'm not." She smiled. "I just like tuna salad."

After lunch, we parked down by the James River and watched the daffodils and blossoms on the trees. She slid across the seat and wrapped her arm around mine and laid her head on my shoulder. "Thanks for coming to see me," I whispered.

"You don't have to thank me," she replied.

"Darling, if it weren't for you and Suzie, the only company I would have had for the past three months would have been the guys that come in from the local veterans groups and Ben."

"But I want to come," she whispered hoarsely. "I do love you." I could not see them, but I knew there were tears on her cheeks. "If I didn't think this was the last Easter I'll spend with my family for a couple of years, maybe…" She paused. She put her hand on mine. "I might get that motel room Suzie said to stay away from and stay with you." She squeezed my arm.

"It's okay. My mom wrote and told me she would be down for Easter." Unfortunately, I didn't believe it. I slid forward on the seat so I could look at her. "Are you scared, of Vietnam I mean?"

"You and Suzie have done a pretty good job making me have doubts."

"Sweetheart, I went through the same feelings before I shipped out. And I went anyway and look how I turned out," I said with a touch of irony and a smile.

She looked and fluttered her eyelashes through her tears. "Oh, yeah, try and cheer me up."

"Hey, you're made of good stuff. You'll be fine." When we got back to the hospital, I got down into the chair. I backed up and she moved to close the door. I wrapped my arm around her waist and pulled her into my lap. We both held the other tightly. Then, she put her mouth on mine so gently and we held the kiss with our lips just brushing. She patted my shoulder and got into the truck and started it up. I pushed to the hospital door and turned to wave, but I only saw the dust. I went through the doors and saw that a couple of orderlies were rolling a bed out of the ward.

I started up the hall. "Can you wait down there until we get this around the corner?" one of them asked me. They brought the bed down the hall until they were beside me and turning the corner. It was then that I realized that there was a body in the bed covered with a sheet. A shudder shook my shoulders and rose to my head. A small gold trophy lay on the bed. My throat tightened and then a sound burst from my mouth with the tears from my eyes. I watched the orderlies moving the bed down the long hall as a bleary, tear-drenched image; they grew smaller until they turned the corner. The hand on my shoulder startled me. A soft voice, full of its own emotions, said, "Come on, Scott, boy, you don't want to be bawlin' out here in the hallway." I tried to push, but my hands were cold and numb. Miss Adams pushed me to my bed. She handed me some tissues. After I had dried my eyes, I could see that she had been crying also.

"What happened?" I tried to ask, but my voice came out as a hoarse squeak.

She sat on the bed and took my hand. "His heart just stopped." She sat there holding my hand for about fifteen minutes. She walked out of the ward.

I sniffed and wiped my eyes and nose with the back of my hand. "Ben, you went and left me behind."

25

A Mother and Child

A Good Friday service was held in the chapel that evening. I had spent most of the day there. I sat and stared. I did not hear the priest's voice distinctly. I was thinking about all that happened in the past year. Maybe each person is only born with a certain supply of tears and when those are cried, you feel emptiness or loss, but you could find no expression or release. Since I had been hurt in October, I had cried a lifetime of tears. The service ended and everyone filed out past me. It grew quiet and the priest had shut out the lights before he sensed I was there. "Are you waiting to see me?"

"No, Father. Goodnight." I pushed through long, empty, eerie halls. I had the idea that Ben was walking beside me, his spirit as unable to leave this place as I was. On the ward, out of twenty patients, only five had been unable to leave, three at the end, me in the middle, and one guy by the door. I pushed to the other side passed the nurses' station. The bed had been rolled back into place. There were clean sheets stretched tightly over the empty mattress. The aide was pushing a bucket down the floor, emptying urine into it. He told me that he would be in to help me get undressed when he was finished. The nurse was scratching on a clipboard a few beds away. The patients were in bed, most asleep. I felt a pressure behind my eyes and had to get out of there.

It was a long, sleepless night, but finally Saturday came. I had to get out of that ward. The day was warming up, so I went to exercise outside. I pushed all the way around to the front of the hospital, every push as hard as I could make it. I stopped every fifty yards to catch my breath and put my head between my knees. The sun was shining through my short hair and burning the top of my head. I started back and worried that I had overdone it. Suddenly, I saw bright colored clouds and felt very light headed. I leaned to the side just in time to throw up. I was disoriented. I did not hear anything but, suddenly, there was a hand on my shoulder and a woman's voice sounded far off and indistinct. She came in front of me, grabbed my shoulders, and pushed me up. She put her hand on my forehead.

"You're flushed and very hot." She pushed me into the shade of a tall pine tree and then put my head back between my knees. I recognized her as a nurse from one of the other spinal cord injury wards. She was driving home and had stopped. She pulled my sweatshirt off over my head. The breeze revived me. "Nobody told you about overheating, did they?" I shook my head. She went to her car and came back with a handful of little envelopes, which she tore open and took out alcohol wipes. She wiped my face and the back of my neck. "A lot of you paras and quads don't sweat so you can't regulate your body temperature. Once you start getting warm, you just keep getting warmer, but you don't notice it. If you're not careful, you could pass out; have a heat stroke."

I pulled my tongue off the roof off my mouth. "Thanks."

"Let me push you back to your ward."

"Aren't you driving home?"

"Yeah, I'll come back for the car."

"Just help me up to that door and I'll push across the inside of the hospital."

"That's still an awful long way."

She started pushing the chair. "Something to think about: the next time you are outside on a hot day, carry a wet towel in a plastic bag and you can wipe down with it. The moisture will act like sweat to cool you off." We reached the door and she held it open for me to push through. "You sure you can make it from here? I don't feel right about leaving you."

"I'll be okay." I began pushing down the hall. I heard the door close and glanced back. She was walking back to her car. I went to a water fountain and took a long drink. Then, I splashed water into my face, over my head, and down my arms and chest. I did the same thing at every water fountain until I reached my ward. Then, I slept.

I bought a Sunday paper after church and went back to the ward to wait. I was not sure she was coming, but I wanted to be there if she did.

I started with the comics, then the news, the travel section, and was thinking of starting the crossword. Between each section of the paper, I pushed to the door and looked into the parking lot. I filled in a few answers in ballpoint pen, read something more, and pushed to the door.

Around eleven o'clock, there were voices in the hall. I leaned forward and looked. An aide walked in and pointed to me. My mother walked into the room and down the aisle. I pushed into the center of the aisle. A broad smile lit up her face when she saw me. Her pace quickened and when she reached me, she knelt and wrapped her arms around my shoulders. "Jake, you look great, so much different than the last time, so much different than I expected." I held her hand and put it up by my cheek. I felt the softness of the white silk sleeve and recognized the scent of lilies of the valley. For a second, I remembered a year before, standing in the front hall of the big house, wearing my dress uniform, giving her a goodbye hug, standing on useful legs.

"Look what I brought you," she said, holding up a small Easter basket.

"Thanks." My happiness was touched with embarrassment as I realized the other guys on the ward were watching, but I could not help but take inventory: one chocolate rabbit, two colored eggs, a can of peanuts, and jelly beans, all green ones. As I dug into the artificial grass to see what I may be missing, I realized that she had not come alone. Behind her stood a woman in a bright yellow dress. She looked familiar, but I didn't know why.

My mother looked at her. "You remember Aunt Ann. Doesn't she look wonderful?" Ann was Mom's younger sister, thirty years old. I had not seen her since my high school graduation, but she must have weighed another two hundred pounds more then than she did today.

Ann stepped forward and hugged me. "How are you doing, Jake?"

"Not bad for a cripple." My mother frowned; she did not like me to use that word about myself. "I'm sorry I didn't recognize you, Ann."

"Thanks, that's the nicest compliment you could give me." The women sat on my bed and looked around the ward. Their noses wrinkled at the odors of urine and antiseptic and cleansers. The smells were only obvious to those whose senses were not dead to them. The silence went on too long. "Come on, let me give you the twenty-five cent tour." They followed me from the ward and down to the weight room. I rolled to the stand-up frame. I told them how to hook the strap behind me. They stood on either side of me and grabbed my belt and then helped to boost me up. I told them what I had been doing for the last four months, but I knew from my mom's remarks that she already knew. "How do you know things?

She looked like she had let cat out of the bag. "Suzie—I mean, Lt. Staunton—told me. She calls after she stops to visit you to tell me how you are doing." I remembered Suzie asking if I called home. I wondered how much they talked and if Suzie had anything to do with this visit. Ann left to find a bathroom.

"She looks gorgeous, doesn't she?" Mom beamed.

"Yeah, Mom, I said she looked good."

"Her weight was such a problem. She had almost become a hermit. She was so ashamed of how heavy she was. She never went out. Then, we both started walking and I got her to stick with a diet. And she started jogging and she's lost over a hundred pounds. I needed someone to help me care for your father and she agreed to move in with us. Doesn't she just look wonderful?"

It was at least the third time she commented on how well Ann looked. I knew we were trying to get to another topic and I thought I knew what it was. "I guess Dad's not up to riding down here, huh?"

Her eyes darted down. She stepped closer and took hold of my arm. "Jake, I tried my best to take care of him, but even with Ann to help, it was very difficult. I think he was giving up. He wouldn't do anything for himself, not exercise or try to help." I kept trying to look her in the eye to get a hint of where this conversation was going but she was averting her face. "Jake, I didn't want to do it but it just didn't seem that there was an alternative. Two weeks ago, I got him admitted to the VA hospital in Philadelphia." I turned my head sharply away so that she could not see the wretched smile that exploded across my face. She thought I was angry and began to apologize. I wiped all expression from my face and looked back.

"It's okay, Mom. It's just the irony of things. I understand." In the mirror in front of me, I saw the door open and Ann entered the room. I wondered if her absence had been pre-arranged.

Mom looked at her watch. "It's noon. What time do they bring lunch?"

"They don't bring lunch. I have to catch it, kill it, and burn it all by myself. I was hoping that if you had room in the car for the wheelchair, we could go out for lunch."

"Can you leave the hospital?" Mom's voice was excited and pleased.

"Every chance I get." I realized that Suzie had not told her everything. Mom and Ann did not have any problem getting the chair into the car and I thought maybe they had practiced with my father. While we sat in the restaurant, I told them about my plans to go to college. "When did the doctors say you would be ready to leave?"

"They haven't said anything."

"Well, maybe you should wait until they think you are ready." I shook my head no. "Mom, I don't want to waste a year of my life in there. I have to get on with life. I know I can do it if I have a chance."

"Why don't you come home for a week or so and see how it works," said Ann looking from me to my mother. It was the first thing that she had said in two hours, but it brought the conversation to a dead stop. Suddenly, all I could see were problems, hooking catheters to drainage bags, emptying containers of urine, and getting around a big old house.

"Well," I said, pausing…"Where could I sleep? How could I even get in?"

"Your mother had the house fixed up for your father. She put a ramp up to the porch, turned the sun porch into a downstairs bedroom, and made the powder room into a full bath." Turning to her sister, Ann asked, "What do you think?" I thought my mother was starting to look a little pale; maybe she was remembering all of the problems she had with my father.

"I'd need to hire an aide," I said, "and get some supplies. That might take a month or so."

Ann detected that my determination had just stumbled. "Jake." She put her hand over mine and gave it a reassuring squeeze. "I took care of your father and he couldn't do as much for himself as you do. If you want a chance to see what you can do, take this one."

I licked my lips. "I'll call and we'll set it up." The drive back to the hospital was quiet. Ann went to the trunk to lift the chair from the car. "Mom, if you don't want me to come yet, I'll wait."

"Jake, do you know what today is?" I knew but I let her go on. "You said goodbye to me a year ago—to go to war. I was scared that you'd never come back. I never dreamed that you'd come back like this, that I'd see you come through the front door like this. Why, Jake, why did this have to happen?"

"Don't ask me, Mom, I don't know." I stopped. Did she have another question? I went on. "Can I come home?"

"Whenever."

That evening, I laid my book aside and thanked my father for having the house made wheelchair accessible.

26

To Look Normal

On Monday, everyone who had been away for the holiday learned of Ben's death. Some patients told stories about Ben, some asked who he was. Joe White cursed the hospital staff for letting Ben die. Flo sat on the edge of a mat, her red eyes staring out of the window. I could not help thinking that who Ben was had separated from his crippled body. I got on a mat and laid back but I did not want to work out. A student sat beside me and took my hand and stretched and rolled my fingers.

I wondered what would happen to Ben's body and about dying surrounded by strangers and no family. My mind wandered away.

One Saturday, my team returned from a mission. The sun was low as the chopper touched the landing strip. A jeep with a trailer and a truck sat waiting to take us to the company area. The debriefing was short. We hadn't found anything but leeches, skin rash, and two-inch bamboo thorns. It was around nine when I collapsed into bed.

The dawn's earliest light was shining in when a loud voice entered our barrack. "Two-five, get the hell up. You got a mission"

"You're out of your tree, you got the wrong damn team. We just came in last night," answered another voice.

The first voice hollered back, "The old man says you're going back out. You don't like it, write your fucking congressman."

I ate three breakfasts to try to replace the weight I lost in the field. I washed my 60 in a tub full of solvent, filled my boxes with clean ammo, and packed my ruck. I picked through a case of C-rations looking for the fruit cocktail and thc peanut butter. Then, we rode back to the airfield. We piled back into the Huey. I grabbed my favorite spot on the left side just behind the pilot. The rotors increased in speed until the chopper lifted about a foot off the ground. Then, it moved sideways, which was forward to me since it was in the direction that I was facing. I was fascinated by the versatility of the big machine. For an instant, I regretted letting my father talk me out of going to flight school, but I let it pass.

Once up, the chopper flew due east to a fire-support base that was taking rockets every night. Our team was to go find the bad guys and put a stop to it. When we got off the chopper, the team leader and the ATL had to go to a briefing and get maps. This meant that the rest of us should find a mess hall and eat. First rule for a Ranger: eat at every opportunity because it can be days between opportunities.

We found the mess hall. The big mess sergeant said that they would not be serving for another hour or whenever the padre finished Mass. He nodded toward a priest who was setting up his altar on one of the tables. I had been out in the field every Sunday for over a month so I figured that it wouldn't hurt to catch some grace. The rest of the team wandered off to find a PX.

The priest was in his late fifties. His white hair was cut close to his sunburned scalp. The crows feet at his eyes were deep black lines. The Mass was quick. The sermon was a short reminder to write the folks back home because it might be what they are praying for. After Mass, I helped the priest to pack his altar accessories into an aluminum footlocker. The priest put his vestments into a small suitcase. He sighed. "I have to catch a chopper back to Long Binh before dark," he said as he reached for his box.

"I'll carry the footlocker for you, Father." It felt comforting to be in his presence. As we walked toward the chopper pad, a tall, thin, bespectacled man came trotting out from between two big tents.

"Hey, Padre," he called, "I'm glad I caught you. I got one over at the aid tent I thought you might say some prayers over." The thin man led the way around the side of the tent to a large metal shipping cube called a conex. The priest set down the suitcase and had me put down the footlocker. The thin man opened the doors. He looked in at the three bodies in the dark body bags on the floor of the conex. The priest put a black stole around his neck and took a couple of containers from the footlocker.

"What happened?" he asked in a voice that was changed and gravelly.

"We took a couple of rockets just before dawn and their bunks took a hit." I remembered I had been sleeping just before dawn. The priest stepped in, bent over, and unzipped the three bags.

"Padre, the Catholic is on the right there," said the thin man.

"The prayers couldn't hurt the other two," the priest said. The chaplain knelt, made the sign of the cross, and then glanced back. The thin man and I knelt too. The priest began praying in Latin. He anointed each body with holy oil and sprinkled them with holy water. When he stopped praying, I said, "Amen." The priest packed his stuff back in the case and the thin man zipped up the bags. The priest sat down on a wall of sandbags and took out a pack of cigarettes. He shook one out and offered one to me. I lit a match and held it out to the priest. The lines in his face seemed deeper and longer than a few minutes before. The priest sucked hard at the end of the cigarette and held the smoke inside before breathing out a long stream.

"You know," the priest said, leaning back and closing his eyes, "their wives, parents, girlfriends…" He paused for a thought before continuing, "…whatever, will be waking up in another couple of hours in yesterday. Fixing breakfast, dressing the kids, going to church, having a picnic, mowing the grass, anything but thinking that the man they sent here is a corpse." He rolled the butt between his fingertips and took another drag of smoke. "Then, some officer knocks on the door." He blew out the smoke for emphasis. "Only you and I know they are dead. To die among strangers who don't care if they see another dead body, that is a very lonely day." He flicked the cigarette butt so that it bounced off of the conex door. "What a fucking place to die!" I had never heard a priest curse. The priest summoned all his will and pushed himself off the sandbags, grabbed his suitcase, and headed for the sound of a landing chopper. I came behind with the footlocker.

"Father, I haven't heard Latin in several years." His pace slowed. "The melody is comforting to me at times like this. It takes me back to a simpler time."

He chuckled. "It also keeps the Protestants off guard. The Jews are onto somethin' there with Hebrew. It keeps us all confused." When I got back to the mess tent, the team was seated at a table with trays heaped with food. "Hey 60, you and the sky pilot talk to God?"

"Are you kidding," I said. "God is a very long distance call from this place."

"Jake. Hey, Jake." It was Flo. "She's finished, you can go." I got off the mat and pushed outside. I found the shade of a tree and sat.

My workouts became longer and harder. I was trying to get the muscles that work to take over for the muscles that did not. I needed more naps. I was just waking up from one when one of the guys came to tell me that a Mr. Waters was on the phone for me. "Waters?" I wasn't making the connection, but I only got two calls a month so I went to see what it was.

"Hello," I said tentatively. "Mr. Scott, this Herbert Walters. I've got your car here with the hand controls. I could drop it off at the hospital—if this is a good time for you."

With Ron's death and my mother's visit, I had forgotten the car. "Yes!" I semi-shouted. I reeled in my excitement. "I mean, yes thank you. Would you bring it all the way around the building to the back lot and I'll meet you there?"

"Fine, we'll be there in about fifteen minutes." I ran into the wall and a doorframe going outside. I sat shielding my eyes from the setting sun, squinting at the far end of the parking lot.

Joe White rolled out. "Hey, I'm on the way to chow. You going?" Before I said anything, Joe launched into the story of how he made out at home over Easter. He was planning to check out of this place in a couple of weeks. It was not registering in my brain. I saw it turn into the lot. It looked bluer and shinier, maybe because it was mine. I owned a car.

"Are you kidding me?" teased Joe White. "You were going to be late for chow waiting for that piece of shit?"

"Hey, don't let me hold you up," I said, pushing forward. Mr. Walters had some more papers for me to sign and then he showed me the manuals, the registration, and some of the gadgets in the car. All the time, I noticed Joe White circling it, looking through the windows.

When Mr. Walters left, Joe said, "So come on, ain't you gonna take a ride?"

"What! And let you get in the chow line ahead of me and eat all those delicious grits? My momma didn't raise no stupid children." I pushed toward the mess hall.

Joe easily caught up to me. "You mean you been waiting all this time for that pile of junk and now you're just gonna let it sit on the parking lot?"

"Later," I said, "I'm hungry." Actually, I had no appetite at all, but if I was about to make a fool of myself with the damn thing and wrap it around a tree, I'd just as soon do it without an audience. I stayed away from everyone after dinner and snuck to the car an hour before dark. I folded the footrests and collapsed the chair. Then, I sat the footrests on the edge of the doorframe. I slid across the front seat, slid the seat forward, and folded the back forward. I reached behind the seat, hooked my hand through the leather toe strap, and hauled the chair in. I took a deep breath, smiled broadly, and said, "Thank you, God."

Then, I backed the wheelchair out, but something went wrong and it fell sideways. I had to lean out the door, while saying, "God, if you give me a decent pair of hands, I wouldn't have to go through this crap," and I dragged it into position. Then, I hooked my hand under it and hooked the other hand on the steering wheel and hauled it up. Every time I started to lose control, I swore and questioned what God was trying to teach me, but I got it upright. I unfolded it and got in. As I examined the side of the car, I invented some new curse words because the chair in falling had scratched the bluer and shinier surface.

I practiced loading and unloading four more times until after dark. I pushed inside and got a towel from the shower room to put on the backseat to protect it from the chair. Then, I loaded back in. I put the keys in the ignition and started it. I felt like a kid in the front car of the biggest, meanest roller coaster on earth. I was afraid that I would lose control of this big V-8. I thought of explaining to the VA what my car was doing parked inside of their hospital. And how would I explain it to the nice lady from the insurance company who had driven out to sell me insurance?

I pushed the hand control in tightly to hold the brake on as I moved the shifter to drive. I eased off the brake and the car started forward. I pushed on the brake. "Whoa!" The car slammed to a stop and threw me into the steering wheel. "Yes, remember the power brakes," I mumbled to myself as I buckled the seat belt. I turned the car so that it was moving down the parking lot. I practiced a couple of times getting used to the brakes so that I brought it to a smooth stop.

Then, I drove the car out of the parking lot. In going around the corner, the force threw my shoulders into the center of the car and pulled my hands from the wheel. I quickly recovered, but not before I found myself going across the lawn. I jerked the wheel back toward the driveway and the tires cut big strips of sod. I brought it to a stop and glanced about to see if anyone had been watching. "Okay," I reassured myself, "relax, you'll get the hang of it." I rubbed my eyes and blew out a deep breath. I would have to lean my shoulders into the curve for balance. I tightened the seatbelt.

I drove to the front entrance and looked at the cars whizzing by on the highway. I kept fighting the excitement. I was a big kid with the best present of my whole life. I rolled down the electric windows. I reached in my jacket pocket for a Beach Boys tape I had bought just for this occasion. I shoved it into the player and cranked up the volume. I clicked on the turn signal and pulled away from the hospital. The car accelerated smoothly and the wind flooded the car. "HOOOOOAAAAHH!" I screamed at the top of my lungs. "Freedom," I said with a smile that spread so large that it hurt my cheeks, but, at the same time, I felt some tears. My happiness grew with each foot I drove from the hospital.

I came to a red light and managed to stop. The music was flowing from the car. A station wagon drove up in the lane beside me. I glanced over. There were three cute young women in the front seat. The one closest to me looked over at the car and then at me. I returned the look. She turned to the other two and said something. They all looked at me and the one in the middle waved. I waved back. Then, the driver puckered her lips and made a kissing motion. I smiled and nodded. The three of them laughed and when the light turned green, they all waved and made a left turn.

It struck me. "They don't know I'm in a wheelchair, they can't see my stupid hands or anything else that says I'm a cripple. They just see a guy in a neat car." I wondered if I would ever get out of the car or just keep driving. Eventually, I pulled into a gas station and drove back onto the highway toward the hospital, reluctantly. When I got out of the car, I examined the scratch again. Joe White would know how to rub it out. I pushed to the door and turned for one last look before I looked up to heaven.

"Ben, you shoulda been with me," I said loudly. "Nobody would have known we were a couple of cripples!"

27

A Bachelors' Party

The next afternoon, when I got to Sam's weight room, there was a new wheelchair sitting by the desk. Sam gestured, "Hey, boy, get on the mat there and let me fit your new wheels to you." I lifted onto the mat. Sam shoved the hospital chair off to the side and rolled the new chair over. The chair was at least three inches narrower than the old one.

"So Sam I guess there won't be a captain, or first sergeant, or a proclamation, huh?

Sam looked at me and said, "What the hell you talking bout?"

"The last decoration Uncle Sam gave me got pinned on my chest; this one gets pinned on my ass." He shook his head.

I lifted into the seat. The new cushion was much firmer than the old one. Sam adjusted the footrest height so that my thighs were just resting on the cushion. "You have to keep the circulation to your legs from being cut off," explained Sam. "Take it for a spin."

I gave it a push. "Wow, it's great. It must be fifty pounds lighter than that truck I had!" The wheels being closer together not only made it easier to guide and steer between things, but it gave my arms a better angle to push from.

"You gotta keep those tires pumped up nice and hard or it will get harder to push," reminded Sam. I pushed out of the therapy room and up the hill to my ward. The push rims on the wheels were coated with a soft plastic that gave my hands a better grip and made pushing and braking easier.

I went outside to the car. I got in and folded the chair. I pulled it in. Even folded, it was narrower. That and the lighter weight made it so much easier to pull in. "With this chair and this car, I am ready to get out of here." I tried the sound of that on my self. That evening, I called Suzie to see when she would be down.

"Hello?"

"Suzie?"

"Hi, Jake."

"Honey, you sound terrible. What's wrong?"

"There's some kind of creeping crud going around the hospital. All the patients and the staff have been catching it. Last weekend, I had to work double shifts so many nurses were out. I think I got run down and now I've caught it."

"It's not fatal, is it?"

"Only if you can die from stomach cramps and diarrhea. I don't think I'm gonna be well enough to come by this weekend."

"Well, it's nothing personal, sweetheart, but the very last thing a guy in a wheelchair wants to catch is diarrhea."

"Oh, yeah, I guess you would have trouble moving quickly."

"Yes ma'am, you just feel free to keep your germs in D.C."

"Look, I'll be down next Friday. By the way, I saw Cathy." Suzie's voice had changed to that "so what happened?" tone.

"Yeah?" I played it as though I didn't see what was coming.

"Did you talk to her?"

"Yeah."

"And?!" Her voice hit a demanding note.

"Suzie, you know the answer. Look, I don't think you're going to change her mind. Don't fight with her about it."

"She doesn't know what she's getting into."

"Listen, Mother Susan, if you keep beating on her, you're going to lose the opportunity to just be her friend and love her in spite of her decision. Do you understand?"

"Yes." Her voice was hoarse.

"Suzie, I love you."

"Goodbye."

"Suzie, don't be angry with me. Please."

"I'm not, Jake. I'm tired."

"Okay. Bye-bye." I started to take the receiver from my ear.

"Jake, I love you too."

"Thanks, sweetie. I needed that."

I worked harder at everything the next few days. Thoughts of going home kept pushing into my head, but I kept finding reasons why I was not ready to go. That Saturday afternoon, I headed for the car to take a drive and get out of there. Joe White was just finishing some work on his car.

"Now what are you doing on that car?" I asked, not believing that there was a single part of that car he had not tinkered with at least twice.

"I just mounted some speakers in the doors."

"How many speakers are in this thing?"

"Just six. I got these when I was home last time. The guy that sold them to me hired me to install speakers and radios and stuff when I get home." He stopped suddenly in mid-thought, but there was more that he wanted to say.

"And?"

"My girlfriend." He busied himself by shoving tools back into their places in a tool kit. "I asked her to marry me." He deliberately rolled the tools and tied the straps.

"So don't keep me in suspense, what the hell'd she say.?"

He broke into a huge smile. "She said yes."

"You son-of-a-bitch, you. Congratulations."

Joe's voice changed. "I'm going home this Tuesday."

"For how long?"

"For good."

I was glad for Joe. I knew how badly he and I wanted to get the hell out of this hospital. At the same time, I felt such loneliness. Since Ben's death, Joe was one of the few guys I felt like being with. Those men who had given up hope of leaving or who were settled here drained my will. I broke out of my thoughts. "Well, we got to have a bachelor party. I'll go get some suds."

"I'll come with you," volunteered Joe, "and show you where to go. I been wanting a ride in this hot car." We could not fit both chairs in the car, so after Joe was in I pushed his chair over by the Charger. Then, I loaded in.

"You have the honor of being my first passenger," I commented. I had the feeling that he was grading everything I did. Joe gave me directions to drive away from Richmond. We drove for about fifteen minutes. There were fewer buildings and more open spaces.

"Where the hell are you taking me?"

"Right there." Joe pointed to a long, low building with a dirt parking lot. Out front, a sign with peeling paint announced that this was "Ray's Grocery and Package Store." The roof had a very noticeable sag in the center. A concrete porch with two steps up ran the length of the front.

"It's got steps. How are we going to get in?"

"Just pull around on the right there and park in front of the window." When we had parked, Joe leaned over and shoved out two long blasts of the horn. A big man with a bull neck and white hair, cut in a flat top, looked out the window. Joe told me to flash the headlights. I fumbled with the knob for a second and then used both hands to pull them on. The big man waved and disappeared. In a few seconds, he came walking around the corner. His large belly hung over the front of his pants, which drooped loosely from a pair of suspenders. He bent down and looked through my window.

"Hey, Joe. I didn't recognize you in this car."

"Hey, Ray. Want you to meet Jake." A huge perspiring hand reached out and grabbed mine.

"Hey, Jake," he grinned through crooked teeth. "What can I get you boys?"

"Give us one of those Styrofoam coolers, put in two cases of beer, fill it with ice, and give us a bag of chips and peanuts," Joe ordered.

"What about you, boy?" asked Ray, looking at me. I knew I did not look old enough to buy booze, but what the hell. "I'll take a pint of scotch. The kind with the horse on the label."

"Be right out." Ray walked inside.

I looked at Joe's grinning face. "That Ray's really a character," I said. "But why did we have to come all the way out here?"

"Are you legal to buy beer?"

"Nope, aren't you?"

"Nope."

"Oohh."

In a few minutes, Ray came walking around the corner, followed by a black man carrying the cooler, the bags stacked on top. I handed him my keys to open the trunk and he handed me the bottle of scotch and a cash register tape. Joe nudged me, "Pay the man, I'm the guest of honor." I counted out the cash and Ray walked back inside. When the other man had finished loading the trunk, he brought the keys back and I handed him a dollar. He shoved it into his pocket and walked away.

When we got back to the hospital, we had a plan to invite some guys to meet us back at the cars after dinner. I saw Dave at dinner and then Duke and Marv. When we got back to the cars, there were about fifteen of us. Joe and I drove our cars to the far end of the parking lot and backed them in so that there were a few spaces between them. Before we finished passing out the beer another ten guys had shown up to see what the crowd was for. Joe had opened both doors to his car and had a country and western station cranking out over his six speakers. We took turns razzing Joe about married life. Two cases of beer did not go very far, but this group did not need alcohol to make them act crazy. Instead of eating the peanuts, we all took a handful, surrounded Joe, and pelted him with them.

In order to make the beer go further, I had been drinking the scotch. Just as the beer ran out, someone sounded a warning. "Look out, it's the bitch!" All the empty beer cans went into my trunk and Dave slammed the lid. She stormed up and quickly walked around, looking into the cars and at our faces. Unfortunately, I was the only one who had had enough to get a little drunk.

"I want to know what has been going on up here," she demanded. We looked at each other. Joe looked at me and shook his head.

"I'm just going to stand here until I get an answer," she demanded. Joe turned and began to push for the hospital just as I started to open my mouth

"You..." I never got the next word out. As Joe came by, he grabbed the arm of my chair and spun me around so fast that I got dizzy and, for a few seconds, as I drifted down the incline, I thought I was going to be sick. Joe continued to hold onto the arm of my chair, guiding me along.

"Shut up," said Joe in a quiet, stern tone. "You may not care if you get thrown out of here, but some of these other guys got no place else to go."

I started pushing, but, due to the scotch, one arm was pushing harder than the other and, eventually, I had made a slow turn and was heading back toward the cars. Joe pushed around in front of me and pushed the front of his chair into mine to turn me back. I kept turning back into Joe. Joe started laughing out loud, then a few others, and, by the time we were halfway across the lot, the whole group was chuckling, sputtering, laughing, crying. Just then, the sky, which had been clouding up, burst open and dumped rain over everyone. The short nurse went running by as fast as her short legs would carry her. The sight sent us all into hysterical laughter and we just sat in the rain and got soaked.

As they filed through the door, each one stopped to pat me on the back and thank me for a great party. "Hey guy," said Joe, "I couldn't have planned a better bachelor party." Sunday, I pulled around by the dumpster and threw all the cans out of the trunk, emptied the water out of the cooler, picked peanuts out of every part of my car, and felt happy.

28

The Ultimate Humiliation

Monday evening, Joe and I cleaned out his locker and the drawers beside his bed. We packed everything in Joe's car. The next morning, Joe rolled over to my bed before I had gotten an aide to help me get dressed.

"Jake." He grasped my wrist. "I'm the hell out of here."

"Aren't you gonna stick around for breakfast?"

"Nope. I'm gonna pull into the first town in North Carolina and have breakfast there."

"Good luck. I might drive down one day and see if I can look you up."

"Yeah. I'll get some of my daddy's corn whiskey and we'll get blind drunk. So long."

He was pushing down the aisle and I called after him, "Hey. Kiss the bride for me." Joe waved his hand over his head but did not look back.

That morning, a different group of students was in the therapy room. Flo brought this beautiful dark-haired woman with creamy, tanned skin over to work with me. She introduced herself and flashed a smile that made me shudder. As she stretched my hand, I could not stop staring at her. Then, she knelt on the mat and lifted my leg and brought it up and out to the side. She had done this twice when suddenly she dropped my leg back on the mat. She quickly stood up from the mat and the smile became a look of disgust as she looked at her hands and stockings. I struggled to find out what was wrong. My pants were soaked and there was a puddle of urine around me on the mat. I pulled up my pant leg and found that the drainage hose at the bottom of the leg bag had pulled off and the bag had emptied. "Oh shit!" I said loudly enough to bring the room to a brief hush.

Flo started over and then returned to a cart of towels and brought over a stack. She gave a couple to the student and piled the rest around me to soak up the urine. Flo looked at the dampness on the student's stockings and told her to go home and change. A couple of other students were trying to suppress smiles. As she started to walk out, I said, "I'm really, really sorry."

"It's okay. It wasn't your fault," she said, and her smile returned, for a second. Flo laid towels on the cushion in my chair and helped me back into it. I pushed into the hall and toward the ward, leaving a trail of drips behind me.

"I can't believe this crap," I muttered as I pushed. "I piss on the most beautiful woman in this whole hospital in front of a room full of patients and staff." I pushed to the nurses' station just as Miss Adams came out into the hall. She looked down at the soaked pants and heaved a sigh.

"Scott, boy, are you having problems?"

I wanted to scream, "What the fuck does it look like?" but I remembered that she was on my side so I just said, "Yeah."

"Well go on back by your bed and I'll have an aide come clean you up." I pushed back to the bed and Lavassuer came down the aisle with a cart with two basins of water and spread one of the rubber sheets they used on the gurney for shower morning on my bed. Then, he pulled the curtains around the bed. The aide pulled on a pair of gloves, helped me up onto the bed, and helped me take off the wet clothes. Everything had to come off. I sat up and took the washcloth and started rinsing off while the aide went to fix the drainage bag.

When he returned, he showed me that he had taped the hose on so that it would not come off again. Lavassuer reached under the cart and lifted out clean clothes. I laid a towel across my groin and laid back. The aide moved to the foot of the bed and started pulling on clean socks. It had been six months that I had lain naked while strangers worked on me and it had not gotten any less embarrassing. I tilted my head so that I was looking out of the window. I watched the wind push little wisps of clouds along in front of a brilliant sky. I could feel my legs being moved as the aide struggled with the elastic stockings, first the left leg, then the right.

Then, I was aware that the aide had moved up beside me. I could feel my left leg being moved as the aide fastened the straps of the drainage bag around my leg. Next, I knew he would attach the catheter to the leg bag and tell me to finish getting dressed. I kept watching the free clouds. I thought of that beautiful student holding onto me, moving my crippled body and, suddenly, the look on her face. The aide did not say anything. What the hell was wrong? I looked back to see what the hold up was.

My penis was very erect, hard and swollen. Only a few inches of the catheter protruded from the tip. The aide had my penis clasped tightly in his hand and was moving his hand up and down. I stared in shock; I could not believe what I was seeing. With his other hand, the aide was fondling himself. I looked at his face. Lavassuer looked back at me and jerked on my penis harder.

I thought, *The son-of-a-bitch is waiting to see if I am going to tell him to stop.* I fought the urge to holler and said with as much anger as my voice would contain, "Get your goddamn hands off of me, queer." As I said this, I struck his arm with the edge of my hand. The aide let go and stepped back, but he kept looking at my erection. I reached around, feeling for the towel. Lavassuer had it draped over his arm. He tossed it to me. I shook it out and covered myself. Then, I rocked from side to side until I got my elbow under me and I could sit up. I leaned forward and put my head between my knees so that he could not see me. For an instant, I felt faint and then thought that I might be sick. What was I going to do?

Several minutes passed. The aide was still standing beside me. Then, I realized that the bastard was waiting to finish dressing me and I had no choice; I had to let this man who had just sexually molested me humiliate me some more. I sat up and fished the end of the catheter out from under the towel and positioned it next to the end of the leg bag. I did not look at the aide, nor did I say anything. The man stepped forward and twisted the catheter onto the bag. The aide then picked up a pair of pants and brought them to the bed. I knocked them from his hand onto the bed. "Get the hell away from me."

The aide pushed the cart down the aisle. I watched him through an opening in the curtain. I pulled the extra blanket from the foot of the bed and covered up. I lay on the bed.

The entire six months had been designed to dehumanize me, to degrade me, to humiliate me to the point where I would give up. And when it appeared that the events in the therapy room were not enough, some creature in hell had devised this ultimate humiliation. My mind went numb; it would not think. My shoulders began to shake uncontrollably and, buried in hopelessness, I began sobbing. When my emotions were drained, I fell asleep and the dream soon started.

29

The Phone Call, the Bathroom, and the Orphanage

I woke in the afternoon. Someone had pulled the curtains open, probably Lavassuer. I shuddered. I thought of lying there and ignoring the world, but, sooner or later, the world would come bother me, so I got dressed. I pushed out to the car and loaded the chair in, but I could not think of anywhere to go. I took the scotch out from under the seat and took a mouthful, swished it around, and swallowed.

I thought about what to do. I wanted to go wash his touch off of me. I wanted revenge. I wanted to tell somebody to fire him. Would they call the cops and have some kind of a trial? My thoughts were all jumbled. I watched the employees leaving as the shift changed. Lavassuer got into a Mustang and drove out. He did not see me. Oh, I wished I had a gun.

I pushed to dinner and sat off alone. I drank some coffee and left the food on the plate. I kept rocking in the chair. I went back outside and bummed a cigarette. People came by, some spoke, I did not answer.

"Hey, Jake," a guy called. He was from Ben's end of the ward. He rolled up in an electric wheelchair and bumped into my chair to get my attention. "There's a phone call for you." This usual cause for excitement was an irritation, but I could not tell the guy to go back and hang up on whomever. I pushed in to the phone.

"Hello?"

"Jake?" It was Suzie.

"Yeah."

"You don't sound like you. You're not sick, are you?"

"Naw, I'm just tired of this place."

"Listen, I called to say I can't come this weekend. I got a call from the lawyer in Illinois. He said that my husband is consenting to the divorce and that they have a hearing scheduled for Thursday. Then, they want to settle on the property. He's buying my share of the house. I'm sorry about not coming down."

I did not care. As crappy as things were going, I didn't want to see anyone just now. "It's okay," I said. "Take care of that and it will be one less thing you have to worry about."

"Jake, tell me what's wrong."

"I'll tell you when I see you. Have a good time getting divorced."

"Okay, take care. Bye-bye."

"Bye."

The sound of her receiver hanging up was the echo of a door closing between me and the world, an empty sound. I brushed my teeth and shaved using both hands. Then, I laid in bed. Suzie's call had cleared the way. I resolved to go home that weekend.

I avoided everyone for the next three days. The anger I felt kept boiling within me. I should report that son-of-a-bitch and have him fired. But then, I thought about an incident that happened just after I arrived at the hospital. An aide had slapped a patient. I hadn't seen it, but it was the talk all over the wards. Even though it had been witnessed by two other patients, they still had a hearing. There was talk that the patients had been threatened if they testified, that there might be an accident. I could not bring myself to testify to what happened to me.

Then my conscience kicked in, saying, "If you do not report him, he could do that to another patient." Then, the other thought crowded in. Suppose Lavassuer did not deny what happened. Suppose he admitted it and said that I asked for it or was a willing participant. He could make me out to be a queer. "Forget it," I told my conscience, "some other patient is going to have to look out for himself." I was partly to blame. They had treated me like a thing for so long that I had stopped caring. To them, I was the job; it made no difference if I was embarrassed by their pokings and probings. So I just found it easier not to know what they were doing to me. I wondered how it would be at home. I had to think of a way to get revenge.

I woke up very early, before Lavassuer came on duty so that I could get someone else to help me get dressed. I started to identify a list of things that I would need help with when I got home. Was there a way I could do these things myself? I went to the hospital store and bought regular support hose. It took both thumbs to pull them over my toes and then I used my teeth to pull them up. It was weird, but it was one less task I needed to ask someone else for help with.

The first day I wore the socks, my feet and ankles were badly swollen. I would have to prop my feet up whenever I could. I went to meet with a counselor about college. He told me that the VA would pay all of my tuition and expenses for whatever I wanted to study. I also found out that I needed a doctor to prescribe exercise equipment for me and the VA would get it for me.

I had to collect supplies to take home: a catheterization kit, an irrigation kit, rubber gloves, blue hospital pads, and bottles of pills. Friday evening, I loaded everything in the trunk of the LeMans, including everything I did not absolutely need when I came back to the hospital. If this trip home worked, I would not be coming back for long. The next morning, extra early, I was dressed and on my way to the cafeteria down the long hallway with pale gray skies outside. I had the first good breakfast in months with lots of coffee to keep me awake on the road, on the drive north.

I went back to the ward and opened my locker. The only remaining item was my camouflaged jacket, the one from Vietnam with the colored patches on it. It had been cleaned, starched, and pressed. I pulled it on. I had a hard time getting the buttons through those stiff buttonholes, but it got done. I rolled to the car and looked back at the building. I joined my hands. "Oh, God," I prayed. "This has to work because I can't come back here to stay." Then, I was in the car and gone. I doubt that the Apollo astronauts felt any more apprehension of the unknown.

The drive started out great. I had a pile of tapes lying on the passenger seat. When I felt like risking my life, I would change the tape. I held the steering wheel against my left forearm and the hand control in my left hand. I pulled the old tape out of the player, which involved a lot of fumbling and swearing. I put the next tape box between my teeth and flipped it open. Then, I tilted my head forward so the tape slid out into my hand, all at sixty miles per hour. As I went north, I noticed that spring was not as far along as in Richmond, but, every so often, there would be a tree or bush filled with blossoms.

I thought of the irony of the events of Tuesday. The first accident of the drainage hose pulling out had convinced me not to ever leave the hospital. What if that had happened somewhere outside the hospital? What if I had been sitting in school somewhere? But then, the assault had convinced me to get the hell out of the hospital and take my chances with the world.

The car ate up the miles. In two hours, I was passed Washington, but it took a lot of effort and I was tired. The strain of holding the hand control in the same position had made my left arm sore and my shoulder ache. Maybe if I got out and stretched and had a coffee, I could stay awake long enough to get home. I pulled off the highway into a shopping center. I unloaded the chair and started pushing into a fast food place when I realized there was no ramp up the curb. I called out to a guy crossing the parking lot who was heading for the door. "Hey. Excuse me! Hey, could you give me a hand up on the side-walk?" He turned his head away from me and quickened his pace. He strode over the curb and, in a second, was through the door.

"I don't believe that guy," said a woman's voice from behind me. She had a young boy in her arms and was leading a girl by the hand. "Can I help you?"

"Well I appreciate the offer, but it looks like you have a handful already."

She sat the children on the curb and turned to me. "Okay, now what?"

"Just grab the handles in the back and when I pop a wheelie, roll the front wheels onto the curb and lift the back." It worked like a charm. *Thank you, God*, I thought. I turned to wait for her. She picked up the little boy and struggled to help the little girl to her feet. "Would you like to ride on my lap?" I asked the girl. She walked to the front of the chair and put out her arms for me to pick her up. I did not have the muscles in my back to lift her from there. "Sweetheart, climb up on my feet." She held on to my pant legs and climbed onto the toes of my boots. I braced my elbows on the chair arms for leverage and reached under her arms and lifted. I brought her up so that she was kneeling on my thighs. She threw her arms around my neck, gave me a hug, and said, "Daddy." I smiled and, just as quickly, swallowed a lump in my throat. I didn't realize how much I needed that hug.

The woman explained that her husband was in the Air Force at Andrews Air Force Base, but was away on a flight. "When he is not around, she calls everybody Daddy." I turned the girl around and sat her on my lap. The woman held the door and I pushed through. At the counter, she offered to carry my food on their tray and asked if I would like to sit with them.

When they sat the food on the counter, I gave the server a twenty-dollar bill. "This is for everything."

"What are you doing?" she protested. "You don't have to do that."

"You did not have to stop outside to help me, but you did what you could. Let me do what I can do." We went to a table and I slid the little girl into the booth. "I gotta run to the bathroom, be right back," I said. I noticed when I pulled the little girl up that the leg bag was getting full. I headed to the rear of the restaurant for a door with a gingerbread man on it.

I hit the door with the toes of my boots and pushed it in. The tension of the spring that closed the door pushed me back at first, but I managed to get it open. As I pushed through, it kept closing on me and steering me into the wall. Later, I would think of this trip to the bathroom while watching a nature film of a fly going into a Venus flytrap, a plant that traps poor insects who think they can get out once they have gone in.

I pushed through a narrow short hall to a second door and pushed through that. Good thing I had gotten the narrowest wheelchair as it just barely fit into the stall. Unfortunately, I got no privacy as the wheelchair held the stall door open. I waited for a man at the sink to finish washing his hands and leave before I pulled the drainage hose from inside my boot. I checked the new tape that had been used to fasten it to the bag to make sure it was not working its way loose.

I pushed to the sink. My knees would not go under the sink so I sat with my side to it. I tried to turn on the faucet. It had a spring-loaded glass knob on it. I could not turn it with one hand. I grabbed it between the palms of both hands. The knob was wet from previous users and my hands slipped. I wiped my palms on my pant legs and gripped harder and turned harder. Suddenly, I was successful. Water gushed into the sink and ricocheted in a spray all over me. I wiped my face on my sleeve.

"Enough hand washing," I muttered. I pushed to the paper towel dispenser. It was about five feet up on the wall. Some clever attendant, not wishing to have to re-stock the dispenser until next year, had crammed the towels in so that they bulged from the bottom. I reached over my head and pried with my thumb to get an edge loose. When the edge came out, I reached up with both arms to catch it between my palms. The towel got wet and ripped. It ripped again. By now, the water had evaporated from my skin. "Enough hand drying."

Now to leave, I pulled the first door open and pushed to the second door. The hallway was so narrow that I could not get off to the side to open the door without it hitting me. I would have to pull it toward me with one hand and back the chair up with the other hand at the same time. The door had a round doorknob. I tried pressing the palm of one hand against it and pulling it. No luck. I used both palms. I pulled. It did not open; instead, the wheelchair rolled forward into the door. I was going to die of old age in the hallway of a men's room.

I had to let go, back up, lock the brakes, grab the knob again, and pull. The door opened. I hooked my right hand behind the knob and felt for the brake with my left hand. It released. Now I tried to reach across my lap for the right brake with my left hand. I could not get the damn brake to release. My right hand slipped and the door closed. "Shit!" I took a breath. "Be patient, you can do this." Lock only the left brake. Grab the knob with both hands, pull, hook the right hand behind the knob, and feel for the brake. The brake released. The chair started to roll toward the door. I reached my left hand out and put my palm against the wall and pushed backward. Slowly, the chair inched backward. Quickly, I slid my palm back along the wall. Palm against the wall, push. Concentrate; don't let the doorknob slip from the right hand. The door was about halfway open, but the chair would not roll back any more. I had backed into the door behind me. I did not have enough leverage to push it open. I just started to laugh out loud.

Suddenly, the door in front of me opened as a boy started into the bathroom, but he was startled to see a man sitting on the other side, leaning forward, staring into his face. The boy started to back out and close the door. "No, no, don't go, help me open the door." The boy came forward and slammed the door into my still outstretched hand and then struck the toes of my boots. I shook the pain out of my knuckles. "Wait a second." I turned the chair as much as I could in the cramped space. The boy got the door open and held it while I went passed. "Next time, I'm pissing in the parking lot," I vowed.

By the time I got to the table, the woman and children had almost finished their food. I started to pull into the table when I saw the man who had passed me on the way in. "Excuse me," I said to her. "I see an old friend." I rolled to his table. "Hi. I wouldn't want you to ruin your lunch worrying about whether I got in or not." He looked up with the hamburger, bun, and lettuce crowding to escape his mouth and said, "Go to hell."

I smiled. "It couldn't be any worse than meeting you." I pushed back to my food. She was smiling and shaking her head, having overheard the exchange. "You're crazy."

"Yeah, it's the one character trait that was developed by the Army that wasn't effected by my disability." I took a sip of my coffee and then extended my hand across the table. "I'm Jake."

She took my hand. "I'm Kristi." Her little girl crawled off the bench and back onto my lap. She reminded me that a year ago, I had been holding Elena on my lap. I wrapped my arms around the girl and gently rocked back and forth. I wondered if Elena would remember me. Would Bibi? I watched Kristi watching the little boy trying to drink from a straw.

I closed my eyes and remembered another little boy trying to drink a soda. About ten Rangers had climbed into two jeeps to visit an orphanage run by an order of French nuns. We were headed toward Long Binh. One of the jeeps was towing a trailer filled with ice and sodas. Stuffed in beside us were bags of oranges, apples, cookies, and chewing gum. We turned off the main highway and went up a road under great old trees. The orphanage was surrounded by a high wall and we had to wait until the gate was opened.

The sisters wore black dresses and veils with little starched white collars. They stood surrounded by, I guessed, between seventy and one hundred children ranging in age from four to twelve years old. From their features or black skin, it was obvious that some of the children had been fathered by Americans and abandoned to the tender mercies of the war. Some wore T-shirts and shorts that had been donated by other soldiers and did not fit well. I was carrying two of the smallest children and found that four others were holding onto the baggy legs of my pants and just going where I went. When I lay on the grass, they piled on and snuggled beside me. They were trying to absorb love and comfort just by touch. One of the girls had a nasty scrape on her knee. I got a medic's bag out of the jeep to wash it off and put a bandage on it. One of the sisters came to me and spoke to me in French. I raised my hands and said, "Je ne parlez," and shook my head. She took my hand and led me into one of the buildings to a small infirmary that they had.

On the only cot lay a boy covered by a sheet. His eyes stared from a skull covered with skin. Hollows filled the spaces between the bones. His dry, cracked lips would not cover his teeth. Until he blinked, I was not sure he was alive. The sister pulled the sheet down. The boy's body was covered with sores. His arms and legs had barely any muscle tissue. Beneath his fallow skin were his ribs and distended belly. I shuddered. I had never seen a child starving to death and, for an instant, I thought I would cry. I was about to tell the sister that I was not a medic, but that would not work. Behind her was a glass cabinet intended for medicines, but it was practically empty.

I knelt beside the boy and got a tube of ointment from the medic bag that we used in the field for skin rash. I sat the boy up. It was like posing a mannequin. I put some of the salve onto my finger and worked over his body, putting it onto the sores. I stood and put the contents of the medic bag into the cabinet.

"Merci," said the sister.

I nodded. "Um, you're welcome." She nodded and smiled at me. I went to the jeep and got a Coke and an apple. I went back. The boy was still sitting as I left him, maybe because he was waiting to be told he could lie down. I squatted in front of him and opened the can. There was a faint glimmer in the boy's eyes. I held out the can and the boy took it in his hands, but when I let go, he almost dropped it; he had so little strength that he could not lift the can to take a drink. I took the can and held it to the boy's mouth. He drank and then he smiled.

I handed him the apple. The boy looked at it and then looked at me. He did not know what to do with it. I pulled the knife from my belt. I cut a slice and chewed it. Then, I cut the thinnest sliver and put it to the boy's lips. He bit off a small piece and chewed it very deliberately, as if it took all the strength he had just to do that. It took twenty minutes to feed him a third of the apple and half the soda. I lifted his legs into bed and covered him. In seconds, he was asleep.

"Is something wrong?" It was Kristi.

"What?" I shook off the trance.

"You're crying," she whispered. I felt my face. My cheeks were wet. I grabbed a napkin and wiped. "Just some old memories." Kristi helped me back off the curb. I thanked her and said good-bye to the kids. I loaded into the car. I wondered if that little boy ever woke.

30
The Feeling of the Grey House

The food and coffee gave me a shot of energy as I started to drive again, but it did not last long. North of Baltimore, I found myself fighting to stay awake—I had to stop for a nap. I pulled off the interstate and found a wide shoulder on the road, locked the doors, put my feet in the right seat, and went to sleep.

I dreamed about the ride back to the States on a big C-141. The huge jet carried me in a stretcher that rocked in a harness slung from the ceiling. There was a knocking in the plane and a faraway voice calling to me. Slowly, I realized that I was in a car and not a jet. I looked in the direction of the voice and was startled to see a Stetson and a pair of sunglasses looking in my window. The Maryland trooper called to me to open the window. I opened the door.

"Are you alright?" the police officer asked.

"Yeah, is anything wrong?"

"I passed here a couple of hours ago and noticed your car, so when it was still here, I checked it out."

"I just got tired and pulled over for a rest." Then, it struck me what he had said. "A couple of hours!" I looked at the clock; 4:15 pm. "Oh man I gotta get going." I got back on the interstate. In a while, I was on a bridge over the Susquehanna River. Just on the other side, I turned north and followed a two-lane highway into Pennsylvania. The trees there had only buds and small leaves. It was 5:30 when I turned and drove back toward the river. The anticipation was growing. I shivered as I began recognizing the landscape. The car began climbing a long gradual hill along a winding road. Many days I had struggled to get my bike up this hill, strong will ordering tired muscles to keep pedaling. The feel of the ridged rubber on the pedals pressed into my bare feet, breathing hard from my dry mouth. I would never feel all that again. As I went around a curve, a pick-up truck going the other way was passing a jogging woman and the guys in the back were whistling and calling to her.

At the top of the hill, my hand instinctively reached for the turn signal. I turned slowly into the white pea gravel lane and heard the pebbles crunch beneath the tires. The sky was a soft pale blue; the long shadows from the old evergreens darkened the sides of the lane. I drove slowly, wondering how my mother would react when she saw me. Then, I saw the great, grey, three story house through the trees. I stopped the car and took a long deep breath. A wave of emotion broke over me and I sobbed. The time I had been away from its comforting rooms had been too long, measured not in days or months, but in events and changes to me. I wiped my wet face on my sleeve. I really should carry a handkerchief.

The white gravel formed an "O" in the green grass in front of the house. The lawn had clumps of garlic grass, buttercups, and dandelions across it. I pulled up by the end of a new ramp that ran down from the porch. The porch went from a sun porch on the right across the front and down the left side of the house. The garage doors were closed. Mom's car must have been inside. I blew the horn and began unloading the wheelchair.

I got the chair out and put the cushion in it. Still, no one came out of the house. I tooted the horn again. I rolled back and opened the trunk and laid my bag in my lap. I pushed up the ramp; it was a little steeper than I was used to, but I made it. I rolled to the front door. I grabbed it between my palms and turned as hard as I could, but it would not budge. I had not expected it to be locked.

I rolled to the short, fat wall that ran along the edge of the porch. I peered up under a bird feeder that hung from the porch ceiling. I reached for the spare key that was held against the bottom by a rusted nail. Using both hands, I turned the key and pushed open the wide front door. I popped a wheelie over the weather stripping and rolled into the front hall. My wheels met with the resistance of the thick Persian runner. I sat the bag down and listened. The house was still.

The front hall was eight feet wide and went in twelve feet before it reached the stairs that went up to a landing and turned and came back toward the front of the house. I sat staring at those steps. I remembered a little boy creeping down in pajamas, peering between the rungs of the banister at the Christmas tree in the huge living room. Then, I remembered a pretty dark-haired girl in a peach-colored gown posing on the stairs for a photo beside the same boy, but he was much older and was wearing a white dinner jacket.

I went to the right into the dining room. I smelled the musty odor of old carpets and lemon oil furniture polish. In the kitchen, I noticed the red oven light was lit. I opened the oven door. Something in a casserole dish was bubbling. That meant she had only gone out for a few moments. I looked into the refrigerator. There were a few bottles of Rolling Rock beer, my father's. It had probably been there for months; my mother did not drink it. I took a bottle and stuck it into the bottle opener bolted to the side of the kitchen counter. Then, I wedged the bottle between my legs and pushed back through the house.

Back on the porch, I pushed around to the side of the house. I looked down a set of steps that ran into a formal garden surrounded by a boxwood hedge. The stone walk ran out to an Oriental lantern on a stone column and then beyond to a trellis covered with wisteria. Looking over the trellis through a gap in the trees, I could see a patch of grey, which was the Susquehanna. I had spent hours of my childhood playing by it and in it.

The beer was good, cold, and welcome. Looking at the woods and river got me thinking about a particular stream in Vietnam. The mission was to go to a fire support base that was being abandoned and wait to ambush any bad guys that showed up to scavenge what the GIs left behind. The problem was that it took us two days to discover that the pilot left us in the wrong clearing, five kilometers east of where we should have been.

On the second day of the mission, we came to the stream. The bank dropped about six feet into the water. On the other side, four feet from the edge of the stream, a solid wall of bamboo rose. The point man went over the bank into the stream and found that the water was about chest deep. I handed my machine gun and ammo to the man ahead of me. I grabbed vines and lowered myself gently, trying not to make any splashing noise that might reach unseen ears. We waded down the stream until we could find a sandy area that we could all fit onto. We rested for a few minutes and drained the water from our pouches and ammo clips. I took a dry rag from a plastic bag in my pack and dried the gun and a belt of ammo so the links would not rust. The team leader had been looking for a break in the bamboo for us to move through but it stretched as far as we could see on either side.

The only way to go through was to low crawl on our stomachs. We took off our packs and tied them to our ankles. The point man took a knife with a saw blade and cleared a tunnel through the low, thorny branches. I was in the middle of the file. I unloaded the machine gun—in the tangle of bamboo, the ammo would have snagged and been pulled out and it would have been almost impossible to aim at anything. I pushed the gun and the boxes of ammo into the tunnel, then crawled in after them and dragged the rest of my junk. In a little over two hours, we had crawled about fifty yards; the whole way thorns snagged our clothing and equipment. Several times, I had to slide the gun and ammo off to the side or crawl over them to get up to the guy in front of me to unhook him from a snag of thorns.

As we came out the other side, we looked at one another. The thorns had torn huge holes in our uniforms and scratched long thin cuts that trickled blood. A black ranger from Baltimore, Mac, looked at me, pointed to my face and then to his own face, and whispered loudly, "Leaches."

"Let's check each other out," said the team leader. "Sixty, you and Mac go first." While the rest of the team made a circle looking out for bad guys, Mac and I stood in the center. We unbuttoned our shirts. I lit a cigarette and handed it to Mac. He used his free hand to steady my head and then touched the glowing end to the gorged worm that was sucking my blood from my cheek. It squirmed at the burn and dropped to the ground. I dropped my pants—no one wore underwear—and while I looked down the front of me, Mac looked down my back, butt, and legs. I burned one off my stomach and he got another off my leg. Then, I got dressed and he dropped his pants and I looked him over.

"Hold still you got one on your butt," I whispered.

"Don't you burn my ass," he whispered in reply.

I started laughing. "Hold still." He shivered. He got dressed and we took our places on the perimeter and two more guys stood up. I flipped open the cover on the gun and positioned the first bullet. I heard someone running.

The white gravel crunched with a quick rhythm. I rolled toward the front porch. It was my Aunt Ann. She had slowed to a walk when she saw the strange car, and stopped when she saw the front door open. I rolled out where she could see me. "Jake!" she yelled and ran, waving her arms. She took the steps by twos and threw her arms around me. It was not my mother, but it was the greeting that I was hoping for.

"What are you doing here?"

"I pinched a nurse and they threw me out."

She looked at me to see if I were serious. "Really?"

I grinned. "There aren't any nurses there that I would want to pinch. You are the one that said come home so I did."

"Come in. I have to get dinner out of the oven before it burns."

"Will you carry this for me, please?" I asked, handing her the beer bottle. She took it and drank the rest of the beer.

"I'll get you another," she said.

I followed her into the kitchen. I watched her as she worked. She was the running woman that the guys in the truck had been whistling at. She was wearing a grey sweatshirt with the sleeves cut off and blue shorts. She had rock-hard muscles in her calves and thighs. I wondered if she only ran or did weights too. "You run much?"

She turned off the oven and left the door open. "Every evening. It makes me feel great, like a high." She grabbed two beers and slid a chair beside me with her foot.

"What time will my mother be back?"

She arched her eyebrows. "Don't you know? She spends weekends in Philadelphia, to be with your father." I felt a stab of jealousy that my mother had never gone to that trouble for me. I shook my head no. "Yeah, you remember Doctor and Misses Parker—well they have a townhouse there. Your mother spends Friday and Saturday nights. Look, I'm going to go take a shower before dinner, you need anything?"

"No." She put her arm around my shoulder and gave me a squeeze. We sat in silence for a few minutes and then she leaned over and kissed my cheek. She walked to a desk by the back door.

"Here's some mail that came for you in the last week, if you want to look at it," she said, placing it on the kitchen table. Then she went up the back steps.

I pushed outside and went to the car. I opened the trunk and took out the box of supplies. Without my mother here, I did not know how I was going to manage; maybe this was not a good idea. I could just sleep with the leg bag on and, when she came home, I could ask her to help me with the catheter. I pushed back up the ramp, inside, and through a door under the stairs into the new bathroom. It was great. The builder had moved the wall out into what had been a small butler's pantry between the dining room and kitchen. The sink sat on a counter that I could get my knees under. The toilet was high and had a grab bar. There was a big tub with grab bars and enough floor space that I could maneuver around. I put the box on the counter and drained the leg bag.

I went through the dining room into the sun porch, where a hospital bed sat on one side and wicker furniture was crowded on the other side. Curtains had been hung halfway up the long windows. I sat for a moment trying to imagine my father in that bed. Then, I went back to the kitchen to go through the mail. The first couple of letters were from the colleges I had written. I tore open the one from Arizona. They needed my high school records. "Good," I thought, "an excuse to visit the old school." One letter invited me to join an association of retired non-commissioned officers. "Great, twenty years old and I'm retired already."

The last letter was battered and covered in post office rubber stamps. The first address to Walter Reed had been crossed through and my home address written on it. I started ripping at it when I saw the APO on the return address. Someone from Vietnam had written to me. I fumbled trying to get my fingers under the flap. Finally, I grabbed an end between my teeth and the rest between my palms and ripped it open.

It was a get-well card with a note inside.

"Hey 60,

Greetings from the land of rice paddies and water buffaloes. Hope this letter catches up to you, Jake. In case you hadn't heard, the company got moved out of Cu Chi in early December."

I shook my head. No wonder I had not heard from them. My letters were probably in Tibet by now.

"Half of us got sent to Long Binh and the rest got sent up north. We heard that one of those teams got the shit kicked out of them, but I still don't who got it and how bad. Anyway, Long Binh is the pits. They got us doing perimeter guard duty. The regular troops are a bunch of potheads; Charlie could walk right past most of them. The boredom is driving me crazy. You know us, we'd rather be in the field. All they do here is get drunk and plan on coming home. The ARVNs let us go for a parachute jump with them, and even a couple of guys who aren't airborne went. It was wild. I'm a short timer. I'll be the hell out of here in a month." I looked at the date. March 12. By now, the writer was home. "Write if you get a chance. Let us know you're not dead. I'll get in touch when I get home. Harry."

Harry had been the assistant team leader. He was a good Baptist who would sit around reading the Bible. I wonder if they thought I might have died. I was in bad shape when I left Vietnam. I had not tried to write at first. Why didn't Harry send his home address? Did the whole team stay down south? Ann touched my shoulder and I jumped.

"I'm sorry. I thought you heard me come down. Are you alright?" She noticed that I had gone pale. She took the letter from my trembling hands and read it quickly. She rubbed my shoulders and slid her hand down my neck inside my shirt collar. It was a different touch than most I had felt over the past six months; it conveyed gentleness, caring, and affection. She ran her fingertips up and down the pale scar on my spine. "Feel better?"

"Yeah, I just hadn't thought of what might have happened to those guys and how much they mean to me."

She patted my shoulder. She took plates from the dishwasher. "You like tuna casserole?"

"Uh huh."

"It's a low calorie recipe."

"Then I'll eat twice as much." She walked around to the oven and pulled on oven mitts. She was wearing a very short dress that came to the top of her thighs. She opened the door, bent forward, and reached into the oven. The dress rode up so that I was looking at her light blue lacey panties. I looked away. I am not supposed to be looking at my mother's sister's behind and thinking it was cute and sexy.

Hold on. Why couldn't I look? I had been living in a hospital for the last seven months. I had been surrounded by nurses whose bedside manner was as stiff as the starch in their uniforms. I was tired of being a cripple who they ignored at every opportunity. I wanted to be a man. I wanted to look at lacey panties. I looked back at Ann. She was spooning noodles onto the plates. She had long, tanned, muscled legs and the dress clung to all the curves of her body. My eyes were not crippled. Women were one of the things in the plus column about being out of the hospital. It was the first day that I was on my own, not just a few hours and then a retreat to the hospital, but in this place where I could feel safe, have a beer when I wanted, read my mail and look at a pretty woman, sit at a table and have dinner with her. Like guys who did not live in hospitals could do.

"Can you set the table?" she asked. I looked away. Did she know I was staring at her?

"As long as you don't care if the salad and the dessert forks aren't in the right place."

"We're not having salad or dessert. They're not on my diet." I put a tray on my lap, went to the drawer, and took out linen napkins and silverware. I placed them on the linen placemats on the table. Ann came in and set the plates on the table and lit the candles. She pulled the chair at the head of the table away for me.

"I'm not sitting in my father's place; I want to sit in my usual place." I dragged the chair to the right away from the table and pulled in. I hit my knees on the table. I lifted my feet off the footrests and then pulled in.

"Do you want another beer?" she asked.

"What are you drinking?"

"Your mother and I are trying wines."

"Then I'll have wine."

She took the tray that I had used and returned with ice water and white wine. She slid her plate beside me and sat down. I grabbed my fork but saw that she had folded her hands. I bowed my head and she said grace. "Nobody ever says thanks for hospital food," I said wryly. I sipped the wine. I did not let her see the face I made. It was too sweet. "Aunt Ann, if you ever have…"

"Wait a second," she interrupted, "if we're going to get along, you may not call me aunt. I was ten when you were born. If anyone asks, you are my younger brother." She smiled. "But you are not going to make me feel old with this auntie crap."

"All right I got it. Ann, if you have any plans for this evening, I'll be fine."

"What makes you think I have plans?"

"Because you are a pretty, single woman." I noticed her blush.

"Thanks for the compliment." She patted my hand. "But my plans are to do some laundry and do some homework."

"What kind of homework?"

"English and Art History, they are required to get my teaching certificate." We sat and talked as the room grew dark. She wanted to know about Vietnam. She talked about her plans for her future. I felt comfortable talking with her; it was like having a sister. While she cleared the table, I went to the sun porch. I cranked the hospital bed down so that the mattress was on a level with the cushion to my wheelchair. Ann came in.

"You need any help?" she asked.

"I just have to get off my butt and stretch out my back." I lifted onto the bed. Suddenly, one of my legs straightened out with a strong muscle spasm and shook. Ann stepped back and her eyes grew big. I laughed. "Don't worry; it's just a spasm—not a miracle." I dragged my legs onto the bed.

"Is there anything I can do for you?" offered Ann.

"Please pull my boots off?"

She pulled on the boot. It was very hard to get off and when it did slide off, I could see that my foot was very swollen. Before I could tell her not to, she slid up my pants leg and grabbed the top of my sock to pull it off. There was the hose to the leg bag. I felt uncomfortable. "It's the leg bag I have to wear."

"I know," she said matter of factly. That made me more self-conscious. She could probably see the outline of the bag under my pants or maybe my father had had to use one. She got the sock off and massaged my foot. The pressure of her fingers left deep indentations in the swelling. Then, she pulled off the other boot and worked on my other foot.

"You don't have to do all that," I said.

"But I like to," she replied. "Do you want me to bring in the portable TV?"

I shook my head. "No, I am going to read the rest of the mail and take a nap."

"Do you want me to help you get ready for bed?"

"No." I could not explain the discomfort I felt. The house was safe. It had provided a refuge from frustrations, anger, and humiliation. I was not ready to undergo the feelings of helplessness, dependence, and embarrassment. I read through the mail and fell asleep.

31

The Body Image

"Jake, Jake." Ann was shaking me. I opened my eyes and was confused that this was not the hospital. I looked at my watch. It was after midnight. Ann was wearing a white robe over a blue silk pajama shirt. She sat on the edge of the bed and picked up my hand. "Let me help you get ready for bed?"

"No. I'll do it later."

"Jake." She sat, waiting for me to look at her. "At the hospital, you said you needed help. Why won't you let me help you?"

I laid my arm across my eyes. I found it difficult to explain what I thought should be obvious. "You don't know what it's like to be ashamed of your body. To be stripped naked and have people treat you like a thing, to have them not care if it hurts, and to have no control of your body." It was silent. After a minute, she squeezed my hand and pulled my arm away from my eyes.

"You're wrong," she said hoarsely. "Of all the people you could possibly say that to, I understand most of all." She turned so that she was facing out the window. It was the same as when I covered my eyes. She went on. "If I tell you something, would you promise never to tell anyone else, especially your mother?"

What could be such a personal secret? "Yeah, I can keep a secret."

"I've seen pictures of myself when I was a little girl. I was skinny then but I can't remember that time. Sometime around when I was nine, I started gaining weight. I think your mother leaving for college and getting married had something to do with it. My parents always compared me to her but I could not compete. I was so alone and miserable." She paused and took a deep breath. She had waited a long time to share this burden with someone. "Anyway," she went on, "I didn't notice until I went to high school. I began to hear the comments in the hall. I hated gym. I was so embarrassed to change in the locker room, to have the other girls see me. I studied and spent a lot of time alone and it just got worse. By the time I finished high school, I weighed two hundred and thirty pounds. I told you I did not go to college before—it was not because I did not want to, but because I wanted to escape that atmosphere. I became a secretary in a tractor dealership. I gained still more weight, but all I met were farmers." She sniffed and wiped her eyes. "All they had to compare me with were Holsteins, so they thought I was thin." I smiled. She did also.

"For the next ten years, I never went swimming, never went to the beach." She started crying. "I never had anyone to give me a hug or a kiss. Do you know what it feels like to never be touched, to be ignored, talked about and treated so cruelly?"

"Yes, I think I do." I rubbed her shoulders.

"I think you do too," she said. "That's why I told you this. It's so much different now. Guys at work, who never noticed me before, are always stopping by my desk. Yesterday while I was running, some guys in a pick-up truck yelled and whistled. They were jerks but it still felt great. You've been feeling shame for your body for a few months, I felt it for years."

Maybe it would help if I could tell someone what was bothering me. Could I trade secrets with Ann?

"Would you promise to keep a secret and never tell anyone, especially your sister?" I struggled to sit up. She turned and her face came within inches of mine and she looked into my eyes. She tried to read my face.

"Yes," she said. I could feel her breath on my lips.

"You can't tell anyone ever," I repeated.

"I promise," she assured me.

Then, it was my turn to look out of the window. I told her what Lavassuer had done to me. The whole time, I felt my face burning hot, but I was relieved to have told her. I had concentrated so hard on what I was saying that I did not feel her put her arms around me. When I finished, I felt her rocking me gently and saying softly, "I'm sorry, I'm so sorry."

"He made me hate myself."

I laid back down and she lay beside me. I don't know if I drifted off; my head was crammed with tumbling thoughts, but there was the grandfather clock striking one in the morning.

"Are you asleep?" I asked.

"No," she answered, "it just felt good being with you. I can help you get ready for bed. If it does not make you too uncomfortable."

"I'd appreciate that, as long as it doesn't make you uncomfortable." She helped me off with the camouflage jacket and put it on a hanger on a hook behind the door. "I'll iron that for you tomorrow." I took off my shirt. All that was left was my pants. I looked at her. I wished that I did not have to go through this again. She nodded. We got the pants off. I got into the wheelchair and I put a towel in my lap. We went into the bathroom. She faced me and leaned forward to take off the leg bag. I found myself looking down the V-neck of her shirt. She was not wearing anything else but her panties. Her breasts moved as she worked and her nipples were hard. She must have known what I was looking at and I did not make any effort not to look.

I took the leg bag and rinsed it out in the sink while she prepared the irrigation kit. She moved the towel from my lap and inserted the syringe into the catheter. I did not watch what she doing until she said, "Oh." I looked down and saw that I had an erection and that only a few inches of the catheter protruded from the end. She was trying to hold the end of the catheter without touching my penis. I saw her blushing.

"I'm sorry," I apologized. "I don't have any control over when that happens."

"Well from what I know, that isn't any different from any other man. I mean," she said, blushing harder, "your father and you are the only naked men I've ever seen."

"Honey, we gotta get you a man."

She finished and covered me with the towel. "You know," she observed, "you don't have a bad body. I'd give anything to get that skinny."

I clenched my jaw. "Ann, you're overdoing this getting skinny. It's plain to see what the guys in the truck were whistling at." I saw her in the mirror watching me. "Do you think we could figure a way to get me in and out of that bath tub this week? I haven't been in a bath tub in over a year."

"Are you sure you won't dissolve?"

"I'm melting, I'm melting!" I cried in a high, squeaky voice. We went back to the sun porch. She hooked the drainage bag on the bed. I climbed under the covers and she connected the hose to the catheter.

"You know," she said, "we're going to have to get you a bathrobe. You can't push around the house with a washcloth in your lap."

I fingered the sleeve of her shirt. "Maybe I could just wear the pants to your pajamas, auntie." She clutched her hands around my throat and started to shake me. I grabbed around her and pulled her over so that she sat on the edge of the bed. I sat up and put my arms around her and gave her a tight hug. "I wish I had been there for you when you needed a hug all those times."

"Actually, you were. When you were a little boy and your parents would bring you to see your grandparents, you would give me a big hug and want me to read you a story." She moved closer and put her arms around me and put her mouth near my ear. "Thank you for feeling that I was enough of a friend to tell me what happened to you," she said tenderly. I felt her hands move up my back between my shoulder blades. I leaned to her and kissed her cheek, "Thank you," I whispered. She drew away very slowly and rubbed her hand down my cheek. "Goodnight." She walked out and I heard her climb the stairs.

"Good night," I called after her.

32
Adventures in Wheelchair Land

Sunday morning was filled with bright sunshine and cool temperatures. I woke to the sound of the chimes of the grandfather clock, but I was unable to count the hours. I smelled the coffee and heard Ann singing with the radio in the kitchen. I heard the swinging door into the dining room open and she came into the sun porch carrying a tray with mugs of coffee, a vase with a daffodil, and a plate with a donut. I rocked from side to side and sat up.

"Oh good, you're up. I was considering a bucket of water." She handed me a mug. I struggled to get my fingers through the handle without burning myself. "Are you going to church?" she asked.

"Yeah."

"Well, we've got to get going. It's after ten. The last Mass is at 11:30. You must have been tired."

"I guess the drive took a lot out of me."

"I didn't know whether you brought clothes home, so I went up and looked in your closet. Are these okay?" She held up a blue blazer, blue dress shirt, blue and white paisley silk tie, and khakis.

"That's fine." I thought how if someone had brought those pants to the hospital, I would not have had to put up with that stupid clerk in Richmond. She put her hand on mine. "Tell me what you need me to do." I had her clamp off the catheter and take the drainage bag and empty it. Meanwhile, I pulled on the knee sock and used my teeth to pull up the support socks. Before she got back, I had a pair of boxers on and the catheter down the leg opening. I talked her through the routine. I got the pants on and put on a pair of loafers. Once in the chair, I sipped coffee while she buttoned the shirt and we tied the tie together.

Last night had established a friendship that made me comfortable when she helped me. It felt different than in the hospital. She passed me the doughnut. "Aren't you having a doughnut?" I asked her.

"It's not on my diet."

"You don't take a break."

"The ground that I won is too important. Maybe I've replaced compulsive eating with compulsive dieting, but I can tell you that I can't get away from the fact that I'm proud of myself."

We started down the lane in the Pontiac. "Nice car."

"It's stolen," I said dryly.

"You are crazy."

"You know, a poll of most of the people who know me would probably get you the same opinion. Put a tape in if you find anything you like."

We headed down the hill into Castle's Crossing, named for Edwin Webster Castle, the son of a Welsh mining engineer. Edwin's older brothers inherited the ownership and management of some slate and granite quarries on the other side of the Susquehanna. Edwin had to find some way to make money. His brothers had to take the long roundabout way to get their stones to the big cities. Most of the river there had high bluffs on both sides. Edwin surveyed the river and found that this spot had long gradual slopes that ran up from the river on both sides. He acquired the land and set up a ferry and shipping company and charged his brothers to bring their slate and granite across. Most of the granite ended up in the older buildings in the town, but the slate went on to cover most of the roofs in Philadelphia, Lancaster, Trenton, and everyplace in between.

On the outskirts of town, I drove by Drier's Building Supplies where I had worked summers during high school. The town had no place to grow, except on the top of the hills, so it had not changed in over a hundred years. The Catholic church, Saint Luke's, was made of granite. Most of the children in town either went to Saint Luke's school or got on a bus and went up the hill to the new county school. We parked in the school parking lot. I pushed to the front of the church. There were six granite steps up the front and no ramp. I waited while Ann went inside to ask the ushers to help me in. A woman's voice spoke from behind me.

"Hi Jake."

It was Valerie Robinson; her older sister Betsey was the girl in the peach colored gown that I had taken to the prom. Her family was our neighbors.

"Hi Val." Her dad and mom walked up. Her dad put both of his hands around my outstretched hand and shook my hand. "Welcome home, son. I don't know what else to say but thank you, Jake."

His greeting took me by surprise. I told him good morning and Mrs. Robinson stepped forward and hugged me and the other two daughters said hello. "How's Betsey?"

"She's still in college," answered Val with an edge to her voice. Just then, Ann came down the steps with Hank and Charlie Drier. They were going to carry me and the chair up the steps. I recruited Mr. Robinson and another man who was on in his way in to help. The Driers had spent a lifetime slinging sacks of concrete and lumber and probably could have handled it without help, but I just felt better with the extra hands.

Once in church, I sat behind the last pew. Ann and the Robinsons sat in that pew. The Robinsons had four daughters all with light brown hair and freckled faces from hours at high school team sports practice. The oldest, Betsey, had graduated with me. Valerie had been two years behind so I figured that made her about eighteen. Of the other two daughters, Diana would be sixteen and Julia fourteen. Despite their ages, they were all roughly the same height of five feet nine or ten. I began the Mass in a very prayerful state of mind, thanking God for bringing me home when others would never know that experience. I did not recognize the priest who was crossing to the pulpit to read the gospel.

I had long ago concluded that God had assigned an angel to pick the gospel readings that, under the circumstances of the moment, were directed to me alone. Like the time in Vietnam I returned from my first mission when we had a firefight. Our patrol had unexpectedly walked into a Viet Cong patrol. Everyone on both sides just stood frozen for a few seconds looking at their enemy. Then, everyone grabbed their triggers at the same instant. The shooting only lasted about thirty seconds. Most of the bad guys ran back down the trail rather than reload, but one young man was rolling on the ground. He died a few minutes later. I went to church that Sunday and the priest read, "Treat others the way you would have them treat you." I wondered if that man had died because of the way that he had treated others or if I was the one who had better watch out.

The priest motioned for the congregation to stand. Ann, Valerie, Diana, and Julia stood right in front of me. I sat marveling at the sexuality of the female bottom. I could see the designs on Valerie's panties through the white dress she wore. No museum could show me paintings or sculptures that were any more pleasing to the eye than the backsides of these four women. Although these bottoms spanned a period of sixteen years, they were all in great shape. Then, I tuned into what the priest was reading. "What I say to you is: anyone who looks lustfully at a woman has already committed adultery with her in his thoughts. If your right eye is your trouble, gouge it out and throw it away!" Suddenly, my hands of their own volition covered my eyes to save them from the excruciating pain of an avenging angel scooping them out in church.

I tried to concentrate on the sermon and keep my eyes in the missal and my thoughts on prayer. I looked up and saw her kneeling there, head bowed and hands folded. The designs on her panties were flowers, roses. Then, I realized that God himself—by not working a miracle—had given me this unique perspective of the female torso; being in a wheelchair put me at eye level with their anatomy from their breasts to their bottoms.

After church, the Driers did not wait for anybody else and took me down the steps. I waited to talk to several folks that I recognized when I rolled back from communion. Mr. Robinson brought the priest over and said, "Father, this is Jake Scott. He just came home from Vietnam." The priest nodded and looked around, anxious to see someone else to speak with, but Mr. Robinson tightened his grip on the priest's arm. As the priest and I exchanged looks, Mr. Robinson said, "Jake could give you an interesting perspective of the war." The priest glanced at the tall man, gave him a weak smile, and pulled his arm free. The priest called to another parishioner and walked away.

"I don't understand," I said, but Mr. Robinson had gone to catch up with his family. Mr. and Mrs. Walls walked toward me. Mr. Walls stopped a few feet away but Mrs. Walls came to me and squeezed my shoulder. I remembered the day in my junior year of high school that their son was called from class to be told that his brother had been killed in Vietnam. It was the first time I knew someone with a personal contact to the war. Mrs. Walls was smiling at me, but her eyes were fighting to contain her emotions.

"Your mother must be very glad that you're home."

"Yes, ma'am.

"This Memorial day, we are going to have a ceremony at Johnnie's grave." She spoke slowly and deliberately to keep the memories from overwhelming her. "We would like it if you could come."

"I'm only home from the veteran's hospital for a week." A look of disappointment shot across her face. "But if I can get back, I'll be there."

"Please forgive my husband that he does not speak to you. He finds it hard." The woman stepped forward and hugged me tightly and I heard a moan of agony. I patted her back. She turned and walked back to her husband, clutching a tissue. I pushed for the car. I could not imagine the feelings of emptiness and pain felt by a parent who has lost a son. I stopped beside a big tree and reached out and felt the texture of its bark and felt a sense of comfort from its long life.

Ann was talking to Hank Drier. They were about ten feet apart. Hank was about thirty-five years old and a big man with a huge neck, broad shoulders, and large hands. He was poised like a wrestler. Ann was smiling, gripping her purse like she was trying to tear it in half and twisting her toe into the dust. They were looking at each other as if the other were growing a horn from their forehead. I had gotten to know Hank well when I worked for his family. He was a non-stop talker once he got to know you.

Ann saw me watching them. She took a few steps toward Hank. Stopped. Then shoved her hand forward as if she wanted to karate chop him in the kidneys. He took her hand and they said goodbye. She walked quickly toward me.

"What's going on?" I asked.

"Hank was inviting me to go out with his brother's family on their boat, but I told him that you had just come home and I couldn't."

"Do you like him?"

"Well," she said, hesitating, "yes."

I turned and pushed to Hank, who had started to walk away. "Hey Hank, wait up." I looked back. Ann was watching us. While I pushed back to her, Hank smiled at her and waved. She waved.

"What did you say to him?" she asked as we walked toward the car.

"I said you asked me if it was all right if he came over for dinner about four."

"You what! And what did he say?"

"He said sure he would be glad to."

"Jake!" By this time, we had reached the car and she helped me roll in the chair. She got in and asked, "What will your mother say?"

"What's my mother got to do with it?"

"I haven't ever asked any man to the house."

"Why not?"

"Because it's not my house."

"Yeah. Where's your house? You're more concerned about whether your older sister will approve of them." Ann looked worried. "We'll just say Hank is an old friend of mine that I asked for dinner," I said.

She nodded, "Okay." She stared out of the window for a few minutes and then she turned to me. "What do you know about Hank?"

"He told me that his family was from Germany and his father brought the family and his parents to the United States in 1938. His father changed the way they spelled their name. Hank was drafted toward the end of the Korean War, but when the Army found out he had grown up speaking German, he was stationed in Germany where he worked on big construction projects with German contractors." I glanced at her to see if she wanted to hear more. She tilted her head, waiting for me to continue. "I know his brother Charlie got to go to college, but Hank is the brains in the business. It'll be interesting when old man Drier dies to see who gets to run the business."

"Jake, his dad died last October."

"Oh." I curled my lips into my teeth. "So, who runs the business?"

"Mama Drier."

"Mama Drier!?" I was surprised. I could not picture her in coveralls.

I drove into the parking lot between a little market and a liquor store. "I'll go in and get steaks for the grill and some other fixings. You pick out some wine and beer." I rolled into the little market and back to the meat counter. I peered through the glass case, over lean red pieces of beef. I could see a woman cleaning a stainless steel cutting top against the back wall. "Hello. Could you help me?" I called. She looked around above the display case, but saw nothing and went back to cleaning the cutting top. "Yoo-hoo. I'm over here." She turned again and still did not see me. She became agitated.

"Ralphy, if that's you playing around, get back to work."

"It's not Ralphy. I'm down here." She slid open the door to the meat case and looked in and was startled to see a man's head looking back. Her first thought must have been about why this crazy man was hiding behind the meat counter. She stepped back, took hold of a cleaver, and stepped onto a short step ladder.

"Oh, you're in a wheelchair," she said with relief. I did wonder what she had planning to do with that big knife.

"Can I have a couple of nice thick Delmonicos?" Then, I got the fixings for my baked bean recipe.

I tried to balance everything on my lap as I pushed to the checkout. I would push the wheels and grab the groceries before they fell; push, grab, push, grab. I laid the items on the counter and the belt carried them to the cashier. The wheelchair would not fit through the narrow checkout aisle. I apologized to the lady behind me who had already started unloading her cart and asked her to back out of the way. Then, I pushed down the row of check out counters and around the end but I found that there was a railing that kept me from getting back to the counter where my groceries were and that the "IN" door only opened in. So I called to the clerk who was waiting for me to pay. She went out the "OUT" door and opened the "IN" door so I could get out. Then she had to bang on the "OUT" door so that another clerk came and opened the "OUT" door so she and I could go in. I noticed that Ann was already sitting in the car watching this. I went in and paid and then came out to the car. Ann got out and took the bag from me.

"What was that all about?" she asked.

"Adventures in wheelchair land." I grinned, shaking my head in amusement.

33
Little Old Aunt

Ann went for her run early and left me at work in the kitchen. I started on my bean recipe. First, I threw a chunk of salted pork into a heavy pot. Then, I prepared to chop an onion, a stalk of celery, and a green pepper. I removed a vicious looking knife and brought it to the cutting board.

"And now," I began narrating the process aloud, confident that I was alone, "the further adventures of Captain Cripple and the Mutant Vegetables from Venus. First Captain Cripple seizes the evil celery leader and subjects him to the water torture." I rolled to the sink and scrubbed the celery, all the while making the sound effects for a drowning man. Then, I went back and laid the celery on the cutting board. I picked up the knife and hooked the handle between my right thumb and palm. I rested my left palm on the back of the blade. I patiently picked the knife up and down for each slice of the celery. The cutting board was at the level of my chest and my arms and shoulders grew stiff from working at that angle.

"Next, Captain Cripple seizes Herr Von Pepper and performs the delicate stemectomy." I had to hold the knife in both hands but the pepper kept sliding away. I took the pepper and sat it in my crotch and put the point next to the stem. "Just remember, Captain Cripple—you slip here, you're gonna be singing castralto." Gently, I pushed the knife down and then pulled it out, moved over, and repeated the process until I had worked all the way around the stem. I pulled the stem and the seeds out. "Captain Cripple reports to the president that the evil Von Pepper's brains have been removed." Then, I tried slicing the pepper, but I became so frustrated that I grabbed the knife between both palms and hacked away at the pepper until it was in pieces.

"Finally, Captain Cripple comes to the dreaded Spanish onion. Buenos dias, Senor Cebolla." The onion was much more difficult. "Hold still, you little son of a bitch—the more you struggle, the more you suffer—and the more I suffer." I put the handle of the knife in my mouth and clenched it between my teeth, steadied the blade with one hand and the onion with the other. Then, I moved my head and shoulders forward and pushed down on the blade with my hand to slice the onion. By the time I finished, I could not see at all; tears were streaming down my face.

"The evil vegetable creatures have launched a chemical attack on Captain Cripple. Captain Cripple retreats for first aid." I rolled to the refrigerator and pulled out a beer. "Look at this! Captain Cripple's little old aunt bought this expensive German stuff. Could it be that Captain Cripple's little old aunt has the hots for this guy?"

"*Who* are you talking to?" asked Ann.

I almost jumped out of the chair. "Damn, woman, don't sneak up on me."

"Well, if you hadn't been in here talking to yourself, you would have heard me come in. And who is Captain Cripple's little old aunt?" The sheepish look on my face answered her question.

"Hey, do me a favor?" I asked. "Finish chopping that onion, please?"

Ann snatched the knife from the cutting board. "I've been gone forty-five minutes and that's all you got done?"

"You try holding the knife between your teeth and let's see how far you get." I dumped the vegetables into the pot with some oil and stirred them, but it was hard to see into the pot sitting beside the stove. Next, came Worcestshire sauce, brown mustard, and a big can of beans. I put a top on it and had Ann set it in the oven.

"What else were you planning to serve?" she asked.

"If you would pry the top off that beer, I thought that I would start with that. I bought cole slaw and steaks."

"You want me to make some biscuits?" she volunteered.

"Good idea, a guy Hank's size needs to know that you can cook." She looked worried.

"You're not going to tease me when Hank gets here, are you?"

"I'll behave myself. How long have you been seeing Hank?"

"He has invited me out on the boat with his brother's family twice, but we've never been alone. Frankly, I didn't relish another afternoon with his relatives—they're not my kind of folks."

"You mean Charlie's a loud-mouthed horse's ass?" I suggested.

"Well, yes—and so is his wife."

Suddenly, I felt faint and I realized I had done a lot for my first full day out of the hospital. "I need a nap. Wake me up before he gets here." I hit the bed like a brick. Two hours later when Ann woke me, I felt as if I hadn't been asleep any time at all.

At 4:00 p.m., I was on the side porch spreading the red coals in a hibachi; Ann had set up a folding table with a checkered cloth and a vase of fresh flowers. A big flat bed truck came driving up the driveway. I smiled. "That Hank knows how to impress a girl." Hank came up on the porch and knocked at the front door. "Round here on side, Hank," I called.

"Hey Jake, you doing the cooking?"

"I'm just burning the cow." The sound of the stereo came through the window; apparently, Ann knew that Hank had arrived. Hank came over and sat on the porch rail. He was wearing a short-sleeved shirt. The sleeves stretched around his muscled arms. His face and neck were permanently red from years in the sun and wind. "How bout a beer," I offered.

"Thought you'd never ask."

I fished into the cooler of ice beside me and pulled out one of the beers. I wedged the beer into my crotch and pulled up the opener that hung on a string that I had looped over the brake handle. The odor of Hank's cologne enveloped me. Good golly, he must have been going all out to impress Ann. I hooked the opener on the bottle and pulled up by putting my hand under the handle. But the wet bottle slipped, flew toward Hank, hit the floor, and the top shot off. The cold beer foamed across the floor. Hank scooped up the bottle, looked at the swallow left in the bottom, and drank it. I grimaced. "So, Hank, you want another beer?"

Hank got up and said, "I better get something to wash this porch off with."

Ann came out of the side door. "What are you two up to?"

I pointed at Hank, "I told you about this guy Ann he can't hold his liquor."

"Me!" protested Hank, "I show up and he starts throwing beer bottles at me while they still have beer in them."

Ann shook her head. “Bad little boys, I have to baby sit bad little boys. I’ll get a bucket of water to wash this off.”

“I’ll come help you,” said Hank. In a minute, they were back. He carried a bucket of water and she carried the tray of red, raw steaks. She handed me a long handled fork. She was wearing a trace of make-up and she smelled pretty good too. When Hank finished rinsing the porch, Ann took the bucket and started back inside.

“Hey why don’t you sit down and relax with us?” asked Hank.

“I gotta get my biscuits out of the oven.”

Hank settled back on the porch rail with a fresh beer. He looked out at the garden. “Jake, can I ask you a question?”

“You can ask it, I may not answer it.”

“What was it like…” He paused and took a sip. “…Over there.” I stabbed the fork into a steak and listened to it sizzle on the grill. I took a swig of beer and let out a long sigh. It was a question I should have been ready to answer, but was not.

“I guess most days it was routine boredom interrupted from time to time by confusion and hell.” I poked the steaks and flipped them to sear the other side. “I remember one day the platoon leader had a formation and asked for volunteers for a dangerous mission.” I paused until Hank looked back at me and I smiled. “Turned out some of our Kit Carson scouts—they were ex-Viet Cong who scouted for us—wanted a couple of us to come to the village for dinner. Me and five other guys figured what the hell, we packed into a jeep and drove to the village.

“The house was basically one big room made out of six by sixes and one by sixes. The roof and walls were corrugated metal and scrap metal off the Army base.” Ann came out, carrying the bread basket covered with a cloth, sat it on the table, and pulled a chair up beside Hank. “We all sat at this big long table. It’s just the Rangers and the scouts; the women did the serving. Over there, the women know their place.” Ann grabbed Hank’s beer, shook it, and sprayed me.

“Anyway, as I was saying before I was so rudely interrupted, the women brought in trays of assorted glass jars that they had rescued from the dump and cleaned. They put chunks of ice in them and gave us all bottles of Vietnamese Thirty-three beer. We poured it over the ice.” I looked; they were holding hands.

“Now, the water that makes the ice is of questionable origin and, as it freezes, things may fall into it. After it is frozen into blocks, it is stored in an ice house and sawdust is sprinkled over it to keep adjacent blocks from freezing together. The effect of pouring the warm beer over the ice is to free small creatures, sawdust, and other unidentifiable objects that foam to the top and float on the head of the beer. I skimmed the head off with my finger and flicked it on the dirt floor. After a glass or two, you don't even bother to skim off the head."

I turned the steaks again and had another swallow of beer. "They served this white stuff that I took for a filet of fish. I picked some up, looked around at the other guys, and put it in my mouth and started chewing. After what seemed like five minutes of chewing the same bite of fish, I notice everyone else is chewing. I swallowed the rest in a gulp. I asked the scout beside me what it was. He tells me it's water buffalo. I ask what part of water buffalo and he draws a line from his throat down his chest to his stomach. We figured he meant that it was tripe."

Eeyyuu, cow stomach," said Ann, making a face.

"Buffalo esophagus," I corrected. The steaks were done and we moved to the table. Ann led the prayer. I insisted on trying to cut my own steak. Ann and Hank would watch the effort from time to time.

"Jake," said Hank as he finished, "you know if you're gonna be home this summer, you could come back and work at the shop." Ann finished eating. I was attempting to saw off a second piece of steak.

"Please, let me help you cut that," she offered. I surrendered the meat.

I looked back at Hank and asked, "Doing what?"

"We could use you on the inside selling stuff and answering questions. You probably know as much about it as anybody working there."

I chewed the pieces Ann had cut. "Thanks, Hank." I almost said no. "I might take you up on it."

Ann got up and gathered two handfuls of dishes and headed for the kitchen. Hank followed her with what was left. In a few minutes, Hank came back. "Where's Ann?" I asked.

"She said she had to clean the kitchen." I started pushing into the house. "The hell you say, wait here." I rolled through the house.

"WHAT are you doing? You can do this later."

"I wanted to get this taken care of before your mother got home."

I had completely forgotten about my mother. "Forget her. The whole idea is to find another guy that you could see naked besides me."

"Jake!" Her face turned scarlet.

"I'm serious, go take the big lug for a walk in the garden." I got behind her and started running into her and pushing her out of the kitchen. She started through the dining room and I called after her. "This time, when you want to kiss him…" She turned. "…Do it."

I shoved the leftovers into the refrigerator, and filled the sink with soapy water for the dishes to soak in. Then, I pushed around to the bathroom. I looked through the living room windows and did not see them on the porch.

I went to the sun porch. I took off my shirt and boots. I laid down and stretched my back. Soon, I went to sleep. A dream began.

I was waking in the hospital. A blinding light hung over me. There were silhouettes of people. A woman leaned over me, pulled my eyelids open, and looked at my pupils. "He's conscious," she called. "Hey Major! Does this guy look familiar?"

Someone moved the light so that it was not in my eyes. "Hi, ranger." I recognized Major Nurse and forced a smile. Pain, like fire, burned over my body. A medic and a nurse stepped up on either side of me and started cutting off my clothes. "Let me help you get your make up off," said the Major. She took a large gauze pad and put some skin cleaner on it and began very gently wiping off the black and green camo stick I had painted my face and hands with. Her fingers were cold and smooth and her grip was firm. She took a small pair of clippers and started shaving my head.

"It's a good thing you hardcore types don't have any hair. I'd be here all day if I had to shave some of these hippies." The doctor came over and started to explain drilling into my skull. I was so tired and aching that I was past caring. Once they started drilling, I passed out. When I awoke, I was looking at the ceiling. Her face leaned over mine and she looked at my pupils and behind my eyes. "Do you know that you have little gold circles between the blue and the pupils of your eyes?"

I wanted to say that, under the circumstances, I could care less, but that took too much energy. I tried to say, "No." My tongue stuck to my lips. I managed to whisper, "Drink."

"You can't have anything to drink for awhile." She took a gauze pad, dipped it into a pitcher of water, and wiped my lips and tongue.

"Jake Scott! Ann Jacobs! What are you doing?!" It was my mother's voice. I was still trying to come out of the fog of sleep. I could not figure out why she sounded so upset. I opened my eyes and looked. Ann was lying beside me in bed. "What have you two been doing?" my mother kept yelling louder.

"I have been sleeping," I said. I turned and looked at Ann. "What have you been doing?"

"I came in to help you get ready for bed," she said defensively. "I couldn't wake you up so I laid down to take a nap and help you if you woke up later." We were both lying under the blanket. Ann got up and she was wearing the blue pajama shirt.

"Don't you think that you should wear some clothes around him?" demanded my mother of Ann. I was shocked at the tone of her voice; you would have thought she caught us in the middle of sex. Ann sat in the chair like a child being put in the corner and pulled the shirt over her knees. *They're not sisters*, I thought, *they're mother and daughter*. No wonder Ann won't have anyone over; they'd never get a passing grade from my mother.

I tuned back into my mother's tirade about how this looked. My mother was telling Ann to leave her house when I cut in, "Mother, can it! Will you? Nothing happened. This woman has been helping me for the past two days, because you did not have time for me." Uh-oh. I slipped. I hadn't meant to say that last part. My mother glared at me. Never before had I spoken to her in that tone of voice. She stormed from the room. We listened as she climber the stairs and slammed the door to her bedroom.

I blew out a deep breath and had a sudden craving for a cigarette. "Well, that wasn't how I had pictured my homecoming reunion." Ann was crying. I threw the blanket off and got back into the chair and rolled over to Ann. I took her hand between mine.

"I just laid down with you," she said, catching a sob, "because I was afraid that if I went to my room, I wouldn't hear you call when you woke up." She was behaving like a little girl scolded by a parent, dependent on her sister's approval.

"Sit over here and let me give you a hug?" I patted my lap.

"I couldn't—your mother."

"To hell with my mother. She's going to sulk in her room." She sniffed and dried her eyes on her sleeve and slid onto my lap. I put my arms around her and gently rocked her. "How'd you and Hank get along?"

She smiled and her eyes brightened. "You know what he likes?"

"No. What does he like?" I expected an answer like professional wrestling.

"He likes opera. He asked me to go to Philadelphia on Friday evening to see one."

"So you're going, right?"

"How will you get ready for bed?"

"Darling, I'll manage that."

"What about your mother?"

"She's my mother, not your mother. It's time you started living the life you want."

"Do you think it's too late to call Hank and tell him I'll go?"

"What time is it?"

"11:30."

"Nah. I think he'd like to get a call. You go do that and I'll get undressed and meet you in the bathroom." The first day home from the hospital had gone pretty well.

34

What I Deserved

Ann woke me and handed me a mug of steaming coffee. She was wearing a blue cotton dress with a white collar. “I have to leave for work. Want me to help you get dressed before I go?”

“Yes, thanks. Have you seen my mother this morning?”

“She came down and went out already. I think she’s still mad. Do you think she really wants me to move out?

“Naa, she ain’t still mad,” I said with conviction, although, inwardly, I admitted she could be.

“I was thinking that I have a lot of leave saved. I could take off a few days and we could do something together,” she offered.

“Well that’s nice, but why don’t you take off a few days and spend them with Hank.”

“Hey, don’t start pushing me. I already have too many mothers.”

“Yeah, mind my own business. Okay, take off Wednesday and we’ll ride around Lancaster, maybe go shopping.” I was in the bathroom when I heard the front screen door close. When I came out, I stopped and listened. There were noises in the kitchen. My mother was frying bacon and whipping pancake batter. She looked up as I came in but looked back down and her arm started working faster. I rolled beside her and put my arm around her waist.

“I’m sorry I yelled at you last night.”

“Why did you speak to me like that?”

I backed away from her so that I could see her face when I spoke. "Mom, did you hear what you were saying? I mean, if you don't trust Ann and me, I would at least think you know us well enough to know that I'm not going to sleep with your sister. Ann is a grown woman. It was humiliating to her to be scolded by you. I've seen enough humiliation that it upsets me to watch it."

She was handling the whisk in her hand like a whip. I could see her clenching her jaw muscles. I asked hopefully, "Are we friends?"

She nodded and said, "Sit down and I'll have your breakfast ready."

"Mom." I waited for her to stop stirring and look at me. "I am sitting down." I finally got to her; she smiled. She was flipping pancakes when the phone rang. She picked it up and walked, trailing the long cord back to the stove. I sat sipping coffee and reading yesterday's paper. I could tell from listening to my mother's half of the conversation that she was talking to Mrs. Robinson.

When she hung up, she sat plates on the table and sat down with me. "Did you see the Robinsons yesterday?"

"Yeah, at church."

"They want to invite us for cocktails on Friday, a welcome home party for you. Isn't that nice?"

"Yeah mom, that's very thoughtful."

"What do you want to do today?"

"I'm going to fill out these college applications." I nodded at the mail I'd opened yesterday.

"Oh, where are you applying to?"

"Penn State, Arizona, University of Miami—maybe Chaminaude in Hawaii."

"What about Princeton? Your grandfather and father went to Princeton."

"Mom, I couldn't get into Princeton."

"Why not?" she said with alarm that I would harbor such a heretical thought. "You got A's in high school and very good SAT scores."

"No, Mom, I mean physically. I could never get up all those steps into those ancient buildings."

"Oh." Her voice registered disappointment that the tradition would be broken. I went into the living room to my father's desk and uncovered the typewriter. I threaded the pages of the applications through the roller. I rested the edges of my palms on the top of the typewriter and used my thumbs to push the keys. I went very slowly, not wanting to send in applications covered in correction fluid. One application asked me to write a paragraph on why I wanted to attend that school.

I tried to get creative but admitted that telling them I didn't want to spend months struggling through snow drifts or that I wanted to see women in skimpy clothing was not going to impress them. Filling in the paperwork took all morning. About 11:00 a.m., I went to the liquor cabinet and fixed myself a scotch over ice. I went back to the desk and shook the cover out to put it back over the typewriter. I knocked a pile of letters off the corner of the desk. I leaned forward to pick them up and the chair tilted forward and I almost went out on my nose. I thrust my hand down and pushed up from the floor. I slid the letters against a wheel and slid them up the frame of the chair until I could get them between my palms. I noticed that some of them were overdue bills and notices. I felt a bit ashamed that I had not thought that my mom was having trouble making ends meet. I would have to find a way to help.

After a whole morning of typing and scotch, I needed a nap. When I woke, I went looking for my mother. She was in the garden, weeding and mulching.

She looked up. "Jake, I put some lunch on the little table there."

"Thanks, mom." I asked between chews, "Do think I could set exercise equipment up on the sun porch so that I can work out?"

"Sure, dear, I'll ask Ann to help me move some of that furniture into the basement and we'll bring your weights and bench down out of Ann's room."

"Ann's room?"

"Oh, yes, besides running, she lifts weights." I smiled; what an aunt. I went and collected the college materials and wrote a check. I went out to the Pontiac and my mother followed to watch the loading operation.

"That's a very nice car."

"Yeah, Mom, it was a get well present from Uncle Sam." I bit my lip and wondered how to approach the subject. "You know, Mom, between social security, VA comp, and my back pay, I've got $4,000 in the bank." Her face registered that she knew where I was going. "I accidentally saw the bills on the desk. I would like you to take this." I handed her the check.

"Jake," she said, looking at it, "I can't take this. It's your money. "I've started a job as a real estate agent. I'll be earning some money soon."

"Mom those are family bills and I'm a member of the family. Now, you take it or else…" I paused. "…I'll go around and pay them on my own."

"Thank you, Jake." She leaned through the car window and kissed my cheek.

I stopped at the gas station and an attendant came out. I looked at the prices; premium was thirty-two cents a gallon. "Fill it up with the good stuff, please." The guy pumped the gas, cleaned the windshield, and checked the oil. I paid him $4.80. I drove to Eisenhower High School. It had been built in 1958. There was a large circular drive in front with the U.S. and Pennsylvania flags flapping from poles in the center of the circle. I parked in the side lot. I pushed around the building, looking for a way up over the curb. *There musta been people in wheelchairs thirteen years ago*, I thought. *How come nobody thought about them when they built this place*? At the back of the building, I found a wooden ramp that was meant to drive the lawn tractor over. I pushed up that and went through the nearest door. I was pushing down a long hall toward the office when the bell rang. Doors burst open and kids poured into the hall. They were hurrying to their next class and kept bumping into the chair or tripping over my feet.

Just as quickly, they were back in other rooms and the hall was silent. I came up to the office. I talked to the secretary and gave her the list of colleges to mail my transcript to. She was new and I did not recognize her.

"Hi, Jake." Valerie Robinson had come in behind me.

"Hi, Val. Somebody send you to the office?"

"I'm here to see Mrs. Swenson," she said to me and the secretary.

The woman went over to a door labeled "Guidance Counselor," knocked, and looked inside. Then, she closed the door and looked at Valerie. "She'll be with you in a moment."

Mrs. Swenson was still the guidance counselor. I mumbled. "What was that?" Valerie asked as she sat beside me.

"I said, what a flake." Each senior had had to see a guidance counselor before graduation. I had gone in and told Swenson that I was going into the Army. She told me I was wasting my life. I walked out. She set up other appointments, at which times she declared that I was going to waste my intelligence and my education. She presented me with alternatives. To get her to leave me alone, I told her that I would consider the alternatives, and I did.

Our last confrontation took place in front of the Army recruiting office in Lancaster. It was the Saturday after my eighteenth birthday. I was going to sign the papers. I would report after graduation. Swenson and six other people were demonstrating against the war in front of the office. I waited until I thought that she would not see me approaching the door and I started. She saw me.

"Mr. Scott. Where are you going?"

She knew damn well where I was going. I made a gesture toward the recruiter's door. "Those people are lying to the American public," she spat. She shoved some leaflets in front of my face. I tried to step around her, but she grabbed my arm. The other demonstrators and passers-by had stopped to watch us. "Do you want to be taught to fight and kill?" She asked me again and again; each time, her voice grew louder until she was screaming. The recruiting sergeant came out of the office and a police officer stepped beside me. The policeman explained to the crowd that they could demonstrate, but they could not interfere with people using the sidewalk. Swenson was glaring at me and either did not hear him or was ignoring him. The sergeant took both of our arms and pulled her hand from my wrist. Another demonstrator told the officer that there would not be any problems and they began marching again, except Swenson, who kept looking at me through the window as I went over the paperwork.

"Mr. Scott!" Swenson called. She walked from her office, leaned across the counter, and looked at the wheelchair. "You insisted on going to war, didn't you? Look what has happened to you. Do you see this, Miss Robinson? This man would not listen to me. He went off to kill people. Do you know what I think, Mr. Scott?"

"I don't care what you think."

"I think you got just what you deserved. I see you in that wheelchair and I think it serves you right." Swenson turned on her heel and retreated to her office. "Miss Robinson, you can come in now."

I sat there, face burning, throat tight, a flood of tears trying to push past my eyes. It all came down to this—I was being punished for serving my country, for being patriotic, for all those ideals I learned in this school. I wanted to scream, but I turned the chair and pushed to the door. I fumbled and fumbled with the knob. Valerie came around and opened it. I pushed the chair as hard as I could. "Jake? Jake," I heard her call softly after me. I pushed harder. Outside, heavy, dark clouds were blocking the sun.

I drove to the river. I got out and sat contemplating the broad expanse of water slowly parading by. I kept forcing thoughts of rolling into the swirling waters from my head. I remembered the bottle under the seat. I took a swallow of the scotch and concentrated on the burning sensation.

It was about six when I got to the house. I went to the sun porch. The wicker furniture was gone and my weights and bench had been set up. I carefully slid from the chair onto the bench and laid back. I started pressing the weights, up and down, until my arms would not do it.

"Jake?" My mother and Ann walked in. "We thought we heard you come in. Do you like this set up?"

"Yeah. Thanks." My voice was tired and flat.

"Did something happen?" asked my mother.

"I don't want to talk about it."

"Did it have something to do with Valerie Robinson?" asked Ann.

"What do you mean?"

"She's called here twice looking for you."

I grabbed the weights and started pushing again. At dinner, my mother and Ann talked about the latest gossip from town. "Oh, by the way, Ann." My mother gestured with her knife. "I meant to tell you that we've been invited to a cocktail party at the Robinson's Friday night." As she finished, she looked at me to make sure I remembered. Ann and I looked at each other in the same instant.

"Ann," I rushed. "Isn't that the night you have tickets to the opera?"

"Yes," Ann gulped, trying to hide behind her forkful of salad.

"Oh, that's nice," said my mother. Then, she put on her mother-daughter face. "Who are you going with?"

It was up to me. "Hank Drier asked me if I knew anybody who would like to see an opera and I introduced him to Ann."

"Hank Drier," my mother spat with sarcastic disapproval. My mother could only be happy if her sister got involved with the doctor or lawyer type. It would not hurt if he were an Ivy League graduate from an old, rich family.

"Mom, I just want you to know that Hank Drier is the nicest guy in this town, a friend of mine, and my guest for dinner here last night." That ended the conversation; my mother got up and started clearing the table.

Ann watched her go into the kitchen and whispered quickly, "Why did you tell her about Hank? Why did you think I was kicking you under the table?"

I burst out laughing, "Honey child, you could set fire to me under the table and I wouldn't feel it. Besides, she had to know sometime. Now it's out. Enjoy it."

She stood and was deliberately folding the napkins. "What have you and Valerie got going?"

"Nothing." My mood raced back to sullen.

"Aren't we friends?"

The phone rang. My mother answered it in the kitchen. "Jake, it's Valerie." Ann raised her eyebrows.

"Tell you later," I said. I rolled into the living room and picked up the phone. "I got it, Mom," I said into the receiver and heard the other phone get hung up.

"Hello?"

"Hi." The voice was husky and sultry; she was suddenly older, but then there was silence. "It was good to see you yesterday at church, umm," she said, inhaling, "and at school."

"Yeah, I guess I should have just phoned the school."

"Where'd you go?"

"I drove to the park by the river."

"I'm sorry she said those things to you."

"Yeah, well, what can I do?"

"Could I stop by Wednesday after school?"

"Yeah, if you want." Then it struck me what she was asking and I perked up. "That would be nice. I'd like that."

That night, my mom came onto the sun porch. "Jake, do you need anything?"

"Mom, how did you get Dad in and out of the tub?"

"Well, we didn't exactly. I put a chair in the tub for him to sit on."

I got undressed and rolled into the bathroom. I pulled the chair straight toward the tub, swung the footrest out of the way, and sat on the side. I lowered myself in and turned on the water. It felt fantastic to lie in a tub, the hot water relaxing my muscles. I slid down and put my head under water and my butt floated and I had to roll sideways to get my head up. I was in there until the water started to get cold and I let it drain. Then, I tried various approaches to getting out, but I was too slippery.

"Anybody! I need some help." Instantly, the door swung open and Mother and Ann came in. I laughed. "Were you guys listening at the keyhole?" I grabbed the washcloth and spread it over my groin to preserve some modesty. After a quick discussion of the options, Ann grabbed under my arms and my mother under my knees and they sat me back in the chair.

After I was in bed, the house grew quiet. Then, I heard someone coming down the stairs. Ann walked in and sat on the edge of the bed.

"You found the pajama pants," I observed. She blushed. "I'm sorry you found them." She blushed more.

She took my hand. "You want to talk about what happened today?"

"Somebody called me a criminal and said I should be punished for going to Vietnam."

"Who?"

"Nobody important."

"Then why were you upset?"

"Because there are a lot of other people just like her."

"Not Valerie?!"

"No."

"What did she say should happen to you?"

"I should be sentenced to a wheelchair for life."

She leaned toward me and held me. "I'm sorry, Jake."

I hugged her tightly. "I only hope I find a woman to love me who is as great as you are," I whispered into her ear.

She pulled back and looked at me. "I can be a good listener if you want to talk about what happened over there or anything that's bothering you." I leaned over and kissed her cheek. "Goodnight," she whispered.

"Thanks," I returned. She turned off the lights and I heard her climbing the stairs.

35

Growing Older

Tuesday morning, my mom and I drove to an athletic supply house and bought a gymnastic tumbling mat. Then, we stopped and got a non-skid bath mat. When we got home, she spread the tumbling mat on the living room floor. I got down onto it and stretched and exercised. I sat up, grabbed my feet, and pulled them back to my butt so that my knees were under my chin. I put my hands on the floor behind me and pushed forward until I was squatting on my feet.

"Hey, mom!" She came in. "Will you please move that footstool beside me and hold it?" I put one hand on the stool and then started lifting with both arms and bouncing on my feet and lifting higher until I could get my butt to the height of the stool and then throw my butt onto the stool. This involved a good number of misses and I would fall to the side or back. My mom put a big chair against the stool to hold it. I managed to get on the stool and then did it again and again until the maneuver went right almost every time. Once I was on the stool, I could lift into a higher regular chair and then back up into the wheelchair.

When Ann came home, I explained to her and my mom the purpose of all this. The bathtub was a challenge. They put the bath mat in and I got in with my clothes on but with my feet bare. I went through the same procedure and ended up on the side of the tub. It may not work as well when I was naked and wet, but at least I had a solution.

That evening, I asked Ann if she had taken off for the next day. “No,” she said, “I wanted to see if you still wanted me to. I can call in tomorrow.”

“I forgot and told Valerie to come over after school.”

“That’s okay, how about Thursday?”

“It’s a date.”

On Wednesday, I practiced lifting from the floor again because I realized it would be important to be able to get up if I fell. When Valerie arrived, I was on the mat trying to do a sit-up. I had my hands under my butt but I kept lifting my legs. “Hey, Valerie. How’d you like to do me a favor?”

“Sure. What?”

“Put your hands here above my knees and hold my legs down.”

She straddled my legs and knelt down, which caused an already short mini-skirt to slide a little higher. I looked up at the ceiling until she was sitting on my legs. Most of the sit-up was accomplished with my arm muscles. When I sat up, my face was only inches from hers. I could smell her scent. My eyes were looking directly at her lips. I did ten sit-ups. “Talk about putting a carrot before a mule,” I muttered.

“What?”

“Nothing, nothing, just talking to myself.”

She looked out the window. “Is that your car out there?” I shook my head but my eyes never left her throat. “It’s neat. Would you like to take a ride after dinner?”

“Sure, I’ll pick you up at your house.” I did two more sets of sit-ups before she left. With her as my therapist, I could be ready for the Olympics in no time.

I was a little surprised when I pulled into the Robinson’s drive and saw four teenagers: Valerie, two other girls, and a guy who was seeing one of those girls. They walked up to the car.

“Hey,” said one of the girls, “we can’t all get in with this wheelchair in here.”

The other girl said, “We could just leave it here and you can pick it up when you get back.”

“Yeah,” said the guy, “how do I get it out of here?”

“I got a better idea,” I growled. “The wheelchair can stay where it is and I can leave you all.” I slid the car into reverse and started backing out the drive.

“Jake, wait, please,” pleaded Valerie. I stopped and she stooped beside the door and looked at me with her beautiful eyes.

"Hey," I said, still pissed, "I ain't no chauffeur and this ain't no limousine."

"I didn't know they were coming by." She spoke softly so that the others could not hear. "They just stopped over and asked me to go to a bonfire by the river and I mentioned that we could all go in your car. I forgot about the wheelchair. Don't be mad, they can ride in their car and I'll ride with you. Okay?" She ran her fingertips over the hairs on the back of my arms and sent chills up my arm. There was no way I could stay mad with those big hazel eyes looking into mine.

"All right," I whispered.

We followed the others to the river. They weren't speaking to me. The area was flat so, with Valerie's help, I rolled to the fire. There was a crowd of about twenty. She introduced me around. I had gone to school with several of their older siblings. I sat for an hour and a half listening to them talking about their plans for the prom, for graduation, summer jobs, and who was dating or breaking up with whom. Somebody brought a jug of rum and Coke. They gave me a cup but it was too sweet and I sat it aside. When the sun went down, it got chilly. I took off my camouflage jacket and wrapped it around Valerie's shoulders. She was still shivering when we drove home.

The lights of the instrument panel dimly lit her face when she leaned over so she could look at me. "You're not angry, are you?"

"No, why did you ask that?"

"You were really quiet back there."

"Sweetheart," I sighed, "surrounded by those kids, I suddenly realized how old I've become. I felt nothing in common with them. I probably have nothing in common with the kids *I* went to school with. They're talking about all the fun that comes with the end of high school. I couldn't exactly stir up the conversation with, 'So what d'ya think of the M-16?'"

"You could have told me about Vietnam?"

"From what I've seen, the people back home don't want to talk about the war. They just want it to be over with. They want people like me not to remind them of where I've been or what I've been through. They don't want to know if I have bad dreams or head problems."

"Do you?"

"What?"

"Have head problems or bad dreams?"

"Yeah."

"Would you like to talk about it?"

"Yes, but not to you."

"Why not to me?" Her feelings were hurt.

"Darlin,' I want to talk about shit that's going to bother me forever, stuff that you can't even imagine. How can I talk to you or any of these nice folks?"

"Is the war all you ever want to talk about?"

"I guess it sounds like that, huh? I want to talk about going to college and having a normal life too, but sitting there and listening to those kids." I looked at the still dark streets of the town, the traffic lights changing for no one, the empty shops. "Not only am I different, but this town's different from when I left and it's not going to go back to the way it was because I came home. I don't know the people they're talking about, it isn't my graduation or summer vacation, and I'm not going to the prom next weekend." I turned the car into her driveway.

"Jake, stop. Please." I stopped and put the car in park. She sat looking out the window while she spoke. "All the years we grew up next to each other, I had such a crush on you. In high school, I tried so hard to get you to look at me and you never noticed me. I was so jealous when you asked my sister and not me to the prom. I remember when you came to pick her up. I sat in my room looking out the window at you in your tux, wishing I could get you to look at me. When I saw you at church on Sunday, I almost cried. I'm so angry for what they did to you."

I was stunned by what she had said. She was the first person to tell me that what had happened to me made a difference to her. I laid my hand on her shoulder and she started speaking in a hoarse whisper.

"When I heard you were hurt, I wanted to go see you, but I was scared that it wouldn't be you anymore. If I had known you were coming home," she said, turning to look at me, "I would have asked you to take me to my prom."

"I'm afraid we wouldn't gotten much dancing done."

She sat back and put her hands in her lap. There was silence for two minutes. "Where are you going to college?"

I shook my head. "To be truthful, I haven't decided yet. What about you?"

"I am going to Notre Dame in Baltimore." It got quiet again for a few minutes. I slid my hand across her shoulder and up her neck.

"I'm looking at you now." She slid toward me and I pulled her onto my lap. We kissed and I slid my hand down her back across her short skirt and along her stockinged leg. "I must have been blind before," I whispered into her ear. She smiled. Suddenly, the light on her front porch went on. "I have the distinct impression we're not alone." She slid back into the right front seat and I drove the car up the rest of the drive to the bottom of the front porch steps.

"Hello, Jake."

"Hello, Mrs. Robinson."

"Young lady, it is a school night."

"I'll be right in Mom." Her mother stepped back inside. Valerie put her arms around my neck and we kissed again. Then, she got out and ran inside.

Ann was waiting up for me when I got home. "Is that pink lipstick smeared all over your face?" she asked with an impish smile. "You sly dog, wipe that smug grin off your face."

Then I really grinned.

Thursday, Mom, Ann, and I went shopping. I wanted a knapsack and Mom convinced me to buy a blue suit for the Robinson's party. We had lunch and then drove to Longwood Gardens, a huge botanical display with water fountains. I pushed as long as I could and then Mom and Ann took turns giving me a boost. When it was time to leave, I was too exhausted to drive. I slid over and let Ann drive. When she pulled out of the parking lot, the tires screamed and she laid rubber.

"Hey!" I yelled in fright. "Wild woman, take it easy."

"It has a little more power than I'm used to."

36

A Thanksgiving Party

Friday, I spent the whole day obsessing about how I would be accepted at the Robinson's party and worrying about how I would get around. There were steps up the front. The living and dining rooms were down two steps from the rest of the first floor. There was a bathroom in what had been a first floor closet. The door was too narrow for me to get through. The door opened in; even if I could get a small chair in the bathroom and transfer on to it from the wheelchair, I could not get the door closed. Suppose they went to all the trouble to carry me up the steps and I had to go to the bathroom or the hose pulled off the leg bag. The inaccessibility of the place was becoming overwhelming. I began to think up excuses why I could not go or might have to leave early.

Around five o'clock, Hank drove up to the house in a black Lincoln Continental. He strolled onto the porch shook my hand and I said, "Hey, Easy Money, where's ja get dem wheels." Hank muttered an answer. I put my hand behind my ear and pushed it out.

"It's my mother's car," he said, digging his toe into the gravel.

I had to keep teasing. "And she trusts you with it?"

"I happened to mention I was taking Ann out and she threatened to disown me if I drove my truck to the opera. You think she's trying to tell me something?"

The sound of the spring on the screen door stretching made us both turn. There stood Ann. She was wearing a jade colored strapless silk dress with a string of pearls and pearl earrings and carrying a matching wrap. Hank made a long, soft whistling sound. Ann and I both heard it. I rolled over to her, licked my finger, touched her arm, and made the sound of escaping steam. "Whoa, hot stuff."

"Well now that you *gentlemen* have embarrass…" She looked at the Lincoln. "You got Mafia connections?"

"Hey," I said, "didn't I tells youse da guy is lousy wit class?" Hank opened the door for her. I looked at my watch. "Now children I want you back here in time for confession Sunday morning." They both blushed. Hank walked briskly to the driver's door and waved to me. I gave him a thumbs-up and a wink. As they drove out, I thought, *at least somebody's going to have a good time tonight.*

I changed into my blue suit, but I shocked my mother's fashion conscience by wearing my boots instead of my father's black dress shoes. My mother nearly strangled me buttoning the top button of my shirt. Then, she tied the tie she had chosen for me and buttoned my collar buttons. I was not going to manage to stay home for long if she insisted on running my life. I went to the porch to wait while she dressed.

It was peaceful and cool. Birds were darting in and out of the garden. The sun was hanging out over the river. I thought of the long drive to Richmond and wished I had another week. "Suzie is a single woman again," I reminded myself. I rolled into the house and let the phone ring about twenty times. I did not want to take the chance that she was in the bathroom and got there just as I hung up. I looked at the desk calendar, April thirtieth. There was less than a month to get my act together if I was going to go to Cathy's graduation. I heard my mother's heels on the stairs. I rolled into the hall. She was wearing a gray dress and the sweater she wore when she came to Walter Reed.

I drove into the Robinson's drive and was relieved to see that it was a lawn party. They had even reserved a parking place for me on the lawn. I got the chair out and started toward my hosts but the wheels kept sinking into the soft lawn and I needed two rest stops before I made it. When I reached them, I said hi. Mr. Robinson said, "I saw you struggling, but I didn't know whether I should go offer some help or not."

"That wasn't too hard," I said, still panting. The tight collar was making it difficult to breathe and for the blood to get to my head.

"Why don't you rest here and I'll bring people over to you?" volunteered Mrs. Robinson.

I nodded. "Okay."

She took my mother by the arm and went toward the drinks. "Maybe later you'd like to see the office I put in my garage," Mr. Robinson offered.

"Hi Jake," said a voice behind me.

"Hi Betsey," I said and I struggled to turn the chair so that there was a tree behind me and people could not come up behind me.

She gave me a kiss on the cheek. She turned to the man with her and gestured. "This is my fiancé, Tad Lawrence."

The man took my hand. "How do you do," he said, but his tone told me he did not really care.

"Fine, thanks," I said.

"That's funny, you don't look fine," he said, snorting at his attempt at humor.

"That's because I just had this sudden urge to throw up," I replied with my best sarcastic smile. He turned and walked off. "It's none of my business," I said to Betsey, "but isn't twenty a little young to be getting engaged?"

Her eyes flashed. "Well it's worse for me, then, I'm nineteen." She swung her shoulders and her upturned head followed and she went to hang on Tad's arm.

Mrs. Robinson came walking over with a large man whose bulging eyes were surrounded by puffy flesh. "Jake, you remember Mr. Cooper with Merchants Trust?"

"Sure he does," he said with his booming voice and he reached out with his fat sweaty hand and patted me on the head and rubbed my hair out of place. I was stunned; no one had patted me on the head since I was a little kid.

The man had started toward Mr. Robinson. "Mister Cooper," I called just loud enough for him to hear, "could I tell you something?"

"Sure, son." He stepped closer. "Could you bend over a little?" I asked, speaking more softly. "A little more?" Then, I reached out quickly and rubbed him on the head. "I'm just fine, sir," I said in a loud voice. Unfortunately, Mr. Cooper's hair didn't take rubbing well; in fact, it all came off in my hand. The crowd around us went silent and then went into hysterical laughter.

"Hey boy!" shouted Cooper, snatching the hairpiece from me. "What the hell'd you do that for?"

"Because I don't like the way you say 'boy.' I'm a grown man and I don't like being patted on the head any more than you do." Cooper blustered into the house.

"Jake, how could you," my mother said sternly.

"Relax," said Mr. Robinson, wiping tears of laughter from his eyes. "Cooper had that coming, funniest damn thing I ever saw." He was still chuckling when he pulled a folding chair beside me and sat down.

"I don't think I'm getting off to a very good start with your guests," I said. "I've also insulted Betsey and her boyfriend."

"Really," said Mr. Robinson with a touch of admiration in his voice. "You'll have to tell me later." Someone inside the house turned up the stereo and played "Stars and Stripes Forever." Then, the side door opened and out onto the porch came Valerie wearing a dark blue mini-dress with white stars. To her right were Julia and Diana wearing mini dresses with red and white horizontal stripes. They walked down the steps with their arms around one another and sparklers in their hands. The crowd broke into applause. "They put that together in your honor," said their father proudly.

Betsey came hurrying over. "Father, they're acting like children," she said petulantly. I understood that I was not the only one who had changed in the past two years. The Betsey I had known would have gotten a kick out of her sisters' antics if she hadn't actually been part of them. Now, she was only worried about impressing Tad with the "right" family image. I said hello to everyone else without any other incidents. Valerie and her sisters brought me a punch and food. They were a matched set and the younger two felt obliged to be by Valerie's side all evening. The crowd began to say their goodbyes.

"Jake, you ready to see my office?" reminded Mr. Robinson.

"Well, I need to see what time my mom wants to leave."

"I've already taken care of it. My wife is going to run her home." He gave me a push up out of the lawn onto the drive and we said goodbye to the rest of the guests. Then, he led me to a door at the rear of the garage and into his office. A dozen beautifully detailed model planes hung from the ceiling. "Recognize any of them?" he asked.

"That's a Flying Fortress, that's a Liberator, and that's a Lightning," I said, pointing to the three I recognized.

"There's a B-25," said Mr. Robinson, pointing to one directly over my head, "and there's a Mustang and a Thunderbolt. Look around." He took great pride in the contents of this room. There was a large map on the wall showing the Allied campaigns in North Africa, Sicily, and Italy. On another wall were photos. I moved closer to get a better look. Mr. Robinson came out from behind a bar in the corner with scotches and handed me one. A group of American GIs was posing on a captured German tank. A young dirty-faced sergeant looked familiar. I turned and looked at Mr. Robinson. "Yeah, it's me," he grinned.

I looked over the desk at a shadow box. It was filled with patches, medals, and a pair of captain's bars. "You were a captain?"

"Eventually, I was a sergeant when we took Sicily, then the unit went to Italy. We had a command post take a direct hit from German artillery. I was supposed to be there, but our patrol was late coming back. We were out of touch with division for a couple of hours and when we got back in touch, someone told me to take command of what was left of the company. A few days later, I was a lieutenant. By the time I got hurt, I was a captain." He held up his scotch. "Here's to the guys who come back alive and keep on living."

I raised my glass. "Here's to us." We tossed down the scotch. I took my jacket off; it was getting warm. "I didn't know you got hurt?"

There was a knock at the door. Valerie put her head inside. "Daddy, can I come in?"

"Sure, sweetie, join the crowd." She came in and flopped in a chair. "Valerie! Wouldn't you like to change first," said her father uncomfortably.

"Why, Daddy?"

"I think what your father is trying to say is that your dress wasn't designed to sit down in." I laid my jacket in her lap. She stood and put it on and it came down farther than her dress. She went and leaned against the bar.

"You were going to tell me about being wounded," I reminded.

Mr. Robinson smiled and shook his head. "Some sniper with a sense of humor shot me in the backside. The bullet shattered my pelvic bone. When the war ended, I was still in an Army hospital in England recovering from a series of operations. Between operations, I was on crutches and worked in a supply unit stockpiling stuff for D-day. Then, they shipped me to a hospital in the States and we finished the war in the Pacific. I missed all the dancing in the streets, the parades. When I got to my parents in Missouri, I was just one more out-of-work veteran. I guess that was why I wanted to have this party for you."

I had a lump in my throat and could only nod. Valerie broke the silence. "I didn't know any of that, Daddy." She walked over and gave him a hug.

Mr. Robinson stood with his arm around his daughter and looked at me. "What do you think about Vietnam, Jake?"

Valerie turned to me. "Do you want me to leave?"

"No." I closed my eyes and collected my thoughts. "I think we should be there. I think the North Vietnamese will kill thousands of those people in the South, especially some of the mountain people and enslave the rest if the U.S. doesn't help. To me, the peace demonstrators are saying that it's okay for the communists to be able to kill and terrorize the Vietnamese people. I don't understand their position. I just don't know. We have a bunch of politicians running the war. The soldiers are fighting and losing lives, but we know with the tactics we're using, we can't win that war. I just don't know," I said, shaking my head and staring at my scotch. "I don't understand. One time, I saw a young Viet Cong rolling around on the ground after he'd been shot. I figured that he was about fifteen or sixteen. I wondered if either of us understood why he was dying."

"Fifteen or sixteen," said Valerie with concern in her voice. The office grew quiet.

When I tuned back in, I realized that I had to drain the leg bag. "Do you have a bathroom out here?"

"Yes," my host pointed to a door that was obviously too narrow.

"I'll just roll outside." I went into the darkness behind the garage. As it was draining, I thought, *All the world is a toilet.*

When I got back to the door, Julia was coming out with her father. He held out his hand to me. "Betsey and her friend are getting ready to drive back to college. My wife wants me to come say goodbye. If I don't get back, thanks for coming."

"Thanks for thinking of me," I responded. He leaned forward and hugged me and I returned the hug. When I went into the office, Valerie was seated facing the wall looking down at herself. When she heard the door close, she pulled my jacket around her and stood up. She had some color in her cheeks.

"I wanted to see why my father did not want me to sit in this dress."

"Apparently, you did," I said, pointing to her cheeks.

She walked over and looked at the photos while I looked at some handwritten notes on the map. When I looked around, she was watching me. "Did you have to kill anybody?"

I thought for a second how to answer that, the corners of my mouth turned down, but I couldn't talk. I crossed the room, picked up my glass, poured some more scotch into it, and drank. Then, I rolled over to her. "Sit in my lap?" She took my coat off and laid it on a chair. She turned her back to me, lifted her leg, and came back onto my lap. She put her face close to mine and brushed her hair back. I slid the tip of my finger back from the corner of her mouth, across her cheek, and to the back of her head into her hair. We kissed and I slid my tongue across her lips. Then, I looked at her with a serious expression. "How much older than you is Betsey?"

She gave me a puzzled look, "Two years."

"You're seventeen?"

"Yes," she said, lifting one eyebrow, "is that a problem?"

"When's your birthday?"

"December, I am not too young for you if that's what you're thinking."

"Come here, mind reader." I slid my arms around her body and kissed her for a long time, until our combined weight on my poor butt made me uncomfortable. "I gotta head home."

"Can I come over tomorrow?"

"Please. In the afternoon, I'm going to five o'clock church so I can get an early start back to Richmond Sunday morning."

My mother was waiting up to help me. It seemed weird sitting there naked in front of my mother and I wished she would stop trying to reassure me or deal with her own embarrassment by saying, "I've seen all this before when you were a baby."

Sunday morning came too quickly. My mother and Ann were wiping away tears when I left. "I'll be home for good by June," I promised.

"Hank said maybe we could come down," said Ann.

"Great, I'll call you and we'll pick a day." I drove down the lane. I was surprised that I was not sad at leaving. I knew the time would fly before I came back. I made it to a rest area in Virginia before I had to take a nap. I was at the hospital by 4:00 p.m. It did not look as depressing as when I had left.

37

Against Medical Advice

Monday morning, May 3, 1971, I started the countdown to getting out on my own. As I was getting dressed, Burnie asked how I had done and I was telling him. I noticed he was using an external catheter. "Hey, who decides what kind of a catheter a patient can use?"

"You have to see a urologist."

I went to Miss Adams and she had the ward doctor write a urology consult. A couple of days later, I went to the urology clinic. The doctor was a visiting specialist from the Medical College of Virginia. He was a tall man with thinning red hair and a hooknose. He helped me onto the examining table. He began, "I guess the doctors here have told you about your sympathetic nervous system."

"Are you kidding? The doctors here haven't told me a damn thing about what's happening to me."

He went on as if he had expected me to say that. "You see, even though your injury is fairly high on your spine, your internal organs are still working. For example, your heart is beating, your diaphragm is pushing and pulling air, your stomach, liver, kidneys, and other organs in your gut have kept functioning. What we don't know is how your bladder will work. A lot of that may depend on the level of the injury. Some low level paras regain bladder control. Others will spontaneously void when their bladder reaches a certain level. The key thing is not to have any urine left in your bladder that bacteria might grow in."

He handed me a pitcher of water with a straw. "I'm going to remove your catheter and give you a lot of water and see what happens." After the catheter was out, I sat around with a towel in my lap, drinking and drinking and flipping through old magazines. After two hours, the doctor came back. "Anything happening?

"I feel like I'm floating and I'm sweating some, which is weird."

He held a different catheter. "What I have here is a straight catheter. It is different from the one that you have been using because there is no place to inject water into it to hold it in your bladder. How are your hands?"

"I manage," I said.

"Do you want to try to get this into yourself and drain your bladder?" With the doctor's instructions, I used some lubricant and got the tube into my bladder and drained it. The doctor looked at the amount of urine. "That's good. Now what you can do is rinse the catheter out and wrap it in a clean towel. Whenever you feel that bloated feeling, or every three hours or so, use the catheter. Do you want to try that?

"You mean no leg bags or irrigating a catheter?" The doctor nodded. "I'll try," I answered. I would regain some control of my body and not need help from an attendant. Pushing back to the ward, I marveled at how something so disgusting could make me feel so happy. I stopped in the hospital store and bought an alarm clock. This was something I did not want to sleep through.

Catheterizing worked all right, but it meant that I had to set the alarm twice during the night. Get out of bed, push down through the dark ward to the bathroom, and put the catheter in. It worked. I was going to the bathroom by myself—most people would not regard that as a thrilling accomplishment.

An invitation for Cathy's graduation arrived. It was on the 27th of May at 7:00 p.m. On Friday evening, I tried to call Suzie again. The phone in her apartment rang and rang. I did not like to call her at work because she could not take time to talk. Just this once, though, it would not hurt; I had to know when she would be home. The phone was answered on the fist ring. "Ward eleven, Walter Reed Army Medical Center, Specialist Hoskins speaking, sir."

"Is Lieutenant Staunton there?"

"Lieutenant, it's for you."

I had to wait for a few moments. I could hear a woman speaking to someone in the background. The receiver was lifted. "Lieutenant Donovan speaking."

I stuttered. "I'm sorry I asked for Lieutenant Staunton."

"Jake!" She screamed into the phone, "Where are you? Are you all right? I called three times last week. Finally, some guy said you weren't there—that you went home. What happened? Where are you now?" Her non-stop questions had me laughing.

"If you'll stop for a breath, I'll fill you in, but first, what's with Lieutenant Donovan?"

"It's my maiden name. Now, tell me," she ordered impatiently," what happened?"

"I went home for a week on a trial visit."

"How'd you make out?"

"I'm not telling you until I see you again."

"Come on, don't tease me, tell me."

"It would take too much time."

"Okay. I have to work Wednesday night, so I'll be there Thursday evening."

"I'll get you a room and you can stay over, all right?"

"Good idea. Goodnight, Jake."

"Goodnight, Miss Donovan."

The only thing I could concentrate on was getting ready to leave. I knew I needed more strength so I lifted weights with a purpose. I was standing up for better than an hour at a time. Sam showed me how I could get someone back home to make a frame to stand in. I thought about asking Hank to get the material and make it. That weekend, I took the car to a car wash and spent several hours waxing all the parts I could reach and wiping down the interior.

On Monday, the cluster of doctors and nurses came onto the ward for the weekly tour. I listened as they talked about the new guy that had been put into the bed where Joe White had been. Nothing ever changed. They walked to my bed and picked up my chart.

The first assistant page-turner pointed out something in the chart to the chief-nodder-and-grunter. He looked at me. "There's a note from the urologist that you are performing intermittent catheterization. How is that working out?"

It occurred to me that if I told them that it was a disaster, they would have a hard time keeping the grins off their faces. "It's working out fine." The doctor made a note in the file and they prepared to move on, but I had a question. "What do you have to do to get out of the hospital?"

"You mean you want to go home for the weekend?"

"No, I just got back from a week home. I mean for good."

The doctor shook his head as if to say, "I have never met such a hardheaded patient." His chest heaved and he began to explain, "All of the doctors on the spinal cord section will get together with you and review your file and assess where you are in your recovery, and then give you an estimate of when you'll be ready to leave."

"Great. When can we all get together?"

"Maybe in a month or so."

"Too late. I'll be ready to leave on May twenty-seventh. Can't we get an earlier date?"

"Well, there doesn't appear to be any point wasting time getting together with you Mr. uh…" He snapped his fingers and my file was handed back to him. "Scott. You've already made up your mind. I do not believe that you will be ready to be discharged then and if you do, I will have your chart marked 'Discharged A.M.A.' Do you know what that means?"

"American Medical Association?"

"Against medical advice," he said with mounting irritation.

"Doc, I don't care if you have it stamped Paranoid Schizophrenic Lunatic. It ain't like I can expect a miraculous cure if I stay here. But I'm gonna be on the road on May twenty-seventh." The chief-grunter-and-nodder snapped the file shut and almost flung it at the nurse. After that, until I left for good, the group just walked past my bed on rounds.

I was getting bored and had to look for some new trouble to get into. Several times, I had seen a sign pointing to a swimming pool, but I hadn't followed the arrow and no one had offered to make it available. One night, well after lights out, I got out of bed. I quietly rolled down the aisle and passed the row of electric wheelchairs that were recharging their batteries. They were plugged into every socket on the ward and into the hall. I pushed through the halls to the sign and through the doors. The huge indoor pool glimmered in the green glow of the exit signs. The sound of the door latching behind me echoed from the high ceilings. I rolled along looking and thinking how I was going to manage this.

There was a ramp going down into the water at the shallow end of the pool. I did not want to roll down in my own chair. I could imagine the effect on the bearings and axels of chlorinated water. There was a hospital chair parked to the side. I positioned it so that the back wheels were against the wall and I locked its brakes. I positioned my own chair and transferred. I took off the T-shirt I was wearing and threw it on my chair. I rolled to the top of the ramp. Was I going to be able to push back up once I was down there?

What the hell, the worst that could happen is that I would have to spend the night in the pool until the staff came in the morning. So they would probably kick me out, who cared. I let the chair drift down the ramp and I slid my hands on the railings on either side of the ramp. The water came up over my thighs. I moved the footrests out of the way and slipped into the water. When the water hit my shoulders, it was much colder than I expected.

Without warning, I had strong spasms in the muscles in my stomach and thighs, which caused me to double up. My face was pulled under water. I panicked. I thrashed out with my arms to pull my face up, but the spasming muscles were too strong. I sank to the bottom of the pool. I put my hands on my knees and tried to straighten my body, but the muscles fought me even harder. I pushed off the bottom as hard as I could but still could not get my head out of water. I was going to drown in four feet of water. My hand hit something. I moved my hand back in that direction. It was the wheelchair footrest. I threw my other hand upward and caught the seat and pulled my head out of the water. I sucked a quick breath and went under again. I rolled my body around, hooked my hands on the frame of the chair, and pulled up so my head came out of the water.

I was coughing, blowing water out of my nose, and shuddering with fear. I could feel my heart pounding. Finally, the spasming muscles relaxed. I let go of the chair and reached for the side of the pool. I grew accustomed to the water temperature. I took a deep breath and let go of the wall. I was floating face down. I looked down the length of my body suspended in the water. I grabbed the side and pushed off, floating on my back.

Cautiously, I put my arms back over my head and then, pulling as hard as I could, brought them to my side. My body slid through the water. I did it again and again. The thrill was tremendous. I was moving—no wheelchairs, no obstructions, no frustrations.

"Ow, shit," I hollered as I swam head first into the wall in the deep end. I hung onto the wall, rubbing my head. I let go and was able to tread water. I looked down at my body hanging below the water. I rolled over and swam back, but I slowed down when I neared the chair. When I got to the chair, I rolled over, face in the water, and swam into the chair. With my shoulders lying in the seat of the chair, I put my arm over the back. I pulled and twisted so that I could get my hands on the arms of the chair and I pulled my butt in. I looked down at myself.

I had lost the blue pajama pants that I had been wearing. I looked around but the blue pants blended with the unlit blue pool. I pushed against the handrails and I began moving backwards up the ramp. I was already tired by the swim and this was a long, slow process. I only make a few inches with each push. Several times, I locked the brakes and rested my head on the rail. By the time I got to the top, I had no strength left in my arms. I rolled back against the wall and leaned forward and put my head between my knees.

I rested there for ten minutes and then pulled my own chair over. I dragged myself from one chair to the other. I spread my T-shirt over my crotch and started back to the ward. I could only push twenty to thirty feet before I had to stop and rest. I was grateful that I didn't meet any staff in the hall. I finally reached the ward just as Miss Adams was crossing from one side to the other. We startled each other. She looked at me—wet hair, shivering, naked, and she burst out laughing.

"Scott, boy, you been skinny dipping in the pool?"

"Well it didn't start out that way, but I swam out of my pants."

She laughed again. "Come on." She took the handles of my chair and pushed me back to my bed. I put my arm through the strap on the trapeze above the bed and she grabbed under my knees and we swung me into the bed. In the process, I lost my shirt. She walked to a cart and brought me fresh pajamas. I put the shirt on but I was too tired to do more and I fell asleep.

38

Lt. Donovan

I was sitting in the parking lot when Suzie drove in. I pushed out to the car and was sitting by her door before she got out. She looked at me. "You have changed in the last month."

"How so?"

"For one thing, you have enough hair for a part. You've gotten rid of that hospital pallor. You have a tan on your arms and face and you've built up your muscles. I flexed my triceps and a pretty smile blossomed across her face that made me smile. She got out and gave me a peck on the cheek. "All these weeks apart and that's all I get?" I took her hand between my palms and pulled her toward me. She turned and sat on my lap. I kissed her to make up for all the lost opportunities. I moved my lips off of hers and brushed them across her cheek and down her neck to the open collar of her shirt. My breath went down her neck and she squirmed closer. I moved my mouth to her ear and whispered, "Suzie, I missed you so much. I thought of you everyday. I love you."

She put her hands on either side of my face and pulled me nose to nose. "I love you," she paused, "but I'm going to be careful and go slowly." I did not understand her, but I let it pass.

"Have you eaten dinner?" I asked. She pointed into her car at a bag of popcorn and a soda. "Come on," I said, "I haven't eaten. I'm going to buy you with a real dinner."

"Is it far? I don't really feel like driving any more."

"You don't have to drive at all. Follow me." I started across the parking lot.

"Hey is that a new chair?"

"Yup." By then, I reached the LeMans. I pulled the keys from my pocket and unlocked the door. I looked back.

She was standing by the front of the car with her mouth hanging open. "What's this?"

"This, my dear, is called a car."

"Yours?"

"How'd you think I got home for the week?"

"I thought maybe your mother had come down and picked you up. You mean you can drive?"

"No, actually I push it."

"Oh, you smart-ass."

I got in and pulled the chair in. She was still standing at the front of the car watching me. I leaned over and unlocked the passenger door and pointed to it. She came to my window. "Why don't you follow me to the motel and I'll change into something nicer and leave my car there?" I nodded. We drove to the motel and she pulled to the side. She took a bag from the car and went inside. In fifteen minutes, she was back wearing a black dress. For the first time, I noticed she was wearing her hair loose and it fell over her shoulders. The dress clung flatteringly to her body. When she sat in my car, I spent several moments staring at her legs.

"What are you doing?"

"Looking at your legs. This is the first time that I've seen you in a dress without white stockings."

She put her hand gently under my chin and pushed my head around so that I was looking out of the windshield. "Drive."

I pulled onto the highway and headed toward a restaurant I had found near the state capitol building. The table was near the window. As the sky outside grew dark, the waiter came and lit a candle. She watched the waiter until he left and began to speak when another waiter appeared with a pitcher to fill our water glasses. She started to arrange her silverware and adjust the spacing between her plates. She opened her mouth when they brought rolls and butter to the table. Finally, when it appeared we might have a moment to ourselves, she got out her question. "So tell me why you suddenly decided to go home."

I could not tell her then about Levassuer and maybe that was not the reason I went home. I loved her and I wanted this to be a special evening. "I thought that it was time to see if I could get the hell out of there."

"And how did it go?" She was becoming exasperated at having to pry every detail from me.

"It went okay. I could get around the house, I took a bath, and I practiced some new tricks. I did some cooking, some shopping, saw some old friends."

"Old girlfriends?"

"One."

"How did you get along?"

The waiter came back to take a drink order and she ordered two scotches and glared at him as if to say, "when we want you back here, we'll call."

"About the same way we're getting along."

She gave me an arched eyebrow look but didn't pursue it. "What else?"

"I drove up and back. Last night, I almost drowned myself." Now, the eyebrow came down into a scowl. "I went swimming in the hospital pool."

"Jake, you're doing terrific."

"Does that mean that your mental health session is about over?"

She glared. "What the hell is that supposed to mean?"

I was in danger of ruining the mood. I held up my hand. "Take it easy." I put my hand across the table over hers. "You know what I mean. I thought that maybe once I was better and you were better, we could work on a normal relationship like normal people."

The waiter came back and sat both scotches in front of her and she growled, "Thank you." He backed away and disappeared.

I reached over and took one of the scotches and asked, "Can I have one of these?" I could see her clench her teeth, so I continued, "When I was home, I did not want to explain what happened in Vietnam, how I hurt, and how I feel. But they can't understand. They see what it did to my body but not to my soul. You do though. You are someone special—I don't have to explain it to you. Don't you feel that way about me?"

She looked out the window. I was afraid I had intruded too far, uninvited, into her secrets. The waiter had dared to approach the table. I ordered a steak. "Would you like a steak?" I asked her. She nodded so I told the waiter two of what I ordered. When he started asking about extras, I told him just what I had already ordered with an impatient voice. He slunk away.

"Suzie, I don't think anyone knows how the war changed you as well as I do." She still did not answer. She pulled her hand away from mine, picked up her napkin, and dabbed at her eyes. She did not speak. The waiter quickly brought the food; I think he was anxious to get rid of us. She was polite when I asked her how the food was. She watched me wrestle my steak around the plate for a while and offered to cut it for me. Rather than embarrass myself further, I accepted. I kept hoping she would say something. I was angry with myself. *You idiot! You moved too fast. You ran your big mouth. You blew it.*

On the drive back to the motel, she told me to pull into a liquor store. I watched her through the front window, thinking, "Great, she wants me to drop her off so she can go in and get drunk." She came out with a bag. I drove to the motel and she pointed to the space beside her car. My heart sank. I felt for sure she was going to drive back. She pulled a bottle of chilled champagne from the bag and a package of plastic cups. "Open these, please," she said, handing me the cups. She twisted the cork out of the champagne and filled two cups.

She raised her cup. "Here's to getting well."

"To getting well," I replied and we tapped cups. I emptied the cup. She filled it again. I collected my courage. "Could we go into your room?"

"Would you like to sleep with me?" The champagne I was sipping came out my nose and she started slapping me on the back to keep me from choking to death.

"And I've been worrying all evening that I was going too fast for you."

"You didn't answer the question."

I could feel my face turning red. "Yes, I would."

"And I would like to go to bed with you, which is why we're not going into my room."

"Maybe I'm more than just a little stupid, but is there some kind of logic at work here?"

She climbed out of her seat and put one leg across me so that she was straddling my lap. The steering wheel pushing into her back pushed her against me. "Listen to me," she said in a no nonsense tone. "When I was a naïve little coed, I met this handsome graduate student, who was nice and attentive, so I let him make love to me. Then, I thought, well I must be in love because we're having sex. So—I married him." She took a big swallow of champagne and went on.

"In the past couple of months, I've discovered I didn't know a thing about him—not his philosophy, not his ambitions, his religion, his politics, his likes and dislikes, and especially whether I could trust him. If I hadn't had sex with him, I would have been able to look at our relationship more objectively." She poured herself some more champagne and went to empty the bottle in my cup.

I shook my head no. "I don't feel like champagne after scotch." She reached in the bag and pulled out a miniature of scotch. She twisted it open and emptied that into my cup.

"There's something," she said, stopping to find the word she needed, "secure about being married, even if it is a lousy marriage. If you're a woman, you don't have to put up with men; you just push them away with the explanation that you're married. You don't have to worry if sex is a sin or a blessing because you're out of circulation. But then." She put her forehead against mine and I could feel her eyelashes brushing mine. "You tell some wise ass you're married and he looks at you with big blue eyes and says that if he was married to you, he wouldn't leave you alone on Christmas Eve. And you know why you're alone, because your marriage and the security are an illusion."

I put my hands on her hips and could feel that the hem of her dress had slid up there. I moved my hands around her and up her back pushing her into me as I went up. I slid my fingers up her neck and massaged her hair. She closed her eyes and purred. I whispered, "You're divorced—you're free to love who you want."

She opened her eyes and shook her head to clear it. She pulled my hands down and held them with hers. "Oh, God, you confuse me. I won't be divorced for another year or more. This was just a hearing to re-title our property. You're soon to be six years younger than me, but you're more responsible and mature than my ex—who's ten years older than you. You want and need to go to college. I've been to college I can't go back to being a coed."

"So what's with this tease, 'do I want to have sex with you?'"

"I was just trying to show you that I feel the same way and if I let you come in," she said, smiling, "then I'd let you come in. I'm never again going to have sex to prove to myself or anybody else that I love them. It ruins a perfectly good friendship. First, I'm going to fall in love and, when I am certain that it's love, then—only then—am I going to use sex as an expression of love. Do you understand?"

"No! I'm confused. Are you saying, even though you say 'I love you,' I should think you don't love me because you won't have sex with me?"

"NO!" She leaned forward and kissed me. "I'm saying we don't really know each other. We know each other's pasts, but I don't know your ambitions, who you are, or who you will become. Whether I can trust you? How can I love you before I know you?"

"I'm a Catholic, Republican, veteran, and I'd never hurt you."

"And where are you going from here?"

"To college."

"And then?"

"I don't know."

"And I don't know what I'm going to do. By mid-June, I'll be out of the Army. I need some time to myself; maybe it is post-divorce shock syndrome. I hope you'll write to me." I nodded and remembered that I had already promised to write Cathy and Valerie, and this from the world's worst letter writer. She poked me in the chest and said, "I'll write you and, maybe in a few years, we can get back together." She leaned to my ear and said, "I hope we'll still feel the same way we feel tonight." She leaned toward me and we kissed very passionately. She put her tongue into my mouth and it was a warm, soft, wet rush of excitement.

She pulled back. "Goodnight."

"No, no, no, wait, wait, let me get this straight. We need to be apart so we learn more about each other."

"No silly," she said patiently, "so we can learn about ourselves. You can't ask me to love you until you know who you are. Now, it's late and I'm tired and a little drunk."

"Tell me one thing. If I weren't crippled, would it be any different?"

"No! Why do you ask that?"

"I know that a lot of women are never going to get passed the fact that I'm in a wheelchair. Hell, Suzie, I don't even know if I can have sex. I mean there's no therapist over there for that."

"Honey." She gave me a kiss on the cheek. "Right now, it's very obvious to me that you don't seem to have any disabilities. I gotta go. I'll come see you tomorrow." She opened the driver's door and climbed out.

"Goodnight," I called after her. I was trying to figure out what she was saying to me. I went to buckle my seat belt and found that I had an erection, which, of course, I couldn't feel. Maybe this was part of my sympathetic nervous system.

The next morning, I headed to therapy and left a note on my bed telling Suzie where to look for me. Florence had me kneeling up when Suzie came walking in. “Suzie, I want to meet the best therapist in the VA. This is Florence. Flo, this is Suzie, the best nurse in the Army.”

“Florence, you are working wonders,” said Suzie. “He’s a much better bullshitter now than when we had him at Walter Reed.”

“Oh, I can’t take the credit,” replied Flo. “Bullshit is a natural product for this one.” The women laughed.

“Oh, thanks. I’m so glad I made those flattering introductions.” Flo asked Suzie if she could keep me from falling off the mat and busting my head open. Assured that Suzie could handle it, Flo left us alone.

“Well, I guess you got a good night’s sleep without me in the bed,” I whispered.

She smiled and shook her head. “You little bastard.”

“I resent that ‘little’ remark.”

“If it makes you happy, I laid awake thinking about you, about us.”

“I had a dream about us.” I caught myself.

“So don’t keep me in suspense.”

“It was a sad dream.” I looked away from her.

“Tell me.”

I sighed. “We were walking along the beach; I could walk in the dream. Sometimes we would run and wade into the surf.” I got a lump in my throat.

“Please, tell me the rest,” she urged.

When I could speak, my voice was hoarse. “My legs collapsed and I fell on the beach. And you kept walking away like you didn’t notice what had happened. I’m sorry. I shouldn’t have told you.”

“Jake, can you understand that I want to make sure that the feelings I have for you aren’t simply because I’m on the rebound?”

“Would I be premature in proposing marriage?”

“You’d get a punch in the mouth for proposing marriage. Take my word for it. You’re too young to get married—to me or anybody.”

“Yes, Mommy.”

“I don’t see why I drive all this way for this abuse.”

“You love me.”

“Yes, I love you.”

I sat back and then scooted around so I could lie on my back. “You want to help me do some sit-ups?”

“What do you want me to do?”

“Sit on my legs and hold my knees down.”

She knelt over my legs and froze. “Are you sure this isn’t some kind of a scheme to get between my legs?”

I felt my face going scarlet. "I am learning a lot about you. You are a raunchy broad."

"ME! You're the guy trying to maneuver me into these compromising positions. Hey, Flo. Come here please?" The therapist walked over. "Look at this," said Suzie, indicating her position on my legs. "Does he ever ask you to sit on his legs like this?

"No, but I might be interested." I could feel more blood come to my face and thought my pores might bleed. I did a set of sit-ups—aware of how close I came to her.

When I finished, I laid back to catch my breath. "Are you going to Cathy's graduation?" I asked her.

"No, I arranged to work that evening. I am afraid there would be too many memories of my own graduation. What about you?"

I lied, "I haven't decided." I did not want to say I would and then have something go wrong to keep me away. We sat looking around the therapy room for a few moments and occasionally catching each other's eye.

I grew uneasy and said, "I thought about us for a long time last night before I went to sleep."

"That's what gives you the bad dreams," she said, trying to make light of my remark.

"I can see we're not going to be serious any more."

"I don't think we should." I got back in my wheelchair and we went out to the visitor's area where she had pushed me the first night she came down. We got coffee from a vending machine. We had said all that could be said. She drank the last of her coffee. "I need to go home and clean house and pick up some uniforms from the cleaners." We went to the parking lot beside her car. She sat on my lap and we kissed goodbye. She wiped a tear from the corner of my eye. "What's wrong?"

"Is this our last kiss?"

"No Jake—trust me, this is not our last kiss." She got in her car and disappeared from sight.

39
Flo's Determination

Sunday, Ann and Hank drove down. Hank was a student of civil war history. We spent the afternoon visiting Petersburg and Appomattox Courthouse. As usual, I was worried that we would not find a bathroom I could use. I sat watching the countryside, listening to Hank talk about the events that had scarred this part of Virginia. "Hey Jake. Jake!" Hank's voice called me from my thoughts.

"Yeah, Hank."

"Ann tells me you were thinking of teaching history. Are you a history buff?"

"I am interested by it. Mostly, I think we study the past to understand what our motives for decisions in the future are. It might be interesting to study the lessons of Vietnam with someone who has been there." We stopped at a Confederate cemetery. Rows of white markers, rows and rows and rows of gravestones making a monument of a green field. I wondered how many of the men had been eighteen and nineteen and twenty years old when they died.

The week began. Flo was stretching my hands. Flo was chipper and chatting with the other therapists. She looked down at me stretched out on the mat. "Did you and your nurse friend have a nice time on Friday?"

"Well, let me put it this way; I don't have any stories like yours about wild weekends."

"You seem kind of far away."

"Just thinking."

"About Suzie?"

"Some, mostly about leaving."

"I heard you were leaving."

I nodded. "Flo, I read in the Sunday paper that there's a little circus in town at the end of the week. Would you and your son like to go to the circus with me this weekend?"

"I don't date patients, but thanks for asking."

"Not so fast now. You see, I'm leaving here next Thursday for good. That means, after this Friday, I'll only have three more sessions. If I were to spend those sessions with another therapist, then I wouldn't be your patient anymore. Besides, it is something I'd like to do to say thanks. Come on, break a rule once in awhile."

"What day you want to go?"

"Is Saturday afternoon all right?"

"Okay."

"Write your address down and I'll pick you up."

"You!" she said with mock alarm. "You want me to risk my child's life with you behind the wheel?"

"Actually, I was thinking of riding up on an elephant."

"Sex on the back of an elephant would make a great story."

When Miss Adams was working that week, I went back to the swimming pool twice. The first time, I let her know where I was going in case I did not come back in a reasonable time. By the time I got out of the pool, I was so tired I needed a nap so I slid onto a bench and took a nap. The next thing I knew, Miss Adams was hollering at me because I scared her to death thinking I had drowned. The next time, I invited Dave to keep an eye on me, but that was the last time.

It was before two on Saturday when I drove up to Flo's house. She and her son were sitting outside waiting for me. I was surprised how small the boy was for seven years old. He was a Mongoloid child. He had a grin and a twinkle in his almond shaped eyes that was a blessing to the beholder. His mother good-naturedly squeezed into the back seat with the wheelchair, because the little boy wanted to ride up front.

"Jake, this is my son, Tommy."

"Hi Tommy, I'm Jake," I said, and the little boy shook my hand and said something. I had difficulty understanding him. I looked over the seat at Florence and raised my eyebrows for help.

Flo leaned forward between the seats and said, "Tommy, what did you ask Mr. Jake?" I listened very hard and was able to make out something about the circus.

"Yeah, Tommy, I like the circus. Are you glad we're going?" The little boy nodded yes and settled back in the seat for the ride. I started the car and congratulated myself for a clever answer that should have taken care of at least four questions.

As we drove along, Tommy began a discussion that was kind of one-sided. Flo helped out by answering some of his statements or prompting me to say the right words. I began to understand speech patterns and many of his words. I gathered that we were talking about the fact that Tommy had mentioned to his teacher that he was going to the circus and that had led to a class discussion of circuses. Tommy was saying that he wanted to ride a horse in the circus. I drove into a large fairground where the circus had set up a tent. The cars were being directed to park at the far end of a grassy field. I stopped by the turn where a man was waving the cars on. When I stopped, the man began waving harder. I rolled down the window and called into a stiff breeze, "Hey, I'm in a wheelchair. Can I park a little closer?"

The man did not hear me. "You see me wavin at ya? Move that thing. Follow dem cars! You're blockin traffic."

I tried again. "Do you have a parking spaces for people in wheelchairs? It's impossible for me to push through this grass."

The man was not listening. He started toward me in an impatient fashion and yelled, "Hey, mister, there're no special places!" By now, he was near enough to hear me.

"Even if I am in a wheelchair?" I yelled back and jerked my thumb toward the wheelchair in the back seat.

The man was humbled. "Hey, we never get no handicaps."

"Maybe it's the warm welcome they get," I said so Flo could hear. The man waved me into a space near the tent.

Tommy was sitting watching the exchange. "He was mad," the boy said.

I reassured him, "He's just having a bad day." I shoved the chair out and climbed in. I looked at the shabby tent with its tears and patches. "Well, this ain't no Ringling Brothers," I cracked.

Flo smiled. "This ain't even one Ringling." The circus was mostly carnival and sideshows. There was an elephant harnessed to a large wagon for which they charged twenty-five cents for a ride. I bought tickets for Flo and Tommy to take a ride but Tommy wanted to go by himself. So he took two rides. As the beast and wagon rumbled past us, Tommy would wave enthusiastically. Flo squatted beside me and put her hand on my arm. "Are you understanding Tommy?"

"I'm getting the hang of it."

"He gets frustrated when people don't understand him, but he gets upset with me if I start explaining what he's saying to people."

"He just wants to be treated like normal folk. I understand that." I watched Tommy leaning over the side of the wagon watching the elephant's backside.

Flo noticed the change in my face. "Is something wrong?"

"I was just thinking how happy he is now. Someday, he'll know that somebody is ignoring him or talking down to him because he is different. I was thinking how that will hurt."

"Jake." She squeezed my arm and I looked from the boy to the mother. "They have already treated him like that and he is such a sharp little guy that he feels the hurt. I sometimes find myself not wanting to take him out and risk the insults, but then I think that people do it out of ignorance and that if they could meet Tommy, they'd know." There was a rage and a tenderness in the mother's voice. There were no horses to ride, so I bought Tommy a large stuffed horse to which we tied a helium balloon. We shared a cotton candy, which covered the horse with wisps of pink.

Flo had to help push me through the sawdust spread around the tent. It was more difficult because Tommy insisted on helping her push and got between her and the wheelchair. We entered the tent. Bleachers were set up on either side of the aisle. The lower rows were already packed with people so Flo and Tommy had to leave me sitting in the aisle and climb to the top row of seats. A man with the circus came up to me, "You can't sit in the aisle. You're blocking it if there were an emergency."

"Your people sold me the tickets, you show me where I'm supposed to sit."

"Can't you get in the bleachers?"

I was aggravated. "Why do you think I'm in this thing? Because it's a fashion statement?"

The man went to talk to the ringmaster, who shrugged. The man came back to me. "If anything happens and we have to get everybody out fast, I'll just grab the chair and back you out, okay?" The circus was mostly a two man show. One man juggled, rode a unicycle, walked a tightrope, and stood on his hands at the top of a ladder. The other man had trained dogs, ponies, apes, and a seal. After each act, the ringmaster pitched another toy or gimmick for the parents to deny their children. I turned around every once in awhile and looked to see how Flo and Tommy were doing.

We stopped on the way home and bought a large pizza, although Flo kept saying none of us could possibly eat any more. When we got to Flo's house, I asked about the bathroom and she pointed down the hall. I went to the door but found that it was too narrow for my chair. "I'm going to leave and head back to the hospital. I have to find a bathroom."

"No, no wait, try something with me," she said. She got one of her dining room chairs and put it into the bathroom by the door. She held it while I got from my chair onto that chair. Then, she dragged me into the bathroom and left. It was difficult to sit up straight in the chair with no stomach muscles and handle the catheter and hold the bucket I drained it into. Then, I could not get my jeans buttoned. I struggled for a few minutes. Flo tapped on the door. "You okay in there?"

"I need some help, please." She came in. "I'm sorry to bother you," I said.

"Don't be silly, you're doing pretty well." She helped me. "You know, if you improvise enough, you can do almost everything."

"Thank you. I'm trying."

We ate pizza. Then, Flo played piano and we sang. She flipped through a large book of songs and we sang for almost two hours. When she got to the end, she looked at me. Tommy was curled up in my lap sleeping. "He is such a heavy load to carry to bed."

"It's okay," I said, turning the chair. "Where's his bedroom?" She led me down the hall. I pushed, balancing the boy on my lap. When we got into his room, Flo gently slipped off his shoes, slid him onto the bed, and tucked a blanket around him.

Just then, he sat up with a big smile and said, "Fooled you. You thought I was sleeping."

Flo tickled him, "You rascal."

"Jake, spend the night," he said between giggles. It was the first time I remember seeing Flo blush.

"Tommy, I can't. I did not bring my toothbrush. If your mom says it's all right, I'll stop back tomorrow."

"Yes, Mom, yes, say yes."

"Okay, okay, if you go to sleep now." Tommy laid down and closed his eyes, but he had a huge grin on his face. Flo walked with me to the front door. She put her hand out and I shook it. She went to open the storm door, but a gust of wind jerked it from her grasp and slammed it back. "If this keeps up," I said, "tomorrow would be a good day to fly kites, say around two o'clock?"

"Okay." She backed me down the one step and I turned and started to push toward the car, but I turned back. "Flo, I want to make sure that I said thank you for everything you've done for me and I think Ben would have wanted me to say thanks for him, too. I never meant to try to get you in trouble." She stepped closer, the wind pulling her curly hair into her face and whipping her jacket out behind her.

"I watched you today, "she said, smiling. "You'll make a good daddy."

"I guess. I got to wonder whether I can ever have kids."

"There are plenty of little boys like Tommy who need a daddy; you'd be great with one of them."

"Yeah, I'll think about them." I remembered the orphanage in Vietnam. She bent forward and hugged me and I reached up and put my arms around her and patted her on the back. The next day, I bought a huge Chinese dragon kite and we drove to a park. It took both Flo and Tommy to get the kite up. Once it was flying, Flo had to steady Tommy as the strong winds and the size of the kite threatened to drag him along. We collected sticks and tried to build a fire in a stone fireplace in the park to cook hotdogs on, but the wind kept blowing it out. We drove back to the house where Flo boiled them on the stove. After dinner, Flo gave Tommy a bath and he came out in his pajamas so that I could read a story to him. I pushed back to Tommy's room and gave him a ride to bed.

The little boy crawled under the covers and looked back at me. "Do you want to live with us? Take care of my mommy?"

The questions took me by surprise and I didn't know how to answer him. "Tommy," said Flo sitting on the edge of the bed, "you can't just ask people to live with us without talking to Mommy first."

"Well, I like him. Don't you like him?"

"Yes, I like him," she said, glancing at me, "but there are a lot of other things to think about."

"Do you like me?" Tommy asked me.

"Yes, buddy, I like you a lot."

"And do you like mommy?"

I smiled at the little matchmaker. "Yeah, I like her a lot too."

Tommy slid to the side of his bed to demonstrate that there was room for me. "You could sleep in my room."

"Tommy, my daddy is in a hospital and my mommy is home all by herself. I think she wants me to come stay with her. You understand I have to take care of my mommy, just like you take care of your mommy." The little boy nodded yes. "I'm going to take your address with me and I'll write you letters and you can write to me, okay?" I rolled out of the room with a lump in my throat. I pushed to the living room and listened. Flo was saying prayers with the boy. Then, the light went out and she came into the living room. She sat on the arm of an overstuffed chair. She looked very tired. Then, she started crying.

I rolled around and backed the wheelchair in beside her. I put an arm around her shoulders and pulled her toward me. She put her arm around my shoulders and lay her head on my shoulder and kept crying. She spoke in a whisper so that Tommy would not hear her. "It just gets so hard and I feel so alone." She was a different person from the one who told funny stories at therapy and smiled and cared for her patients. "I have to fight all the time. I have to fight the school system, public attitudes, being a single parent trying to always find time and money." She cried some more. "I'm sorry, I didn't mean to put this on you."

"I don't mind if I can help by listening. It makes me feel useful."

She leaned away and took a tissue off the table to dry her eyes. "You'd better head back to the hospital it's getting late."

"You gonna be all right?"

"Yeah. I think all this running around trying to get that four hundred pound kite off the ground wore me out. I'll feel better after a good night's sleep."

I gave her a strong hug and said, "When I'm feeling discouraged, that's what always works best for me."

"Thanks."

For my last three days in the hospital, the clocks seemed to have slowed down. On Wednesday afternoon, I went shopping. I bought cards for Tommy and Flo, Sam and Miss Adams, and I bought a bag of sugar. I stopped by the bank and closed my account. I had several thousand dollars—most of which I put in a bag under the spare tire in my trunk.

That night, I took a shower, packed my knapsack with everything that was left in my locker, and went to bed early, because I had to be up very early.

At 4:00 a.m. on May 27, 1971, my alarm went off. I shut it off quickly, went to the bathroom, shaved, and got dressed. At 5:30, I was sitting outside in the doorway to a furnace room watching the parking lot. By six, all of the employees had parked their cars, especially Levassuer's Mustang. I rolled up beside it and opened the door to the gas fill spout. I grabbed the cover in both hands and twisted it off. I shoved a rolled up piece of newspaper in it to act as a funnel and then I poured five pounds of sugar into the gas tank. It was not as violent as I would have liked, but I had some revenge.

I went in and got my knapsack and put it in the back of my car. In the mess hall, I got a coffee and sat by myself to write cards. "Dear Flo, I really thank you for everything, especially the chance to meet Tommy. He is a lucky little guy to have a mom like you. I can't help with a lot of your fights, but I hope this will help. Love, Jake." I put three hundred dollars into the card. Then, I wrote the other two cards. I ate ham and eggs and toast and juice for breakfast. Then, I went back through the line and got a plate filled with grits. I rolled to the trashcan and let it slide in. It was my way of saying goodbye to this hospital. I rolled to therapy. It was reassuring to see that Flo was her wild and chipper self.

"I'm leaving. I just came by to say goodbye. I put a card in on your desk, but do me a favor and read it when you're alone."

She handed me a slip of paper with her address on it. "Good luck. Remember you promised to write Tommy. I know he'll remember."

"And I'll remember." She leaned forward and gave me a kiss on the cheek and a couple of guys whistled and hooted. She started to blush but quickly went into a comic explanation. I figured that was her defense mechanism.

I stopped across the hall and said goodbye to Sam. I pushed back up the hall to the ward. Miss Adams was in the nurses' station. "Today's the big day, Scott boy."

"Yes ma'am. I wanted to say thanks for everything. I swore when I got out of this place I'd never come back, but I might stop back to see you." I paused. "And to remember Ben."

She shook my hand. "Goodbye, Scott." As I turned the corner into the hall, I heard her call, "And you be careful with those women, boy, they're gonna git you in trouble." I smiled.

40
Graduation

I was nearing Washington and I had to piss, eat, and get gas, in that order. I got off the interstate and drove over to Fort Belvoir. I was heading for the NCO club. I remembered an evening in Cu Chi. I was waiting in a line outside to get into a club that was crammed full of soldiers. Suddenly, two explosions rocked the area behind the club. All the doors flew open and men were clawing their way out. Those of us in the line started running just to avoid being trampled in the stampede. As I ran past the corner of the building, two pairs of strong hands grabbed either arm and I ran out from under my body and sat down. It was Bumper and Croz from my unit. They dragged me back out of the way of running feet. They were doubled up laughing and I think they'd had more than a few drinks already.

"What the hell is so funny," I demanded. They tried to get serious but then looked at each other and started coughing, and laughing and choking and crying and wiping their faces on their sleeves.

They pulled me onto my feet and led me to the rear of the club where a window had been blown in from the explosion. "Come on, come on, come on, hurry, hurry," they were both spouting in a jumble of words that included some profanities. We watched as men came out the window and the door and ran for sandbagged shelters.

"Shouldn't we be running for shelters?" I yelled over the bedlam. This only occasioned a fresh round of choking guffaws as they dragged me into the club and pulled me to the bar.

"Take this, take this," they whispered out loud and threw two cases of beer into my arms. They proceeded to grab as many full bottles of liquor off the shelf behind the bar as they could carry. Then they yelled, "Run, moron, run. Don't just stand there." Watching these two drunks run with their arms full would have caused me to laugh if I hadn't been scared to death that we were about to caught and have the crap beaten out of us. We staggered between some darkened buildings and put our booty into a jeep. I grabbed Bumper and pulled him away from the driver's seat and threw him in the back; the last thing we needed was to have some drunk drive us into a ditch.

One of them handed me an open bottle. I couldn't see the contents in the dark. I took a swig, warm gin. I pulled over at the end of the airfield. I turned and looked at them. They were hopeless; every time one of them started to tell me what happened, they both went into convulsions. Finally, between snorts and gasps, I was able to make out that they had come into possession of some artillery simulators, which they had set off behind the club with this very outcome in mind. They grabbed me when they saw a chance to have an extra set of arms to carry stuff. Luckily, we predicted the commanding general's response and hid the loot in a drainage culvert, because, by the next morning, the base was being turned upside down.

When I got to the NCO club, it was two in the afternoon. The club was empty. I headed for the bathroom. I could not get into the stalls, so I hoped no one else would come in, and I used the sink for everything.

There was a heavyset guy stocking the cooler at the bar. I cleared my throat. He looked up, picked up a towel to dry his hands, and asked, "What can I do for you?"

"Can I get something to eat and a beer?"

"I got these ready-made sandwiches wrapped in cellophane here. Let's see." He looked in the refrigerator. "You got ham and cheese on whole wheat, roast beef that's been cooked for a year and a half on soggy white bread, and cream cheese and green olives on a bagel. If I was eating this stuff, which I never do, I'd eat the ham and cheese."

"You twisted my arm. I'll have that and a draft." The man sat the sandwich at the end of the bar at the level of my shoulder. "You are military, right?" I pulled out my ID card and showed the man. The man sat two drafts on the bar. "I only ordered one."

"I can't let you drink alone." He raised his glass. "Here's to the United States of America."

I raised my glass. "To the United States." We drank. I had a hard time finding an end of cellophane that I could pull open, so I bit a hole in the cellophane, but I still had problems.

"Lemme get that for you," said the bartender, producing a kitchen knife. He slid the knife into the hole I had bitten and cut the wrapping.

I took a bite of the sandwich. "This tastes like cellophane."

"The roast beef tastes like cardboard and I ain't never ate no bagel." The big man talked while I finished the beer and half the sandwich. The next thing I knew, my head snapped back. I had fallen asleep. "You all right, bud?"

"Yeah, I been up since four-thirty this morning and checked out of the VA hospital in Richmond. I gotta go to a graduation tonight at seven in Washington. I better go out and take a nap in the car, then I'll be all right." I laid some money on the bar.

"If you want to take a nap, I got a couch in my office. You're welcome to use it," the bartender offered.

"You sure? Thanks." I rolled into the office. I fell from the chair onto the couch and dragged my legs up. As soon as my head was down, I was unconscious. I woke to the sound of men outside the office talking and laughing. The clock on the wall showed a little after five. I grabbed my legs and threw them back on the floor. I sat up and pulled the chair next to me. I went to lift up but the couch was old and when I pushed against the cushions, they sank to the floor. After four attempts, I was too tired to attempt another one. I shouted, "I can use some help in here." The sound of talking and laughing went on. "HELP!" The door burst open and three guys in khakis stormed in. "Hi guys," I said sheepishly, "can you give me a hand back in the wheelchair, please?" They swarmed around me, but before I had a chance to explain what help I needed, I was scooped up by the three of them and deposited in the chair.

"You okay?" one asked.

"Yes, thanks." They headed back to their beers. There was a bathroom off the office. I could get in but I could not close the door so I worked as fast as I could and hoped no one came in to the office.

The club was full of GIs. The bartender looked over, saw me, and threw me a salute. I returned it. I got to my car, got gas, and headed up Route 1. Unfortunately, my nap meant I ran smack into D.C. rush hour traffic. Including a stop for a large black coffee, it took me an hour and a half to reach the graduation.

The wind was picking up and dark black clouds were piling up over the college. It was a long push from the parking lot to where the graduation was supposed to be. I found a crew of men collecting the chairs and hastily pulling down the decorations before the storm hit. One of them directed me to the college theater and explained that the graduation had been moved indoors. It was another long push. When I finally got to the lobby, the graduates, dressed in their nursing uniforms, were lined up to process into the theater; there were only three men. Cathy saw me and threw me a kiss. I waved back.

I waited until they had processed in and then pushed to the door. The capacity of the theater could not accommodate all the guests. Someone from the college invited the people standing in the lobby to an area where they were setting up a reception for after the graduation. They had run a loud speaker into that room and you could listen to the speeches and presentations. The ceremony moved along pretty quickly. All the while, thunder was rumbling and the wind was rattling the windows.

By eight o'clock, the graduates and their families were coming into the big room. Tables with red punch and cookies were set up against one wall. A disc jockey started playing records in the corner. I was sitting at a table watching for Cathy; maybe she was looking for me in the lobby. I pushed across the room and was looking for an opening in the flow of people coming in.

"Jake, Jake." Cathy had come in the door next to the one I was trying to go out.

"I was going out to look for you."

"Come on over. I want you to meet my family." I followed her through the crowd to a table of tall, blonde people. Her three brothers were all younger than she. Her parents had streaks of grey mixed through their blond hair, but the family resemblance was eerie. Their children looked more like they had been cloned than born. "Mom and Dad, this is my friend Jake that I met in Walter Reed." I saw the expression in Mrs. Creel's face change. I had seen that same expression on my mother's face when I told her I had orders for Vietnam. It was the expression of a mother who has just found that they are about to send their child in harm's way.

"These are my brothers, Peter, Michael, and Mark." I shook hands down the line. Cathy, her parents, and I moved around a table. There were not enough chairs for her brothers so they headed for the refreshment table and loaded up plates with cookies, then they stood by the window watching the storm.

There was an awkward silence at our table. I felt that I was intruding on a family affair. I licked my lips and said, "Um. I think I ought to get going."

"No, no," said Cathy, getting to her feet. She stepped behind her mother, looked at me, and nodded to her mother. "Come on, Daddy, let's dance."

He resisted, "Honey, nobody else is dancing."

She pulled his hand. "Well somebody has to start." She led her father onto the floor. She was right; soon other fathers and daughters and other couples came out and danced. I knew she had wanted me with her mother, I looked at her mother. She was trying to ask me something and I knew what.

"She'll be okay. In Vietnam, I mean. The bases where the nurses are stationed are surrounded with security." Her mother looked relieved, maybe because she had not had to ask the question. "Just make sure you write her a lot of letters, even if she doesn't write back. You don't have to have anything special to write about. Tell her about sunrises and sunsets and the colors of the leaves in fall, how white the snow is and how gray the fog is, and what's happening to the flowers in Maryland when spring comes. Don't let her think that a week went by when you didn't think about her and she'll come back just fine."

The woman reached across and took my hand. Her hands were cold and trembled slightly. I knew that it was taking all of her will to control her emotions and not take away from the celebration of her daughter's graduation. Cathy and her dad came back to the table. Another song began and he invited his wife to dance. Cathy slid her chair beside me. "Is that why you invited me to your graduation, to reassure your mom?"

"No." she bit her lip and blinked away a momentary tear. "I'm not using you. I don't have a steady boyfriend and I thought, I mean, we're good friends."

I put my hand on hers. "I told her not to worry and to write often."

"Thanks."

"Wanna dance?"

She looked puzzled. "I guess?" I backed away from the table and when she stood, I took her hand and pulled her onto my lap. I put my arms around her and she laid an arm around my shoulders and put her face against mine. Although the music stopped, we sat like that until her parents came to the table.

Her dad spoke to me, “Son, we’re going to take our children to dinner before our sons eat another case of cookies. You’re most welcome to come along.”

“Thank you, sir, but I have to get home to Pennsylvania and I have one more stop to make. I better get going.”

When we reached the outdoors, we found the rain had stopped, the sidewalks were covered with puddles, and there was lightning in the distance. They walked in silence as I tried to find the shallow parts of the puddles. My hands and sleeves got soaked and my hands slipped on the wheels. I realized that Cathy was gently pushing the chair to help me. When we reached the parking lot, her mom kissed me on the cheek and her dad and bothers each in turn shook hands with me. No one spoke. They turned toward their car and Cathy said she would catch up to them. She walked with me. The car next to mine was parked too close for me to be able to wheel up to the door. I had to give her the keys and ask her to back mine out. I took a bag from the car and removed a piece of paper. “This is my parents’ address.”

“I know. I saved it from the letter you had me write.”

“Send me your APO and I’ll write to you.”

“Are you going to see Suzie?”

“Yes.”

“Tell her I said hi and I’ll call her.” A gust of wind blew her hair across her eyes and she pushed it back in place. “Maybe I was wrong about you and Suzie,” she said.

“Well you were right that we could not cure one another, but you were wrong because the feelings that we have for one another helped us find the cures in ourselves.”

She sat on my lap and we kissed. Our tears mixed and ran around our lips. I pulled her tight against me. She whispered, “Jake, I’m kinda scared.”

I wiped the tears from her cheeks. “You’ll do all right, kid. You got good people who love you.” She stood and walked toward her parents without looking back. “Look me up when you get back,” I called hoarsely, but I was afraid this would be the last time I would see her. I made the sign of the cross. “Please, God, take care of her.”

41

Looking for a Love

I started the car and turned on the interior light. My watch said nine o'clock. I felt around under the seat and remembered I had drunk the last of the scotch. I headed toward Walter Reed. I had never seen the hospital while sitting up. The only views of the outside I had were flat on my back in an ambulance. I had trouble finding the right entrance. I parked my car across from the door. I wished I had a cigarette; not smoking could be very uncomfortable at times.

Maybe I should not go in. We said goodbye in Richmond. What was left to be said? Did I love this woman? Hell, did I even know what love was? Why did I feel this way about her? What would everyone back home say if I got involved with a woman six years older than me? Back home, there was Valerie—young, beautiful, affectionate Valerie. Not that Suzie wasn't beautiful or affectionate. Actually, the real problem was that she was divorced. Good Catholic boys did not chase divorced women; not that I was a good Catholic, but my mother did not know that. Damn, I was confused. Did I know what the hell I was doing? It did not make any difference anyway. Now, I had to go into the hospital; I had to go to the bathroom.

I bounced the chair out of the car and I was halfway to the hospital door when the storm, which had been stalking me, caught me in the open. I pushed as hard as I could, but, by the time I got inside, I was soaked. I rolled past the ward and found a bathroom. I used handfuls of paper towels to dry off. I came back to the door of the ward and looked at my watch. She would not be ready to leave for another hour.

Suddenly, I was bothered with a thought; maybe she switched with somebody—maybe she wasn't even here. I pushed slowly and quietly onto the ward. That was one thing about wheelchairs; they could move very quietly. I looked around the corner of the hall. An aide was pushing a bucket down the aisle, emptying urine. Then, I saw her. She was handing out pills and helping a patient take a drink from a pitcher with a straw. I pushed out and went along until I came to a bank of vending machines.

I made a dinner of a cup of coffee and a pack of peanut butter crackers. I should have taken time to stop for something more substantial to eat. I went pushing to the main entrance and stopped by a large window. I watched the raindrops trying to find paths down the panes of glass. A bright flash of lightning silhouetted the trees. When I was eleven, my parents gave me a bedroom on the third floor. One night, a storm had beaten on the roof of the old house. I sat up half the night, afraid and fascinated by nature's tantrum.

When I first arrived in Vietnam, I was assigned to perimeter guard duty at the base camp in Cu Chi. A series of forty-foot towers surrounded the base. Two of us were sent into one of the towers for the night. At about ten o'clock, we could see the lightning and dark clouds rumbling across the flat countryside charging straight at us. Once the storm hit the tower, it rocked back and forth. It did not come crashing down. God bless the engineers.

Another rumble of thunder brought me back to the present. It was 10:40. I wondered if I had fallen asleep sitting there. I pushed to the ward. The lights were out. My eyes strained into the dark; she was standing by a set of doors that went out onto a porch. She was watching the storm. I was sitting in the light from the nurses' station. She turned and stood looking in my direction, but she did not move. I pushed down the aisle and came within ten feet of her when I saw the smile frame her white teeth. I whispered, "You know, if you stand around like this, Santa Claus won't come."

"I've told Santa all about you; he won't be bringing you any presents." She put her hand on my shoulder, leaned forward, and kissed my cheek. "You're not very wet," she observed. We went toward the nurses' station.

"I've been waiting down the hall for about an hour."

"I was hoping you'd come by."

I gave her a puzzled look. "How'd you know?"

"Elementary, my dear Scott, tonight was Cathy's graduation and I was curious if you were going. I called Richmond and they said you'd left."

"Yeah, for good this time," I said. We reached the light in the hall and there was a minute of silence. "I was hoping maybe we could visit for a few minutes before I started home."

"Hi, Suzie!"

Her relief startled us. "Hi Teri. Jake, would you wait out by the door for me?" I pushed away.

§ § § § § §

Teri and Suzie watched him push down the hall. "That's the one, huh?" asked Teri.

"What do you mean 'the one'?"

"The one that you traded days off for. The one Cathy told me about, used to be on this ward."

"What did she tell you?" Suzie glanced at her and went back to straightening papers on a clipboard.

"That you have a thing for him."

§ § § § § §

I was sitting by the door, pulling a pair of gloves from my bag. I hoped they would help me get a grip on my wheels in the rain and keep my hands from slipping. She was coming down the hall, buttoning her raincoat and talking softly to herself. "Jake." Her voice got loud enough for me to hear. "You can't drive home in this weather. Come to my apartment and I'll pull out the sofa bed."

"Okay, but let's take my car and tomorrow I'll bring you back for yours." She agreed. Before we went out, I handed her the keys. "Your hands will unlock the car faster than mine. We ran to the car but, by the time I had lifted in and she had helped me load the chair, we were both soaked. She directed me off the hospital grounds. I took a broad street and, in a short time, I saw a sign that said we had crossed into Maryland. "Turn here," she directed and I followed a drive to the back of a large building. I drove down a ramp into an underground parking garage and she directed me to her parking space, 1015.

I got my knapsack out of the trunk and sat it on my lap. I followed her to the elevator. She had to pop a wheelie to get me onto the curb. Once in the elevator, she selected a button and stood back, watching the floor indicator signal our assent. I struggled to get the chair turned around. I put my hand into hers and she gave my hand a gentle squeeze. The doors opened and I gave several strong pushes into the hall and ran into the wall.

"Damn, there's something about the weave of the carpet that pulls the wheelchair to one side. Would you please carry this knapsack?" I had to push the wheelchair with one arm; even then, it still kept turning into the wall. She walked ahead and put her key into the lock. When I reached the door, I was out of breath and had to shake some blood back into my arm. We went in and she flipped on a light. She put the knapsack on a table. I rolled up behind her and put my arm around her and pulled her back onto my lap. We kissed until a strand of her wet hair fell across my nose and we started laughing.

"I have to get out of this wet raincoat and shoes." She hung her coat on a hanger from the top of the open closet door. "Here, give me your jacket." I twisted and hooked the inside of the top of my sleeve on the wheelchair handle and leaned forward, pulling it off my shoulder and down my arm. She slid her hand across my shoulders. "You're soaked clean through your shirt." She took another hanger and put my jacket on the door.

"I'm going into the bedroom to change. Look around if you want. I'll be out in a couple of minutes." She walked out of the entry hall and into a long rectangular room and through a door halfway down the right wall. She looked back and pointed to a door beside the one she had gone through. "That's the bathroom." I nodded. I was still in the entry hall and to my right was a compact kitchen. I pushed into the big room and maneuvered between the dining room table and a secretary in the corner of the room. Practical arrangement. She could just swing a dining chair around when she wanted to use the secretary. I put my feet against a stuffed chair and pushed it against the wall to get past the coffee table.

I rolled to the sliding glass doors that opened onto a small balcony. Far below, I could see the tops of the trees thrashing about. I backed up by her couch and crossed my leg to pull off my soggy boot. I leaned over and grabbed the heel of the boot between my hands. I was struggling with it when a box of framed and loose photos caught my eye. I edged the chair closer. The first one was in an ornate silver frame. It was Suzie in her wedding gown and veil. She was gorgeous. I looked at the one under it. It was Suzie and a man—her ex-husband, I guessed. I felt jealous. The bedroom door opened and I went back to pulling on my boot.

"What *are* you doing over there?"

"I'm trying to get this damn boot off." Suddenly, it gave and slid off and I almost slid out of the chair behind it. I changed the positions of my legs and started on the other boot.

"Want some hot chocolate?" she called from the kitchen.

"Sure, sounds good."

"Do you want something to eat?"

"I don't want to put you to a lot of trouble."

"Peanut butter and jelly?"

"My favorite." I pushed to the kitchen door. She was wearing a long flannel nightshirt and heavy woolen blue knee high socks. She handed me the sandwich and I balanced the plate on one leg. She kept stirring the saucepan on the stove. It was silent but for the sounds of the spoon scraping on the bottom of the pan and the hissing of the gas flame.

She poured the cocoa into big mugs. "Let's go in to the couch." She carried both mugs in and set them on the coffee table. She sat on the couch, tucked her legs up under her, pulled a blanket around her, and picked up her mug. For that instant, she looked like a little girl. I wished I knew how to interpret her body language.

"How was the graduation?"

"I really wouldn't know. It was so crowded I couldn't see and the speeches were the usual 'you have to get out there and save the world.' I met her family. Had you ever met them?" She shook her head no. I took a sip from my mug. "They seem like nice folks. When her mother saw me in this wheelchair, I think she was two seconds from telling Cathy she could not go into the Army."

"Maybe she'll talk some sense into her."

"Suzie, she'll have to find out for herself."

Her eyes blazed. "Don't you understand?" she said angrily. "She will never be the same after she sees that shit."

"Sweetheart, she could work in some big city emergency room or on some cancer ward watching children suffer and die in front of their parents and never *be* the same. You can't save people from a world of suffering that's all around us."

She set her mug back on the table, got up, and walked to the window. She stood looking out with her arms wrapped around herself. "It's different," she said hoarsely. "I thought I didn't need to explain it to you." I rolled up toward her and she backed away from me into the corner where I could not get closer to her.

"I know what war is. Every morning when I drag my ass into this wheelchair. Every night when I have bad dreams. When I start crying for friends who are dead or memories of the Vietnamese who are still there." She turned and stared out the window. I waited for her to say something. Nothing.

"I think you're frustrated because you can't make Cat see how bad it's going to be. No one can imagine war." I turned and started for the bathroom. I felt her hand on my neck. She sat on my lap and laid her head on my shoulder, the same one Cathy had laid her head on.

She reached up and pulled a long blonde hair from the front of my shirt. "Did you kiss her?"

I didn't know where this question was going, but I thought she already knew the answer. "Yes."

"Do you love her?"

"Do I feel the same way about her that I feel about you? No. I can't explain my feelings, but they are different. We understand one another and when I'm with you, I believe I will make it. I love you."

She stood up. "I better fold out the couch. It's getting late." I went to the bathroom. I could get the pedals and the front wheels through the door, but no further. She slid the coffee table by the sliding doors and stacked the cushions on it. Then, she grabbed a handle and heaved the mattress out. It folded out almost to the wall. She looked at me. "You want some help?"

"Could you carry one of the dining room chairs into the bathroom and hold it?" Suzie positioned a chair and braced herself against it. Just before I lifted from my chair, I looked at her. "The feelings you have for me, are they the same as you felt for anyone else?"

"Yes, and I got hurt."

I was slighted that I was not special. Defensively, I said, "You know I would not hurt you."

"Do you know that you're the same age that I was when I got married? I'm the age that my husband was when I married him. You're the young innocent and I'm the one who is wise in the ways of love."

"I'm not sure I think of myself as the young innocent."

"Trust me on this, honey," she said, patting my arm. I lifted onto the other chair. She dragged me into the bathroom. She went out the door into her bedroom. She came around, moved the wheelchair back, and shut the door. *Privacy*, I thought, *from a woman who has already seen more of me than I have*. I brushed my teeth, struggled to get the zipper down, and used the catheter. She helped me back into the wheelchair.

The mattress of the sofa bed sunk into gaps in the frame, but it was so good to stretch my back. She went to close the curtains. "Don't do that. I like to look outside," I requested.

"Do you need anything?" she asked. I arched one eyebrow. "No sir," she said, smiling.

"Then a drink of water," I replied.

She put a glass on the table next to the bed. She sat on the edge of the bed and kissed me goodnight. She went into the bedroom and closed the door. I rolled from side to side to get my pants off. I picked my feet up in front of my face and pulled my socks off. I got my shirt off and spread my clothes across the wheelchair to dry them out. I really needed to break down and buy pajamas. I reached over to the lamp and, after winding the chain around my finger (and having it slide off four times), I turned off the lamp. I could see the light in her bedroom shining beneath the door.

§ § § § § §

She sat on the edge of the bed and pulled off her socks. Tomorrow, he would get in the Pontiac and drive back home. In three weeks, she would be out of the Army. All of the structure, direction, and stability she had known would be gone. She had met thousands of men in the military. This one had said he knew her better than any man she had known and it bothered her that he was right. He talked to her differently. She liked it when he was with her; she looked forward to it. But was that love? Did she even know what love was?

§ § § § § §

I rolled onto my stomach and lay there looking at the light under her door. It went out. I turned and looked over through the sliding glass doors at the glow of the lights over the city. I heard her door open. She was moving past the foot of the bed. She walked in front of the window and pulled down the blankets on that side of the sofa bed. She crossed her arms in front of her body and took hold of her nightshirt. My eyes followed the hem as she drew it over her head. I saw her naked silhouette in front of the glow. She lay down and moved to me. I rose up on my elbow and reached for her. My fingers moved slowly across her thigh and up her side to the middle of her back. Her nipples pressed against my chest. We kissed, softly at first, then I tasted the lobe of her ear and I moved down her throat. I whispered, "You said you wouldn't have sex with a man until you decided you loved him?"

She slid her hand across my chest and up to the back of my head. She pulled my ear to her lips. "I know I love you."

42

A Last Goodbye

Twenty minutes had gone by since she had gotten into the bed. The parts of my body that could feel Suzie's caresses and kisses were telling my mind that I was ready to make love to her. It was the half of my body that had no feeling that I wanted to react. I slid my hand down my body to find out what was happening. "Damn it to hell," I said softly but angrily. Sudden cursing during foreplay has a way of disrupting the tenderness of the moment.

"What, what did I do?" Her eyes grew big in the dark wondering what she did wrong.

"You didn't do anything wrong, sweetheart," I reassured her. "For the past seven months, at every embarrassing, inappropriate, inconvenient, unappreciated opportunity, I have had an erection. I have them during bed baths, catheterizations, and when people were helping me get dressed. I've had them in front of nurses, orderlies, students, even my mother and aunt. I've been mortified and humiliated by them. After all those times, when I want one—nothing." I laid back.

"You're not going to give up," she said in exasperation. "After all the soul searching I went through to decide I wanted to make love to you."

"Well darling, I'm the young innocent. What would you suggest?"

"Improvise! You're the one who is always figuring out new ways to do things." The only thing that came to my mind was a night in the barracks when a soldier, just returned from his honeymoon, recounted in great detail all the ways he had made his bride happy with his tongue. “All right,” I said, “I’ll improvise. I’ve never done this before so you better…”

“I better what?”

“You better like it. I have a very fragile ego.”

She laughed. “Fragile ego, my ass.” I kissed her mouth and moved down.

§ § § § § §

At dawn, she had helped him get into the bathroom; she put on a pot of coffee and closed the curtains. They went back to sleep. Now, daylight blazed around the edge of the curtains. She moved her hair back from her face. It had been two years since she had awakened with a man beside her in bed. She had never had sex like that. He got an A for improvisation. She thought someone calling her name had woken her, but it was quiet. Then, it started again—a soft, singing whisper. “Wake up a little Suzie, wake up. Wake up a little Suzie, wake up.”

She started laughing, “You are a maniac.” She tried to tickle him.

“You can’t tickle me,” he scoffed. “I can’t feel it.” She slid her hands to his neck and he started laughing and trying to push her hands away. “Stop, stop I can feel it.” She pulled herself up so that she was on his chest and kissed him. “Good morning. What time is it?”

He looked at his watch. “Almost ten. Do we have to get up?”

“Not right away.” She kissed him and enjoyed the feel of his hands massaging her back. She whispered into his ear, “You know what you were upset about last night, well it’s not a problem now.”

§ § § § § §

She sat up and moved the blankets down. I looked down my body. I was hard. She knelt over me and took me in her hands. “Can you feel me touching you?”

“No,” I answered, “but my eyes are telling my brain I’m being touched and my imagination is taking care of the rest.” She moved down on me. I watched with fascination as I disappeared. *I’m doing it*, I thought, *I’m making love to her.* She leaned forward and dug her fingers into my chest and started moving up and down. I put my hands on her hips. *She must love me*, I thought.

Later, she put on a white satin robe. She pulled open the curtains and went into the kitchen. Then, I started arguing with myself. “You shouldn’t have done that.”

"Why?" The other me asked. "I love her."

The conscience said, "It's still a sin."

The other me blurted, "I'll marry her."

"You idiot," said the conscience, "you hardly know her."

"But at least I know I can have sex," said the other me.

"Who are you talking to?" Suzie asked. I blushed. I didn't realize I was talking aloud. She handed me a mug of coffee.

"I was working up the nerve to ask you to marry me."

She lay beside me and I put my arm around her. "I won't be divorced for a few more months and I need time and you need time for school."

"But now I know I can make love to you."

"And I know I can make love to you." She scooted around so she could see me. "We both needed that to heal." She looked me in the eye. "Are you feeling guilty?"

"Yes," I admitted. She shook her head. She kissed me on the forehead. "I believe there are guardian angels who, at the darkest time of your life, when you think you don't want to go on, touch you with the right person. You were that person on Christmas Eve, who changed my life, but I don't owe you and you don't owe me."

I was lying there feeling very contented. She snuggled her head on my shoulder. "Suzie? What are you going to do when you get out of the Army?"

"A couple of days ago, a partial property settlement came in, a check for over twenty thousand dollars. I'm going to take off and hike around Europe until the money runs out."

"Now I am really envious. Sure you don't want company?'

"I just want to be Suzie Donovan for a year. No one trying to make decisions for me or criticizing my choices."

"What happens when the money runs out?"

"I move back in with my parents and get a job. What about you, what next?"

"I got a letter from my cousin Sheila in Tucson. She's already been apartment hunting for us. She wants to fly into Philly and drive out with me. I thought I'd take summer classes and get used to going to school. I haven't told my mother yet. Sheila wants to catch up with family so we'll probably head out at the end of June. She told me some of the houses she has looked at are huge. If you get back from Europe and you want a warmer climate, you could come out."

"I'll think about it." She helped me back into the bathroom. She had to help me to shave because the mirror was too high for me to see what I was doing. We got dressed and had breakfast. I was aware that our time was growing short. She handed me my dried jacket and I shoved it into my knapsack.

"Suzie, there's something I want you to have." I pulled my beret from the knapsack.

"Not your beret?"

"I can get another. Please, take it to remember me by." She sat in my lap and I fixed it so that it did not fall over her eyes. She handed it back to me. "I can't keep it. Another beret won't be this one."

"There's something I'd like from you. A photograph." I looked toward the box by the couch. "Maybe one of those over in that box."

"Not those, they're another part of my life. I don't want to share them with anyone else. They are *my* memories. I have one for you, the way I'd like you to remember me." She reached up on a shelf and pulled down an album. She opened the cover and removed a 5 × 7 photo and held it against her chest. She walked to me and held it out. It was Suzie with very short hair wearing her Vietnam style fatigues and seated on some sandbags.

"You are really cute; I've always had a thing for women in uniform."

"I want a picture of you," she said, taking an instamatic camera from a drawer.

"I wish we could get a picture of both of us," I said.

She nodded. "I can arrange that," she said, crossing to the door. She opened her front door, crossed the hall, and knocked on that door. A small woman with bright orange hair (with gray roots) answered. Suzie took her hand. "Misses Hochberg, could you please do a favor for me?" asked Suzie, leading her across the hall. Suzie pushed a flashcube onto the top of the camera and explained to the lady how to hold it and push the button. "Now you have to hold it still. Here, lean against the wall." Suzie skipped over to me and sat in my lap and smiled for the camera, but Mrs. Hochberg did not snap the picture right away.

She looked through her glasses at us. "So this is your young man?" Her Brooklyn accent was so thick that the words rolled into your ears like waves.

"This is Jake, Mrs. Hochberg."

"Hi Suzie's young man. And how long have you been in a wheelchair?"

"About four months."

"My husband, Saul, God rest his soul, used a wheelchair for about six years. He broke his hip on the ice. I told the super there was ice and he said no. Well, I told him, 'My Saul was lying on the sidewalk and I was calling my son the lawyer to sue.'"

"Excuse me, Mrs. Hochberg, but her sitting on my lap is cutting off my circulation. Do you think you could snap the picture?" Mrs. Hochberg brought the camera to her eye but kept talking during the whole process. "You should have such bad circulation as I have." We managed to get her to shoot four photos between a complete recap of the progress of her husband's hip operations, the incompetence of the surgeon, and the efforts of their son the lawyer to set them up for life. After the last photo was taken, Suzie gently steered Mrs. Hochberg back to her own apartment.

When Suzie got back into her apartment and closed the door, we burst out laughing. "Now that is a character," I said.

"What's this crap about me cutting off your circulation?" she demanded and shoved my shoulder.

I pushed toward her, chasing her into the kitchen and cornering her. "I had to say something to hurry her along or we would have been there all day." I started trying to tickle her, but she straddled my lap and it became an embrace and a kiss with a lot of tongue and heavy breathing and moaning.

"You did not answer my question and, before I leave, I have to know the answer or I'll spend my whole life wondering what it might have been." I put my hand beside her cheek so she would not look away. 'Will you marry me?" She put her hand over mine and held it against her cheek.

"I am so honored that you would ask me. I know what your feelings are for me and I have the same love for you; otherwise I would not have come out of my room last night. But I can't marry you now."

"Later?"

"Maybe." We held each other very tightly. She gave me her parents' address.

It was silent in my car as I drove her back to pick up her car. The lump in my throat was making it difficult for me to breath. When I stopped beside her car, I wanted to say anything but goodbye. I sobbed and then the dam broke and I cried. I felt my heart breaking in my chest. She slid into my lap I saw that her face was also streaked with tears. I hugged her and rocked back and forth until I had gained control of my emotions.

One last kiss and then she slid across the seat and got into her car and started the engine. She looked over to wave and she drove away. I checked the urge to follow her. "I know what love is," I whispered.

43

A Father and a Son

I sat in that parking lot for another thirty minutes. Suzie had pulled me back from despair and made me believe in myself. She had helped me start loving the cripple I am and made me realize others could too. Now her support was gone; I was unsure what to do. Flo, Sam, Miss Adams, Cathy, and Suzie. Maybe I should not have said goodbye to so many friends in such a short time. I shivered and took a breath. I turned the key and started driving.

I found the parkway and headed north. I was going to do one more thing today. I must not lose my nerve. I stopped and paid the toll for the tunnel that ran under the Baltimore harbor. I drove from the bright sunshine into the dim coolness of the tunnel. It was that tunnel that triggered a memory that I had long buried. I was twelve. My teacher had sent a letter home to my parents. At eight o'clock in the evening, my father came into the dining room where I was doing my homework on the table. He seized the upper part of my arm in a grip that gave voice to rage. He pulled me off the chair and led me to the basement stairs. At the top of the stairs, he took hold of a yardstick.

In the center of the basement he had placed a stool. He sat on the stool. There was no expression on his face. My throat was dry and my heart was pounding with the dread of what I knew was coming. "What did I do?" my trembling voice asked. He made no answer. He pulled me across his lap and extended his arm above his head and brought the stick across my buttocks. I flinched but I did not cry out.

When he struck me the third time, the stick broke. He glanced around for something to replace it with and seized on a six-foot length of hose he siphoned homemade wine with. He grabbed the two ends. He stood and brought it down with all his might across my back.

For a second, I thought the pain was going to make me lose consciousness. I struggled to get away from him, all the while pleading with him, "Tell me what I did. What did I do?" He continued to swing the hose, striking my back and legs. I screamed and pleaded with him to stop. Finally, when he figured he must have accomplished something, he pushed me in front of him upstairs and sat me in the chair in front of my homework.

"I don't want to get any more letters from your teacher," he said as calmly as if nothing had just happened. He walked from the room.

At about ten o'clock, my mother came into the dining room and found me still sitting there. She took my hand and led me to my bedroom. I stood in a daze and felt her unbuttoning my shirt. She took it off. Then, her hands began to tremble when she saw the stripes of blood on my undershirt. She took off all my clothes; blood that had dried to the clothing pulled away with the clothes and wounds started to bleed again. My back, bottom, and legs were criss-crossed with welts of purple and black and red.

I shivered as the car drove back into the sunshine. "What the hell did I ever do to deserve that?" I asked aloud. I never knew what was in the letter from the teacher. All I had learned from that was to be intimidated by my father and to avoid confrontation with him. I crossed the Susquehanna but I did not turn toward home. I continued past Wilmington and followed the signs for Philadelphia. I glanced at the map on the passenger seat. I located the red dot that I had marked on it and where I had to get off of the interstate. I was not looking at the scenery.

I was rehearsing, one more time, a speech I had been practicing for almost two years. It was bound to be a tough audience. The closer I got to the stage the more nervous I became. I spoke aloud to the empty car. I repeated the lines but changed the timing, the tone, the volume, the cadence of delivery. I looked for reasons not to go, but I kept on. I found myself pulling into the parking lot of another VA hospital. I parked and sat looking up at the building. Then, slowly and deliberately, I pushed the chair from the car and then slid back into the driver seat. Then, I sat looking at my wheelchair, a prison cell I would occupy for life. I hated this inanimate, mindless device, the symbol of my helplessness, of the effects of war. I wished for a gun, my machine gun. I would shoot it, again and again, until it disintegrated into bits of metal and vinyl.

I pushed up the sidewalk and into the building. The first thing was to find a bathroom; I must not forget my body's schedule. Then, I rolled to the information desk. Two men wearing V.F.W. hats were sitting there. They smiled at me. "Can I help you?" asked one.

"Do you have a patient named Scott?" I felt as if I were asking for myself.

"Scott who?"

"No, his last name is Scott."

He flipped open a directory. "David?"

"Yes," I said, "that's it."

"Room 226."

"Thanks." I took the elevator and followed the signs down the hall. I found the room and paused outside. I summoned my courage and rolled in. There were two beds, both empty. The lucky bums, they had semi-private rooms, no sharing your privacy, your guests, and everything else with nineteen other guys. There was a cleaning woman backing out of the bathroom, dragging a mop.

"Are you looking for somebody?"

"Is there a guy named Scott in here?"

"Down in the dayroom at the end of the hall."

"Thanks." I pushed down the hall slowly, not anxious to arrive. I could see through the open doors into the big room and through the windows on the opposite wall. I stopped at the doors. In the center of the room sat a man in a wheelchair. The brown hair was almost completely white and he sat slouched in the chair. I knew him. Maybe it was the shape of the back of the head, but I was sure it was him. I pushed cautiously toward him, expecting him to turn suddenly and confront his offspring. There was no movement but the rhythmic rise and fall of the shoulders. I stopped to the side and slightly in front of the man in the wheelchair. There was still no movement; no turn of the head, no shift of the eye. I pushed in front of him and turned to face him.

I was shocked by the appearance of the right side of my father's face. The upper eyelid was closed over the eye, while the lower lid sagged away revealing the lower portion of the eyeball. The eye had crusted drainage at the corner. The muscles under the cheek had atrophied and the pale gray skin hung limply from the cheekbone. The corner of his mouth drooped down and a trail of saliva had run over his lower lip across the stubble on his chin. I shuddered.

"Hey, Dad." I waited. "It's me, Jake." I felt the eyes stare through me and out the window on the other side of me. I went to a table and got a Kleenex. An old man standing, faced into the corner, mumbling to himself, was the only other person in the room. I returned to my father and wiped the spit from his chin and wiped his eye. The fixed stare never changed.

"Can you hear me?" I raised my voice and then I looked over to see if the other man was listening or if anyone was by the door. Then, I spoke louder. "I came here to say something to you. Do you know that I am here?" The straight stare continued. "If you can hear me, then blink." I watched his face and, after a few seconds, he blinked, or at least one eye did. I pushed slowly around my father. He was dressed in a set of hospital pajamas and his own bathrobe. A urine drainage bag hung under his chair and the hose went into his pajama pants. I stopped my wheelchair beside his and looked out of the window to see if there was something out there that he was looking at. I blinked into the bright sunshine.

"Do you know that I'm twenty years old now?" I did not look for a response and, in fact, turned my head so that I could not even see him from the corner of my eye. "In all that time, I never remember you telling me that you loved me. Even when I was a little boy. Why couldn't you have ever said that to me?" I worked at keeping the speech coming from my head and not my heart, no emotion, nothing to interfere with what I had waited so long to begin. "You could never see any good in me. When I got an A on my report card, you condescendingly pointed to the C. When I limped off the football field, you didn't ask how I was. You launched into a rant of what I should have done.

"Do you know why you never told me you loved me?" I waited for the answer, and then I gave it to him. "You didn't love me. You were waiting to love the person you were trying to make me into." I looked sideways at him and then I pushed around so that I was directly in front of him looking at that expressionless face. "You never, *never* listened to what I wanted or what I decided." My voice wavered between pleading and anger. "You never said, 'Good luck, son, nice going, boy.' Never a pat on my back or an arm around my shoulders. We never had a conversation, you lectured. All you could hear when I spoke was how wrong I was, how I was making a mistake, how I would not be what you wanted me to be. All you could do was nitpick and find fault. You could never accept and love just me."

I pushed in a halting circle around him as I spoke. "I wanted to be a chopper pilot. I wanted to fly, but that wasn't what you wanted. It wouldn't look good on your resume." I finished the first circle. "Sure, I might have gotten shot down, crippled, or killed, but it would have been my decision, my responsibility and my triumph or blame. Do you know the frustrations I go through every day? Are you sitting there raging with anger in your mind because you can't walk, get into bathrooms? Do you piss in your pants or shit yourself? I do. Do you have frustrations? You want to know the worst frustration?" My voice rose to a shout. "I don't know why the hell I am in a wheelchair."

I stopped and faced him and said fiercely, "It was my goddamn life, but now neither of us has our lives to live because they belong to these fucking wheelchairs. Did you want me to love you or hate you or didn't it matter?" I pushed back to the table and got Kleenexes, one to blow my nose and some more to wipe my eyes. I took a breath to calm down and glanced at the open doors. I pushed back.

"I want to know something. Is this how your old man treated you, or was it to the other extreme?" I searched the face in front of me to see if it was registering, but I could see no change in the eyes. "Did your old man make it clear to you that he just didn't give a damn who you were? Is that what you learned?" I reached over and put my hand on his arm. I lifted it and drew his hand into my lap and put it between my hands. "I don't know whether I will be lucky enough to have a son, but if I do, I will hug him and I will tell him that I love him and I will love him for being just what he is. The whole time we lived together, did you ever open the door to my bedroom while I was sleeping and whisper that you loved me?"

I laid his hand in his lap and pushed to the window to clear the lump in my throat. Looking into the bright sunshine, I remembered bright sun on a snow-covered hill. My father pulled me to the top of the hill on a big sled and we would ride down together. We went up and down that hill for hours. When I started to shiver, my father gathered dried branches and lit a fire and rubbed my arms and shoulders to warm me up. Then, he trudged home, pulling the sled and me under a purple and pink winter sky. The sense that I was being watched caused me to jerk my head around. I saw no one but my father. Maybe it was wishful thinking, but his stare seemed to have shifted slightly.

I rested my forehead on my hands. "I met a little boy named Tommy last week and I realized how much he is like me. The only thing he needs is a father to love him." I looked into the pale face—

the hollow cheeks, the sunken eyes. "You know all those years in Catholic school, high school, and with you and mom and no one taught me that the hardest thing to do is to love someone the way they are—crippled, retarded, whatever. It is probably something you can't be taught—and only a few people learn it." I rolled to him and put my arm around his shoulders. I did not want to cry now. "I love you—just the way you are—or in spite of it. But I love you."

I turned to leave and almost ran over the aide who had come up behind us. "Man, he don't understand a word you sayin'," said the aide.

I licked my lips. "Are you sure?"

The aide thought. "Well, no, I ain't for sure."

"Well, I don't want to take that chance." I pushed to the table and got a Kleenex and came back to the man in the wheelchair. I wiped the drool from the corner of his mouth and then wiped a tear from his eye. I turned and left

After I had pulled the chair into the car, I lay across the front seats and went to sleep. I was in the Michelin rubber plantation, rows on rows of rubber trees. We were in a circle in total darkness. I held my hand in front of my eyes and saw only black. The luminescent hands on my Timex told me it was midnight. I arranged the ammo belt to the machine gun by feel and moved some vines away so that they would not get tangled with the belt. Suddenly, a hand shook my leg and a whisper said, "A light." We looked into the blackness. There was nothing. Somebody asked, "Do they have fireflies in Vietnam?" But it flashed again for a second, a flashlight. Then, off to the side another and on the other side of the circle another. "Everybody stay still," whispered our team leader. "They know we're out here, they are trying to draw our fire to see exactly where." We watched the lights come on and off at different points around us for maybe an hour.

Slam! The door of a car parked beside mine closed. I woke up and started driving in time to get caught in Philadelphia rush hour traffic. It was around seven when I drove up in front of the big old house. I was puffing up the ramp to the porch when the front door swung open and Ann came bounding out. "EEK," she yelped, startled to see a head coming over the edge of the porch. "Jake, I didn't know you were coming home."

She glanced at her watch. "Um, your mother drove into see your father, and I'm supposed to meet Hank for dinner. Do you want me to help you fix something to eat?"

"No, you get going. I need some time to myself."

"Bye, honey," she said with a kiss on my cheek and she skipped down the steps. I pushed through the huge, quiet house and dropped my knapsack on my bed. I headed to the bathroom. Then, I went to the kitchen for two big glasses of water. Our well water was always the best. Then, I fixed a scotch chaser and took it out to the sun porch. I slid onto the bed and rolled onto my side. I pushed the curtains aside and, just outside the window, a beautiful red rose bud hung at the end of a long stem.

My shoulders began shaking and I began crying. Between sobs, I kept repeating, "Why, God, why do you keep messing with me?" Someone sat on the edge of the bed and put their hand on my shoulder and gently pulled me onto my back. Through the tears in my eyes, I saw the blurred face of Valerie.

She answered my question before it was asked. "Ann drove by the house and told me that you had come home. Why are you crying?"

"Could you please just hold me?"

She lay on the bed beside me and we entwined our arms around the other in a tight embrace. I inhaled the scent of her hair and felt the pressure of her hands on my back. "This was all I needed," I whispered, "someone to welcome me home. I'll be fine." We lay there for a long time. *What a day*, I thought, *I started in bed with a beautiful woman and ended the day in bed with a different woman. There will never be another day like this.*

She pulled back and leaned on her elbow to look at me. Her soft fingers wiped away a tear. "What are you thinking?"

I could not answer that honestly. "I was feeling sorry for all the cripples in this world who don't have anyone to give them a hug when they need it." She squeezed me again. "And I was thinking of a friend named Ben and wondering in two years how many hugs he got." Valerie pressed her lips against mine and her mouth opened. I slid my hand over her shorts and rubbed her thigh.

It was 11:30 when Ann came home. She came into the sun porch and was surprised to see me there. "What are you doing here? I mean, where is your car?"

"I let Valerie drive it home. I didn't want her walking in the dark."

"Oh no! It's bad enough when you give a girl a ring, but when you let her take the car home," she said teasingly, "you might as well have set a wedding date."

"Get out of here and go to bed," I said with a laugh.

"Are you ready for me to help you get ready for bed or did Valerie do that?" She blushed when she realized what she was suggesting.

"I am ready for bed. I made some changes in the last three weeks so that I don't need as much help. Although, if you think we can mange it, I'd like to try the tub tomorrow."

"Well, if I can't get you out by myself, I can always call Valerie."

"Yeah, right. Go to bed." She kissed me goodnight and turned off the light. I heard her heels on the steps. As I was falling asleep, I thought, *I told my father I love him.*

44

Back on the River

I was sitting on the porch sipping coffee when I heard music from the road, then saw my car coming up the drive. The windows were all open and music with a heavy beat was blaring from it. Valerie stopped and she and Diana and Julie climbed out. Valerie was carrying a bag of doughnuts. "I was beginning to wonder if I would ever see the car again," I said.

"Valerie said she wanted to bring you breakfast, but," said Diana, moving away from her older sister, "Julie and I know she just wanted to drive through town so that all of the seniors could see her in that car." Valerie hit Diana in the breast with a powdered sugar doughnut, leaving a white ring on her navy shirt.

"You, brat," they shouted simultaneously. I stared laughing. We all went into the kitchen for coffee. Ann came running through the kitchen holding a towel around her naked body. She ran to the dryer and dug out some clothes and turned to see us staring.

"Oh, I didn't know you were here. Well, do what you were doing." She ran out.

The girls turned to look at me. "I don't know what this looks like," I said, waving my hands, "but it isn't what it looks like. She doesn't run around the house naked." Just then, Ann came back in wearing a shirt and panties and dug into the dryer and pulled out a pair of shorts, which she slipped on. As she was toweling off her wet hair, she said,

"I'm sorry but I overslept and Hank will be here any second." On cue, Hank walked into the kitchen.

"Are you getting married soon?" I asked in jest. The looks they shot each other answered that question.

Hank was there to take her out on the boat. "You guys want to come fishing?" Hank invited me and the Robinson girls. Ann and the girls went to the garage to get our fishing poles. "Hank, wouldn't you rather be alone with Ann?"

"Jake if we were going to the theater or to dinner, yeah, but pulling slimy fish out of a muddy river isn't exactly the place you plan to be alone with a woman."

We drove to the marina in two cars. Hank managed the chair down the steep ramp to the pier. When he had the boat in the water, he brought it up to the pier. I swung the footrests out of the way. Ann and the girls each took an arm or leg and lowered my butt to the wooden planks, which was kind of a controlled fall. I started to slide my butt toward the edge of the pier when Hank said, "Look out for splinters."

Julie nudged Diana. "It's all right, Jake, Valerie will help look for splinters." For a second, I thought one of them was going to get pushed into the river.

"Is this going to go on all day?"

Valerie retorted coolly, "Not if they would just grow up." The girls pulled the boat against the pier while Hank and Ann got me into the boat. It wasn't very dignified. Ann put my chair back into the car. The boat pulled away from the pier. The roar of the engine, the gurgling of the exhaust into the water, the rush of the wind in my face, the smell of wind, water, bait buckets, the spray on my face; there were a million memories of years of fishing on this big river. Hank maneuvered between some rocks where the fish were known to hide. He tossed a rope over a downed tree's limb to hold us from drifting. Six lines went into the water and six people settled into the reflection that makes patient fishermen. Ann was talking softly to Valerie and Hank was giving Diana and Julie a hand. I wondered what was happening twelve thousand miles away, a Sunday evening in the war. I had not read or watched any of the news coverage of Vietnam.

The tall trees on the bank made me think of the tall towers on the perimeter of the base camp. Four huge poles supporting a platform, about forty feet up, with low walls of timbers and sandbags and a tin roof. I could see those trees being cut down and shipped to be used for the poles. One night, the ARVN troops had a fire fight with the Viet Cong in the village outside the base camp. An armored personnel carrier opened up with a machine gun. Whatever he was aiming at caused his bullets to ricochet and I watched as red tracers came floating in wild paths at me in that tower. I hit the floor and heard the bullets whine by and thud into the sandbags.

Suddenly, the strike of a fish on my line brought me back to the river. It jerked the pole from my hands, but I was able to save it by hooking a hand on the reel and pinning the pole against the boat. I had to catch myself with my other hand and push.

"Quick, somebody grab it!" I shouted. Julie reached over the side and grabbed the pole and held it out to me. "I can't do it," I said.

"Go on, bring him in," said Ann, taking the pole from her and helping me to get control of it. I put the butt of the pole between my legs, put my palm under the pole, and used the flat of my other palm to turn the reel. It was a slow process, especially with everyone watching and calling encouragement. Hank netted the fish and I felt proud of the accomplishment.

"Just like the old days," I said.

We didn't stay out too long since there was no bathroom for both sexes. The job of getting me back onto the pier had been thought through by Hank. Julie and Diana held the boat against the pier. Hank got onto the pier. I sat on the edge of the boat with my back to him and put my arms above my head so he could grab my wrists. Valerie and Ann each grabbed a leg and on the count of three they heaved me up. Then they lifted me into the chair.

Hank could not get my chair around the corner into the men's room, so we stopped at the sink and he stood guard at the open door while I got the catheter out. Later, as we sat around a fire, dangling hot dogs on sticks into the flames, I looked around at the sunburned faces of my friends. "Thanks, everybody, for helping me today," I said sincerely. "This is what coming home is about." And yet, it was not the same; doing what I used to do did not erase the paralysis or the wish to be able to do it on my own without their help.

45

Widows, Orphans, and Cripples

May 31, 1971, Memorial Day, I was up early. My mother was still in Philadelphia. Ann was sleeping in on the holiday so I did not worry about pushing through the house naked. In the kitchen, I made two cups of coffee and balanced one on the arm of my chair as I pushed back to the sun porch. "If I spill this, I am going to have a lot of embarrassing burns to explain." I sipped the coffee between struggles with my socks and pants. I put on my boots and then closed the door. On the back of the door, my camouflage jacket was hung, pressed, and starched. I put it on over a white short sleeve shirt. I glanced at my watch; I had to get a move on. I had seen the Walls at church on Sunday. They reminded me. I pushed to the kitchen and gulped down the other coffee. I made a phone call.

I went to the bathroom. I looked into the mirror. I put the black beret on my head and adjusted it just so. I drove my just cleaned blue car to Drier's store and around back to the lane that lead to their house. Hank was sitting on the steps. He stood and entered the passenger side. I drove back to the highway but, shortly, I turned and drove up a steep hill that led to a bluff that overlooked the river. I parked and unloaded the chair. It was a struggle to push the chair through the lush grass around the gray headstones. I had to rest my arms many times. Hank started to help me. "Not this time," I refused.

"I need to get there on my own." I stopped by a small stone that had a bronze Marine Corps emblem on it.

A troop of boy scouts and some men from the American Legion Post moved quietly among the rows of stones. They stopped at different graves and pushed a small metal holder in the earth and put a flag into it. The Walls drove up. Mr. and Mrs. Wall got out and moved slowly through the stones toward their son's. Mr. Wall wore the brown uniform of a Marine major and he carried a small wreath of white flowers. Mrs. Wall was clutching his arm. It appeared that they were holding each other up. A few steps behind them walked a pretty young woman carrying a little girl. The little girl wore tiny white gloves and a black dress. I looked back at the grave and read, "John R. Wall, 1948-1968, Beloved son, husband and father."

The little group stopped at the grave. The grief surged inside of them and fought to escape in quiet tears that streamed down their cheeks and lips that trembled with the strain. Mr. Wall stepped forward and tried to get the wreath to stand on the little tripod that was attached to it. Hank stepped around me and adjusted the legs so that the wreath stood there. When Mr. Wall straightened up, a boy scout asked, "Could I put a flag on the grave?" The man nodded his head. I looked around. The scouts and veterans had formed a circle around the little party at the grave. The boy placed the flag beside the stone and someone in the group called, "Attention." A scout raised a bugle to his lips and played "Taps." As the notes floated through the silence, Mr. Wall brought his shaking hand to his cap in a salute. I brought my hand to my beret and held the salute until the last note died away.

The Walls shook hands or embraced all of the scouts and veterans one by one. Mr. Wall walked to me and said, "Son…" but his voice faded in a hoarse croak and he was unable to go on. He patted my shoulder and walked away with his wife toward their car.

The young woman walked to me and stooped beside me. "Did you know my husband?"

"No, ma'am," I said, taking her hand, "but I know your loss." She stood and hugged me. I reached up and returned her hug. She turned and picked up her daughter and took her to the car. The others went back to their tasks. I sat there, staring at the wreath. Then, sobs burst out of me. I put my head between my knees and cried for a few minutes. Then, I wiped my eyes on my pants leg. I sat up. Hank was squatting, looking out at the river. He pushed me back to the car. Once we were loaded in the car, I turned to Hank.

"You asked me once what Vietnam was about. It was about contradictions; two ideologies who each claimed to be fighting for freedom—a small country, a big country—deceit, camaraderie—bravery, cowardice—determination and incompetence." I pointed to the graves. "But someday, that is all we'll remember it by." I twirled a small flag one of the scouts had handed me. "The parents, widows, orphans, and cripples that it left us will do the remembering."

As much as I had wanted to go home, I suddenly felt smothered by it. I needed to move on.

46

October 1987

Suzie walked into the cramped office and sat at her desk. She reached up and tried to work the tension from her neck by kneading the muscles with her palms. She looked at her watch. Damn, she should have been out of here an hour ago. Whatever the bug everyone had was playing havoc with her nurses' schedules. Two more had called in sick. She had pulled one off another ward and had been able to call in one. She hated supervising and longed to get back to taking care of people.

"Suzie!" It was Dr. Ross, a resident who was always too full of energy. "Some of us are going out for a drink. You wanna come?"

"Thanks, but I'm beat. I've got to get home." The doctor took off her lab coat and hung it on the rack behind the office door. She sat on the edge of the desk and crossed her long legs.—

"Come on," she urged, "you need some social life. You've been working too hard."

"I'd like to, Hannah, but my dad wants to go to a meeting at the base and I have to go home and take care of Mom."

"How's she doing?"

"No better, no worse. The tumors are pressing on her spine. She loses feeling in her legs and cannot walk."

"Listen, if you want me to sit with her some night so you can chase a man, I'll be glad to."

"You're a real pal, but she's my mom."

"Okay, see you tomorrow." Dr. Ross was out of the office when she leaned back in. "Tell that new nurse if that kid we sent up to PICU comes back down, page me."

"You work too hard," said Suzie. The doctor stuck her tongue out and disappeared. Suzie rubbed her eyes and looked at the photo on her desk of her mom and her. It was taken in 1978, just before her second tour with the Peace Corps. She had taken a job in the States after her first tour, but she needed to go back to where people needed her. For them, she was the only medicine for a hundred miles or more. She remembered the day when the jeep came to the clinic to pick her up. The driver explained that she had to come back to the city. There was an emergency phone call from home.

She bounced in that jeep for three hours before they reached a phone. The message was to call her father. She could hear the strain in his voice. Her mother had passed out while driving and wrecked her car. The doctors had found a tumor restricting the flow of blood to her head. The flight home was a long one. Since then, she had lived with her parents, nursing during the day and caring for her mom at night when her dad went to work. His retirement had been short lived. The nest egg they had saved for the house in San Diego was needed, so they sold the house and got an apartment. He went back to work to get health insurance. Her mom had been through years of radiation, chemo, and surgery, but it only slowed the disease.

She thought her dad liked the work at the Navy base, partly for the escape it provided. Yet it was hard working a screwy shift until 4:00 a.m. and then catching bits of sleep all day.

She took a brush and mirror from her desk drawer. She looked at the few grey hairs in her short dark hair. She brushed her hair vigorously, looked to see if the grey hairs were still there, and then replaced the mirror and brush. She stood and took her coat from the rack, switched off the light, and walked to the door. She paused. She walked back and sat at her desk. She picked up a slip of paper, which she was able to read by the light from the hall.

She had been in the library last month and had seen a shelf of phone books, one was for Tucson. She needed a friend, maybe more than a friend. She needed someone to hold her; someone to help her with the dreams that had come back. She picked up the receiver and dialed the area code, then she paused, and then she dialed the number. There were beeps and clicks and then the buzzing of the phone ringing. It rang. It rang. It rang.

Then, there was an answering machine. A woman's voice said, "Hi, this is Lisa Scott. Neither Jake nor I can come to the phone, but leave a message and we'll call you back." Suzie closed her eyes. She hadn't expected a woman to answer, or maybe she hoped a woman would not answer. She felt very alone. A loud beep startled her. She had a problem seeing the phone to hang up. She dried her eyes with a Kleenex and walked into the hall. She needed to check on the new nurse before she went home.

47
The Reunion

It was the end of June 1992, a Friday morning. The temperature at Fort Benning, Georgia was already into the high eighties by mid-morning. Ever since she had gotten to work that morning, her curiosity had been driving her crazy. Would he be there on the fort, so close after all these years? She thought it would be the wildest of chances—going over to see would be a waste of time. But she thought if she did not go, she would spend the rest of her life wondering if he had been only a mile or so away.

She visited the last ward on her rounds and told the specialist in her office that she was going out for a few minutes of fresh air. "Too much anniversary party last night, ma'am?"

"It's just such a beautiful day. I need some sunshine." The specialist had been referring to a first anniversary party that her nurses had thrown for her the night before, one year since she had made full Colonel. Twenty-one years in the Army—it seemed like only yesterday that she had taken the oath. She had behaved herself and was home at a reasonable time. Her children were waiting up for her. Her teenage sons were such worriers when she was out, it was a shame they didn't understand it in reverse.

Her husband was in New Orleans at a conference and would not be back until Sunday. She kissed the boys goodnight and went to bed. She took a shower and was dressing in the bedroom watching the late news on television. The local Columbus station did a piece about the fiftieth anniversary of the modern Ranger being commemorated for the next few days at Fort Benning. There would be Rangers from World War II, Korea, Vietnam, Grenada, Panama, Desert Storm, and Somalia. She thought of Jake. Would he come from wherever he was for the reunion? She had a restless night.

She drove to the Ranger headquarters where the morning ceremonies were scheduled. An MP saluted her and then directed her to a parking space. She walked slowly toward the reviewing stand, looking through the crowds for a man in a wheelchair. The young sergeant marching a formation of Rangers in the opposite direction threw her a smart salute. She liked Rangers—they were so military and the young sergeant was definitely cute. She turned around to take another look at him, and found that he was marching backwards looking at her. He spun sharply around and continued to march.

"You still got it, honey," she said with a huge smile. The ceremony began. She looked slowly around the crowd under the big trees. She would see someone in a wheelchair and move around for a better look, but it would not be him. She was a little surprised at how many veterans were in wheelchairs, on crutches, or on canes. It was a sobering reminder of the danger of their profession.

She walked behind the crowd, looking, occasionally remembering to return the salutes of the troops who saluted her. She saw another man in a wheelchair. It was difficult to get a look at him because a woman stood close beside him. She crossed behind him. He wore a black beret and a camouflage jacket. She caught sight of a scroll patch above the red and yellow of a 25th Division patch and her pulse quickened. If it wasn't Jake, maybe it was someone who had been in his unit and would know where he was.

She waited for the ceremony to end before she went any closer. A few of the young Rangers came to him and he turned to speak with them. She caught her breath. It was him. He had hardly changed in twenty years. She felt a lump in her throat. She was impressed with the fraternity between the young and old Rangers, how interested they were in him. She looked at the young woman whose hand rested on his shoulder. *That dirty old man*, she thought, *if she's twenty, then I'm a goose*. The young woman was deeply tanned with short brown hair that had bleached to an orange tint in the sun.

He glanced in her direction for a second and looked back at the men he was speaking to. She watched his face as the eyes widened and his mouth fell open and he looked back. He recognized her.

§ § § § § §

I stared at the tall woman in white coming toward me. "Cathy?!" It did not sound like my voice saying the word. "Oh my God." She quickened her pace and came up and put her arms around me. I wrapped my arm around her and pulled her onto my lap. We kissed each other and hugged tightly and I felt tears on my face from me and from her, tears of joy and relief. A photographer from the local newspaper snapped our picture.

I looked at the surprised faces of the young people around us and explained, "This is a nurse who took care of me after Vietnam." The young Rangers smiled and nodded. They wondered if they were supposed salute under the circumstances. They decided discretion was in order and they just wandered away.

"Hi, Jake," said Cathy, getting up from my lap and straightening her uniform. She looked at the young woman. "If you introduce her as your wife, I'll slap you silly."

"She's my daughter, Kara. Kara, this is Colonel Cathy," I said, squinting to read her name tag, "Muir."

"Hello, ma'am." My daughter extended her hand. Cathy took it.

"Kara, it's very nice to meet you."

Just then, a teenage girl ran up. "Mr. Scott, my dad is taking us over to the jump tower for a ride. Could Kara come?"

"You want to go up a two hundred fifty foot tower?" I asked my daughter. At first, she grimaced, but then she batted her eyes and said yes. The two young women ran off through the crowd, followed by the eyes of several dozen Rangers.

"Jake, she's gorgeous. How old is she?"

"Seventeen," I said with a sigh, watching the young men watch my daughter. "I feel like I brought a lamb into a shark tank."

"They're probably no different than you were," she tried to reassure me.

"That's what worries me."

"Jake, I've got to get back to work."

"But we just got together after twenty years," I said with exasperation. "I have so many questions." I was pleading with her to stay.

"I was going to say, why don't you come to my house for dinner."

"How accessible is it for wheelchairs?"

"Well, it's up a few steps."

"And the bathroom doors are too narrow?"

"Maybe."

"Let me take you and your family to dinner, please?"

"My husband is out of town, but I have two boys. One is your daughter's age."

"Great. We're staying at the Hilton. Come by at six for drinks and we'll decide where to go for dinner."

She kissed my cheek and took a few steps away but she turned. "Jake?" I tilted my head and stuck out my jaw. "Is your wife going to be there?"

I smiled and shook my head. "We're divorced." She turned and started walking. I noticed a swish to her dress. "Still the same old Cathy."

I drove to the jump tower to watch Kara. I got there just in time to see her and the other girl get strapped onto the bench. Then, the cable started to pull them up, up, and up. I could hear my daughter squealing all the way up. At the height of a ten-story building, the cable released and they fell for about thirty feet before the parachute above them filled with air and lowered them. The jump sergeant at the bottom asked who was next.

"Hey Jake, you wanna go up?" I turned to see who had called. Three of the guys from the unit came walking up.

"This wheelchair don't climb steps real good."

"Not a problem." They scooped me out of the chair and carried me up the ten steps to a platform and sat me on the bench. Kara got back on the bench beside me. The sergeant put a strap across our laps. I watched as the ground dropped from under us. The sergeant flipped the platform of steps out of the way so we could bounce when we reached the end of the cable. I wrapped my arm tightly around the support cable, loving the thrill, the view, the memories. I had this sudden rush of terror that my legs would start spasming and shake me off the bench. My crippled hands could not grab anything if I started to slip, so I gripped with my arms that much tighter. I loved the drop and felt like yelling all the way down, but I was afraid to startle Kara.

After the ride, I drove to the firing range. Kara headed back to town with her friend to find a mall. Then, I drove around Fort Benning, just remembering. It was pig hot and humid when I got back to the hotel and I headed for my room to change and fall into the pool. At the pool, I had lunch and read some. Then, I performed a controlled fall into the deep end of the swimming pool. After an hour of laps and hanging on the side, I swam to the steps and lifted my butt from step to step until I reached the top.

A couple of guys with the reunion were sitting at a table and I asked them to get my chair and lift me back into it. I could feel the sunburn to the top of my head so I headed to my room. I fumbled with the key and got it into the lock and was holding it between my palms, wiggling it to get the latch open, when Kara's voice asked from inside, "Daddy, is that you?"

"No, it's the house detective." I heard giggling. "We're changing. You can't come in." I wondered who "we" was. In about a minute, the door opened and three other teenaged women in bikinis and bathing suits filed out in front of my daughter.

"Okay, Daddy, you can go in."

"Why does everybody have to change in our room?"

"Victoria didn't have a bathing suit, so I lent her mine because I bought a new one." She dropped the towel she had on. "You like it?" She spun around to model the suit.

"It looks like its all straps and no suit, your fanny is hanging out. You're not going out in that?"

She gave me a kiss on the cheek and said, "Sorry." Then, she disappeared into the elevator the other girls were holding open for her.

I remembered to call after her, "I want you to be back by five to change for dinner." A hand waved through the closing elevator doors. I sat there wondering if "Sorry" was for the inconvenience of keeping me out of my room, or for buying an imaginary bathing suit or for ignoring me. "Her mother was right. She has me wrapped around her little finger," I muttered.

We met Cathy and her sons in the lobby. The teenagers went to a pool table. Cathy and I got a table in the bar. The waitress came to the table. Cathy ordered a white wine and I ordered a glass of water with a scotch chaser. A couple of guys from my unit stopped by our table and I introduced Cathy. They sat down and asked her what kind of pain in the ass patient I had been. The drinks came to our table, followed closely by our three teenage offspring. I could tell by the looks on their faces that some plan had been hatched. My daughter opened her mouth to speak for the group and I cut her off. "Whatever it is young lady, the answer is no."

"Daddy, how do you always know?" she said with a pout.

"When I see you come toward me with that 'ain't I just the cutest thing' look on your face, I know something's up."

Cathy's older son took over the effort. "Sir, we were supposed to go to an amusement park tonight," he said, avoiding his mother's frown. "If we could go, we could get pizza on the way."

My daughter joined in, "And I could ask Francie and I wouldn't be out too late and you guys could catch up on old (she emphasized "old") times and …"

I interrupted, "You better stop for a breath."

I looked at Cathy; she was glaring at both sons. The younger one responded with, "I didn't say anything."

"You three wait over there," I gestured. When they had moved out of earshot, I asked, "Did my invitation mess things up?"

"I think I ruined a couple of hot dates by telling them they had to come, but I'm not happy about them weaseling out."

"We probably couldn't have talked in front of them anyhow. Should we let them go?" She nodded. "By the way, is my daughter safe with them?" I asked in jest.

She returned the smile. "As safe as I was with you."

"Oh, now I feel better," I said sarcastically. I pushed across the room. I handed my daughter a twenty-dollar bill. "Young lady, I want you back in this hotel by midnight, and I don't mean a second later. Is that understood, gentlemen?"

"Yes, sir," they answered in unison.

"Because, I will come looking for her," I added for emphasis.

"Daddy, you're embarrassing me." While the boys went to say good-bye to their mother, she kissed me and pulled on a jacket that I hadn't noticed she had brought from the room.

The bar was filling with generations of Rangers so we moved to a quiet table in the corner of the restaurant. I looked at her and wondered about all the years. Each of us was waiting for the other to start. I launched in.

"What happened to you in Vietnam? I mean, about spring of the next year, I get a letter back with post office rubber stamps all over it. I could see that it had been forwarded through hospitals in Vietnam, Japan, and the States before they lost track of you. I was scared to death to write your parents and ask what happened. All I could think was that I was the guy who assured your mother that nothing would happen to you."

She reached across the table and patted my hand. "I was in the O.R. for like this forever shift and all of the sudden in the middle of this surgery, I had this terrible stomach pain. At first, I thought it was food poisoning, but I couldn't leave this doctor while he was fishing metal out of this guy. Anyway, I passed out and they found I had a ruptured appendix. I almost ***did*** die. I ran a fever for weeks. What happened to you? When I got better, I wrote to you in Tucson, but my letter came back."

"I moved after my first year. The VA helped me buy a house up in the foothills."

"How are your parents?" she asked. "I tried to write you at their house."

"My dad died during my junior year in Arizona. My mom rented their house out. She went for a trip to Paris and ended up with a teaching job there. She gave the house to my aunt Ann."

"And what happened to you? Did you become a teacher?"

"No. When I got to college, I felt out of place. I couldn't relate to kids whose most harrowing experience was having a zit for the senior prom. Then, some anti-war professor went off on a lot of crap and I raised my hand and said 'fuck you' and rolled out. I got a job as an emergency services dispatcher on the midnight shift and took mostly evening classes with older students." The waiter brought our salads.

"I had to take psych classes. When they started teaching about shock and prolonged stress and the after effects, parts of my life started making sense. I could see it too with the cops and firemen I worked with. So I changed majors to psychology. When I went for my Master's, I had to do an internship, so I worked at the veterans' hospital. I realized those guys were going through the same shit. I got a job there and went for my doctorate."

She arched her eyebrows, "You mean you're Dr. Jake Scott?"

"Yeah, but most people can't tell me from the patients. How about you, career Army,"

"Yes."

"I guess Vietnam didn't chase you out."

"No." Her look was far away for a second. "But you were right. I could never have imagined." I thought for a second she might cry, but she drew a deep breath and took a sip of her drink. The waiter cleared the plates and brought the entrees. I sat studying her. More Rangers came to our table. I introduced her and said that she had been stationed in Vietnam.

"Thanks, Colonel," said one of the men and he handed her a Ranger crest. All the others thanked her in their turn.

When they left, she asked, "How did Kara happen?"

"Well when I started at the VA hospital, I met her mother, Lisa. Lisa's father was a long-term patient there and I would see her in passing. One day when I was leaving, I found her crying in the parking lot. Turns out some Air Force guy had shipped out, leaving her seventeen and pregnant. I started helping her out and was there when Kara was born. Then, we realized that I could get an allotment from the VA for her and Kara if we were married, so we got married. Not much romance. Someone once told me you have to know who you are before you get married, guess I didn't know who the hell I was.

Cathy inquired, "I guess you weren't interested in Suzie?"

Her question hurt me. "I loved her very much. After my dad's funeral, I drove through Chicago looking for her. I found her parents' house; there was a for sale sign in the front yard. The neighbor told me that they had moved to California and that their daughter was in the Peace Corps. I didn't know her dad's name and I didn't know where to look."

"How long have you been divorced?

"'Bout two years. Turns out my ex had been writing this Air Force guy for years and, one day, he shows up. When I came home from work, she and Kara were gone, no note, no nothing. Kara was twelve then." The waiter cleared our plates and I ordered more drinks. The drinks were making it easier to talk.

"I went crazy after that. I didn't give a damn about Lisa—our marriage was dead for years—but Kara was the only child I would ever have. I quit my job at the hospital. I took off for weeks looking for them. I got another dispatcher job. I started drinking. I was planning ways to kill myself. One night, I was sitting in the dark house with a revolver in my lap when there was a knock at the door. Kara had run away from her mother."

"Didn't her mother come after her?"

"Yeah. My ex said I was a cripple and could not take care of Kara. Kara dropped the bombshell. She said Mommy's boyfriend was coming on to Kara and if the judge made her go back, she would run away where she couldn't be found. So I got custody. Her mother lives in Reno, so we don't see her too often."

She reached over and took my hand. "So how are you doing?"

"Well, everything seems to happen for a reason. When I went back into counseling, I worked with teenagers in private practice, doing court evaluations and teaching. This reunion is the best medicine for some of my symptoms. You?"

"Mostly, I stay busy with three boys."

"Three?"

"Two sons and a husband, he was a chopper pilot in Nam. Now, he designs and installs computer systems in airports." The waiter brought the drinks and the check. I swirled the brandy into a small whirlpool and bit my lip. "Go ahead," she said with a twinkle in her eyes, "ask me."

"Do you know where Suzie is?"

"She's in San Diego."

I felt a shiver. "What happened to her?"

"Well, you already know she went in the Peace Corps, to Africa, then back here, then back to Africa. She was still trying to find herself." She sipped the brandy. "I saw her a few years ago at a nursing administrators conference. She moved to San Diego to care for her mother, who had cancer. Her mom lived about eleven years. When she died, Suzie stayed on to look after her dad."

"Did she get," I said, halting, "married?" Cathy shook her head. "Did she ask about me?"

"Somehow she knew that you were married."

"Knew I was married? I wonder how."

"Maybe she tried to look you up." All of a sudden, an avalanche rumbled through my brain. Suzie found out I was married and did not try to get in touch with me. I was still sitting there with my mouth open and thoughts bumping into the side of my skull when Cathy fighting a yawn brought me back.

"Long day, huh?"

"That and I was out celebrating last night—one year since I got the bird."

"Congratulations."

"I should have brought my own car and let the boys bring theirs."

"I'll run you home. I got a rental car with hand controls." We drove through the dark Columbus streets. The cool summer air blew her hair. She directed me to a nice two-story house in the suburbs. "Wait here," she said as she opened the door, "I'll be right back." In a few minutes, she was back, handing me a piece of paper. "It's my address. This time, don't lose it."

"This time, don't get shipped out in the middle of the night."

"You will let me know what happens," she directed.

"Whaddya mean, what happens?"

She unfolded the paper and put it back in my hands. I turned on the interior light. There were two addresses; the second was in San Diego. "You're going to find her, aren't you?"

"Maybe."

"Maybe hell! You let me know." She opened the door and started to get out. Then she said softly, "Oh, what the hell." She leaned back. I took her in my arms and we kissed. She closed the car door. "Don't chicken out," she said through the open window.

When I got back to the hotel, I sat in the bar with another brandy and a cigar. I was watching the front door. I pulled out the piece of paper and read it again. Suzie Donovan. There was writing on the back. A phone number, not a Columbus area code. Kara and Francie came walking into the lobby at midnight. I followed them onto the elevator.

§ § § § § §

It was July Fourth weekend. Cathy had to work that Saturday, but it was so boring. She had brought her address book to work hoping to catch up on some letters. She opened it. Should she? She dialed. "Hello," said the voice at the other end.

"Suzie, it's Cathy."

"Hey! Everything okay?"

"I saw him."

"Jake?"

Cathy could hear excitement in her voice. "Yeah, he was here at Benning for a reunion."

"How is he?"

"He looks great. And by the way, he's divorced."

There was a pause at the other end. "Did he ask about me?"

48

No More Goodbyes

The room was full of brilliant moonlight. The green light of the numbers on the alarm clock lit the edge of my bed. I watched 2:59 become 3:00. I had been back from Benning for almost eight weeks and every night had been like this. I would be awake for two or three hours.

Kara had started classes at the University in mid-August. When we got back, there was registration and moving her into a dorm. Tonight was the first night she had been home since school started. I sat up and threw off the blankets. I reached toward the foot of the bed and grabbed a pair of shorts and pulled them on. I got in the wheelchair and rolled to a desk. I flipped on a lamp. I opened the drawer and pulled out a photo album. I opened the cover. Inside was a yellowing photo, one that Mrs. Hochberg had taken. I turned it over and read the back. "Love always, Suzie."

I hadn't called. I kept finding excuses. I did not want a polite dismissal. I guess I had spent so long not telling my father I loved him because I did not want rejection. I had conditioned myself to avoid the possibility.

I pushed across the room to a rowing machine. I lowered my self from the chair to the seat of the machine. I dragged my legs into position and put my feet under the straps on the footrests. I pressed my palms against the handles and began pulling and pushing as hard as I could—back and forth, back and forth. The years had changed me.

My neck and shoulders were bigger. I had more control over the muscles in my back, which enabled me to lift my lower body more easily. My hands had not gotten any stronger. I still used two hands to pull up zippers and hold pens when my hand grew tired. I occasionally used my teeth to pick up awkward objects that I could not control with my hands.

After about fifteen minutes of rowing, the hall light went on. Kara came shuffling in my room, rubbing her eyes. "Daddy," she said with exasperation, "what are you doing?"

"I'm sorry; I just couldn't sleep."

"What is it? You've been prowling around ever since we came back from your reunion. I've even seen you sitting outside in the dark."

"I guess the reunion triggered a lot of old thoughts and feelings. I'll quit rowing and read so you can go back to sleep." I got off the machine and pushed to a drafting table that faced through a sliding door looking up to the mountains. There was a watercolor pinned to it that I was working on. Next to it was that slip of paper. I stared at the phone number. I had started to dial it a number of times, but I never finished.

"This is crazy," I muttered. I looked back at the clock. Two more hours and the sun would pour over those mountains. I pushed to my daughter's bedroom and knocked on the door and then opened it a crack. "Kara, are you asleep?"

"No" was the groggy answer from beneath the blankets.

"I am going for a drive and I won't be back until Tuesday or Wednesday. Would you take care of the house and feed the cat?"

"Where are you going?"

"San Diego."

"When?"

"As soon as I can get dressed and packed."

"In the middle of the night!?"

"Might as well, can't sleep."

She grunted. "Uh-huh." Then, I heard her sleeping breathing.

By four o'clock, I had filled a knapsack with jeans, T-shirts, a razor, toothbrush, and catheter. I rolled out to the garage to a big customized Ford van, which I only used for long trips. Beside it was the blue Pontiac, shined to a high gloss. One thing about Tucson, it was a great place for old cars.

I opened a panel on the side of the van, put in a key, and pressed a button. The side doors opened and an electric lift folded out and descended. I backed my chair onto it and was raised so I could roll into the van. I maneuvered my chair and got into the driver's seat. I started the engine and flipped a switch that folded the lift and closed the door. Just then, the door to the house opened and Kara came out with a cup of coffee. I rolled down the window. She handed the cup to me. "Thanks, sweetie."

"I hope you find who you are looking for."

Her remark took me by surprise, since I had not said anything to her about Suzie, but I should have known. "And don't fall asleep driving," she added. She stood on tiptoe and gave me a peck on the cheek and then shuffled back into the house. I drove through dark streets going west until I reached the interstate. Outside, a huge moon ran along in front of me. I ran the van up to eighty and set the cruise control. I fished up a headset and turned on the radio. Then, I sipped coffee. I adjusted the steering wheel and the seat and sipped more coffee. It would be about an eight-hour trip.

Why hadn't I just phoned her or written her? No, I had to make my best effort. Suppose she doesn't want to see you? It was such a long drive. "You idiot," I assessed myself. The sun had oozed over the hills to the east, spreading light and heat over the tops of the saguaro cacti and working its way down onto the shorter plants and onto the flatlands and into the ravines. I was grateful to be heading west; otherwise, the sun would be blinding me for hours. By the time I hit the town of Gila Bend, I was ready for breakfast.

The waitress surveyed the damage I had done to a plate of biscuits with sausage gravy, scrambled eggs, and home fries, with juice and coffee. "Is there anything else you want?" she asked.

"Listen, I have to go to the bathroom. If I'm not back in fifteen minutes, send someone to open the door and let me out," I said. She gave me a strange look. I rolled in. Things had changed a lot in twenty years, but people were still devising frustration for cripples. There was a huge stall with a door I could not close except by leaning backwards out of the chair and sliding my hand underneath it. There was a little knob that I could not grab with my crippled fingers.

When I went to the sink, I rolled my knees under it, but the paper towel dispenser was five feet up the wall. I had learned to pull the towels out before my hands got wet. I reached above my head, caught the towels between my palms, and pulled a couple down. I was getting the hang of life.

Back behind the wheel, I started thinking of my marriage of fifteen years. I had driven my ex-wife crazy with Vietnam. There were photos and stories. There was spending every Memorial Day and Veteran's Day at commemorative ceremonies or visiting cemeteries that interfered with her plans. She could not understand what it had done to me or meant to me. I struggled to find value in my sacrifice.

I pulled into a truck stop to get gas. The lift lowered and I rolled onto it. The Arizona heat got to me quickly and I hurried to get back into the air-conditioned van. The gas pumps were on a concrete island and I could not get close enough to reach the pumps. A trucker who was filling up beside me gave me a hand and I demonstrated the lift. "I'm gonna need one a them in a couple years," the trucker said. "I'm getting to old to climb up inta dem semis."

Sitting behind the wheel, I felt sorry for my ex-wife. I remembered one of our strained discussions. "When I married you, I didn't know I was marrying that," she said, pointing to the wheelchair. "Our friends don't invite us to their houses because they can't figure out how to get you in. Nobody asks us to go on trips or to dances 'cause you're just gonna sit there. I like to dance, but I haven't been asked since I married you. Guys would ask me, but they see you sitting there and they don't. That wheelchair is as much a pain in my ass as it is a pain in your ass." I did not know what to say in response. She was right.

Mid-way across California, the road started blurring and I pulled over, got in the back, and fell asleep. The lack of sleep for the past week must have caught up to me because when I woke, it was dark. I drove on to San Diego, to a motel, got a wheelchair accessible room, and slept soundly through the night—except for a quick bad dream where my ex-wife showed up and said she was coming back to me just as I was about to talk to Suzie. I used the coffee maker in the room and drank four cups of coffee

I got a city map at a gas station and found Suzie's house. I parked in front. I sat in the van staring at the house. "This isn't going to work," I muttered aloud. I deserved a lot of blame for my divorce. My lousy temper, my cursing and swearing every time the frustration got too much. I went into a depression whenever I realized that the miracle I was praying for was not going to happen. My ex did not know how to handle me. I must have been a jerk to be with then.

I had not really changed. I was afraid that one day I'd be sitting there, fighting to pull my boot off of my swollen foot and drag myself out of the wheelchair. I'd start cursing and screaming and Suzie would walk out the door. When Suzie got to know me, it would ruin any chance we might have.

A man walked out of the front door, but I did not see him until he walked over and looked into my windshield. He walked to the driver's window. "I noticed you parked out here awhile. Can I help you?"

"Are you Mr. Donovan?" He frowned and was hesitant to answer, suspecting I might be a Jehovah's Witness, a process server, or a student working his way through college selling insurance.

"Who are you?"

"Sir, my name is Jake Scott." I paused to see if that meant anything to him. "I'm trying to find Susan Donovan." I could feel my pulse throbbing in my throat. The man was mentally reviewing all the photos he'd last seen in the post office.

"She's at work," he said. I had a reprieve.

"Could I call when she gets home if it's not too late?"

"She works until eleven."

"Could I call her at work?"

"Who are you?"

"I'm a friend. I knew her when she was an Army nurse."

There was a long silence. "You're the patient that wrote to her when she got out."

"Yes, sir."

"She's in neo-natal intensive care at Mercy hospital."

"Thank you, sir."

I found my way back to the freeway and headed into the city. Cars whizzed past me. The closer I got, the slower I drove. I found a parking lot about a block from the hospital and pushed up the sidewalk. I entered the coolness of the hospital and got directions from a volunteer at the information desk. The woman traced the route on a small diagram of the hospital.

I came to the elevators, but I watched several cars come and go before getting onto one. The doors slid closed and I sat there. 'Her father would have told me if she was married or dating or involved, wouldn't he?" I mumbled. "Suppose she just politely shakes my hand, says it was nice to see me, and says good-bye." The doors opened and two nurses started to get on but saw me and backed out of the way. "No, I'm going up."

They got on the elevator. One of them turned to me. "You haven't pushed a button."

"Three, please." I started mumbling to myself, "Maybe she can't stop. There's probably all these critical kids on the ward."

"What?" one of the nurses asked.

"Nothin," I replied. The doors opened and I rolled into the corridor. The lights were dimmer here. I rolled to a row of windows and looked through. My chin just cleared the lower edge of the window. I could see tiny bodies in plastic bassinettes. What marvelous creations we humans are. A nurse with short silver hair wearing a light blue scrub suit walked past carrying a tray and started working on one of the infants.

I turned and rolled back to the elevator. I should just go back to Tucson and realize you can't turn back the clock and find things the way they used to be. "You can't just leave now," I muttered. For one thing, she would get home that night and her father would tell her I had been there. "Go on, you idiot," I scolded myself. I turned back toward the windows. The nurse with the short silver hair was staring at me. "Oh my God!" I gasped.

She walked to the window and then turned and began walking to a door; the walk became a jog and the jog became a run. She emerged into the hall and, with me pushing toward her, the distance closed rapidly. She slid onto my lap as if she had been there yesterday. We hugged. It felt so wonderful to feel her hands pressing my back. We kissed, pressing our faces together. Then, she put her face into my chest to wipe her tears on my shirt.

"Where have you been?" she asked in a hoarse whisper.

I looked past her at the group of nurses that had gathered in the hall. "I've been afraid that if I found you that you wouldn't want me," I said into her ear.

"I want you, I really, really want you," she replied. We kissed and I felt her hands gripping my shoulders.

Epilogue

Yes, we got married, but first, we went into therapy together for about a year and a half. Then, we spent the next eight years after the wedding in therapy. We would joke it was our honeymoon. When I realized how much good therapy did for me, I marveled that, as a professional in the field, I never realized how much I needed to heal myself.

Her father announced that since I was there to take care of Suzie (and she thought she was taking care of him), he was going to travel. He gave us the house and the mortgage. I found I liked being near the ocean and we bought a boat together and I got some special equipment for fishing.

Kara studied computers in college and got a job for Hewlett in England. It was a good excuse for us to travel to the British Isles. I had always wanted to see where the Scotts came from.

Ann and Hank ran the lumber yard and had six children, all girls, so the trucks had to be painted "Drier and Daughters."

I went back to Richmond and the old hospital had been demolished and replaced with a modern, spacious building. It seemed sad that other patients would not be chased by food carts, or chase them with air horns.

We drove up to Washington D.C. and went to "the Wall." It was a huge black magnet pulling our memories and emotions from us. We found the names of friends and we cried for a long, long time.

I looked at our reflection in the polished granite and closed my eyes in a softly spoken prayer, "Thank you, God, for this woman who loves me."

Printed in the United States
143417LV00003BA/61/P

9 781606 937013